CLAUDIA VAMPIRE

ALFONSO MORET

EC Publishing LLC
11100 SW 93rd Court Road, Suite 10-215
Ocala, Florida 34481-5188, USA

www.ecpublishingllc.com
info@ecpublishingllc.com
+1 (352) 234-6201

Printed in the United States of America

CHAPTER 1

CLAUDIA

MOST INHABITANTS OF OUR PLANET earth probably do not believe or even know that the undead exist and are roaming around this planet. So, it doesn't matter to the humans at all if vampires have feelings or emotions or if they can mourn or cry. Claudia Brocolac, the wife of Colonel Demetrius Gannet Brocolac, found out that, indeed, vampires can suffer from emotional pain. She knows now that the undead could feel sadness, could mourn, and could weep. The aftermath of Demetrius's demise found Claudia isolated and mourning in her room. It was now three days and she had neglected to respond to any contact from others of her brethren.

Her grief had disheartened her deeply, a fear dwelled in her black heart and she believed that it was useless to exist any longer. Demetrius had been her deity, her Gibraltar, her companion, and her only lover for two hundred years. Together, in all that they imbedded and committed themselves to, the injustice and immoral acts they had performed, were only for survival and pleasure. Claudia felt that she was not responsible for what fate had turned Demetrius and herself into and now, for it was each vampire's responsibility to survive in anyway possible if they wish to exist. With Demetrius, he found his rituals were all justified and with Claudia by his side, his world was complete. Together they existed, traveled, killed and let live, and had loved one another for over two hundred years.

So now, with the lack of her nourishment, her elixir, human blood, Claudia had become weaker. Dark circles formed around her eyes and her hair was in disarray and dry. Her pale demeanor became paler, it now resembled that of a ghost or ghoul.

On the third day, she lay on her bed, declining in health. She was ready to let go, ready to perish, ready to be with Demetrius. Now the cramps in her body caused her to moan and toss with agony. She would get chills off and on that made her body shudder and jerk. She would be in pain, but soon, she would ceased to exist. These thoughts crossed her mind. These thoughts made the agony bearable. *Let it come*, she contemplated, *let it come*.

She screamed out, "Let it come!"

Alphonse, one of Demetrius's old friend and protégée and was the foreman of the horse farm, received the news of Demetrius's death, and he also mourned his companion and employer. And now he was told of Claudia's isolation and her despondency. He had been mourning away. The word came to him from the horse-ranch workers, they, in turn got the news from the housekeeper. The housekeeper, Martha, knew if Claudia died, she would not have a job anymore. Martha hoped that some old friend would come by and try to get Claudia to respond and get involved with existing again.

On the third evening of her despondency, and as Claudia lay in bed looking at Demetrius's portrait on the wall, she saw how Liberte had captured Demetrius in all his full glory. His fierce stare, his strong nose, and vibrant cheekbones were mesmerizing while his soft cruel mouth condemned you to kiss him. As she stared at the portrait and shook her head and wondered if existing and the hiding were worth the troubles, but then she was startled by a loud knock on the door. She then sat up quickly, but now she tilted her head and she continued to view the portrait. She was taking in all of Demetrius's features, ignoring the knocking.

The knocking irritated her, she shook her head and put her face in her hands as she mumbled, "How could they have done this to you, my Champion?" Around her eyes, there was smudged eye make-up, her lips were chapped, and her hair was a mess as she just held her hands to her face. Now she could not cry anymore, her body was lacking moisture, blood. Her body was drying out and she would soon perish.

The knocking continued, and Claudia's untidy head and extremely pale face turned to the knocking, and she finally responded weakly in a whispered voice, "Go away. Just go away. I cannot go on anymore without Demetrius."

The door was pushed and forced open and Alphonse stepped in. He cringed as he viewed this once beautiful creature that now resembled a despondent corpse.

He took in a breath and walked in. As he held on to a thick rope and then he pleaded, "Please, my queen, listen to me."

Claudia looked up at him and her head drooped to her chest and she whispered, "Alphonse, they have taken our king away. I will soon be with him—my pet, my love."

With an imploring look and manner, Alphonse responded, "My queen, Demetrius made me promise that if anything ever happened to him that I must make sure that you would carry on in his absence."

Claudia looked up at him, a frown crinkling her expression. She shook her head slowly and whispered, "I cannot, Alphonse. I cannot. I have no will."

Alphonse half smiled and stated, "Ah, madam, you are royalty in our world. A queen cannot let her subjects down. Demetrius's teachings will vanish and the new vampire ways of surviving will be gone, and then we will all vanish, perish. It was not of choice, but fate and destiny that created our brethren. We have a right to survive here too. We are here for a reason, a reason we will not understand until we meet our maker. We need you, my queen, we live for you."

At that point, the rope that Alphonse had been holding tightened and pulled at him. Alphonse gave it a tug and there was a *thud* outside the door. Something hit the floor then the rope stopped moving.

Claudia's expression went to puzzlement, and she pointed and asked, "What are you holding there, Alphonse?"

Alphonse's face brightened, and he smiled and bowed down to his queen. He jerked the rope and said, "Your elixir, madam, your life blood to our continuing new world."

And then a young blond man staggered into the room. He was bare chested and blindfolded; his hands were tied behind his back and he was gaged.

The captive stood there legs apart, his neck craning to the north and south, trying to fathom what was going on. His golden hair disheveled and his muscular chest and arms were shiny with perspiration, accenting his fine physique. He moaned through the gag and tried to speak.

The back of her hand went to her mouth, and again, she shook her head slowly and implored to her foreman, "Oh, Alphonse, I do not think I can again. I, I…" Her stomach churned with anticipation, and now the sight of this perfect specimen aroused her senses. She tried to fight the needs her body yearned.

At that point, Alphonse brought up his index finger with its one-inch manicured fingernail and slit a small cut across the artery of the captive's throat. Blood began to seep out and then it began to squirt a three-foot arch as the young man wiggled to get free and went to his knees, moaning through the gag.

Alphonse placed his hand on the wound and looked at Claudia and stated, "Lovely lady, be our queen. Drink."

At the sight and smell of this man's blood, Claudia's will power rapidly diminished. Claudia became powerless to fight the need, the demand. Her eyes narrowed, her lips curled, and she became fixed on the man's throat. Her tongue quickly swiped at her lips, her mouth opened, her eye-teeth became prominent and needing, and saliva moistened her mouth that she almost gagged. With a loss of control, she sprang from the bed, and in a flash, she was on the young blond captive. She held him up and turned his head, and then her mouth was on the wound, sucking and slurping. Blood ran down the man's neck and his chest and some spread on Claudia's cheek. His struggles were useless as he twisted and turned in her grasp. Soon, that mysterious sexual arousal overcame him also, now the blond captive seemed to be enjoying the depletion of his life-giving fluids. At the end, it made him smile, and then he collapsed in Claudia's arms. Claudia let the body fall to the floor, and as she wiped her mouth, she seemed to have gained a new will and reason to exist. In seconds, her face looked younger, wrinkle lines disappeared, and her lips were moist and tender again. She stretched her neck and patted down her hair. The young victim moaned again through the gag; he was not dead yet. The dark circles around her eyes disappeared. Although she was pale, there was some color to her face and her magnificent baby blue eyes sparkled and her dry blond hair now seemed to be filled with luster.

Claudia stepped over the body and then looked into the mirror. She patted her hair again here and there and tilted her head back and forth, looking at her reflection in the mirror.

She took a deep breath and looked at Alphonse and said, "Alphonse, how could I have forgotten how incredibly wonderful it is to drink blood. The emotional and physical eroticism that over-whelms our being and floods our brain and body with sensations is so incredible and just indescribable." Claudia took another breath.

Alphonse lifted the body over his shoulder and asked Claudia, "Then you will continue with Demetrius's teachings and be our queen?"

Claudia gave a small curtsy, nodded yes, kissed Alphonse on the cheek, and said, "Thank you for breaking me out of my stupor, my friend."

Alphonse bowed his head and said, "You drank but you let him live. I'll hide him in the barn. You can indulge with him tomorrow." As he walked away, he turned and stated, "I will die for you, my queen." He turned and went out the door to go take the body to the barn. The blond man would wake up tomorrow and be weak, but he will survive. A doctrine of Demetrius.

Claudia loudly claimed, "That was Demetrius's teachings. With that, we shall survive, my friend."

Claudia turned to her friend and told him to leave so she could change clothes. She felt exhilarated and wanted to go into the village tonight. She was still hungry. She had gone three days without nourishment. After she finished dressing, she went into the kitchen area, and Alphonse was sitting at a chair reading the newspaper.

Claudia sat down and asked, "Alphonse, why don't you and Matilda come to the village with me. It is still early. I feel lively tonight."

"I was hoping you would want to do something more than just sit around here and count the horses. I'll get the limo and we will go pick up my woman and head to town."

San Moreno was a small hamlet just outside of Valencia. It was celebrating their annual roundup and shearing of their sheep. The small landowners herded their animals into the large barns that led into fenced off sections in the barn and readied the sheep for shedding. This was the town's main produce and means of survival. The small stores and venders would soon collect the tabs they had rendered through the past year after the selling of the wool.

There had been a small parade that afternoon, and now several families were in the midst of barbequing lamb on open pits where the whole town will surrender to their appetites tonight. They were street performers and shops open for business. A clown-dressed juggler was tossing lit torches into the air as wide-eyed children gawked in awe. A young man sat on a boulder and strummed his guitar in a flamenco tune. Soon a traditionally dressed beauty danced to his tune, clacking her maracas to his beat. Her flashy red, green, and blue tinted dress swayed to her movements while her stamping feet also kept tune to the playing guitar. A small crowd gathered there. An overdressed vendor stood on a small platform, his old beat-up Ford station wagon stood parked next to it. He was orally vending his product as he flashed smiles and swore how his potion relived headaches and rheumatism. There was a box next to him with several bottles of the elixir.

Claudia, Matilda, and Alphonse sat in the front seat of the limo and watched the crowds mill around the town's square.

Matilda spoke, "Come on, Phonso, I want to dance."

Alphonse nodded.

Claudia looked at the couple and stated, "Go on, have fun. I'll join you in a moment."

Alphonse and Matilda got out and walked over to the large gazebo where a band was playing rock music. The crowd were mostly young adults, several couples were rocking out on the dance floor while others milled around moving their bodies to the music and drinking wine in paper cups.

Claudia looked into the rear-view mirror and adjusted her hair and straightened her lipstick and then left the vehicle. This was new to her. As a vampire, she had never been out in public without Demetrius.

Claudia got out of the vehicle and walked over to the crowd and music. She lingered at the back of the group who were standing in front of the dancing couples, she eyed Alphonso and Matilda slow dancing to an upbeat song. They seem to be in rhythm to the tune; it was their favorite soul number.

Months before, she and Demetrius had been watching dance shows on TV and tried to rock-n-roll and fell laughing into each other's arms and then on the bed. Claudia found that the rhythm of the rock-n-roll numbers was easy for her to adopt and that she had a knack to dress to the styles of the younger generation.

She had been turned to vampirism when she was only twenty-two and now, two hundred years later, she still had her youthful looks. The jeans-and-loose-blouses style were entirely to her liking. The form-fitting jeans accented her adorable physique and added to her youthful demeanor. Claudia stood there looking at the young couples' dance and moved to the hip-hop music. Her head bobbed with the drumbeat and her shoulders dipped with the tune.

The evening was mild while a cool, gentle breeze fluttered through the air. The stars were just beginning their exhibition while a three-quarter moon began it's journey through the night sky. The music completed a scenic picture of allurement.

A young man approached her and kept his eyes on her. His mouth took on a lopsided grin. He was tall and thin but not skinny. His bushy curly hair swayed in the air and he wore a thin black beard. His dark hair and eyebrows brought contrast to his fair skin face.

He had brooding dark eyes but as his smile broadened, his whole demeanor glowed with warmth.

He stepped closer and remarked, "Hi, hello, there. Please excuse the intrusion, I'm new in town and I saw you here moving to the music and it seems that you are ready to be asked to dance, ha-ha. Am I correct in assuming this?" He smiled even broader, making Claudia step back. But then she smiled and she involuntarily nodded no and then yes.

Reaching for her hand, he stated, "*Ah, fantastico!* My name is Roberto Clemoso. I'm here from Valencia to buy, no, I'm sorry, mademoiselle, to rent horses for a film that is being made, as we speak." As they maneuvered their way through the crowd and on to the dance floor he looked sideways at Claudia and with one strong eyebrow arced he asked, "And you are?"

Claudia looked straight ahead and cleared her throat and responded, "Here in Spain. I am called Señora Claudia Brocolac."

They were on the dance floor but he stopped and then faced Claudia. He had an innocent surprised expression on his face, but then smiled and asked, "No, are you from the Superior Brocolac Stables?"

"I own the stables, Señor Clemoso." She stood there standing proudly.

The band ended their number and a female vocalist took the mic and began singing, "Midnight at the Oasis, send your camel to bed. Shadows paintin' our faces. Traces of romance in our heads."

Roberto's surprised look went to content as he reached and brought Claudia to him and began dancing slow to the music. He brought his head back to looked at this lovely maiden and stated, "I cannot believe how lucky I can be. Your farm is the stables I was sent to inquire about." He pulled her in closer and they kept to the rhythm. She laid her cheek on his chest.

The vocal continued, "Let's slip off to a sand dune, real soon. And kick up a little dust."

Claudia pulled her head back and asked, "What is the name of the movie?" The yellow moon highlighted her cheekbones and deep penetrating dark blue eyes.

Roberto stood at arm's length, mesmerized for a moment and then shook his head. He spoke, "Forgive me, Señora Brocolac, for a moment you had captured me." He smiled and went on, "Just like in that movie, *The Godfather*, I was struck with a lightning bolt."

Claudia looked into his handsome face and said, "You flatter me señor. The name of your movie, Roberto?"

He cleared his throat and continued, "The movie, yes, the movie." He smiled again and responded, "The movie is a remake of an old Cary Grant movie called *Gunga Din*. The director wants all the front officer's horses to be white stallions. You have the best-looking and well-trained horses, we are told."

Claudia was enjoying the warmth of this man's body and the feel of his arms around her waist. She clutched him a little tighter and let her cheek lay on his chest again and told him, "Yes señor, I have the best horses in the land. We will negotiate tomorrow. Tonight, no business."

Roberto looked down at her and nodded. He now let the music do its work while he moved seductively to the tune.

The songstress continued, "You don't have to answer, there's no need to speak, I'll be your belly dancer and you can be my sheik."

After the song ended, they walked off the dance floor. Roberto's arm was around her waist and he guided her to a refreshment stand. There was some perspiration on Roberto's brow. Claudia took a hanky from her back pocket, faced Roberto, dabbed his forehead, and stated, "You move very well on the floor." She looked at him up and down and continued, "It makes a woman wonder." She stared at him, an eyebrow arched, and she grinned.

Roberto was about to respond when Claudia put up her hand and said, "Get yourself some wine and cool down. I am going to the ladies' room." She walked off and then turned and stated, "Roberto, I don't drink alcohol but enjoy yourself." She continued walking.

Claudia was taken by this vibrant young man, but she knew she couldn't indulge in Roberto yet, there's business to deal with first. Claudia went around back to where the small men's and women's restrooms were. The women's restroom was empty, so she went around to the men's and entered. There was a man standing in front of the sink and mirror combing his greasy hair. He was tall and well built, and his big bushy mustache covered his lips.

He eyed her walking in, and at first, he frowned and turned slightly and stated, "Señorita, the women's is on the other side." he smiled broadly and continued, "but I don't mind if you use ours here. It's the same as yours isn't it?"

Claudia broke a small smile and responded, "I do not know. I've never seen a man's bathroom before."

"Ah, let me be your guide, señorita." He turned and swayed his arm and said, "This way my dear," he walked over where two booths sat side by side, opened one door, and said, "At your service, my little pretty one, I'm ready to help in any way." He bowed and winked at Claudia as he looked up."

Claudia came up to him and turned him to face her and pushed him hard. He stepped back, and the force made him trip back and made him sit on the commode. Claudia jumped on him and bit on his neck. Her arms pinned his arms to his waist. He was amazed at the strength in this petite female. He struggled and tried to yell. His vocal cords had been severed, and Claudia lavished in drinking his blood. The erotic vibes trembled in her body, and soon, an unknown pleasure streamed through the man's veins and body. Then Claudia let loose her grip and his arms now hugged Claudia in pleasure. As his warm blood seeped through him and into Claudia, he climaxed as he died sitting on the commode. She found she couldn't stop that Roberto had aroused her, so she sucked him dry until she reached eroticism.

Claudia searched him and found a large buck knife. She opened it and began cutting his throat. She took his watch and all his valuables, making it look like a robbery. Claudia went to the sink and cleaned herself up and went to find Roberto.

CHAPTER 2

ROBERTO

ROBERTO WAS SITTING ON A bench with Alphonse and Matilda. They seem to be in deep conversation.

As Claudia approached the group, Roberto rose and offered her his seat and proclaimed, "Ah, the señorita has returned." Claudia sat down looking at Alphonse with a curious expression. He just gave a thin smile as Roberto continued, "Claudia, I was waiting for you when Alfonse here approached me and asked if I was enjoying your company. He had observed us dancing." Roberto took a drink from the wine glass he had been holding and went on, "As we began conversing, I found out Alphonse works for you, so we were talking about the horses, my dear señorita!"

Claudia looked over at Alphonse. He gave a slow nod. Claudia then turned to Alphonse and stated, "Well then, are you satisfied with the components of the transaction, Mr. Clemoso? I assume we can accommodate what our man here requires."

Roberto nodded and responded, "Your foreman strikes a hard bargain, but he states the horses are well trained and obedient. The horses are needed to complete the movie, so we came to an agreement." He looked around and cleared his throat and continued.

"Time is money in this world. Contracts will be drawn up tomorrow. Uh, can I drop on by for signatures?"

Claudia nodded and responded, "By all means, but come over for evening drinks, maybe a bite to eat."

Claudia then placed her arm through Roberto's arm and said, "Enough of business, let's go dance some more." She looked at him smiling.

Roberto gave a closed mouth smile and went to the dance floor guiding Claudia though the large crowd that had gathered.

The band was now playing an old number and the female was singing again, "Let me go why don't you Babe, you keep me hanging on."

They slowly rocked to the tune. Claudia snuggly adjusted her body to Roberto's and with contentment, pressed her body to his, grinding with the music. Claudia then felt that Roberto was becoming aroused. Claudia, too, felt that desire, but she has never made love with someone and not drank their blood. She did sexually get involved with Demetrius all the time but that was different. The vampires both had sufficiently embedded themselves in blood and then made love. Making love to Demetrius was the highlight of their existence.

As Roberto held her close and she felt her body respond to his movements, she wondered what would it be like to have sex without drinking blood. Would it feel sensual? Could she restrict herself from penetrating his neck, drink his hot blood, and indulge in the highest form of passion she had experienced?

Claudia smiled to herself and pulled her cheek away from Roberto's chest and whispered in his ear, "Roberto, take me to your room, now."

Roberto's expression revealed surprise and glee and he managed to hold her at arm's length and stated, "Anything you request, my queen, I am yours tonight."

They walked away hand in hand to his vehicle.

As they entered Roberto's room, he turned on the light, but Claudia turned it off and said, "The moonlight is ours tonight. Hurry, it is high and bright tonight."

Robert grinned and began disrobing as Claudia went to the windows and opened the blinds allowing moonbeams to glitter the dark room. Roberto was now fully nude and laid on the bed, waiting for his woman to join him. Claudia stepped back, half her body was in the shadow and the other half in the moonlight. She disrobed slowly, her blouse opened and fell to the floor, her breast hiding behind her dark red bra. Standing, she unbuttoned her jeans and stepped out of her ballerina slippers and the pushed down her pants and stood there almost nude in the dark, and then twirled quickly and then her bra and panties came off and paused there for a moment.

Roberto tried to speak and uttered and then found his voice and pleaded, "Claudia, oh Claudia, come to me. I am exploding here."

Claudia grinned and the quickly stepped up to him and laid atop of him where they kissed passionately and rolled around on the large bed.

They made love to the orgasmic state and Claudia discovered a new treat and pleasure for her vampire existence. An unforeseen pleasure, an inclination to educate the vampire brethren. Having sex and not killing was almost as complete as sex from their dying prey.

After they caught their breath. As she rolled off him, she turned and looked into his dark black eyes and asked, "Roberto, what is it like to live in America? The movies reveal modern cities, snowcapped mountains, deserts, and beaches with hot suns and clean sandy beaches. Is this true, Roberto?"

Roberto's perspired face turned to gaze at Claudia. He grinned, nodded, and said, "America is the most modern of the world, my dear. There are huge buildings everywhere filled with people performing all the duties to make their elaborate world exist."

Claudia's face showed wonder and interest, her eyebrows arched up.

Roberto continued, "In California, is where Hollywood, movie stars, and palm trees are, madam. Ah, and it is almost sunny all the time. You can drive from the beautiful beaches of Malibu to the snow-capped mountains of Big Bear in three hours." Roberto continued as his grin broadened to a flashing smile, "You should take a trip there." His eyebrows arched and a serious expression covered his face. The moonlight showed light perspiration covering his face, he added, "A small vacation, Claudia. I live there now." His expression went back a grin.

It was now two in the morning, and Claudia wanted him again, she turned on her side and nodded to him and stated, "Perhaps I will, my love, but now thrill me again. The night grows short."

Roberto took on a puzzlement look for a second and then smiled and rolled atop of Claudia. As they grunted with pleasure, he brought her face to his and they kissed.

At eight in the morning, Roberto awoke and found himself alone. He sat up and shook his head awake, he stretched and said out loud, "*Mi preciosa*, where are you, my love?" He swung his legs over the side and saw the note on the dresser. He stood up and grimaced some. His muscles ached. He uttered, "Ay, mi amore, you are a strong little lady."

He turned his body and glanced and at the full mirror attached to the dresser and seen some small bruises on his back and upper arms where she had squeezed him at moments of high passion. He smiled, thinking he had did a great job in bed last night. He took the note and read it.

> My darling Roberto, I needed to leave you sleeping. You had accomplished a man's quest to the ultimate and I/we needed rest. I had important business in town this morning. Last night was an unforgettable adventure. Please, if you care to, come to the Rancho tonight for dinner and bring the contracts. You have etched yourself into my core. Tonight is ours. Bonne jounee, mon amour.

Roberto folded the note, kissed it, and put in in his dresser drawer. He then opened another drawer and took out a little medicine box and opened the lid and picked up the small cardboard flap that contained enclosed blue pills of Viagra and whispered, "Tonight will overshadow last night, my friends."

*　*　*

At the ranch, the caballeros had been given instructions to roundup the white stallions and prep them for their journey. The gardeners had instilled their weekly duties while the two housemaids tidied up the hacienda insides. A cook was brought in and was cooking up *arros con pollo* (rice with chicken), beans, and rice. The cook was also told to make enough for the workers for the next day. All was set.

As the overcast red sky darkened and the hazy orange sun began its decent behind the Montcaber mountains, Claudia woke from her daytime slumber, she stretched her nude body and gave a painful yawn and rubbed her stomach. She was back to the routine of the undead. The hunger controlled her life as the ritual mandated her as a drug addict. She was powerless over her condition, so she would succumb to it, causing as less damage as possible. Demetrius taught her that. He was not overjoyed that he needed to take human blood, but he had surrendered to its calling. There were times when taking the life of someone overcame him and he performed his burdens with a fierceness and callous bravado that made him appear as if he was a monster. A monster he was, but the nobleman in him was still a part of him, and Claudia tried to maintain the virtuous side of a lady's womanhood as much as possible.

Claudia was thrilled with Roberto and planned to take him as a lover. She will not turn him but use him as a caretaker when she moved to the United States. Yes, she decided to move away from Valencia and stalk a new land. She would keep the farm and continue to allow Alphonse to run it and trust that the profits would be submitted into her accounts.

Roberto drove into the long cul-de-sac driveway that led to the front of the Brocolac Hacienda. He was impressed by the Japanese garden landscape. The small running streams, the assorted rock formations contrasted to the various colors and hues of the flower beds. The quaint bridge over the still pond that housed large Koi Carp fish was a statement of wealth of the home's owner.

As he closed in on the exquisite pull handle door knob, it sprang open by a heavyset woman dressed casually with an apron around her front.

She exclaimed, "*Señor Roberto Clemoso, si?*"

Roberto gave a quick bow and uttered, "Si señora."

"*Bueno, entra, yo me llama Maria.*"

She explained to him that Claudia had taken a spill while jumping an obstacle in the field and landed in the mud. She was not hurt and would be down shortly. He was to eat dinner and she would join him in the library for wine.

Roberto was now in the large dining room at a table with twelve chairs. The dining ware consisted of fine china and expensive-looking silverware that had a sort of dragon design handles. He ate his *pollo-con-arros* while listening to tunes performed by Frank Sinatra and friends. Roberto was upset that he had to eat alone but the dinner was good. It was pleasant to eat a home meal. After he had finished, Maria led him to the library where she picked up a brass box and offered him a cigar. Roberta picked one and Maria took it, she snipped it, and as he was holding it, she lit an end till it seemed lit and Roberto puffed on it, blew out a cloud of smoke and nodded it was fine. Marta poured two glasses of sherry wine. Roberto sat down on a huge maroon fluffy sofa.

Maria then said, "*Señor Roberto, ya me voy a ir. Claudia viene en un momento.*" With that she went into the kitchen. Roberto heard clanking and thuds as she put things away, and then he heard the front door open and close.

He was one third done with the cigar and had sipped half his wine when the music amped up and the tune resonated through the room and then Frank's voice captured his ear. The lights went down which let the incense candles create a fervent atmosphere.

"*The summer wind, came blowing in, from across the sea. It lingered there, to touch your hair and walked with me. All summer long we sang a song and then we strolled that golden sand. Two sweethearts and the summer wind.*"

A sliding door swished, and Roberto turned toward the sound of the opening door. Claudia stood there with her hands on her hips, she wore a brown-netted body suit the color of the sofa. Her body reeked underneath the fabric with touch me, adore me. Her raspberry red hair was teased up and flowed around her face in large curls. Her makeup consisted of darkened eyebrows, mascara outlined her vibrant blue eyes that sparkled like a running river in the sun hitting small boulders. She wore lipstick that matched the color of her nail polish hue.

Roberto sat there stunned, his eyes opened wide, one eyebrow arched, his mouth in a twisted grin. The cigar burning between his fingers burning long ashes.

"Well, Roberto," Claudia broke the trance between them. "Aren't you going to ask me to dance?" She tilted her head slightly trying to look naive. There was not one ounce of innocence in her.

Roberto put down the glass of sherry, stubbed out the cigar, got to his feet, and stated, "My dear Claudia, I am mesmerized by your entrance and the beauty you bestow upon me. I am unworthy. Forgive me, may I have this dance?"

Claudia seemed to float toward him and into his arms. They embraced for a moment until Claudia drew back her head and told Roberto, "Kiss me now. Kiss me hard and deep. I need you, Roberto, I need you now."

Roberto looked at her and began to say, "And I…"

Claudia didn't wait for him to finish. She went forward and their lips, mouths, and tongues met.

They swayed with the tune as Sinatra sang, *Like painted kites, those days and nights went flying by. The world was new beneath a blue umbrella sky…"*

They fell onto the inviting sofa and between kisses, fondling, moans, and groans they began disrobing each other. As they hugged there, their nude bodies found each other and the crescendos went from high to low, high to stillness, and then to fierceness with yelling and cursing and grasping and hugging. The music had stopped, and the candles had burnt out, and they lay there, stroking, kissing, and hugging. Claudia held him close until Roberto fell asleep.

Claudia unclenched herself from him and got dressed and went out into the late night to obtain her needed elixir. She drove down to the next farm five miles away, the Cabrillo Estates. She parked by the trees behind the small bungalows that were lived in by the farmhands. The Cabrillo farm was an olive oil plantation and had an ocean of rows of olive trees and then the terrain swooped up onto a hilly countryside. Claudia went to the first dwelling and tried the door. It was unlocked. She went in and she viewed someone sleeping on a sofa bed. The room was small and open with a small kitchenette in one corner. An open door led to a bedroom and a bathroom. She glided to the open doorway and peeked in, there were two beds on the opposite sides of the room, one was empty. She then noticed a light under the bathroom door. She held still. The toilet flushed, and she heard the faucet go on and a human's groan. The door opened and then the light went off. In that moment of illumination, she saw the workhand yawn and then he took a step toward his bunk. In the dark, Claudia swooped behind him and gave him a hard judo chop behind his neck. He slumped and Claudia caught him and easily carried him to his bed. There, she laid him face down and bit into his nape, sucking and drinking enough to fulfill her quench but not enough to leave him in demise. As she slurped that erotic sense shot through her body, but she just thought of Roberto and that maybe she will wake him and lay with him before the sun rises. Claudia broke her trance and knew that tomorrow this poor soul she had depleted of his blood will be weak and will feel ill. She hoped he would not be let go because he did not show up for work. As she drove home, she thought of what was ahead for her and all the things she wanted to complete in life but never had the chance. She knew now what she would do and how she would do it.

Claudia went back to her home and when she entered the bedroom, Roberto was awake and smoking a cigarette.

He looked up at her and asked, "Mi amor, where have you gone to?" An eyebrow arched and a suspicious state engulfed his face as he quizzed her, "You have another lover? I am not enough for you?"

Claudia smiled broadly and responded, "Don't be insane, Roberto." She gave a little laugh and continued, "You fulfill all my needs and satisfy the hidden lust that you have unlocked. I couldn't sleep. I went for a drive to think about what I have decided on." Claudia walked over to him and sat next to him. He was nude but had a pillow on his lap.

Roberto put out the cigarette and asked, "And what have you decided, my love, about California?" He frowned as he stared at her.

A grin flashed on her face as she responded, "I have decided to move to America and pursue a career in writing. Don't ask what I will write about. I just know that there are stories, tales that are shuffling through my head. I have accounts of historical events, my love."

Roberto frowned deeper as he inquired, "What do you mean, Claudia, you are in your early twenties. Historical events?" He shook his head slowly.

Having existed over two hundred years, Claudia had become an expert in lying, "Oh, you see. I was born in France and my grand-fathers, uncles, and cousins go back before Napoleon, and in Spain, my husband's family has much history here. In family gatherings, stories were bestowed upon me many, many times. I have letters, diaries, and paintings that can collaborate my tales, Señor Clemoso."

Roberto nodded his head and said, "I see, my dear, I see. Well, you are relocating to America. I am glad about that. Am I going to be lucky, and perhaps, you will reside not too far from where I stay."

Claudia smiled, her eyebrows went into moon slivers as she said, "Perhaps? But right now, my precious one, devour me before I leave. I must leave early for matters that don't concern you. I do not know when I will see you again. Make love to me Roberto as if I was a condemned woman and as if it was our last time together." She stood and began disrobing.

Roberto was still felt a little puzzled, but he realized this was a self-made woman, an independent woman, and a woman of desire. He tossed the pillow aside and as Claudia tossed her blouse away Roberto stood up and lifted Claudia in his arms and began kissing her. She just responded heartily, and then he laid her on the bed and they overwhelmed one another with touching, licking, kissing, grop-ing, and lovemaking.

Later that night, she rose from the bed and slipped on a trans-parent white negligee and sat on a chair facing the French doors that lead to the balcony. The doors were ajar, and the sheer draperies slowly waved as the breeze flowed in. The night was dark and the moon lay gently on her body. In the moonlight, she was a portrait of innocence.

Claudia's thoughts echoed in her mind of what was going on. She knew one thing as she thought, *I do not want to lose this man.* She turned to view her sleeping Adonis. He lay on his side, the blanket pulled to the side one arm in front of his face. He was an ample and handsome human. She wondered how he would respond if she revealed to him what she truly was. Would he be revolted and disgusted? Would he rebel against her? Would he want her destroyed?

It was almost morning now, she looked to the fading stars and shook her head slowly and said out loud, "I don't know. I don't know. I do not know what to do."

Her lover stirred and woke up and looked at her; he seemed content.

She turned quickly as Roberto exclaimed, "You don't know what, my darling?"

Claudia quickly rose and faced him. As she smiled, she responded, "Oh, Roberto, I am sorry for waking you. You seem so peaceful there."

"It's okay, my love, I need to relieve myself. Pardon me."

He got up and went into the bathroom. Claudia quickly gathered her belongings and wrote him a note and then went to her chambers.

Roberto came back into the room and then wondered where she had vanished to. He saw the note, read it, got dressed, and left the hacienda. When he got to his hotel room, he laid back down and quickly feel asleep.

Roberto began dreaming. He dreamt that he was back at his apartment and then he and Claudia had just made love.

Claudia said, "Sorry for waking you. I have to leave."

Roberto swung his legs over the bed and said, "I needed to get up anyway, my dear. I have an early engagement at the Pac-Mar Studios in Hollywood at eight in the morning. I must go to my place and freshen up and get some papers."

Claudia put the back of her hand to her forehead and remarked, "I don't know, I don't know."

Roberto took her hand and told her, "Tell me, what were you speaking of? It sounded serious."

Claudia smiled and got up and walked toward Roberto, the nightgown swayed with her movements. Roberto's left eyebrow arched as he viewed this magnificent beauty approach him, he grinned and stated, "Tell me later." She fell atop him and they rolled on the bed and made love to the early morning birds were chirping in the trees.

Roberto woke up and he thought, *What has this woman done to me? There is something very different about this woman. Different but intriguing.*

CHAPTER 3

LOS ANGELES

THREE WEEKS LATER, CLAUDIA WAS on a jetliner headed toward the United States. Her destination, Los Angeles. In those past weeks, she organized her life to make the transition to the USA—her bank accounts, credit and ATM cards, and a new fake passport. Alfonse and Matilda would stay behind and handle the horse farm and her olive tree orchards. Claudia had managed to acquire a flight that left Valencia at five am and arrive in LAX at one in the morning the following day. Roberto arranged for a car and driver to be at the airport and take her to her new home in the hills of Pasadena. He had interviewed and hired a part-time college student to head the household and handle all the daytime activities. The small mansion was on a cul-de-sac street and sat at the base of a small hill in Pasadena.

As the driver drove to the house, Claudia was impressed with what she could see in the city streets of Los Angeles and as they headed down the street of her new home. The homes here were spread far apart on this street and were on large lots. As she entered the home and the driver brought in all her luggage, she saw her housekeeper asleep on the couch. The noise made the girl turn. She looked young and was pretty. Claudia had sent her a letter explaining her ailment and condition and what she expected from her and the staff.

The girl stirred as she heard the commotion of luggage being placed on the hardwood floor.

She rubbed her eyes as her feet hit the floor and sleepily stated, "Hi, I'm Marta, your housekeeper."

Claudia smiled. She put out her hand and said, "Hello, sorry to wake you. Go back to sleep, I'm going upstairs and rest. I'll see you tomorrow."

Marta yawned and stated, "Oh, all right, tomorrow then." She laid back down and fell asleep quickly.

Claudia tipped the driver and took her special suitcase with her upstairs. In the suitcase was a small igloo container. She opened it and took out the heavy plastic bag filled with blood. She drank it all and started putting things away. Roberto and the decorator had done a superb job in adorning her new home. All the windows had venetians blinds and heavy drapes that would be drawn during the day. Claudia had experimented and found that she could function during the day if she protected herself from the sun. She had experienced being outside during the day, but her body was well covered, she wore a veil, sunglasses, and sunscreen lotion on her hands and face. She did not like doing this and only had done it for special reasons.

At five in the morning the next day, Claudia went outside and inspected her backyard that had an exquisite Japanese garden. The sun was still behind the San Bernardino mountains, which gave her enough light to view her surroundings. It was lovely, she thought, and she imagined how she would enjoy the scenic setting in the nights to come. Just as the sun threatened to break over the mountains surface, she went to bed and slept. She had been awake all night putting things away.

Later that day, around 2:30, as Claudia lay resting in her enclosed bedroom, Marta, her head housekeeper knocked lightly at her door, "Mademoiselle, Mademoiselle, are you awake? There is a message for you from Roberto."

At the sound of Roberto's name her eyes sprang open and she was wide awake. She sat over the bed and said, "Come in, Marta."

Marta entered, and she went over to Claudia and exclaimed, "I'm sorry, Miss Brocolac, for the intrusion, but Mr. Clemoso said it was urgent."

Claudia smirked and asked, "What is the message, Marta?"

Marta smiled and stated, "He said that Pac-Mar is having a party tonight to celebrate the completion of their new movie and would like you to attend. A car will come for you at seven tonight. He added, dress semi-formally and womanly." Marta hunched her shoulders slightly and said, "Whatever that means."

Claudia smiled and hunched her shoulders too and then told Marta, "Perhaps you can assist me with that. Can you return around six this evening, please?"

Marta nodded and said, "Of course, Mademoiselle Brocolac. I'll just stay till then." She then turned and walked toward the door and stopped when Claudia stated, "Please, Marta, address me as Claudia."

Marta turned and gave a small curtsy and responded, "Of course, uh, Claudia," and left and closed the door.

Claudia twirled around the room and went to her wardrobe and viewed her assortment of dresswear. She stood there and picked out three different outfits and placed them on the huge bed and then she laid on her bed and rested.

*　　*　　*

That evening, Claudia was in a limo going down to Hollywood Way by the Bob Hope Airport in Burbank on her way to the Marriott Hotel. The gala was being held in one of the large conference halls of the hotel. She viewed the neighborhoods and how they changed from large homes to residential areas were houses seemed to be right next to each other. She noticed the boulevards had these small malls with a variety of businesses.

She looked through the moon-roof, the sky was filled with stringy light gray clouds. The moon was just making its way through the heavens.

The driver drove into the hotel entrance and then into the cul-de-sac driveway and stopped in front of the hotel's registry entrance.

He now turned and stated, "Ma'am, Mr. Clemoso will be waiting your arrival in the hotel bar. Just go in the entrance doors, turn right, and walk through the lobby past the elevator section right into the restaurant. You'll be facing the bar, ma'am."

The driver eyed her through the rear-view mirror as Claudia gave a tight-lip smile and opened her small silver with gold clasp purse but stopped when the driver told her, "No need, ma'am, it's been taken care of." He smiled. He got out and opened the door for her. As she walked away, the driver shook his head slowly as he kept his eyes on her. He then smiled and shook his head in admiration and then he got into his limo.

As Claudia walked down the lobby, the receptionists, one male and one female, both young, and a bellboy could not keep their stares off her. Claudia was not tall, just five feet five. She was petite in a way, but her flat stomach conflicted with her woman body parts. The silver sleek silk dress clung to her body but allowed her hips, derriere, and bustline room to breath. The spaghetti straps lay loosely on her smooth shoulder, holding the dress enough to reveal charming, spotless cleavage. Her silver and black boa flowed from her neck matching her patent leather high heels. Her perfect limbs carried the ornate torso to its destination gallantly. Her golden red hair was teased and piled high which gave her more height. It twisted into a beehive with one thick strand laying on her alluring shoulder that was next to her purse strap and down from her chest a few inches. Her make-up was flawless and her demeanor provoked confidence, beauty, and strength.

As she walked into the restaurant and toward the bar, eyes turned her way. Roberto was at the end of the bar on a stool, a drink stood on the bar next to him. He had been looking at the television displaying a basketball game. His eye followed the bartenders and then he found himself being approached by a goddess.

Roberto's lower lip dropped a little as his eyes widened and then he slid off the stool and opened his arms and uttered, "Claudia, Claudia, you look gorgeous or should I say" — he mimicked a Fernando Lamas cliché— *"Jew look mavoles."*

Claudia went into his arms and said, "Oh, Roberto, I feel so much better now." She placed her arms around him and lay her cheek on his chest. He wore a black suit and straight black tie.

Roberto held her at arm's length and smiled and exclaimed, "Ah, my dear. I'm such a fool. This is your first day away from home into a different country. I haven't even given you time to unwind and get adjusted. And still you came and with such bravado. You are a gem, my dear, a gem. Please forgive me."

Claudia pulled away and looked up at him. She shook her head and stated, "Oh, you brute, how can I be upset with you?" She pulled his head down and kissed him and then said, "You can make it up to me tonight." She smiled devilishly.

Looking down at her, he said, "With pleasure." He grabbed her hand and began walking but stated, "Come on, my dear, we will make a grand entrance."

They had to walk through the lobby into the second tower building that had a wall of elevator doors and then out into the open air across a short walkway to a large dwelling that housed several large conference and meeting halls, some were separated by movable sliding separators.

Around the bend, they saw several individuals standing outside two open doors. The women were dressed formally as the men were in suit and bow tie. As they approached, the females smiled and gave their hellos, the men just stared. Roberto nodded to them and escorted Claudia through the doors as she took a covetous peek at the girls.

The large ballroom was crowded with men and women, they were sitting and standing around talking, chatting, and taking pictures of one another. The celebrities were scattered here and there.

The main stars were at the front tables. There were at least twenty round tables with ten chairs at each table. In front of the stage, there was a twenty-by-thirty dance floor of linoleum, while on the stage a five-piece band lingered, adjusting their instruments. On the tables were small stands with numbers printed. Waiters and waitresses roamed around, serving baskets of rolls and filling glasses with water. At the left wall was a homemade bar.

Various individuals took notice of them as Roberto pulled Claudia through the crowded aisles as he looked at a card he held in his hand with a number on it. He found their table, number fifteen, and saw several mixed drinks stood on the table. He quickly introduced Claudia to the group.

The room was noisy, so Roberto had to speak up, "Everyone, this is Claudia Brocolac, freshly arriving from Spain." The men stood up as the women smiled and nodded. Roberto continued, "Here to my right is one of the writers, Jack Bernstein and his lovely wife Roberta," he nodded and she smiled. "Next is Jonathon Breck a cameraman, uh, I don't know your partner."

Jonathon said, "My girlfriend, Julie Stone." They nodded at each other.

"Next, here is Hamilton Brail, another writer, and his wife Samantha. Here, we have Julius Irving head carpenter and prop man and his date." Robert looked at her and asked her, "You are?"

She responded, "Cynthia, Cynthia Wade. We're engaged."

Roberto turned and said, "Here on my left is Harold Mantry, one of the executive producers." He held a hand up which held a big cigar and waved. Everyone sat, some took their glasses of water and quenched their thirst while others took a roll and buttered it.

Harold was slicing his roll as he asked Claudia, "Brocolac. You can't be the horse owner, can you?"

Roberto cut in, "You guessed it, Harold. Didn't think you saw those vouchers with the credits."

Harold buttered his roll and stated, "Some of my money is paying for this movie, I want to know all the costs." He chomped down on the roll.

Claudia picked up a roll and told him, "You have received the best horses in Europe, Mr. Mantry. I assume they performed all that you wanted them to do," she cut her roll and buttered it.

Marty nodded and said, "Well, yes, they did, I was told. Yes, they were just fine."

Cynthia asked, "Oh, Miss Brocolac—"

Claudia interjected, "Claudia, please."

Cynthia went on, "Claudia, oh my, Spain, Europe. We plan to visit there on our honeymoon."

Hamilton coughed a little as he drank from his glass. Cynthia nudged him with an elbow and continued, "Perhaps I can get your number and you can give me some pointers on places to see and visit."

Claudia smiled and said, "It would be a pleasure, Cynthia. I have visited many countries but for my personal reasons only at night, that is when Europe is most beautiful and lively. Everyone stays out late, eats dinner at ten at night, and dances till morning."

"Oh, how marvelous and how romantic! Yes, I will get together with you and you can tell me all about Europe."

They were all interrupted by the waiter putting plates of food in front of them.

"Great, I am starved," came from Hamilton. There were mixed conversations coming from around the room and Roberto leaned to Claudia and told her, "I ordered you chicken, I wasn't sure what you like, can't go wrong with chicken," he smiled and drank some water,

"It's fine Roberto, I don't think I can eat anything anyway. I'm just getting over the jetlag."

The band started playing. they started off with an instrumental version of "Yesterday" and Roberto leaned closer to Claudia and said, "How thoughtless of me. I apologize." He bent down his head and made a sad face.

Claudia patted his hand and shook her head. She smiled and stated, "Oh, don't be ridiculous. I'll be fine. Eat your dinner while I find the ladies' room. Eat mine as well."

Roberto leaned back and told her, "It's outside the doorway across the hall, hon."

Claudia got up and went toward the doorway. Roberto told the group, "Jetlag, stomach stuff." Heads nodded, and the group contin-ued eating.

Claudia was on the wide hallway, it was almost empty. She saw a young woman came out of the restroom holding a tissue to her eyes. The young woman turned and walked toward an exit at the east end of the hallway. Claudia followed her and saw her walk toward the parking lot. The night was dark, cloudless, no moon, and the stars twinkled their glitter. A cool wind swept through the lot. The young woman was standing by a Volkswagen Beetle, fumbling with her keys. She opened the door and then, *rrrring-ring*. She pulled her cellphone from her purse.

She looked at it and then said, "David, I don't want to talk about it now. I'll call you tomorrow." She hung up and took a breath. She felt a chill and rubbed her arms and a shadow engulfed her and just as she began to turn, a hand covered her mouth and yanked her head to the side while an arm wrapped around her and pinned her to the VW. Claudia bit into her exposed neck and drank new flesh blood, it has almost been two days. Claudia embellished in the luxury and she felt the warmth shoot through body, felt the erotic euphoria. She drank and drank. The woman's struggle had stopped, and this woman now slumped in Claudia's arms. Claudia stopped herself. No she did not want to kill anyone. She hoped the woman would survive. Holding her up with one hand, she opened the door and she placed the girl in her car. Claudia then got her purse and took any valuables and then as the pretty young girl lay unconscious, she socked her on the chin, leaving a bruise. All this to make it seem as a robbery. Claudia went back to the ballroom feeling strong, alert and content with herself. She looked at the makeup mirror in her purse and wiped the blood from her chin with tissues and straightened herself up.

As she arrived at the table, Roberto got up and pulled her chair and asked, "Are you all right, my dear?" with a concerned look on his face. The band was now playing "Beyond the Sea," a young clean-cut lad was crooning the tune, Bobby Darin style.

She smiled and answered, "Oh yes, darling, much better now." She sat, the group were almost done eating, and the helpers were up and down the aisles, picking up dishes, pouring water and coffee. Other helpers were bringing the dessert, cream cheese slices with strawberries on top.

Mms, ohs, and yeses echoed around the tables.

Roberto put his hand on Claudia's and patted it. They smiled to one another. The tune ended and then there was a tapping on a microphone.

A bearded middle-aged man spoke into the mic, "Good evening, fellow workers and guests. First of all, I want to thank you all for giving up one of your evenings and attending our dinner. Yes, and I really want to show my gratitude for all your superb work on our new film. The FX team did marvels with all the fascinating extra-terrestrial arrangements, the writers with their excellent material, and the cameramen with their incredible filming. I can't forget the actors on their magnificent portrayals and giving me their best dialoging. I can see some Oscar nominations here. I can't exclude the film editors, fine job!

The audience applauded.

Claudia was thrilled at witnessing this celebrity celebration. Roberto was clapping and eating his dessert, Claudia stared at him and wondered, *What am I going to do with this man?*

The speaker toned down his pitch and ended with, "All right, let's party down and dance the night away. Have fun, everyone."

Roberto looked to Claudia and asked, "You feel good enough to dance, my pretty friend?"

Claudia gave a tight-lip smile then nodded and responded, "Let's see if you can keep up with me."

Roberto gave a short laugh and got up and took Claudia from her chair and led her to the dance floor. The band started playing a Huey Lewis number, "Heart and Soul." They got on the dance floor and moved to the music. As the night went on, the more the people drank alcoholic drinks, the looser they became. Even Roberto had too many drinks, but he maintained his coolness.

The last number was a Smokey Robinson number, "Cruising." It was slow and sexy. Claudia melted into Roberto's arms and flushed up against his body with her head on his chest. Both of his arms clutched Claudia close to him and they both were aroused with the moment and with one another.

Finally, Roberto pulled away and said, "Hey, babe, let's jam this place. I want you really bad."

Claudia didn't understand all the jargon, but she sensed the urgency and said, "Yes, I want you to make love to me. Let's hurry."

Roberto took out his cell phone and called the limo driver.

The driver pulled up and they got in the limo and headed for Claudia's new home. They ran up the stairs, disrobing as they went. They fell onto the bed and made love to each other until Roberto fell asleep from exhaustion.

In the morning, Roberto woke up to an empty bed. He got out of bed and searched for his clothes and found that his shirt was missing. In the hallway, he heard the tune "Tainted Love" resonating through the house. He smiled to himself and thought, *Those electricians did a great job.*

As he entered the kitchen, he smelled the overpowering aroma of coffee and the bacon in the air. Claudia was at the stove, humming to the tune. He noticed all the windows had the drapes closed, keeping the daylight from entering. She was wearing Roberto's shirt with the sleeves rolled up and it revealed her slim firm limbs, keeping in time with the music.

"What's on the stove, my lovely dove?"

His voice slightly startled her, but she turned to face him and remarked, "Ah, you are up. I was going to serve you breakfast in bed. I hope you like scrambled eggs?"

The shirt was unbuttoned but covered most of her front. Her belly button winked at him, but he saw it was the small gold ring that she had pierced there; the wink was a reflection.

Leaning on the nook's table top with his arms crossed across his chest, he grinned and stated, "Looking at you, I don't know if I want the eggs or you for breakfast."

Claudia giggled and responded, "Roberto, you make me feel like a little girl. Anyway, it has been quite a while since I've made breakfast for a man, so you better eat the eggs first." Her forehead frowned as her eyebrows rose up.

Roberto nodded and said, "Bring me my breakfast, woman, and go get ready for me. You will be my desert."

"Ooh la la, this man is a beast. Yes, my love, I'll shower and be ready for you but then you will have to leave when we are satisfied." She winked. "I need to rest this day."

Roberto sat down, and Claudia brought the dish over with a cup of coffee and then she flashed opened the shirt briefly and then ran to her room laughing.

CHAPTER 4

ROMANCE

DRIVING HOME AND FEELING SOMEWHAT tired and sore, Roberto shook his head as he thought, *This lover was extremely strong and left bruises on my arms and back again where she held or squeezed me, but the healing felt good.* Roberto began to ponder again about the oddity of this woman he was involved with. Yes, she was attractive and witty. She was a passionate, exotic lady and well off and wasn't looking for a sugar daddy. On all outside appearances, she would be a hell of a catch. Something was not right though. A piece of the puzzle regarding her demeanor and behavior didn't fit or was not quite right. She never ate or drank liquids while he was around. This daylight dilemma was too strange and it banned her from a day-time life. Something didn't figure. He scratched his head as he drove and said to himself, *Gonna check on some stuff, babe. You're keeping something big from me. This ailment concerning albinism, how bad and fatal is it?* He nodded and turned into his driveway.

*   *   *

Claudia lay on her bed, the right-side nightstand housed a jasmin incense candle, it was the only light and it flickered shadows on the walls. She was reading a Vogue magazine, a CD player was on, an old Momma and Papa's tune filled the room, "Monday, Monday" was playing. She closed the magazine sharply and took a breath and shook her head.

Out loud she expressed, "What am I going to do with this man?" She took another deep breath and then took out a legal pad and a pen began to write.

1. Tell him the truth. Kill him if he panics and wants to run.
Then what to do? She shook her head no.

2. Tell him the truth. If he panics and wants to run, keep him locked up and keep him imprisoned.

Again, she shook her head.

3. Tell him the truth, and if he understands but wants to go, allow him to leave.

She made a frown and hunched her shoulders. She knew she cared for him.

4. Tell him the truth and let him decide if he wants no further involvement, then turn him into a vampire anyway.

Claudia smiled, *Maybe.*

5. Keep circumstances the way they are and play this game with him until—

She stopped writing and let out a breath and stated, "Until what?"

Claudia got off the bed and began to pace. She thought back two hundred years and recalled when Demetrius turned her. He did it for revenge. His mate was burned to death and extinguished from this earth by her fiancé, Inspector Beaudin. Claudia shook her head a few times and said, "Ah, my love, Beaudin. You were a brilliant detective." Again she shook her head slowly and said, "Oh, but too smart for your own good. Yes, Demetrius took me and introduced me to a new world. A world of darkness, secrecy, sacrificing lives, and drinking humans' blood for our survival. Oh, but what a pleasurable, erotic, and sexual compliment the act is." She shivered and wrapped her arms around herself and squeezed herself. "Yes, that is my life now, my only pleasure of existence, my sole purpose of survival." She banged her fist on a dresser and shouted, "I did not choose this life, but now I will pursue this orgasmic pleasure of drinking blood until I do not exist."

Claudia looked at herself in the mirror a moment and then she covered her face with her hands and then she ran and jumped on the bed and wrapped a blanket around her and stuffed her head in a pillow and cried herself to sleep.

After hours of rest, Claudia got out of bed and went through the regular rituals of human beings' getting out of bed. When with Demetrius, they wanted to portray themselves as much as possible as normal humans. She showered, brushed her teeth, and used deodorants and perfume regularly. Claudia relished doing her personal hygiene. She was still a female. She smiled as she realized she did not have to shave her legs or underarms anymore. Everything about her has remained itself as it was the day Demetrius bit into her neck and she drank his blood, and turned her. It was still early today, three-thirty in the afternoon.

Marta was a Caucasian-Asian college student and just turned twenty but mature for her age and liked her duties as the head housekeeper. There were two other part-time houseworkers there. She had one class in the morning, an anthropology class. She came in at eleven in the morning and stood until seven at night. The house was huge but only Claudia lived here. Her duties were to keep the house clean and insure the housemaids and landscapers maintained the house and its surroundings and take care of all the day-time essentials. She was also there if anyone came to the door and to answer the phone and take all messages. She was informed that the owner was ill with some type of skin disease and should not be bothered during the day and to keep the house shaded from the sun. List of to-dos were left on the kitchen table. She would have to do some light grocery shopping for herself and if there was going to be company, which so far, that hasn't happened. Her mistress, Mademoiselle Brocolac, used medicines, vitamins, herbs, and elixirs of some type to live, she was directed to believe.

Usually, around three in the afternoon Marta would make herself lunch and sit outside in the patio and enjoy the California sun. Today, Roberto had called and left a message that he would be working on a set tonight and tomorrow, he will be in touch with Claudia tomorrow evening.

Claudia was now downstairs at six-thirty and found Marta washing a glass in the kitchen, a radio was on and the newscaster was commenting on the weather.

"Good evening, Marta, have you viewed the evening skies tonight?"

"Oh hello, Mrs. Brocolac, no I haven't.

"You will when you leave. The stars are just beginning their journey along with the moon. It's beautiful."

Marta put the glass away and stated, "Ms. Brocolac, it's none of my business, since you have no employment," Marta grinned, "you do have a lot of time on your hands."

Claudia frowned and was wondering what this was leading to, "Yes, my dear."

"And you know, you seem to be like an educated person. I saw your library and there are some interesting readings and old books. My classes have me studying ancient times. I was just gonna suggest that if there is something you are interested in maybe you should take a class. All the schools around here have night courses. You're too young to be cooped up all the time. Sorry if I—"

Claudia cut in, "Don't apologize, Marta. I believe that's a wonderful idea. Thank you for bringing this up and the suggestion."

Marta let out a breath and smiled and said, "Oh good. I hope you find something that you're interested in."

They both turned toward the radio when the newsperson stated, "Los Angeles Detectives reveal that another body was found in the LA aqueduct by the third street's bridge. From an anonymous source, the statement proclaims there's an oddity to the situation. The body seemed to be depleted of its blood. This coincides in the eeriness that two other bodies were found in the LA region in the last six weeks. It also should be noted that the missing persons bureau states that a rise in numbers has been noted in their recorded logs. This—"

Marta switched the radio off and said, "Oh, that is dreadful. The news is always depressing. Hit and runs, high-speed chases, robberies, home invasions, murder, and mayhem. My God, when is it going to stop?"

Claudia leaned on the counter and folded her arms across her chest and remarked, "Never, Marta. This is part of everyday life throughout the world."

Marta leaned on the fridge and listened.

Claudia made up a story. "My parents and grandparents told me stories of these kind of atrocities in France, Spain, and other parts of Europe, Africa, and Asia. It is not just occurring here, Marta." Claudia's two hundred years of existence made her a witness to the continuing chaos of the planet.

Marta took her hands out of her pants' pockets and said, "Well, yeah, but this is America. We should have a hand on these kinds of things."

Claudia hunched her shoulders and told Marta, "Just be aware of your surroundings, stay alert, and try to have a nice day, my dear."

Marta smiled weakly and responded, "Yeah, you too."

Claudia then asked her, "Marta, how do you get around? You don't have an automobile."

Marta smiled and told her, "Oh that's simple. Right now, I have Uber, but I am getting a car."

With a puzzled expression Claudia said, "Uber?"

"Oh, that's a company that has all these independent drivers roaming around. When someone calls and wants to go somewhere, they come to wherever you are and pick you up and take you where you want to go. It's all set up with your credit card, the charge goes to your card. Once you are registered, then it's only a phone call."

Claudia just nodded her head and Marta asked, "You want me to set it up for you?"

Claudia smiled and nodded yes.

"Here, give me a credit card, it'll only take a couple minutes."

*　*　*

It was eight fifteen in the evening and Claudia was in the back seat of a new sleek Toyota Camry on her way to Hollywood and Vine. Her Uber driver had been quiet on the drive, but he had taken several glances at his adorable passenger. She had read and heard enough of these Hollywood Boulevards and now she was going to be part of the going-ons, even if it was for one night.

He finally asked, "Ma'am, are you meeting someone in Hollywood tonight?" He kept a straight face.

Claudia looked at his reflection in the rear-view mirror. He was young and attractive, and his vehicle was immaculate, "Oh, I'm hoping to." Claudia grinned.

"Sorry if I'm nosey, but Hollywood at night could be a hazardous place to be for a lovely young lady to be roaming alone. Is there some nightclub or restaurant you would like to be dropped off at instead of the corner of Hollywood and Vine?"

Claudia took out her cell phone and looked to see what his name was and then reached over and patted his shoulder as she remarked, "Why, thank you for your concern, Freddie. I'm gonna be fine. I've taken lessons in martial arts. Believe me, I can take care of myself."

The driver hunched his shoulders and said, "Okay, almost there. Hope I don't read about you in the papers tomorrow."

Claudia cringed up her nose and then said, "You'll probably read about somebody found somewhere. I heard it may be a serial madman out there."

He had to slow down due to traffic. There were many people walking on the streets and vehicles heading both ways on Vine Street.

He answered, "Yeah, I heard about that too. Spooky."

Claudia lowered her dark-tinted window. She saw the street ensembles of the packs of young teenagers who cluttered the walkways along with tourists carrying their cameras and dressed in contrast to the local inhabitants. There were parked vehicles and motorcycles sticking out from the curb. Men and women in leather jackets, some in faded Levi jackets and some had their jacket sleeves cut off. Eateries and nightclubs cluttered the avenues as well as guys standing out front with signs stating "Valet Parking." The lights and noises canvased the evening air and various odors scented the night—cigarette smoke, burgers, pizza, and hot dog aromas mostly.

Claudia gave a tight-lip smiled and replied, "Yeah, spooky."

The atmosphere was not new to Claudia. She had experienced different countries and city night celebrations. Her elixir was out there trying to have fun and unknowingly will experience a traumatic episode tonight; she was powerless about that.

Freddie pulled over to the curb and stated, "All right, Ma'am, here we are, Hollywood and Vine. Can you give me a rating on your phone and have a safe and nice evening?"

Claudia got out of the vehicle and tapped on his window, he lowered it and Claudia gave him a five-dollar tip, he smiled and said, "Thank you, Claudia, I appreciate this."

The night was clear and cloudless. The evening skies took on their normal display of a dark mosaic of glitter and moonlight.

Claudia smiled and walked away. She walked by a small group of guys huddled up in a store alcove of that sold tobacco and marijuana souvenir shop. There were two big black men, one wearing a headband the other with a shaved head, they were conversing with a tall Caucasian man who had his hair in a ponytail. He was holding hands with a blonde girl with long brown hair parted in the middle. The blacks wore Levies and denim assorted jackets that were faded blue and black.

One of the black guys called out to Claudia, "Hey, mamma, whatever you're looking for, we have it here." He stepped away from the group and spread out his arms, hands out, and his jacket was unbuttoned, revealing a bare muscled chest.

Claudia halted and turned her head and stated, "I'm looking for a nightclub with a live band. Do you know where one is?" She half smiled at them.

The long-haired girl stepped over near her and told her, "Hey, we're headed over to the Academy down Sunset. It opens up in a while. Come with us, we're gonna have some coffee."

Claudia looked at the men. They were involved in some type of transaction. The girl got closer to Claudia and stated, "Oh, Mickie is just buying some weed. Come on, let's walk a little."

As they rounded a corner, ponytailed guy ran up to them and the girl asked, "Did you get some?"

Grinning and nodding his head, he answered, "Yeah, babe, but they only sold me three joints." The girl frowned, wrinkling up her nose and the boy continued, "But they laced with opium, hon. A few drags and we'll be there. Fifteen bucks a joint. Anyway, they said they'll be all kinds of people selling whatever at the club."

The girl replied, "Ah, all right. By the way," she looked at Claudia and asked, "I'm Carolynn and this is Michael, what's your name?"

Claudia answered, "Samantha," she smiled,

Carolynn then said, "Michael, Samantha is coming with us to the club."

Michael looked at Claudia and replied, "Cool," he patted his breast pocket and claimed, "We gonna get high tonight!"

Carolynn and Johnny gave each other a high five. Claudia just smiled as she nodded.

Down the street, they went into a crowded café but found a small table near a hallway that led to the restrooms. The table was tall, and the stools fit the table. Michael went to the counter to get coffee while the girls sat themselves on the stools.

Carolynn asked Claudia, "Why you down here all alone, Samantha?"

Claudia took a breath and answered, "Well, you see, I just moved here, and I really don't know anyone."

"Oh, I see. What are you going to be doing while you're here in LA?"

Claudia smiled and said, "See the sights."

Just then Johnny came with the coffee and said, "Hey, this stuff is hot."

Claudia asked, "Where are you from?"

Carolynn answered, "We're from Laguna Beach, way down the 101."

Claudia tight-lipped smiled and just shook her head slowly.

They chit-chatted until it was ten o'clock and then they went to the club.

At the entrance, Claudia stepped forward and told them, "Let me get the cover charge. You two have been exceptionally nice to me." Carolynn and Michael stepped aside and let Claudia pay with her American Express card.

As they went into the nightclub, the tune as "Cold as Ice" by Foreigner smacked them in the face, and then Claudia had to stop to take in the audacity of the nightclub. To the rear of the huge eccentric club was a big stage with at least nine performers, all involved in playing their instruments as well as the leaders singing into stand-up microphones. The shaggy or long-haired performers were in short-sleeved tee-shirts or vest and the vocalist seem to be yelling out their music. What was more amazing to Claudia was that the dance floor was packed solid with individuals, the front half were standing in front of the stage, urging on the band while the back half were dancing and moving to the music. Nearly all had their arms in the air waving to the tempo of the music. There was a balcony that horse-shoed around the club with tables and chairs. On the outside of the dance floor there were also tables and chairs.

Michael turned to the girls and loudly said, "Awesome isn't it?" They nodded, and he told them, "Hey, why don't you guys find us a table, I'll go get us some drinks. What will you have, Samantha?" The music and the constant chatter from everyone was loud.

Claudia gave a weak smile and shook her head briefly and stated, "Water, Michael, I don't drink alcohol."

Johnny's eyebrows lifted, and he just said "Wow."

The girls went into the crowded room and squished through the aisles. From one wall, a group of girls got up from their table, they gathered their purses and jackets, and talked with each other as they made their way to another table where two young men were seated. Carolynn hurried over and placed her jacket on one chair and sat and Claudia did the same. The lighting was all colored lights that kept the room somewhat dim. After a few minutes, Michael found them and placed the glasses on the table and sat next to Carolynn, an empty seat was next to Claudia.

The band ended their number and the leader grabbed the mic and yelled out, "Is everyone having a good time?"

The crowd exploded, "Yeah."

The leader yelled into the microphone, "What, I can't hear you?"

The crowd exploded louder, "Yeah."

"All right now. Our next number is a hit song from that bad ass group, the Rollin Stones." The crowd erupted with yays. He continued, "Under my Thumb." The crowd erupted again with yays.

Carolynn took a sip from her drink and looked at Michael and asked, "When and where are we gonna smoke that doobie? Everyone here is already feeling good."

Michael grinned and explained to the girls, "While waiting for the bartender, I asked this guy next to me where we can smoke since this is a no-smoking establishment. He knew what I was referring to and told me by the restrooms down the hallway there's an exit door, but once you go out, it locks. You have to have someone on the inside ready to open it for you."

Claudia cut in, "Listen, why don't you two go outside. I'll stand by the door." She smiled.

Michael nodded and said, "Hey, that would be great. The dude wants to come out with us. He has some shit too. Hey, here he is."

A tall blond fellow came to where they were sitting, and he put his drink on the table. Claudia noticed he was good-looking and his thin wrap-around beard made him look like a young professor.

"Hi, guys, my name is Greg."

Michael stuck out his hand and replied, "I'm Johnny, my girl Carolynn, and our friend Samantha."

His eyes went to each individual and stopped at Claudia and his head nodded and he exclaimed, "Hey, now. You alone tonight, honey?"

Claudia straightened herself and responded, "Yes, by choice, and you can call me Samantha."

His lips pursed, an eyebrow arched, and he said, "Ooh, touché. Okay, uh, can I call you Sam for short?"

Claudia looked at him, her eyes settled on the vein on his neck as it pulsed, and she said smiling, "Sure, but say it nicely."

Greg smiled and stated, "Oh, just like in that movie, *A Few Good Men*."

"Oh yeah, Jack Nicolson to Tom Cruise. A great movie, man," came from Michael.

Greg nodded and then looked at Claudia and said, "Uh, Sam, I see you're not drinking, are you the designated driver?"

Claudia frowned and asked, "What is that?"

Carolynn put down her drink and answered, "Oh, that's a person who drives their friends around and doesn't drink."

Michael then said, "Hey, come on, let's go smoke. Are you still gonna mind the door for us, Samantha?"

"Of course, go on, I'll follow."

The four partiers got up and made it to the hallway in a single file. Greg was in rear and liked what he viewed in front of him. At the exit door, they looked around as though they were pulling some type of robbery and then went outside. Claudia crossed her arms across her chest and leaned on the wall and listened to the sounds of the band. They were now playing a Three Dog Night hit, "One Is the Loneliest Number."

She closed her eyes and thought of Demetrius. He was such a viral man and so very handsome. He provided for her, he protected her, and he taught her so many, many things. For two hundred years they existed, hiding their secret from the world. He had set everything up and made provisions to live as humanly as possible. Claudia kept her eyes closed and thought to herself, *Will I ever find a man to replace Demetrius?*

"Hey, do you mind if I talk with you?"

She flinched as her eyes opened and a young man was standing in front of her.

"Sorry if I startled you. I see you here by yourself, and you looked like a person in need of company."

Claudia gave him a feeble smile and said, "Oh, I seemed that gloomy, huh? No, I was just here waiting on some friends—" she jerked he thumb toward the door and said, "—they're smoking." She nodded.

He smiled and nodded his head and then said, "I see. You're on a date, okay. Look, I would like to get to know you if this thing—" he jerked his head toward the door "—isn't serious. Here's my business card, home number is on the back. Call if you need to be rescued." He looked around and stated, "Or just want company. Can I at least have your name?"

Claudia took the card, smiled, and said, "Samantha. Thank you."

"Great, Samantha, hope to hear from you." He walked away and went into the men's room.

She watched him walk away. he was dressed in a sports coat and had a clean-cut haircut, and then there was a knocking on the door. She quickly opened the door and first Carolynn came in, there was a light cloud of smoke drifting upward, the open doorway breeze gushed the smoke away. Claudia noticed the glassy look in Carolynn's eyes and her silly smile. Carolynn was fanning her face with her hands as Michael followed her in. He had the same expression on his face and blurted out, "This shit is bomb, man."

Greg followed but he seems to be more settled and just had a straight tight-lip smile across his face. They went back to their table as the band were putting down their instruments and the leader announced, "We're taking a short break to drink and pee." Assorted laughter broke out. The foursome all sat down.

Greg leaned over toward Claudia and asked her, "Hey, babe, you want to blow this joint and go for a ride?" I have a new Corvette that's yearning for a cruise."

Claudia really didn't like his company, but she knew it was time for her medicine. She looked at Michael and Carolynn and said, "You know I really liked being with you two, but Greg and I are going for a ride," she looked at Greg and said, "The beach, yes?"

Greg didn't think it would be this easy, he nodded his head quickly and then smiled and responded, "Hell yeah, the beach. I'll put the top down, so we can enjoy the stars and the lover's moon." He thought he was slick in adding the "lover's moon."

As they were leaving, the band started playing, *"We've got to get out of this place, if it's the last thing we ever do."*

*   *   *

Claudia and Greg were finally on the 101 headed north. The night was cool, but Greg had taken off the fiberglass top and was cruising a cool fifty-miles-per-hour speed down the highway. The dark night had sprinkled an array of glittering stars tonight. There was a fading string of thin clouds hovering over the horizon as they reluctantly dipped into the sea. The sliver of a moon stood still directly above them, one cloud stood at its base. The radio was on the Pandora system and played tune after tune with an advertisement every so often. An old number was playing, *"Sweeten my coffee with a morning kiss, soften my dreams with one of your sighs, tell me you love me for a million years. If it don't work out, if it don't work out, then you can tell me goodbye."*

Claudia had a scarf over her hair, she sat back and pretended she enjoyed the cool breeze hitting her face. She was hungry and then she said, "That song is so deep and meaningful."

Greg looked sideways at her and said, "Yeah, it's a great song to dance to with that special someone."

Claudia smiled and listened. *"If you must go, I won't grieve, if you wait a lifetime before you leave."*

Claudia sat up and asked, "Greg, can we stop and park somewhere, so we can enjoy the night view?" She smiled.

Greg smiled and nodded slowly and exclaimed, "Hey, I know of a sweet spot, hold on." He made a U-turn and went up a hilly street. There was an array of sporadic nice homes here and there. He turned on Mulholland Drive and then turned on a small side street. It was too dark for Claudia to read the sign post. He went over a dirt pathway and stopped. They were on a secluded cliff overlooking Malibu beach.

Greg turned off the engine and turned to face Claudia and stated, "How do you like the view, hon?"

Claudia looked around and responded, "It is adorable." Then she sprang over on top of the console and on his lap, and she began kissing his face and mouth. He responded quickly and began pulling at her clothes. Claudia helped him and when finally he was inside her and moaning, Claudia bit into his neck.

"Hey, what the fu—" Claudia smothered his mouth with her hand. He tried to push her off, but her strength was great. She held him at bay, he was not giving up and tried to twist and turn but Claudia's vampire strength held him down. Claudia was now experiencing a sexual climax and sucked harder and pumped harder. Greg's arousal forced him to surrender to the eroticism and responded to Claudia's humping. She had not experience the exuberance of this act since the days with Demetrius. Greg's body gave a final push and then subsided and Claudia's body vibrated with pleasure. She could not stop drinking his blood, and finally she screeched, "Demetrius!" She slumped on Greg's dead body. She kissed and hugged at him as her orgasm lessened.

It was now three in the morning. The moon was now covered with black clouds as Claudia stuffed Greg's body into the trunk and straightened up her clothes. She put on a black sweater she had in her large purse and tied the scarf tightly on her head, and then drove back to Hollywood. The town was almost empty but there were stragglers here and there. Most people were at fast food stands. Claudia saw a McDonald's that had an alley. She drove into the alley and parked and went through Greg's wallet and then used Greg's cell phone. She saw an Uber app and called it using his credit card. She walked over to the McDonald's and waited. Ten minutes later, the Uber driver showed up, she got in hiding her face as much as possible, and had the driver dropped her off a block before her house. The streets were bare and she waited for the Uber vehicle to drive out of sight and then she walked home as the skies began to shed the night away.

CHAPTER 5

DETECTIVE MORRIS

WEEKENDS USUALLY LEFT CLAUDIA BY herself in the big four-bedroom home. She got out of bed and now was in her living room. The curtain windows kept all rays of the sun out, her air conditioning was kept on when needed. Claudia sat on her couch with her legs curled under her and was watching a news channel. It was six in morning, Eyewitness News was on.

The camera scanned the McDonald's and then went to the reporter. "This is Corrine Summers, reporting to you from West Hollywood. Authorities informed us of a dead body found stuffed in the truck of a vehicle this morning. A neighbor reported the vehicle was parked in front of her garage and could not retrieve her vehicle to attend a church service. Apparently, the culprit committing this horrendous deed killed the victim and took his wallet and valuables. The registration to the corvette belongs to a Greg Portman. The medical examiner has to use the victim's fingerprints to actually ID the body." An Uber driver claims he picked up a woman at McDonald's at around three-thirty in the morning and took her to an address in the hills of South Pasadena. He also claims she was attractive wearing a black sweater and jeans.

The camera scanned the vehicle and the alley and then went back to the reporter. "We will have more information for you later today. This is Corrine Summers signing off and back to the ABC studios."

The screen now viewed a female newswoman back at the studio, "Well, this is an interesting crime to investigate. What do you say, Matt?"

Camera viewed Matt. "Well, looks pretty eerie, Cathy. Let's get to something a little more gleeful, Cathy."

Cathy replied, "Yes, there's news from the happiest place on earth, executives report—" Claudia used the remote to switch the TV off.

*   *   *

Michael and Carolynn were in a motel in Silver Lake and they too were watching Eyewitness News and saw the broadcast regarding the murder. Michael elbowed Carolynn next to him in the bed and asked, "Wasn't the name of the guy who took off with Samantha?"

Carolynn just nodded and said, "I think so."

*   *   *

Freddie was driving his car to the car wash when he heard the news. He switched the radio off and rubbed his chin, he squinted his face as he thought, *Hollywood, la-la or ca-ca?*

*   *   *

Marta turned off the TV after she heard the news of the dead body and just stared at the blank TV.

*   *   *

Lieutenant Jason Morris sat across from the Uber driver. He was writing down the description of the passenger he picked up at the

50

McDonald's as Sergeant Mark Stevens, the police artist, drew on his artist pad the details the Uber driver could remember.

Jason tapped his pencil on the desk and inquired, "Come on, man, try and recall a little more detail. What we have now can match any young pretty girl." He looked at the Uber driver with an eyebrow raised.

David winced and responded, "Aw, come on, Lieutenant, it was three-thirty in the morning, the end of a twelve-hour shift. She had her hair down covering a lot of her face. I was in no mood to pry that night. I told you the address of where I dropped her off. Haven't you guys checked that out yet?"

"Yeah, it was an elderly couple. They were sound asleep at that time. No one else lives in that home and the description you gave doesn't fit anyone they know and or that they have seen in the neighborhood," answered the Lieutenant.

"Go on, get out of here, but remember, when we catch this woman, we'll need you to ID her," stated Lieutenant Morris.

As David left the room, Morris leaned over to take another look at the drawing. Flowing red hair covering one eye, petite nose over perfect lips. "He didn't know what color her eyes were, damn it," huffed Morris.

Oberron looked at Morris and said, "I'll run this through the computer using California files. See what comes up." Sergeant Lou Oberron was Morris's partner.

Morris huffed and stated, "Probably every young woman that has ever been arrested will come up."

Oberron giggled and said, "Well, we know she's not Black or Asian or Latina."

"Yeah, that cuts in down a few thousand," Morris smirked and then got up and put on his jacket and said, "Gonna ride through them streets in them hills in Pasadena. There are some pretty fancy homes up there."

Oberron closed his note pad and said, "Morris, we don't even know if it was a woman who did this. She could be a girl out late, maybe jilted or broke up with her boyfriend and gets a ride from Uber."

"Yeah, but remember she used Greg's credit card. What? So some strange girl finds the card and because she's broke, she uses the stolen card and uses a fake address. Hell, this woman lives up there. If not the killer, she knows something. I'll scan the area on my way home. I live in Monrovia, it's kind of on the way," he winked at Oberron.

*   *   *

Marta was taking some clothes out of the dryer and folding them in the laundry room when Claudia peeked down the hallway and announced, "Marta, are you in here?"

Marta responded, "Hey, you're up. Yeah, just finishing up some of your belongings."

"Oh, thank you, dear."

"What happened? I found a little blood on your blouse."

"Oh, a glass broke and this guy I was with stubbed his finger and some blood fell on me. Did you managed to get it out? I love that blouse."

Nodding her head, she replied, "Uh-huh. The blood hadn't fully dried yet."

She finished folding the last article of clothing and walked into the kitchen carrying the basket of laundry. Claudia was staring out the kitchen window overlooking the sink. It wasn't dark yet; she ducked away.

Marta asked, "What are you going to do tonight, Claudia? I came in today to be here when they delivered your car. It's a nice-looking vehicle. How'd you pick that one?"

"I went through those brochures. I like the sleekness of the Optima."

"Well, you're gonna be white on black in black. Windows are all tinted."

"Yes, I like that. I think I'll go for a ride to the casino off the 210 Freeway tonight. It is about an hour from here. It seems easy to get to from here, straight freeway."

"Oh, you mean San Miguel. It's nice, I've been there but only once. Didn't win anything but it was fun. Them slot machines get you. I was there for hours, went up and down, finally it beat me."

Claudia then said, "I'm going to get ready, Marta, thank you for being my friend. I'll see you Monday."

Marta smiled and said, "Okay and goodnight. See ya Monday."

Marta was out on the cul-de-sac driveway, dusting off her car with a car brush when Lieutenant Morris drove by. He did a double take on her and made a U-turn and drove up behind her.

Marta stopped brushing her car off and waited to see who this was. Lieutenant got out of his vehicle and walked toward her. He thought she as a very attractive young woman, and she thought that this gentleman was very appealing considering he was in his thirties.

Marta went to her trunk and placed her brush in it and as she closed the lid, the policeman stated, "Hello there, ma'am, nice place you have here."

Marta was still puzzled and asked, "Yes, and well, what can I do for you?"

"Oh," he smiled and shook his head as he explained, "excuse me. I'm a police officer with the LAPD and I'm in the process of investigating what may be serial crimes."

Marta's face brightened up, her eyebrows arched, and her lips made a small circle.

Earlier that day, the Lieutenant found out that the body had been drained of his blood. This mode of operandum coincided with two other bodies found in the Los Angeles county vicinities.

Marta regained composure and asked, "Crimes committed around here?" She made a funny face, she squinted her eyes, and asked, "What kind of crimes, may I ask?"

Morris liked the way this girl was acting and wanted to know more about her, "Uh, well, let me ask you this, how long have you lived here?"

Marta grinned and replied, "Oh, I don't live here, I work here. Does that get me off the hook?" she grinned.

Smiling and nodding his head, he answered, "Not entirely. Where were you last night around three in the morning?"

"Asleep in my bed in Arcadia."

Morris clinched his mouth and then asked, "I'm sure that can be verified." His right eyebrow lifted as he continued, "By your boyfriend, lover…" he tilted his head back and forth waiting for her reply.

Marta squinted at the detective and kind of irritated, she answered, "My mom. I live with my parents."

Morris made a dopy expression and said, "Hey, forgive me for being rude. I'm usually questioning, well, not sympathetic, sensitive individuals such as you seem to be. I'm sorry, okay."

Marta took in a deep breath and said, "Yeah, sure, okay. So what kind of crimes are you investigating?"

Morris clenched his face again and looked down and then looked at Marta and answered, "Murders."

Marta's eyebrows rose, and she said, "You had stated serial. Does that mean continuing murders?"

Morris gave a tightly closed mouth smiled and nodded and said, "You catch on. Yeah, we believe some killings were done by the same person, maybe. Everything doesn't match up, but final touches do. Hey, look, I've divulged more then I should. What's your name?"

Marta smiled and said, "Marta Yamamoto, I'm also a student at Pasadena College." She tilted her head to one side and asked, "What's yours?"

Morris put out his hand and announced, "Lieutenant Jason Morris, homicide division."

"Ooh, Lieutenant. You seem young for a lieutenant, aren't you?"

He breathed in and remarked, "Been in the force for ten years. Anyway, Miss Yamamoto, who lives here?"

"Oh, my employer, Mademoiselle Claudia Brocolac. She comes from Spain, uh, actually born in France and is wealthy and a nice person."

Morris nodded and immediately though that this nature person would be an elderly spinster.

With a creased forehead Morris asked, "You think she'd be up at three in the morning. Being elderly and all. Old ones don't sleep well you know."

Laughing and covering her mouth with a hand, Marta finally stated, "Mademoiselle Brocolac is not a senior by any means. She's only twenty-two and going for a drive right now."

Slightly embarrassed and red of face Morris replied, "Oh, how ignorant of me to think your boss was a senior just because, well just because." He laughed a little. "Oh, I'd better catch her before she leaves."

"Oh, the big policeman can laugh at himself. That's a positive sign."

"Positive sign?"

Blushing and grinning, Marta stepped away and said, "Oh, for a girl to know that a man, you know, that he has a sense of humor."

"Hmm, well then, I think I should know more about you, Miss Yamamoto."

"Call me Marta, please."

Smiling, he said, "Marta, uh, perhaps I should get your number in case I have further questions." He tilted his head while smiling.

"Perhaps you should. And I should get your card just in case I think of something."

Morris liked this girl. "Yes, yes, you should." He reached into his jacket and gave her a card but wrote his cell phone number on it and said, "Just in case I'm off duty," he smiled.

After giving the lieutenant her number, they said their goodbyes and the lieutenant went to the front door as Marta drove off home waving out the window.

CHAPTER 6

FIRST ENCOUNTER

THE SUN HAD COMPLETELY HIDDEN itself behind the Hollywood hills as Lieutenant Morris rang the doorbell. Chimes rang as he stood there slapping his notepad on his hand.

The door opened, and the lieutenant stared a moment in surprise as this delightful lovely young woman who stood at the doorway brushing her long red-gold hair. Her devilish green eyes trying to sum up who was this stranger at her door. Her form-fitting jeans clung to her figure nicely while her bright red blouse accented her pale complexion and her attractive face. The red heels stood apart in a stance of defiance.

"Yes, how can I help you?" came from her ruby-red mouth. Her eyes quickly gave him the once over.

Morris finally broke out of his trance, cleared his throat, and asked, "Are you Mademoiselle Claudia Brocolac?"

Claudia was now surprised that this good-looking gentleman at her door knew her name. She nodded and responded, "Why, yes. How do you know me?" That European accent made her more appealing.

"My name is Lieutenant Morris of the Los Angeles Police Department and I'm here just to ask you a couple of questions. Uh, yeah, I was just talking to your employee, Marta Yamamoto. She informed me that you reside here."

"I see. What would you like to ask? Wait, please step inside and sit down."

Surprised Morris smiled and said, "That will be nice, okay."

Claudia smirked and said, "Fine, follow me." As she walked, she stated over her shoulder, "You Americans use that word 'okay', a lot. I now find myself using it now."

"Hmm, yeah, I guess."

He followed her into what seemed like a study or library. One wall had bookcases lined against the wall. The tall windows all had floor-length drapes smothering the openings. Sofas and stuffed antique chairs all faced one another, others faced a large fireplace. Paintings decorated the walls. A few end tables had vintage lamps on them, a hard-carved coffee table stood in front of the sofa, and a hand-carved wooden leaf lay in the center of it with wrapped candies in it.

As the officer followed her in the room and looked around noting the décor, he nodded slowly. She sat as she pointed to an over-stuffed chair. He sat, and she crossed her legs. The chairs stood at ninety-degree angles and they were not facing each other. He continued to scan the room and noticed several pictures on shelves, one had a good-looking man with a beard.

The Lieutenant opened, "Miss Brocolac, where—"

Claudia corrected him, "That's Mrs. Brocolac, even though my husband passed away a year ago."

Morris moved the chair to face Claudia and said, "Oh, okay," He smirked and said, "There's that word again. Uh, were you home last night, or should I say this morning at three, three-thirty?"

Claudia looked at the Lieutenant and said, "Yes. At those hours I was very much asleep."

Morris took out a notepad and flipped a couple of pages and stated, "Earlier yesterday evening, an Uber driver picked you up and dropped you off in Hollywood, Hollywood and Vine. Is that correct?"

"Yes, I met some friends and we went to the Academy Night Club. What is this about?"

"You see, there's been some killings going on and I'm just following up on something. If you don't mind, I can't divulge much more."

"Oh, I see. What else do you need?"

"All right." He looked up from his notes and smiled and she smiled back. "These friends, can I have their names and how I can reach them?"

Claudia took in a breath and said, "Their names are Michael and Carolynn. That's all I know. I just met them, and we became friends."

Morris squinted an eye a little and continued, "What time did you leave the club?"

"I became tired and bored so the man I met there, a Richard something, gave me a ride home. It was just after midnight."

"Oh, okay, all right. I'll try to verify all this. You have a very nice place here, Mrs. Brocolac. You're from Europe, huh?"

Claudia smiled and said, "Yes, I am. If you don't mind, are we done Lieutenant Morris. I'd like to leave before it gets too late."

Morris put his pad away and stood up and began walking toward the door and Claudia followed, and he said, "Of course." He kept walking and then stopped. She almost ran into him. He turned and asked, "Oh, have you seen anyone around here who resembles this woman?" He took out the flyer from his inside pocket and unfolded it.

She held it up to the light and then shook her head and said, "No, never. But I'm new here. I've been here only a couple of days. I came from Spain on Thursday."

Morris stood there a moment and contemplated, *The other bodies were found way before*. He nodded and said, "Goodnight, Mrs. Brocolac. I don't think you'll be bothered by me again. Have a lovely evening."

"Goodnight, Lieutenant, hope you catch your man."

Claudia closed the door and leaned against it and let out her breath. She quickly turned and peeked out the side window.

Morris strolled to his vehicle rubbing his chin and thinking, *Hmm, she's almost apprehensive but she wasn't even here when the other bodies were found, she's filthy rich.* He shook his head and loudly said, "Naw," and got in his cruiser and drove the streets a little more.

*   *   *

Claudia was now driving on the 210 Freeway east. She followed the GPS directions and excited on Highland avenue and came up to the large structure of the Indian gambling casino, San Miguel. She looked up and the skies had become cluttered with heavy dark-gray clouds. There was a dampness in the air. The moon was swallowed by the gray mushroom clouds. There was a multilevel parking structure connected to the gambling building, and there was a lane to the valet section also. She slowed down and thought it would be better to park in the structure since it was more isolated. She realized that she needed to be more cautious here in America. With all the electronic capabilities of criminality screening, the smallest of clues leads to more clues. She recalled how her former finance Inspector Beaudin would sit up at night examining pieces of paper, faded photographs, and pictures of victims' clothing. These detectives, their minds shuffle evidence and clues around like pieces of a puzzle. She will be careful. No taking of lives here even when she's experiencing that stupendous erotic orgasmic pleasure. She smiled at herself. She drove into the parking structure and the first three levels were full.

Hundreds of automobiles of all makes and models. The next level also had cars but there were sporadic empty stalls here and there. She chooses one between two large four-door trucks. She stood seated a moment and wondered about those other bodies that were found. The newscaster stated that each body had been depleted of their blood. Is there another vampire in Los Angeles? If there is, she must locate him and teach him the way of Demetrius. Drink to live but not take lives. Dead bodies mean more authorities searching, seeking, and asking questions. She must find him, this demon.

The concrete walkway that connected the structure to the casino was long. Several scattered individuals were on it, some walking swiftly towards the casino, others dragging away to their vehicles probably with empty pockets. Couples and individuals were everywhere. Toward the entrance, there were several small stands. Some vendors were selling hot dogs, others pizza slices, and one was selling sweets such as donuts and cake slices. Small groups of people were at the stands.

As Claudia entered the casino, she found herself on the second level. Slot machines lined the walls and to her right was a glass wall. The doors led into a room where the tables were filled with people playing poker. She gazed in and was amazed that so many players were at the tables all with somber expressions. Claudia knew nothing about card playing and just smirked and walked on. She got to escalators, one coming up and one going down. At the bottom, she gazed around the room. Everywhere you looked there were slot machines, various animated colors and cartoonish characters jumped around on screens. Some just had symbols, some had still pictures of various landscapes. People were sitting in front of machines putting in money and pressing buttons. The screens would whirl and stop to the disappointment and or approval of the gambler. It appears all the slot machines had someone sitting there. The maze of walkways also had individuals cluttering the floors. Smoke rose from everywhere and dissipated quickly. This establishment was not at smoke-free establishment.

She walked on, keeping close to the wall. She passed eateries, cashier stables, and money machines. She stopped in front of a large restaurant and looked inside. It, too, was crowded with people. The dwelling was hidden from the world. No clocks, no daylight. She summarized that she could well be in here during the daytime. Daylight hours made her a little foggy, but she still maintained her wits.

Claudia turned quickly as she heard this girl scream. A woman sitting at a slot machine just stood up and yelled, "Cashier, cashier! I won, I won!" A small group of people went over to her machine. Claudia walked over to see what the commotion was about.

She got there and a uniformed woman with a thick belt around her waist that had leather pouches was at the machine and speaking with the woman.

"Well your luck is with you tonight. You won $2,000.00."

The woman put her hands to the sides of her face and exclaimed, "Oh my God, oh my God."

The small group there applauded and then dispersed.

The cashier gave her a voucher and explained what she needed to do. At that moment, a young man came over and the girl jumped into his arms and told him, "Ronnie, I won $2,000.00."

He smiled ear to ear and said, "Hey, that's great, Molly. That's great. Let's cash in and get out of here before we give it back."

As soon as they walked away, another woman sat at the machine and immediately put a bill into the slot and started pressing buttons.

Claudia walked away and then saw all the gambling tables in the middle of the casino. People were sitting around the tables as a dealer maneuvered the game. She walked by the tables to see what and how they were playing. She saw four rows of tables where people played Black Jack with different money denominations of playing, there were Three Card Poker, Four Card Poker, Pai Gow, Craps, and Roulette tables.

She peeked in at a Three Card Poker table. She noticed there were three spots to place chips in front of each player. Ten dollars was the minimum bet. The top spot is where you place your bet if you want to receive the winnings if you get a pair or more. The middle spot is the ante and the third spot a bet spot that is played if you want to play against the dealer. If you don't play that spot, all bets are lost. If you bet all three and your card beats the dealer, you win one to one. If you get a pair you win two to one, a straight, six to one, a flush four to one, and three of a kind pays thirty to one. Straight Flush pays forty to one. Those odds keep people playing.

Just then, a young man in front of her slapped his cards on the table and got up and left. Claudia took his stool and sat down. She pulled a money clip from her pocket and took out a hundred-dollar bill and slid it over to the dealer. He checked it for authenticity and slid her four stacks of five-dollar chips. Claudia glanced at the other players bets, some place two chips on the first and second spots some placed three or four chips on those spots. To get a feel of the game Claudia did the minimum, two chips on the two spots and waited for her cards. The dealer was classy and dealt the cards without a flaw. Claudia picked up her cards and the dealer told her to only use one hand. She frowned and picked up one card at a time. The first was an ace of spades, next card was a king of spades, she held her breath. She let out her breath. She placed her chips on the play spot.

Dealer cards were face down. He then flipped three cards, an ace, a king and a ten. The players aahed or oohed. The dealer claimed, "Oh, we have a hot one here." He flipped another ace and then a two and the river card was a king. He paid her the chips.

Claudia stood there for another twenty minutes and lost her hundred dollars. She got up went into the ladies' restroom. She sat on a commode and hugged her body. She needed her replenishment. She decided to go to the parking lot and ambush some lone individual.

She sat in her backseat and waited. People walked by in two's and three's coming and going. Then she seen a white Porcha drive in and park two cars from her vehicle. The structure appeared deserted at this time. The driver got out and stretched. He was a big man, barrel chested and he wore a full black beard. Claudia got out of her car and crouched between the cars. As he got near her, she braced herself to pounce on him. He was one step away when he stopped, mumbled something, and went back to his car. He went to his trunk and opened it. There he fumbled with a jacket searching the pockets. Claudia swiftly went over to him and slammed the trunk door on his head. She gave him another crack on the head. He slumped over and then Claudia picked him up and dragged him between the vehicles. There, she sucked at him and got her fill. He was still breathing. She searched his pockets took his money and watch. She went to the trunk and went through his jacket and took out his credit cards. She would never use them, but she wanted it to look like a robbery. As she got into her car and drove away, she lowered her window to feel the rain, didn't feel like anything to her but she pretended. She sighed and drove home in the pouring rain, content that she did not kill tonight.

Sunday went by quickly, she stood in bed all day. Evening came, and she got on a computer and did research on the three bodies the authorities had found with their blood depleted. It seemed they were discovered all east of the LA River reservoir, a section of Los Angeles known as East LA. She Googled where the main business locations were. There were two main boulevards, Whittier Boulevard and Caesar Chavez Boulevard. The Whittier one ran deep into East LA. The main commercial area was from Indiana Street to Garfield Avenue. The Caesar Street's main businesses ran from Soto Street to Evergreen Avenue. Reading on, Atlantic Boulevard had a lot of stores and eateries too. Claudia dressed in jeans, a red and black checkered lumberjack shirt, boots, and her hair in a ponytail.

She was about to leave when her cell phone buzzed. It was Roberto. "Hello, honey, what is going on?"

"Hey, babe, I'm just doing studio work. I miss you though."

"I miss you too, sweetie."

"You know, one of these evening shoots, you should come down and hang out. Find out how movies are really made."

"Really? I would love to. Tell me when and where."

"I'll do that when we are on local location. Hey, I'll be involved in locating areas in the East LA area this week."

"Oh, what kind of story is that?"

"Well, it's about these young hoodlums, trying to pull off a big-time bank robbery like the one their dads tried to do twenty years ago. True story, it occurred three years ago."

"Ooh la la. What a traumatic escapade that will be."

"Yeah, anyway, hon, I have to leave but can we get together tomorrow night?"

Claudia thought and responded, "Yes, indeed, but it was to be late like nine or ten o'clock. I'm doing some shopping at the mall in Arcadia."

Roberto nodded and answered, "Okay, that will be fine. I'll eat something before I go up there."

"All right, Roberto, I'll see you tomorrow. Goodnight."

"Goodnight, Hon."

CHAPTER 7

SUSPICIONS

FREDDIE WAS READING THE NEWSPAPER as he sat sipping coffee at a Starbucks on Huntington Drive in Monrovia. He was waiting for someone to call for ride. He sipped his caramel macchiato as he read the inside story regarding a man being mugged in the parking lot at the San Miguel Casino. He just made a mental note of this.

* * *

Marta was drying her thick black hair with a towel in her bedroom as she watched the channel seven evening news. She froze when the newscaster stated the news about the man being mugged and robbed at the parking structure in the San Miguel Casino. Doctors claim he lost a considerable amount of blood. The victim is still recuperating in the hospital. She sat on her bed and wondered.

* * *

David was driving to pick up a fare when he heard the news on the radio. It sounded odd to him. Killings and muggings, scary.

*   *   *

Lieutenant Morris was on the phone with the Highland Police Department waiting to speak with the officer in charge of the San Miguel robbery case. He held the bulletin report in his other hand as he read it again.

"Yeah, this is Martinez."

"Hey, bud, this is Lieutenant Morris, LAPD. I'm interested in that mugging at the casino."

"Oh, yeah. You have similar going-ons down your way?"

"Uh, could be. Listen, have you spoken with the victim?"

Martinez shook his head and replied, "Yeah, but not much help. He doesn't know anything. Says he was hit from behind, never saw who it was. His head is all bandaged up."

"Doctors report states he lost a lot of blood. What's that about?"

"Don't know, man. He almost died. The parking lot cop found him at six in the morning. No other cars around. His jacket was sticking out of the trunk. Ambulance picked him up, he had two transfusions. Doctors were puzzled why that much blood was lost."

Morris rubbed his chin. "Has anyone checked his car for evidence and to see where the blood went? Fingerprints?"

"I'm headed down to the evidence room now. If anything comes up, I'll call you. Or, yeah, he did have a bandage on his neck too, some kind of wound there."

"Hmm, head wounds, huh. Neck had bandage. All right, Martinez, hope to hear from you. Later."

"So long."

Morris got up and went to the file cabinets and pulled out the files on the other three corpses and began going through them again. He rubbed his chin as he viewed the pictures of the dead bodies, and then he called the two morticians who handled the autopsies.

"Hey, Williams, this is Morris down at LAPD."

"Oh, Lieutenant, it's been a while. What do you need?"

"Well, those two bodies you have that are depleted of their blood. What do you think of that and how was the blood siphoned out?"

"Hold on a minute." Dr. Williams went over to the file cabinets and pulled out the two files. "Yes, here it is. It appears some type of apparatus was attached to their necks. There's small wounds on the neck. It must be one of them new European siphoning gadgets I heard of."

Morris rubbed his jaw and asked, "Doc, what would someone do with blood?"

Williams put down the files and hunched his shoulders slightly and remarked, "My guess is he maybe sells it to some hospital or this killer is deranged and collects the blood as most serial killers like to do. You know, souvenirs. They keep some type of memento. You know that, of course."

Morrie nodded and answered, "Yeah, I thought of that. Well thanks Doc, I—"

"Oh, Morris, here's one more detail. I don't know if it's a clue or evidence but on the latest body and only on this one," he looked through the file, "uh, Gregory Sander's body, I also found a lipstick smudge by the wound. Then I thought he had been with a woman earlier but now, well, I don't know."

Morris squinted some as he replied, "Hey, listen, everything is a clue. They lead nowhere, and they lead somewhere. Do me a favor, can you analyze it and find what kind or brand. What about the DNA, can you get that from it?"

Dr. William's nodded his head and stated, "Possibly, if there's enough body DNA chemicals there."

Morris smiled and said, "Great, Doc. Call me when you have something. Later."

"Later, Lieutenant."

Morris now called the second mortician who was at the East Los Angeles location. "Hello, this is Lieutenant Morris from LAPD Homicide. May I speak with the mortician who handled the Marquis Sandoval corpse?"

"Yes, Lieutenant, this is Dr. Garcia. What can I do for you?"

"Ah, great, Doctor. I'm involved in investigating these corpses that have been found with drained blood. After examining the corpse, did you find anything unusual in the Sandoval body?" Morris stood up a paced a little.

Dr. Garcia's brow wrinkled as he thought and said, "Why, yes. Besides being most of his blood gone, his head was bashed severely, and he had small wounds on his neck and thigh. The body was found nude. Here's another thing, the guy was killed elsewhere and dumped at the wash."

Morris sat at his desk and began writing and then questioned him some more. "You say wounds on neck and thigh. What does that tell you?"

Garcia had been vaping and let out a gigantic cloud of smoke. It surrounded him a moment and then faded as he spoke, "My summation, Lieutenant, is that Marquis Sandoval was involved in a bisexual episode at the time of his death."

Morris eyebrows rose and he commented, "Bisexual episode. Is this getting more interesting and complicated or what?"

Garcia smiled, "The small wounds appear to be bite marks and are of two sizes. The smaller one, most likely a woman. Marquis had semen on him, his own. I believe he was in the act of making love when the culprits decided to murder and rob him."

A puzzled look overcame Morris as he said, "Whoa, that puts a whole new light on this case, Doctor. Hmm, did you find any lipstick or any kind of makeup on or near the body?"

"It's there in the report. On the back of the title page. Sergeant Tristell noted that on the top of the wash he found a pair of women's panties. He didn't know if they had anything to do with the case or not. They've been analyzed, and the DNA shows no such person is in our records."

Morris looked at the report and nodded and stated, "Wow, I didn't see that. Okay, Dr. Garcia, thank you for the info and for your insight."

Garcia answered, "My pleasure, Lieutenant. Catch that bastard, will you?"

"Gonna try, Doc. Gonna try my damnest."

As Morris sat there rubbing his chin his phone rang. "Morris here."

"Jason, you're still there. Good. Another body just came in. It was found in a motel room on Atlantic Boulevard, The Tic Toc Motel."

"Yeah?"

"The body is depleted of blood."

Morris sprang to his feet and said, "Close up shop, Doc, meet me at our old watering hole." Morris put on his jacket and hurried out of the precinct.

*　　*　　*

Marta was at home doing homework in her room when her mother yelled out, "Marta, dinner is served, what will you drink?"

She had been doodling on a notepad:

1. Won't go into daylight.
2. Young but mature.
3. Never eats.
4. Never drinks.
5. Body found depleted of blood.
6. Took Uber to Hollywood where body was found.
7. From Europe.
8. Filthy rich.
9. ?????????

Marta shook her head and then looked up and answered, "Okay, Mom. Just water." She got up and went to eat.

*　　*　　*

Freddie was driving a passenger to San Miguel the night Claudia went there. As he was on the crowded entrance way to drop off passengers when he happened to see Claudia drive away in her automobile. The way she reacted to feeling the rain seemed odd to him. At the time, he thought seeing her that night was just a coincidence, but the rain thing bothered him. After he heard about the mugging in the parking lot and remembering he took her to Hollywood where there was a killing, he began wondering.

*   *   *

Michael was driving himself and Carolynn back home when Carolynn turned the radio down and looked at Michael and said, "Gee, I believe I just remembered the name of that guy who was with Samantha. It was Greg."

Michael looked over at her and asked, "So?"

Carolynn answered, "That is the name of the body they found in Hollywood that night."

Michael hunched his shoulders and asked, "What's that got to do with the price of potatoes in Europe?"

Carolynn winced and responded, "Don't you remember? The guy who was with that girl Samantha, his name was Greg. They left early to go for a ride."

Michael nodded and then blew out a breath and said, "Samantha leaves with Greg. Greg ends up dead. Wait a minute. This girl we met."

Carolynn said, "Samantha…"

"Samantha kills this guy—"

Carolynn cuts in again, "Greg?"

Michael looks over at her and states, "Greg, naw. She was a small girl. This guy—"

Carolynn mumbles, "Greg."

Michael grimaces, says, "was like two hundred pounds. She couldn't overtake him."

Carolynn puts a hand on the dashboard as she turned to view Michael and exclaims, "Are you suggesting that women are too frail to overwhelm a man? Are you saying I can't beat you up if I wanted to?"

"Hey, hold your horses. I'm just saying that on the norm, it would be difficult for her to get the better of him. Maybe by surprise.

Hitting on the head with a frying pan when he was asleep." Michael was grinning and then laughed a little.

Carolynn just turned, sat back and huffed, and then mumbled, "Men."

*   *   *

Lieutenant Morris was at the LA morgue's building looking over a body with Dr. Williams. The doctor was pointing to small bite wounds on the victim's upper arms and thighs and stated, "It seems as though there were two assailants. This woman was strapped down with duct tape and rapped and mauled by two individuals prior to her blood being drawn."

They looked at one another and both breathed in and Morris stated, "We have a maniac couple who are having sex with their victims before they murder them and withdraw their blood," the doctor nodded his head.

"Would you like to go have a drink, Doc?"

"Okay, let me put our friend away here. I'll finish him tomorrow."

*   *   *

Roberto called Claudia. She looked at the name on her cell phone and answered, "Roberto, when am I going to see you?"

"Oh, my sweet, I am so sorry for being away from you. Work, you know. But I want to see you tonight. What time can I drop on by?"

Claudia wanted enough time to go out and get her blood, so she responded, "Ah, Roberto, you're so hard to refuse, and yes, I miss you too. Let me see, I promised Marta to go to the mall with her, but we should be back by eight, my love."

"Okay, Claudia, I will be there by eight."

CHAPTER 8

CLAUDIA DROVE DOWN TO FOOTHILL Boulevard and on to the Glendale Mall on Colorado Boulevard. Once there, she allowed the valet driver to park her Kia Optima and went into the mall. It was another fascinating experience for this country woman of Europe. The lights were galore, the shops, small stores, and aisle stands were plentiful and the large department stores were sensational with all their wares, clothes, and employees. She envied those who were eating sweet rolls, ice cream, and burgers. This old yearning forced her insides to ache for her medication. She looked around and followed solo shoppers. The first man she followed met up with a female with two children, all carrying bags with store logos. The second man went into a men's shop and allowed an employee to show him some shirts. Claudia was getting frustrated.

She thought to herself, *Perhaps this was not a good idea.* She breathed in and went into Macy's and then went to the ladies' department and was looking at negligees. This section of the store was not so crowded.

As she was feeling the silkiness of a dark red nightgown, a female's voice spoke behind her, "I see you have excellent taste, ma'am. That gown is so sexy."

Claudia turned and viewed a pretty boyish-girl three feet away from her. The young girl raised an eyebrow and tilted her head as she looked Claudia over.

Claudia calculated she was an attractive thirtyish young female, she then responded, "I love the way this feels. Does it come in other colors?" Claudia asked smiling seductively.

The young female hipster had short black hair, a skimpy white blouse, and baggy pants. Claudia also noticed a small tattoo on the back of her wrist. The universal sign for the female sex but in double form. A signal stating she was a lesbian.

The girl hunched her shoulders and stated, "They must have, but this color would look terrific on you." She smiled closed lipped.

Claudia sniffed her, and she smelled of soap and baby powder, and then asked her, "What makes you think so?"

The girl had her hands on her hips and she tilted her head to the side and said, "See that manikin there? She's about your size and figure. She's sexy as hell."

Claudia turned, viewed the lifelike doll and then smirked and said, "You're very kind. I guess you don't work here. You know where the attendant is?"

"Yeah, I saw her go up the escalator with her phone glued to her ear. I was gonna get something for a friend. Is this nightgown for you or for *your* friend?"

Claudia shook her head slowly and said, "Oh, for me, of course."

The girl nodded and said, "Why don't you try it on? I'm a good judge on styles."

Claudia's stomach churned, it seemed to say *feed me.* Claudia smiled and said, "What a good idea. You will be honest with me now, won't you?"

The girl made a upside down smile as her brow frowned and she simply said, "Totally."

As Claudia walked to the dressing room, the girl followed and exclaimed, "The name's Sally, by the way."

Claudia wen into the dressing room but before she closed the door she said, "And I'm Samantha."

From inside the dressing room Claudia heard Sally say, "I love that name. I was thinking of changing my name to Samantha. You know? And then you could call me Sam or Sammy, ha-ha."

"Sally, would you come in here and help me with this?"

Sally straightened up, took her hands from her pockets and nodded. She smiled and said, "Sure will, Samantha."

Sally went into the small room, Claudia was standing naked and smiling and stated, "You like?"

Sally's mouth dropped, and she nodded slowly and stepped closer to this magnificent-looking woman.

Claudia opened her arms and Sally melted into her embrace, their lips met and their skin touched, they both quickly began feverishly fondling each other. Sally's clothes fell off quickly as their sensations heightened and they both groaned and moaned with delight as their bodies rubbed together. Soon, their emotions came to a crescendo. Claudia grasped Sally tightly and bit into her neck. Sally moaned loudly with pain and pleasure as Claudia sucked in Sally's blood. They hugged each other for dear life. As they both sensed an orgasmic awareness, Sally quickly opened her eyes and for a quick second panicked but then collapsed into Claudia's strong grasp. Claudia stopped feeding and sat Sally on the bench. She cleaned herself and then quickly dressed and left the mall. It closed at ten. Sally would wake up in a while and she would feel weak and lightheaded. She may need a medic and transfusion, but she'll live. She may be too embarrassed to report anything. Who would believe her? Claudia drove home to meet Roberto. Her senses were at a stimulating state.

*   *   *

Lieutenant Morris was sitting across from Dr. Williams at the Lamppost bar on Atlantic Boulevard in East Los Angeles.

Morris lit a cigarette, blew the smoke up in the air, and asked the mortician, "Well, Doc, give me the details." He took another drag and smashed it out in an unfinished cup of coffee. He looked around and stated, "LA laws don't let you smoke anywhere."

Williams smirked and nodded and then remarked, "It's not good for you, Jay. Ah, you know that. Anyway, the body came in nude and had bite wounds in the same similar places as the other one. Neck, thigh, blood depleted. His name is Ferdinand Arroyo. A businessman, worked at IBM." Williams dipped a chip into the salsa and said, "Whoa, this stuff is still good here."

Morris took a long drink from his beer and asked, "The IBM office in downtown LA?"

"According to the business card, it's the one in Anaheim."

"Shit. I'll call his secretary and see what his schedule was. So you found a business card?"

"All his belongings were thrown by his side. The valuables were missing. They'll probably end up at a pawnshop."

Morris's eyes closed and his mouth stretched straight, and he remarked, "Yeah, but what city? These maniacs are becoming smart asses." He shook his head.

Williams nodded and stated, "Yeah, and what's peculiar. Any DNA we've come up with reveals nothing. These jokers have never been arrested, no military service, huh. Killers and have never been in trouble, that's hard to believe."

Morris banged the table with the side of his fist, the drinks shook, and patrons in the bar looked their way.

The bartender came over and nodded to them and asked, *"Que pasa, compadres?"*

Williams smiled at him and answered, "Ah, Manual, Jason is upset over a case. We're okay."

Manual nodded and wiped the bar top and moved away.

Morris finished his beer and then told Williams, "I'll be over tomorrow. Don't let anyone touch his belongings."

Williams face tightened and he nodded okay and said, "See you tomorrow. I'm eating a sandwich here."

Morris rose and stated, "Don't you mean a burrito?" He smiled and walked out.

CHAPTER 9

VAMPIRES?

T HE SMALL BACK HOUSE ON Ditman Avenue in the Belvedere District was beginning to appear as if it was abandoned. Its front yard of dirt and patches of dry grass were in disarray and the lovely front garden that had a wall of large colored boulders was dying. The huge elephant ears plants had shriveled and turned brown. All the other plants had died, the only plants alive were the cacti.

As the sun sank over the horizon, there was movement inside the house. Victor rose first. He sat straight up and took a deep breath and patted his long dark hair. He looked over at the other twin bed, the body lay still. He got up and opened his mouth wide and stretched his arms. He lit a candle and peeked out through the venetian blinds and nodded. Victor was about thirty when he was turned. He had black curly hair and wore his hair long, and he used to be the stand in for Tony Curtis when scenes required some dangerous feats. He was turned into vampirism in Ukraine while he was there starting his career when HH productions was making a remake of the movie *Tarras Bulba*. Victor had a difficult time being a vampire and getting back to America. He traveled from the East Coast to

Los Angeles, leaving bodies in swamps and forests. Along the way, he turned Olivia Mackenzie who was only eighteen years old at the time. She was waitressing at some greasy-spoon café along Highway 66 in Arizona. She was quite pretty and had a wonderful body.

Victor then said, "Olivia." She stirred. "Olivia get up. It's night and I'm hungry."

Olivia stirred again, she turned over and then put her legs over the side of the bed and sat up. She had no clothes on. She liked sleeping nude.

She yawned and then said, "Victor, that man last night had been drinking a lot, I felt it on the way home. I liked it." She stretched her small arms up and yawned again, she tilted her head and asked Victor, "My love," she used that term when she wanted something.

Victor stopped looking outside and turned to view Olivia and asked, "What, baby?"

Olivia smiled and said, "Can we find a druggie, a girl, and do her while she's high? I've never done drugs. I'm curious."

Victor nodded his head back and said, "As a teen, I tried them all. I found heroin to be the best, so I stood away. I see the addicts and how they live in the ugly parts of Hollywood, Echo Park, and Silverlake. It's bad shit, babe. We can do one occasionally. There's plenty addicts in East LA." He grinned.

Olivia went over to Victor and hugged him and said, "Oh, Victor, I'm hungry too. I'll get dressed and we can go."

Victor nodded and said, "Yeah, me too. Hey, dress like a druggie girl." She smiled.

*　　*　　*

Now, Victor and Olivia were driving down Whittier Boulevard, scanning the streets for their next prey. Victor quickly turned on a side street and then turned into an alley that led to the back parking lot of the Beehive, a neighborhood bar. He parked toward the rear and they both put down their windows and watched for customers as they went into the bar.

After a while, Victor finally said, "I'm going in and see what's happening. You look too young, babe. Keep a watch."

She smacked him on the arm and exclaimed, "That's your fault, you got me when I was just a kitten, you bastard." She smiled.

As he got out of the vehicle, he remarked, "You were old at heart, baby." He stopped and looked in the window and stated, "You had an old soul and a body of an angel." He then walked toward the back door of the establishment.

As he approached the building, a vehicle sped down the alley and stopped in front of him, blocking his path.

A woman yelled in Spanish, *"Pinche, dejame salir de aqui!"*

Victor understood Spanish.

The man yelled back, *"Vayase cabrona, jew fooken hore."*

The passenger door opened and as the girl was scrambling to get out but then the driver pushed her hard. She screamed as she flew out of the car, but being quick with his reflexes, Victor hurried and manage to grab her before she hit the ground.

In his arms, she looked at him and was somewhat fascinated at being saved by such a handsome individual and she managed to express, "Oh my God, they sent me an angel."

Victor loosened his hold on her and her body slid down his and her legs touched the ground, but she kept her arm around his neck. Looking at each other, she finally let go and said, "Thank you, mister. How can I repay you for your help?"

Victor look down at this fetching young spicy lady with bright red hair and fierce green eyes and smiled and then said, "I'm sure I can think of something."

She backed away and brushed herself off and while patting her hair, she stated, "I'm sure you can." She put her hands on her hips and asked, "Where you going anyway? A *vato* like you isn't spending his night in this dumpy place, are you?"

Victor grinned and said, "Me and my girl," he jerked his head towards his car, the girl followed his gesture with her gaze, "want to get high tonight and have some wild fun with another body between us for extra fun. What kind of drugs can you score, babe?"

The girl kept one hand on her hip and waved the other arm as she spoke, "The name is Yolanda, dude, and how do I know you aren't some cop?"

Victor drew in a breath and said, "I am no cop. There, the law says I have to admit if I'm a police officer."

Yolanda looked him over and pulled out a reefer and said, "Here, puff on this."

Victor put the joint between his lips and Yolanda came out with a lighter, put it up to the joint, and Victor drew in the smoke.

He took a couple quick puffs and said, "Hmm, good shit."

Yolanda took the joint from his fingers and took in a couple puffs and the put it out and put the stub in her small purse.

Yolanda then nodded and asked, "Okay, uh what is your name ese?"

Victor put his hand under her chin and said, "They call me Bronco Billy 'cause I can ride." He humped his thighs a couple of times.

Yolanda stepped back and said," Oh, a caballero, huh?" She nodded and stated, "I like dat. You say you have an old lady, huh? Well, if she's a looker, maybe you found your trio mate. You okay with that?" She humped her hips like Victor did.

Victor smiled and said, "Mm, yeah, sounds like it's gonna be a perfect night. What can you get to heighten things up?"

With her hands on her hips again she put out her chin and said, "You got the money? I can get whatever you want." She smiled broadly.

Victor responded, "Let's go to the car and you can meet Seattle Sue. She can ride too."

Yolanda gave a surprised look and an upside-down smile, shook her head, and followed Victor to the car.

Once there, Olivia's smiling face dominated the open window. Victor exclaimed, "Seattle Sue, meet Princess Yolanda."

Olivia sounded off, "Glad to meet you, Princess. You are pretty."

Yolanda gazed at the new stylish vehicle and at Olivia and then grinned and stated, "All right, Seattle Sue. I think we will get along pretty good."

Victor then said, "Why don't you two get in the back and get acquainted and Princess here can give me directions on where to score."

Olivia crawled over the front seat and Yolanda got in the back seat and they knocked fist together. Victor got in and asked, "Which way, Princess?"

Yolanda exclaimed, "Hey, cut it with the Princess okay. My name is Yolanda. Yollie is okay."

Victor hunched his shoulders and stated, "All right, Yollie, which way?"

Yolanda sat up and with her hands on the seat, she said, "Okay, go west down Whittier Boulevard and turn right on Farris. I'll let you know when the pad is coming up."

Victor nodded, drove down Whittier Boulevard, and turned on Farris.

After a block, Yolanda told him, "Stop here."

Victor parked the car and Yolanda inquired, "What's it gonna be, people?"

Victor reached into his pocket and took out a wad of bills and said, "We want to try heroin. We've never done it, so you're going to show us how."

Yolanda nodded and said, "Sure. We can do it without the spike. That's gonna be two hundred dollars."

Victor slipped her two fifties and five twenties.

Yolanda got out and went down this long driveway and knocked on the garage door. From the side of the garage a person showed up. It was dark, and they look like shadows interacting. They both went around the side, and around five minutes later, Olivia came out and she trotted back to the car.

"Okay, let's party," Yolanda loudly stated and smiled.

They drove up Whittier Boulevard to a motel near Pico Rivera. They couldn't go back to the Tic Toc Motel. Victor had changed the license plates again with stolen ones just like he did every day. He also sent Yolanda in to register the room.

In the room, Yolanda and Olivia sat on the bed while Victor sat on a chair facing them. Yolanda took out two small round balloons, they were tied at one end and they were the size of a small jawbreaker. She untied the end of one balloon and poured the white powder on a small mirror. She exclaimed, "China white!" Her eyes shined with delight. She took out of her purse a credit card, she chopped at the substance, spread it, then formed a little pile, and from the pile made three long lines. She then took out a cigarette and rolled it in her finger, loosening out some of the tobacco. She now stuffed the cigarette with the white powder and twisted the end shut.

Yolanda licked the cigarette and then asked, "Who's first?" she looked from one to the other.

Victor grinned and said, "You do it, hon. Show us how it's done."

She nodded quickly and then smiled and whispered, "Cherries. Okay, when you light it, you have to inhale fast because it burns quickly." Her eyebrows rose as she continued, "Keep it in your lungs, don't cough if out or you'll lose your high. Dis is China white. Good shit, man."

With that, she put the cigarette to her lips and lit the smoke. There was a little fire at the end of the cigarette as the paper burned. She inhaled, and her eyes bulged. Ashes dripped off the cigarette, half of it was gone. She kept holding her breath and now her eyes closed and then she blasted out her breath. A light shade of silver-gray smoke dissipated into the air and she shook her head and then smiled.

"Wow, you're going to trip on…. dis…" Yolanda's eyes closed, and she slumped back on the bed. She laid there lifeless.

Olivia looked at Victor and he hunched his shoulders, and then he checked her pulse and nodded his head and said, "She's alive, she's just knocked out."

Olivia began disrobing and said, "Let's make love and do her. I want to feel high too."

Victor started taking off his clothes, when naked he then started taking off Yolanda's garments. Soon, the three were rolling on each other. Yolanda became semi-awake and tried to engage her desires with the vampires. Victor entered her, and she moaned with delight as Olivia kissed and licked her all over her body. Finally, Olivia found the spot on Yollie's thigh and nipped there and then bit into the vein and began sipping slowly, heightening her eroticism. Yollie jerked but Victor held her down and then bit into her neck. Yolanda writhed and twisted as the vampires took in their feed. After a minute, Yolanda groaned with pleasure as the fiends sucked the rest of her living fluids. Finally, Olivia writhed a final jerk and screamed yes with delight. She was now drowsy from the heroin. Victor laid back on the bed and closed his eyes.

"Yeah, this is a nice high, momma. Come here and suck me off."

Olivia crawled over to Victor like a cat and laid over him and began kissing his neck and went down toward his chest and down to his groin. They both lavished in their high and their feed.

Washing the blood off their faces, Olivia slurred her words, "Baby, I'm feeling so good. How about you?"

Victor nodded, smiled, and said, "I'm fucked up. I can see why these druggies become addicted. What a high. Come on, let's vamoose. The sun will be up in an hour or so."

*　　*　　*

Yolanda's body was not found until eleven in the morning by the clean-up matron. The Montebello Police were the authorities involved with the killing. The information of the murder did not get to Lieutenant Morris's eyes until five in that afternoon. He knew he couldn't get to the Montebello Morgue that night and he did not know anyone there personally, so he would go home tonight and go straight there tomorrow morning.

*　　*　　*

The night of the killing of Yolanda, Claudia went out around 6:30 and went directly to a Shell gas station and put in gas and then parked by the women's bathroom. She waited. Two teenage girls walked into the bathroom giggling and talking to each other. A half hour went by and a heavy-set lady in red shorts and a blue short-sleeves blouse went into the bathroom. Claudia went to the room carrying a small sign and a short club. As she entered, she placed the "out of service" sign over the outside doorknob and then hid her face as best she could, and went inside. The woman was at the washbasin, wiping her face and arms with paper towels. Claudia leaned against the door and locked it.

The woman stated, "Warm evening, huh?"

Claudia didn't answer, she just swung the club down on the woman's head. Claudia dragged her into the commode booth and sat her on the toilet bowl. There, she bit into her neck and got her fill. She cleaned up and went home to meet Roberto. The woman was still breathing.

As she drove into her driveway, she saw Roberto standing by his car. He had his phone to his ear and put it down when he saw Claudia's vehicle rolling into the driveway.

As Claudia exited her car, Roberto told her, "Where you been, hon? I've been calling you?"

Claudia was vibrant and full of life. She ran into his arms and kissed him many times on his neck and face and then smilingly she commented, "Oh, darling, I went to put gas and left my phone on the kitchen table."

Roberto held her at arm's length and with his face all happy, he remarked, "I've missed you too." He released her and turned her around and hugged her close to him and stated, "We have to do something about being apart, when I'm with you I feel so alive." He leaned over and nibbled on her neck.

Claudia closed her eyes and savored his thick lips on her neck, and then she turned out of his arms and then she held on to his upper arms and said, "Roberto, later tonight, I want to have a serious talk with you."

Roberto looked at her grasp and then at her and responded, "By all means, my dear. Yes, after we ravish one another and are all sweaty and tired, we'll have that talk." He smiled from ear to ear.

"Come, Roberto, start a fire and I will go change especially for you."

"Ah, *como no?* Yes, hurry." He pushed her off and gave her a swat on the butt. Claudia jumped forward and laughed and ran into the house.

*   *   *

The day after the Yolanda killing, Lieutenant Morris was at the Montebello Morgue talking with a Dr. Bradley, "Doc, the initial report on the death of a Yolanda Rodriguez states she died of a possible overdose of heroin but there's remarks of multiple bite wounds. Has anyone done an autopsy on her yet?"

Dr. Bradley was an older medical officer in his seventies. He was burly, bald with a strand of gray hair from one ear to the other ear, bald on top, and wore glasses. He put a closed fist to his mouth and coughed into it, and then said, "It's being done now. Come, follow me to the lab."

The lab was a huge room with four metal slab tables. One wall had two large flat-screen monitors, the others had shelves and cupboards; vials and jars were plentiful. There were two desks, bookcases, lean tables with assorted bottles with various colored liquids, and there also were microscopes on the shelves.

On one table, Yolanda's body lay flat. Her stomach and chest were wide open with the layers of her torso folded over. A female doctor was drawing fluid from a kidney as the two men stepped in and got close to the table, The doctor looked up briefly. Her hair was concealed with a surgery cap and a surgical mask covered her lower face, but two large lovely oval dark colored eyes behind glasses looked out from the opening, they emitted curiosity as they quickly evaluated the visitor and then went back to her duties.

"Dr. Morales, this is Lieutenant Morris from Los Angeles and he's interested in how Miss Rodriguez was, well, the cause of death and what else you have found."

Dr. Morales finished drawing up of the liquid from the kidney and laid down the syringe. She then pulled off her rubber gloves and her mask and said, "Glad to meet you, Lieutenant." Without out the mask, the doctor revealed that she was an attractive woman about thirty with a straight Cherokee nose and a nice mouth.

"The pleasure is mine," Morris smiled while his eyes admired the woman. Although she was outfitted in the doctor's smock and rubber apron that went down to her knees.

"This young lady actually met her maker too soon in her life. Death was due to the extreme loss of blood." Elizabeth took in a breath of air and continued, "Heroin was also in her system and would have probably killed her anyway, depending on her overall recovery system but the lack of blood is what really finished her."

In his detective voice Morris asked, "Are there any other significant details about her death doctor?"

Dr. Morales made a strained expression, her eyes narrowed, her lips spread tightly and then she commented, "All corroborating signs and marks reveal that she was sexually abused, while she was probably semi-unconscious, and bitten all over. She was groped very hard to the extent of causing bruises and she was also sodomized," The doctor again took in a breath and looked at the policeman and said, "You're going to catch theses sons of bitches, aren't you?"

Morris's left eyebrow rose as he stated, "I surely hope so, Doctor," Morris reached over and touched her arm and asked, "Your convinced there were two culprits involved in this?"

Dr. Morales rubbed her arm and nodded and said, "Definitely. The bite marks are from two different people. Most likely a male and a female."

Dr. Bradley cleared his voice and said, "Excuse me, I have matters awaiting me in my office, please excuse me. Dr. Morales can answer all your questions."

Dr. Morales walked over to a desk and sat down. Morris followed her and pulled a chair over and said, Tell me, Dr. Morales—"

She cut him off and said, "Please, call me Elizabeth." Her eyes had turned soft and maintained a sadness about them. Her lips were moist from her licking them, and they looked very inviting to Morris.

Morris gave a tight-lipped smile and the said, "Elizabeth—"

She cut him off again and said, "And what may I call you?"

Morris swallowed and said, "Jason or Jay. Uh, Elizabeth, what do you think about these killings? Let me add that there are other similar killings in LA with depleted blood."

Elizabeth squinted her eyes as she thought, and then with one eyebrow arched and her mouth kind of up on one side, she placed one hand on top of Morris's hand and she stated, "Don't laugh. Vampires."

Morris did not react; he kept looking at the doctor a second, he then nodded slowly and then repeated, "Vampires." He drew in a breath, patted her hand on his other hand, smiled, and he said, "You know, that was banging around in my brain for days now, but I wouldn't let it mature. My God, could it be?" He squinted and shook his head and looked at Elizabeth.

Shaking her head, Elizabeth again took on that serious expression and then commented, "It could be a cult or somebody acting like vampires or even maybe believing they are vampires." She looked at the detective, her head tilted a little, her mouth in that straight tight smile at that angle she appeared angelic.

Morris took on a serious manner and stated, "Why the sexual assaults though? Most vampire theories have them creatures only wanting blood to survive?"

She gave a curt laugh and stated, "I guess you not aware of the TV series and novel *Twilight*, are you?"

Morris shook his head no.

"It's a three-segment love story. Vampire sees girl, vampire wants girl, girl sees vampire, girl falls for vampire, blah, blah, blah."

Morris's eyebrows arched and then he said, "What time you off? You want to go have dinner tonight? We need to explore this."

Elizabeth slid over her business card to him, tilted her head, and said, "I can't tonight, but please call me later. We can get together and should talk about this."

Disappointment colored his face. He stood up and remarked, "Hmm, hot date, huh?"

A slight smile made her dark eyes sparkle as she answered, "Uh-huh…" She let that response hang in the air and then she added, "It's my mom's birthday. We're taking her to the Sizzler. She loves that place."

Morris's paleness halted and color returned to his composure. He couldn't control a slight grin developing on his face. He swallowed and stated, "Well, happy birthday to you mom and congratulate her on producing such a witty and lovely daughter."

Elizabeth giggled and looked downward, slightly embarrassed, and said, "I'll let her know she has a fan."

Morris stuck out his hand and told her, "I am very glad to have made your acquaintance, Doctor, er, Elizabeth."

She rose, took his hand, and responded, "My pleasure. May I have a raincheck on that dinner?"

Morris nodded and said, "By all means. I'll call you tomorrow." He turned and walked out the door.

She watched his stroll and smiled.

CHAPTER 10

CONFESSIONS

ROBERTO LAY NUDE ON TOP of the disheveled blankets on Claudia's king-size bed. He then sat up and lit a miniature cigar as Claudia sat propped by the pillows on the backboard, looking at Roberto with adoring eyes.

Roberto let out a stream of blue-gray smoke. It slithered upward and faded as it hit the ceiling, and then he commented, "I don't know if we'll ever reach old age making love like that." He smirked and then grinned and said, "Right now, I really don't care. You are incredible, Claudia. Incredible."

Claudia's tight-lip smile broke as she said, "Remember, Roberto, it takes two to tango." She smiled, her white teeth gleamed in the candlelight. "Roberto, I have something very important to discuss with you." She breathed in and let out her breath slowly. She wasn't sure if she should reveal to him what she was and if she should offer him the opportunity of immortality. She shook her head slowly.

Roberto tilted his head, drew in some smoke and blasted it out quickly, and commented, "Ah, my dear, I too have been contemplating what has been riveting around in my brain for days."

Claudia grabbed a pillow and clutched it to her chest and said, "Fine, my love, you go first."

Roberto snubbed out his little cigar and turned to look at Claudia and said, "All right, you know my work hours are unpredictable," Claudia nodded, "and I have this little apartment twenty miles from you," again Claudia nodded, "and I want to be with you every day you know." Roberto took in a breath and let it out and exclaimed as he nodded, "I think I am in love with you."

Claudia's jaw dropped a little, her eyelids fluttered some, she hugged the pillows tightly, and said, "Roberto, oh, Roberto." They looked at one another and reached out for each other. As they held one another, Claudia gasped, "I have something very vital to talk to you about."

Roberto's forehead creased as he squints and nodded his head. He whispered, "Go ahead, my love."

Claudia swallowed and began, "You see, Roberto, I have not been totally honest with you, sweetheart." Roberto now had a questionable look. "You see, this sunlight avoidance dilemma I informed you I had."

Roberto nodded and answered, "Yes, my love."

"Well, it has all been a lie."

Roberto nodded and softly said, "I know."

Claudia sat up abruptly and loudly said, "You know?"

Roberto got up, wrapped a sheet around his torso, and went to the minibar Claudia put in for him. There, he poured himself a drink and drank it down in one gulp and continued, "I always thought that this skin thing sounded fishy so I looked it up. It really doesn't exist the way you explained it."

Claudia jerked forward and was about to speak when Roberto put out his hand and his other hand put a finger across his lips as he smiled. He continued, "Things were bothering me about that, and then the news reported deaths with depleted blood. I'm an old movie buff and I remembered those films on the blood drinkers."

Claudia gasped and her hand went to cover her mouth.

Roberto held a thin smile and said, "So I did more homework"—he took in a breath—"and I checked on your birth." Robert poured another drink and drank it down. "Claudia Anne Marie Roscrea was born in Paris, France, in the year of our Lord, 1795. That makes you way over two hundred years old."

Claudia straightened her posture, held her chin up, and said, "Yes, but I look well, don't I?"

Roberto stood there with his hands on his hips and asked, "So, my dear, what are you? A witch? A ghost? Or a vampire?" his eyebrows arched and his head tilted waiting for Claudia's reply.

Claudia moved off the bed nude and reached for a candelabra and lit all three candles and held it high, the light flickered on her slim hard body. The candlelight captured the beauty of her face with her ocean-blue eyes, the fire-red curled long hair, her long elegant neck, the firm cone breasts as her pink hard nipples pointed up, the flat unblemished stomach that led to small round tight thighs that kept vigilance to her perfectly shaped mound covered with a small patch of lighter red hair, and on to her beautiful face. She had a flat stomach and smooth perfect legs. "I'm a woman vampire, Roberto. A vampire who will not age and who has the strength of a demon," she exclaimed.

In a flash, she was in front of Roberto and grabbed him with two hands and quickly lifted him up over her head.

"Hey. Hey, put me down. Put me down."

Claudia threw him on the bed where he bounced once, and he quickly went into his pile of clothes and slipped on his pants and fell. "If you are to kill me, I want to be found with my pants on," he said.

Claudia grabbed a sheet, wrapped it around herself, and stated, "Kill you? I am going to offer you eternal life." She breathed hard, turned a chair that faced her dresser with a large mirror, and sat on it.

Roberto shook his head and said, "My darling, I would do anything for you." He took in a deep breath and continued, "But the taking of human lives, I…I don't know."

Claudia stood up, shook her head, and stated, "No, no, my love. We do not have to take lives. We drink enough to stay alive and leave the body. They wake up weak and need a day or two to get their strength back."

Roberto nodded and replied, "But the bodies they are finding, what—"

Claudia cut him off, "They are not the ones I have used. There are others like me here in Los Angeles. I want to find them and educate them. There does not have to be any more killings."

"Hmm, and if I choose not to be turned"—he looked at her with one eyebrow arched, his head tilted—"then you'll have to quiet me, hmm?"

Claudia nodded quickly and responded, "I love you Roberto. I will have to trust you with my secret. Can I?"

Roberto sat on the bed, he clasped his hands together and rubbed them, and said, "I won't be the one who reveals your secret, Claudia. I don't know if I can still be with you. I don't want to be without you also. I'm torn." He put his face into his hands.

"Let me divulge to you the good and the bad of becoming a vampire, my love. Then, you decide to stay or go."

Roberto looked up and nodded and smiled weakly.

Claudia went on like a used-car salesman, "Eternal life, heightened senses, super strength, extra erotic activities, never having to be employed due to her fortune and income, etc., etc."

Roberto sat on the bed, nodding his head as Claudia went on. She began divulging scenarios of important events that had happened in the last two hundred years.

Claudia was an in-depth storyteller. She began with Napoleon's Waterloo and divulge that two hundred years ago, life expectancy was forty years old and the average yearly income was three thousand dollars. She continued and it held Roberto's interest. Morning was coming up and Roberto yawned. Claudia stopped her narratives and let Roberto nap.

CHAPTER 11

DECISIONS

Marta was in the kitchen drinking a cup of coffee when Roberto entered the room. She looked up from the table surprised and remarked, "You must be Roberto." She couldn't help giving him the once over as Roberto stepped in with just his pants on. His chiseled hairy chest was a main feature. "Claudia talked a lot about you."

Roberto rubbed his hand through his hair, smiled, and said, "It would be an embarrassing moment if I was not Roberto."

Marta put the back of her hand to her mouth and giggled.

Roberto then asked, "Is there more coffee?"

Marta nodded and voiced, "Uh-huh. I always make a pot, in case someone drops by. No one has yet."

"Ah, I shall be your first guess then."

Marta began to rise but Roberto told her, "Don't bother. I can get it, thank you."

Roberto poured himself a cup and sat opposite Marta.

"How's Claudia? She sometimes comes down when there's heavy overcast and I remember to keep the drapes closed." Marta asked.

Roberto nodded and said, "Yes, she has an odd dilemma. What do you think about that?"

Marta put down her cup and looked at Roberto. At first she had a puzzled look and then she smirked and responded, "At first, I thought it was really weird, but now I've just accepted it. I kind of feel sorry for her."

Roberto took on a surprised expression and stated, "Sorry for her?"

Marta gave a wide smile and said, "Yeah, there is so much beauty on this earth to be experienced during the day, so much living." She took a breath and continued, "She's stuck up there while life goes on."

Roberto just nodded his head.

Claudia had been in the hallway leaning against the wall, listening. She winced at the words Marta shared. Claudia was now getting angry. Last night, she had just about convinced Roberto to become a vampire and now that little bitch was spoiling it all.

Marta then got up and, while walking to get more coffee, she exclaimed, "I'm gonna check into this skin thing. In today's modern world, science can do just about anything." She came back to the table and sat. "I am—"

Just then, Claudia showed herself and interrupted, "Oh, I see you both have met."

Both Roberto and Marta glanced at Claudia. She was wearing a flowing thin pink negligee. When she stopped, the material clung to her body.

"Oh, my darlings, I did overhear your conversation Marta, and I appreciate you thinking of me. And yes, I have checked into all avenues for cure or remission and it has been useless. My disease is rare and uncommon, and it hits one in every 850,000 births. Mostly in Asia where the babies rarely make it out of childhood. So sad. I've contributed tons of money for research to no avail," she stated.

Roberto sipped his coffee and then remarked, "Oh, lets change the subject. It seems to be a powerless situation. I need to clean up and get to work. I will leave you two, lovely young ladies, to do whatever you do." He got up and walked away, but Claudia caught his arm and said, "You will return tonight and come to a decision, eh, my love?"

Roberto nodded yes, leaned over and kissed Claudia. "Yes, I'll be here about eight," he said.

Claudia smiled and Roberto walked away and up the stairs.

As Claudia watched him disappear, Marta expressed, "He's some magnificent man, Claudia. Where did you find him?"

Claudia turned smiling and answered, "In Spain, at a carnival."

Marta gave a closed-lip smiled and responded, "Nice."

Claudia nodded and said, "Yes, I think I'll marry him."

Marta just smiled.

"Honey, I'm going to lay down, no interruptions, please," Claudia stated.

Marta nodded and said, "No problem." She then started cleaning up and put on the radio.

An old Rolling Stone tune was playing and then the DJ began a dialogue, "Hey, Susan, did you hear the news about that obese woman who got mugged in at that Shell gas station in Pasadena?"

"No, Mark. What happened?"

"She not only lost her watch, she lost her blood."

"How'd she do that?"

"I think her Tampax wasn't finished yet."

"Ha-ha-ha, you're sick, Mark."

"That's the—"

Marta turned off the radio as her eyes widened.

*　　*　　*

Carolynn and Michael were leaving to go back home. As they were packing, Carolynn looked up and said, "Michael, look at the news."

"And there has been a total of four blood-depleted bodies found in the county of Los Angeles. I've been assigned as an investigating reporter to these abnormal killings. Authorities maintained a hushed conduct pertaining to their knowledge or indications of suspects or at least a person of interest."

Michael was now in front of the TV, while Carolynn sat on the bed.

"These callous murders cannot go on without immediate and unlimited manpower form our police department. The public needs to be aware of the importance of any kinds of information and or evidence. The ABC Network, along with the Los Angeles Police Department, is offering $50,000 reward for information that leads to the arrest of this or these culprits. Another note, a man also complained of being attacked at the San Miguel Casino. No other information except that he was diagnosed with a loss of blood. This is Leonard Sanders, ABC News, back to—"

Carolynn had pressed the remote control off and said, "Michael, I think we should let the police know what we know about that night in Hollywood. Samantha may know something important to find this murderer. They may locate her with a broadcast." She looked at Michael with pleading eyes.

Michael turned, sat by Carolynn, and said, "Thinking about it now, I think we should." He turned to face her and stated, "The way they are finding these bodies, well, it would take a powerful person. Samantha could be some type of…of…oh, I don't know. Maybe like an evil witch stuff that puts people under hypnosis. Then, she can do whatever she wants."

"Uh-huh." Carolynn took in a deep breath and let it out and then continued, "Samantha left with Greg and two hours later, he's dead. We should find out if she has contacted the authorities. I'm sure she's seen and heard the news."

Michael nodded and remarked, "Yeah, let's find out."

*   *   *

Lieutenant Morris was at Manual's, a Mexican restaurant in Monrovia, waiting for Elizabeth to show up. He was dipping corn chips in the salsa bowl and munching when Elizabeth came to his table.

Morris stood up and took pleasure at what was walking toward him. Without the white lab coat, Elizabeth took on an entirely different appearance. Her long wavy brown hair with reddish highlights cascaded her oblong face that had a light-tan tone. Without her glasses, her light-green eyes sparkled, while her nicely arched eyebrows guarded her lateral long dark eyelashes. Up close, the tiny gold specs in her garden-green eyes resembled flecks of glitter. Her fine straight nose took vigilance on perfect lips that she tinted with a red lipstick. She wore a smart woman's tan business outfit. A white blouse with frills down the center was mostly covered with a matching vest and jacket. The matching skirt draped on her body perfectly and revealed shapely tan legs that entered dark-brown high heels. Jennifer had a natural sway to her walk that most women are unaware they have and emits sexual waves out into the atmosphere.

As she approached the table, Morris noticed she was carrying a notebook. He reached out his hand and said, "Uh, where's the medical examiner, Elizabeth?"

*　*　*

Marta was doing her homework in the living room, while her mom was sitting there drinking tea and watching the news."

"Oh, Marta, there is some awful demons out there. You know not to associate with strangers."

Oh, Mom." Marta then looked up at the TV and started paying attention.

They listened to the report.

"Another note, a man also complained of being attack at the San Manuel Casino, he also was diagnosed with loss of blood. This is Leonard Sanders, ABC news."

Marta's mom clicked off the TV and said, "I didn't tell you, but the other day, they found a girl unconscious in one of the dressing rooms. I'm glad I'm in charge of the jewelry and perfume section. No dressing rooms there."

Marta put down her pencil, closed the book and fretfully confronted her mom, "Mother, why didn't you tell me about this before?"

Moms hunched her shoulders and remarked, "Honey, you have enough on your mind. I didn't want you worrying. I was going to tell you though, just at the right time, hon."

Marta breathed hard and asked, "Tell me, what this girl said, Mom."

Mom nodded and explained, "I didn't question the girl. I wasn't there, but word came down that the girl admitted to flirting with another woman and went with her into the dressing room. That's all she remembers. She was in a hurry and didn't want to put in a complaint with the managers and wanted to leave. She was helped out and put in a taxi at the store's expense."

"Mom, did she describe the girl in the dressing room?"

Mom nodded, smiled, and said, "In fact, she did." Mom's grin expanded as she spoke, "Marta, I think this girl was gay." Marta's eyebrows rose. "She describes the woman with a man's eye."

Marta replied, "Really."

"Yes, she said the woman was a fox. Red hair, sparkling blue eyes, and had a bitchin petite figure—these are her words." Mom took in a breath and continued, "This is the—how do they say it— oh yeah, the clincher. The hippie girl says that the woman kissed was like sticking your tongue into hot melted fudge." Mom giggled.

Marta smiled and said, "Momma!"

Mom hunched her shoulders and left the room.

After her mom went to her bedroom, Marta began thinking, *Hollywood, San Manuel, Pasadena, never in sun, coincidence? Coincidence?* Marta went to her dresser and searched inside a muddled drawer and finally took out a small gold crucifix on a thin gold chain and placed it around her neck. She looked in the mirror, it sparkled at her, and then she patted her cross and smiled.

*   *   *

Lieutenant Morris was at his desk reading autopsy reports. A cigarette lay smoldering in his ashtray and an empty coffee cup was near his typewriter when Sergeant Oberron came in the room with three files in his hand, a cup of coffee in his other hand, and a cigarette in his mouth.

Morris looked up, grinned. and then remarked, "Hey, Jesse, finally earning your paycheck, huh?"

Out of the side of his mouth Jesse replied, "Fuck you. They have me running all over town, man."

Morris curiosity sprang up and asked, "Whacha got there, Sarge?"

"I've got battery cases. Someone is going around town knocking people out and robbing them."

Morris stated, "Well, that isn't anything new."

Oberron laid the files on his desk, snubbed out the cigarette, sipped the last of his coffee, and exclaimed, "Yeah? Well, they are not just knocking them out, people are losing blood too. They almost died."

Morris straightened up, got up, went over to Oberon's desk, and said, "Let me see those reports. Loss of blood, huh?"

Oberron nodded. "There's not much in there. The victims didn't report the muggings except for a lady over in Pasadena. Here's one from the May Company store on Foothill. The supervisor thought it should be reported and one from security at San Manuel. The victims were embarrassed, I guess. I'm gonna have to track these two down," and warned Morris as he pointed to the May Company and San Miguel reports.

Morris picked up the files and placed them on his desk. He held the other one and stated, "I'm gonna help you out, buddy. I'll go interview this chick from the May Company caper. Reading over this casino one, the guy never knew what hit him. No use talking to him. The girl might remember something. The store took down her name and phone number. Good."

Oberron nodded and asked, "You think they have something to do with those depleted bodies that keep turning up?"

Morris nodded his head slowly and said, "Maybe. Hmm, Sally Jennings. I wonder if there's anything on file. I'll check." He put on his jacket and went into the records room.

*   *   *

Victor and Olivia were in their darkened bedroom when Olivia got out of bed and paced the floor some. Victor turned over and sat up and asked her, "What's up? You need some feed already?"

"Uh…uh…just thinking,"

Victor laid there and watched her.

They had left a trail of bodies from the Midwest to the Pacific Ocean. She did not want to be caught and persecuted in whatever way the law would deal with them. But she was wise enough to understand that they couldn't keep the pace they were on for too long.

"We're demons, you know?" she said over her shoulder.

Victor gave her a puzzled look.

"Yes, we're the bad guys, Victor. If they catch us, it will sheer torture for me."

Victor braced himself against the backboard with a pillow and let her talk.

Olivia took in a breath and continued, "Look, babe, we are going to have to leave LA or change the way we do things."

Victor put his fingers through his hair and asked, "What do you mean, honey?"

She looked up and stated, "Cops are finding the bodies. They gotta be investigating what's going on. Every place we hung our hats, we had to leave 'cause it was getting hot for us. LA is big and California is bigger, but I'm tired of moving and living like gypsies."

Victor giggled.

"What I want, Victor, and you should want it too, is that we settle down someplace." Victor was going to say something, but Olivia stopped him, "Wait, let me finish." Victor relaxed back to the backboard. "We can do this, Victor, but the first thing we have to do is stop killing people."

Victor cut in, "We'll die, honey."

Olivia shook her head and said, "No, we won't. No, we won't. The last two times, Vic, I've cut myself short. I was experimenting. We don't have to take all their blood until they die, Victor."

Victor's brow frowned and he stated, "Baby, when we're drinking blood and making love, well, it's the utmost, babe, and it's the only pleasure we have. We can't eat all the foods of the world or enjoy beverages. We can't enjoy the sun at the beach and surf. All daytime activities are lost to us. Fuck, nothing to do but drink blood and have sex, thank God."

Olivia took in a deep breath. She sat on the bed, faced Victor, and announced, "God? If there is one, he has forsaken us. I'm going to live this way even if I have to do it on my own." She looked away.

Victor's eyes widened, and a fearful look came over him. "What? You'd leave me?" he asked.

"No, you'd be making the choice. You're pushing me away. I know this is the only way to survive. We'll blindside people, get our feed, and rob them. We'll get money and fix up this place. This house can be cute. After your great aunt died, she willed it to you. It's ours. Let's fix it up. We'll almost be regular humans."

Victor shook his head. He smiled and answered, "Okay, I'll try it. No more killing, babe."

Olivia's face gleamed with joy and turned and jumped on Victor. They kissed and made love and waited for nightfall.

CHAPTER 12

SALLY

ORRIS WAS DRIVING DOWN COLORADO Boulevard crossing over Arcadia into Monrovia looking for Sally's address. He passed Monrovia High School and then he saw the house. Morris parked the vehicle and looked at the house. Most homes on the block had no fences, this one had a chain-link fence. The grass was turning brown but neatly cut. He opened the gate and went up the walkway. There was a small porch with two chairs and a small round table that had a glass top. He knocked and waited.

The door opened, and through the screen door he saw an outline of an elderly woman with a batch of curly gray hair. Then a voice stated, "Yes, what do you want? We don't want to hear about the Lord and we're not buying anything."

Morris smiled and said, "Uh, ma'am, I'm a police officer, and I'd like to talk to Sally, please."

"A police officer? Oh, God, what has my Sally done?"

"Oh, she hasn't done anything, ma'am. I'm here to speak to her about the mugging she experienced."

The woman put her hand to her mouth, gasped, and said, "Mugging? Oh, that's why she was so tired and has slept for two days. I thought she had been partying. I was gonna scold her when she wakes up. I—"

"Ma'am, I need to see her now. There's a clown out there, hurting people."

The woman took in a breath and mumbled, "Clown? Oh yes, yes, come in, officer. There, the first doorway. Just knock and go in."

"Thank you." Morris walked to the door and knocked. There was no sound, so he knocked again.

"Go away, Gramma."

"I hope you're decent. I'm Lieutenant Morris. I need to speak with you." He opened the door and went in.

Sally was lying on top of the blankets on her stomach wearing pink panties only. She turned over, grabbed a pillow. and put it in front of her. She rubbed her eyes and said, "Is this about that bitch that fucked me up?"

Morris smiled and responded, "It sure is."

Sally had a puzzled look and asked, "How'd the cops find out? I didn't make a report."

"Yeah, well, the store put in a report for insurance purposes. Anyway, tell me about this woman who mugged you."

Sally leaned forward and said, "If you catch the bitch, you gotta give me five minutes with her alone."

Morris nodded and smirked and stated, "You want to beat her some, eh?"

Sally shook her head and said, "Naw, I want to fuck her. She's a fine bitch."

Morris laughed and said, "Wow, that's a new one on me. Anyway, I'd like you to come down to the station and have our artist do a drawing of her. Maybe we can get her before she hurts someone else. The store nurse says it seemed like you lost a lot of blood. Is there a wound anywhere? It's not noted."

Sally shook her head and said, "I don't know how that happened. I was weak for two days. I have these sores here on my neck though."

Morris went to her quickly and examined her neck and then said, "Sally, can you describe her for me, best you can remember what she looks like?"

Sally lips curled as she spoke, "I remember her. She was about five feet five, red flowing hair, and deep blue eyes. She had a perfect movie-star face and a small well-shaped body and all class and money. I wanted her."

"Hmm, a real looker, huh?"

Sally nodded.

"Okay, look, I'm going to send a car for you to take you to the station and we'll get that drawing done."

Sally nodded and said, "Hey, you're not a bad looking guy"—she looked him over again—"for a cop." She smiled and said, "Too bad I like women."

Morris's eyebrows rose. He nodded slowly and said, "Yeah, too bad." He left and went back to the station.

* * *

Roberto was at the studios on Santa Monica Boulevard, standing with the cameramen. They were all discussing the neighborhood that Roberto had scanned and selected for the recent movie they were shooting.

"That one scene where Brad and George have that argument is gonna film nicely," Henry remarked.

Billy added, "How'd you find that old-time gas station, Roberto? It's like in the middle of a rural neighborhood. Many years ago, it must have been the neighborhood spot for the men in the area."

Roberto was leaning on a fake boulder and staring into space.

Billy nudge him and asked, "Where you at, man? You dreaming about that hot woman you've been seeing?"

Roberto shook his head and then smiled and responded, "Hey, sorry, fellows. Man, I just have something very important that I have to make a decision on. Oh, that old gas station? I've known about it. My grandparents live in that area. I would pass it when I went to the Vons's market nearby."

Henry stated, "From them photos, it's going to need a paint job."

Roberto nodded and said, "Yeah, we have permission to renovate. Don't know why someone hasn't purchased it, knocked it down, and put up an apartment building."

Billy and Henry nodded and hunched their shoulders.

"You thinking of getting married, Roberto? That is a big decision?" Billy asked.

Henry looked at Roberto and nodded while Roberto answered, "Gee, guys, I wish it was as simple as that. Well, it is kinda in that category." He took a big breath and continued, "No, it's a change-of-life thing."

Billy and Henry looked at Roberto with puzzled expressions.

Roberto looked at his companions and realized he was getting too deep and knew he couldn't reveal much more. He forced a closed-mouth smile and told them, "Oh, it's just that I've been offered a new employment that would take me abroad and do a lot of evening stuff."

Billy scratched his head and was about to respond when the director announced, "Okay, our stars are back from makeup, so let's get rolling."

There were lots of bustle going on, and Henry and Billy went to their work stations. Roberto let out a breath and went to a table in the studio and sat down. He found a legal notepad and drew a line down the middle and wrote "Pro" on one side and "Con" on the other. He took a breath and began listing what he thought would be good and what would be bad about becoming a vampire.

*　　*　　*

It was late in the day, and Marta was at the kitchen table going through the mail. There were a couple of charity organizations asking for donations. The children's hospital and the disabled veterans routinely sent their requests. There were loan companies willing to loan you money and there were neighborhood magazines and eatery brochures also. Everything went into the trash receptacle except for the gas and electric bill. She took out the checkbook from a drawer and began writing. She would leave them out so Claudia could endorse them.

She flinched when Claudia suddenly appeared and said, "What did you throw in the trash, my dear?"

Breathing normal again, Marta answered, "Just following you orders, Claudia. When I started, you told me you did not want to be bothered with anything but bills." She smiled.

Claudia nodded but took out the envelopes from the trash, looked through, them and said, "Yes, my dear, but today, I would like to donate something for those little children that are sick or suffering."

Marta smiled and said, "Sure, that is really good of you, Claudia. It's simple. The statements have a place to jot down amounts, so I'll write the check for you." Claudia smiled, and Marta continued, "The only drawback is once you give to one charity, every charity organization starts sending you request. My mom told me that."

Claudia smiled and said, "Oh, well, we'll just deal with that when it happens."

Marta asked, "Okay, give me the amounts and I'll make out everything for you."

"Yes, my dear, leave the checks when you are done, and you may call it a day. I'm going to get ready for Roberto." She turned and went to her bedroom.

Marta shook her head and thought, *What the fuck? If she's some sort of vampire, demon, or witch, why is she donating to charities? A monster with a heart. This is so strange.* Marta began filling out the paperwork and the checks.

* * *

Lieutenant Morris was at his desk looking over the autopsy reports of the latest the depleted bodies found and the muggings reports. He was trying to formulate some type of pattern. The areas were spread in a seventy-five-mile circumference. The victims were of various ages, gender, and body type. The actual assaults were similar. That was the only sign that was the same. Reading thoroughly, he found another indication that the culprit copied. The bites on the neck and body. One body only had one set of bites on the neck. The others had two or more sets of bites. He rubbed his chin and wondered what that was about. Medical examiners state that the multiple-bite wound victims were from two people. Lieutenant Morris decided to submit a National BOLO request asking for similar unsolved murders with the same MO as the LA deaths. For this, he had to get FBI authority. For this, he had to go through his superior, and he will attempt that tomorrow.

He lit a smoke and then smashed it out and said, "Ah, I need to get home. I need some sleep."

At the reception desk, he was checking his messages when a young hippie couple stood at the glass reception counter, waiting to speak with someone. The officer-in-charge was not behind the glass at the moment. There was a mother and a child sitting on a bench who seemed to be waiting also.

He was about to leave when the young woman approached him and said, "Excuse me, that lady there told us the sergeant went to check on someone for her in custody. Do you work here?"

Morris grinned and responded, "You can say that."

"Oh, good. Uh, do you know where the receptionist is? We'd like to give some information on the Greg…uh…something killing."

Morris's hands dropped. He faced the couple and said, "Well, you've reached the right person. I'm in charge of that case." Morris turned and went to the door, opened it, and stated, "Come in. It's more private in here."

The couple seemed a little frightened but followed him to his desk. He pointed to two chairs and they sat down.

"Well, now, please give me your names, first and last." Morris's eyed narrowed some as he viewed the couple.

Carolynn gave a weak smile and stated, "I'm Carolynn Mathews and my boyfriend is Michael Robins. We're from the Laguna Beach area." She smiled weakly again.

Morris looked from one to the other and nodded. He knew Laguna Beach had a lot of wealthy people. Morris took out a legal pad and wrote their names. He looked up and exclaimed, "What do you know about Greg and his fatal demise?" Morris asked, his eye-brows high on his forehead and his eyes showing interest.

Carolyn looked at Michael quickly and then she wrung her hands and spoke, "Well, we came to Hollywood on like a minivaca-tion and wanted to experience the nightlife here."

Morris nodded and said, "Go on."

Carolynn took in a breath and began, "Well, on the night that this Greg character was killed, we met him at a night club in Hollywood."

Morris interrupted and asked, "Name of club?"

Michael put his hand on Carolyn's arm, reassuring her. She answered, "The Academy, it's on—"

Morris cut her, "I know it well, go on."

Carolynn nodded and smiled and continued, "Earlier that night, we were walking in Hollywood and we saw the pretty girl get out of a vehicle and begin walking—"

Michael spoke out, "It was an Uber driver. I saw the big U sticker on the windshield." He smiled.

Morris looked at him and wrote.

Carolynn had looked at her boyfriend then continued, "So this girl was walking by herself and these group of, well, they looked like mean guys, they began gaming on her." She looked at Michael and asked, "Is that the right term?"

Michael tilted his head a little and nodded yes.

Carolynn smiled and continued, "So I went over to her and we talked. She seemed nice, so I invited her to join us. She seemed really glad to hook up with us, seeing she was all by herself."

Morris asked, "Her name is?"

Carolynn smiled, her eyes smiled too, and she said, "I was get-ting to that." She breathed and said, "Samantha. That's all she gave us."

Morris wrote and with his head he indicated to go on.

"Yeah, so us"—she pointed to herself and to Michael—"and Samantha went to have coffee, we needed to wait the club to open at ten. And then we went to the club. We're there for a short while and while Michael and I are"—she paused a moment, took a quick glance at Michael who stood with a straight face—"uh, were dancing, Samantha met this guy, Greg, and brought him to our table."

Morris stopped writing and looked at Carolynn and asked, "How do you know that Greg is the same Greg who was killed?" He looked at Carolynn and then at Michael.

Michael stated, "Eyewitness News aired a picture of him asking for anyone who saw or knew anything about the killing."

Carolynn's head nodded quickly, and then she tried to see what the Lieutenant was writing. He cleared his throat and said, "What happened at the club with this Samantha?"

Carolynn's face brightened and she spoke, "Oh, nothing, but they seem to get along and liked one another, huh, Michael?"

Michael clenched his lips and nodded yes.

Morris looked from Michael to Carolynn and indicated for her to go on.

Carolynn smiled and continued, "So, right away, Samantha told us that she's leaving with this Greg. We tried to warn her that he was a stranger, but she was all enthusiastic about riding in his car. She had told us that she was new in the States and just wanted to go for a drive with him." Michael nodded.

Morris squinted his eyes and asked, "Do you know what time they left the club?"

Michael spoke out, "Yeah, I looked at my watch it was eleven fifteen."

Morris stopped writing and looked at the couple and asked. "Do you have any more information about this Samantha?"

The both shook their heads no.

Morris took in a breath and told them, "I'm going to need a complete description of her. Everything, height, weight, hair color and length, eye color—" He put up his hand and got on his phone and pressed a number. No answer, so he hung up and said, "Our artist has gone for the day. I'm gonna have to ask you to come in again tomorrow. All right?"

They looked at each other and Michael nodded.

"Okay. We want to help you catch this guy." Carolynn said.

Morris got up and they both followed. He gave them his card and said, "I really appreciate you guys coming in and reporting what you know. Hope to see you guys tomorrow." Morris shook their hands and escorted them out. The lobby had an older couple talking with the sergeant behind the glass. They all glanced at one another and went back to their business.

As the couple were exiting the building, Morris overheard Carolynn saying to Michael, "See, I told you we should…" the door closed and shut out the rest of what she was saying.

Morris looked at the rest of his messages, crumpled them up, dumped them in a trash receptacle, and left the building.

In his vehicle, he called Elizabeth.

Two rings later, "Hello."

"Hello Doc…er, ah, Elizabeth. This is Detective Mor—er, ah, this is Jason."

"Well, hello, Jason. You sound a little muddled, you having a hard day?"

"Don't know what it is but you kind of get me disorganized."

Elizabeth giggled and stated, "What do you mean? You think because I'm a doctor? Do you feel intimidated?"

Morris smirked to himself and responded, "That's not it at all. I'm kind of overwhelmed by you that's all. I never met such an attractive doctor before."

"Oh my, what a nice compliment, Thank you."

Morris blushed as was glad he was on the phone and then asked, "So I'd like to know if you can meet me for dinner. We need to discuss the matters of these corpses."

Elizabeth nodded and responded, "Yes, we do. There's something crazy going on out there."

Morris smiled and said, "Well then, glad you want to discuss this with me. Listen, I'll text you in a bit telling you where, okay?"

Elizabeth looked at her phone, smiled, and said, "Uh, ten-four Jason."

Morris smiled and replied, "Ten-four. Over and out." They both clicked off.

CHAPTER 13

CLAUDIA WAITED FOR ROBERTO TO arrive. She was so sure that he would want to be turned and live the night life with her. She sat at her dresser and viewed herself in the full mirror. She squinted at her reflection and realized that her little girl looks were not quite there anymore. She still appeared youthful and lovely but there was a mature look now with a tint of hardness and loss of innocence. She continued to brush her hair and reflected back to 1800s and her teenage years—the flowing light dresses, the running through the grass and trees being chased by her friends, the blue skies, the white fluffy clouds, and that magnificent glowing hot sun. How wonderful it felt when you came out of the cool lake and lay on the grainy large rocks and allowed the sun to evaporate the droplets about you. The burning would start and then you'd jump into the lake again, feeling the coldness slap you and relieve the heat your body had adsorbed. Oh, that gentle tickle of a butterfly landing on your nose as you lay in the warm grass baked by the brilliant sun.

Her cell phone rang. She looked at it and it was Roberto.

"Hello, my sweet. Are you close by, my love, and letting me know to be ready for you?" Claudia smiled from ear to ear.

There was silence for a few moments.

"Darling, are you there?"

Roberto was in his vehicle but was not headed for Claudia's home. The phone was on speaker mode. He then managed to respond, "Claudia, my dear, I have been thinking about your offer all day long. I am tormented by wondering if I want to surrender my

God-given rights to stay human. My religious upbringing tells me this kind of sin is unforgivable to my maker."

Claudia looked at her phone with one eyebrow arched up, and she took on an apprehensive expression. She then said, "Yes, so now what do you want?" Claudia put the phone on speaker and placed it on the dresser.

Roberto cleared his throat and stated, "Yes, all day, my dear, the pros and the cons has been bouncing in my head." He took a breath and wiped his brow, "and I cannot make that kind of a change in my life, my love."

Claudia's eyebrows rose, and her expression changed to being provoked.

"You see," Roberto continued, "although what you have offered—eternal life, wealth, a life where we would not worry about taxes, the superb strength—I know you have and all those keen senses. It sounds, uh, wonderful," he lied, "but you see, I have always wanted a family. Children at my feet when I come home from work. Getting old with the person I love and having grandchildren. And my religion forbids it. I cannot give up that dream, my love."

Through gritted teeth Claudia said, "I see."

Roberto continued, "And you do not have to worry about your identity. You are like," he laughed a little, "those superheroes who hide who they are for the protection of their loved ones." Roberto smiled and said, "Like Superman, Batman, and Spiderman. I will never give you up, I do love you, and you say you do not take lives, just the blood, he-he."

There was an eerie quietness till Roberto stated, "You still there, my love? Do you understand what I am saying? Does it make sense to you? Can you forgive me?"

Claudia tightened her grip on the phone, she breathed hard, and answered, "Yes, yes, yes, and yes. I can understand. I too wanted those things. Roberto, we can have children. They will always be children. We would have a family forever." Her expression took on a pleading look.

Roberto nodded and answered, "Yes, I thought that, too, but I couldn't take away the scenario of a child growing up and turning into somebody. When I was a young boy, all I wanted was to grow up. No, my dear, it won't work for me."

There was silence again and then Roberto asked, "Claudia?"

"Yes, Roberto."

"Do I have to worry about my life?"

Silence.

"Claudia, will you give me a head start if I am to run from you?"

Silence. Then Claudia spoke, "Roberto, in our short time together, I have fallen in love with you. What I want for you is to be happy. Go, live your life. Find your mate and live your dream, for that dream will be mine through proxy. Let me live mine until my demise, however it may come." She hung up the phone and she looked in the mirror with an annoyed expression. She grabbed her hairbrush and stroked through her hair angrily. She stopped brushing and closed her eyes and contemplated what she was going to do. Her eyes opened and a slight smile broadened her face a little.

Claudia stared at herself in the mirror. She looked away and then looked some more and then yelled, "Yes, but that was two-hundred years ago. Today, I am wealthy, I live in the new world, and take who I want. I do what I want. I live by night and rest by day. I am a vampire and I will live forever." She threw the brush and the blow put cracks in the mirror. She clenched her fist for a second and then she laid her head down on her arms and cried.

Marta was about to leave when she heard breaking glass. She looked up and ran up the stairs and burst into Claudia's bedroom. She looked at the mirror and then she looked at Claudia sobbing on the dresser.

"Claudia, what happened? Why are you crying?" A thought ran through Marta's mind, *Vampires don't cry, do they?*

Claudia lifted her head. Tears and mascara ran down her cheek. She shook her head a few times and answered, "Roberto has broken up with me."

Marta's face wrinkled up as she responded, "Oh no. Did he say why?" Marta kneeled and put an arm around Claudia's shoulders. "Gee, I thought he really liked you."

Claudia turned and looked at Marta and responded, "He did. He does. He doesn't want to get serious. He was frightened to commit, and his family is against us since we are of different religions."

Marta's eyes squinted. *That didn't make sense,* she thought, *oh well.* "Oh, let's go out tonight and have a good time. What would you like to do? We can go see a movie. A comedy would be fun. It would take your mind off him for a while."

Claudia took some Kleenex and wiped her tears and nose and said, "Oh, Marta, you would keep me company tonight?"

Marta gave a weak smile and answered, "Yes, I will. Come on, get ready. I'll call my mom and let her know I'm hanging with you tonight and I won't be home."

Claudia smiled and said, "Yes, we will, uh, hang out tonight."

An hour later, they were at the Arcadia Mall AMC theater. Claudia used valet parking, and they were now going up the escalator toward the theater entrance. Claudia was observing the mall's activity. The mall was crowded, and Claudia's vision concentrated on the men. There were few single ones and many with a female. Some men shopped with their family and some had a male companion. Marta had picked a comedy with Adam Sandler.

Once situated in their seats and the trailers were showing, Claudia told Marta she was going to the bathroom. In the ladies' room, Claudia stood at the washbasin, waiting for a prey. Two women came in conversing with one another about boyfriends and went into the stalls. Claudia went into another stall and waited. The women finished, washed their hands, and left. A single lady came in and went into a stall. Claudia waited in front of her door. The woman finished, and when she opened her stall door, Claudia blocked her exit.

The woman was at first astonished and stepped back and stated, "What the fuck do—"

Claudia immediately socked the woman on the jaw. The woman fell back and landed and sat on the commode. Claudia went to her and began depleting her of her blood. Claudia was now becoming energized and excited. The erotic sensations vibrated through her body. She was also angry. She drank and couldn't stop. She did not want to stop. She drank, and the woman collapsed in Claudia's grasp. Claudia took out her pen knife and slit the woman's throat, across her bite marks. Claudia then took what valuables the woman had and locked the door and washed up at the washbasin. Her exhilaration was high, and then she joined Marta in the darkened theater.

Marta exclaimed, "It just started. You haven't missed much." They looked at one another and smiled.

The movie ended, and out in the lobby, there was a commotion going on. From the women's restroom, two medics came out rolling a gurney that had a white sheet over a body. There was a little blood stain in the head area. The concession stand area was crowded with people wanting to know what had happened.

Marta's eyes opened wide and felt a chill freeze her body. She stopped walking. Claudia took her hand and said, "Come, let's go home and get to bed."

Marta felt hypnotized and let Claudia pull her along. After a few steps, she shook her head and looked at Claudia and asked, "Did you do this?"

Claudia looked at her smiling and stated, "Don't be ridiculous. Why would I hurt anyone?"

Marta turned and asked a lady standing close by, "Do you know what happened?"

The woman hunched her shoulders and exclaimed, "Someone cut that lady's throat, is what I was told."

Claudia pulled Marta forward. At the escalators, there was a uniformed policeman keeping everyone from leaving.

They reached the down escalator where the policeman held up his hand and stated, "Ladies, before you leave, I need to get your names and addresses."

The officer took their names and addresses and allowed them to depart.

On the way home, Marta felt a fear she had not felt before. She talked nervously about her school work as she continued to glance at Claudia as she drove. Marta was trying to envision that beautiful face biting someone's neck and sucking blood out like all those vampire movies. Marta shook her head slowly and thought, *Naw, couldn't be.*

She did feel threat though. Those recent killings and Claudia being in the vicinity. That was scary. She believed if she cooperated with Claudia that she would be safe.

They arrived home and went inside and Claudia told Marta, "Well, dear, I'm so glad we went out. I'm hoping, no, I'm asking you to spend the night. It's late and you have classes tomorrow and then you must be here after class. I've made up my mind, you're staying here tonight."

Marta did not want to upset Claudia, so she just nodded her head okay.

"Good, come on. I have a nightgown that was made for you. Come, dear." Claudia went up the stairs and Marta followed, not knowing what else to do.

In the bedroom, Claudia went to her dresser and took out a shear pale yellow negligee and handed it to Marta, "Here, dear, try this on."

Marta took it and went into the bathroom. The material was smooth and silky, it almost melted in your hand. She disrobed and slipped it on. The coolness of the material brought to her skin was stimulating. She looked in the mirror and she twirled slowly and smiled at her reflection. She looked sexy. She thought of the one time she had a sexual encounter with a female. It was all by accident after she and her friends were drinking and smoking marijuana. She ended up with a strange woman, and when she woke up in the morning, she didn't remember anything but felt content and not guilty.

She remembered she looked at this woman next to her, who was still asleep, and sneaked out of bed and found herself nude. She dressed and left, not knowing the girl's name or if the encounter was good.

Marta went into the bedroom. It was dark but lit with candles and incense. Claudia was under the covers on her side, facing away. Marta thought, *Oh good, maybe she's asleep and I'll be safe tonight. Tomorrow, I'm leaving for good.*

She slipped under the cool sheets and lay toward the edge of the bed. She closed her eyes, and then, at first, she smelled Claudia's perfume as the blankets ruffled slightly. Marta's eyes opened quickly as she felt Claudia's body moved closer to hers. Then, she felt Claudia's arm reached around her and drew her snug against Claudia's nude torso. Marta closed her eyes tightly and knew what Claudia wanted. Marta knew she had to go through with it and hopefully satisfy Claudia, and then she would survive the night and get away in the morning.

Claudia's hand moved to her breast and gently stroked her. Claudia pulled her closely and then whispered in her ear, "You will enjoy this night, my sweet. Just let yourself go and find contentment in making love with me."

Mara froze and just nodded.

Claudia was a connoisseur of lovemaking; it didn't matter if it was male or female. Claudia knew all the areas to massage, grope, kiss, suck, and lick. Pretty soon, Marta couldn't help but to respond and give back what was given to her. To her amazement, Marta experienced several orgasms that night. The room was cool, but their bodies perspired, and gracious moans echoed in the room. Alas, Marta finally fell into a deep sleep, smiling.

Morning came, and Marta sat up quickly. She was still alive. She looked over to this beautiful woman who lay motionless. Her hair was in disarray and partly covered her face. Marta brushed the hair away and looked at Claudia and wondered what it would be like to be like her.

Marta's thoughts went wild. *What's this? Did this woman discover in me what has troubled me since that first unintentional encounter? Oh my God, last night was so beautiful. I want to be in this woman's life, I think. No, no, what am I thinking about? This is crazy, but this woman can do things to me and make me reach new wonderful heights. She crossed all boundaries and I enjoyed it, no, I love it. Oh, what should I do now?*

Marta got out of bed, took a shower, and got dressed but continued to touch herself and reminiscence about last night. She left for school thinking about Claudia all day. Marta was hooked on Claudia.

* * *

Claudia woke up around two in the afternoon. She immediately looked over and found the space empty. She leaned over and took in Marta's scent and smiled. Last night was wild and fulfilling. Claudia squinted as she thought, *Who needs Roberto? I can be satisfied and be content with whom I please. Ah, but Marta was something else last night. We just followed each other's lead as if we had been together forever.* Claudia got out of bed and peeked out the window. The sun was hidden by scattered clouds and most of the blue was in overcast. Claudia quickly showered and dressed. She put on her sunglasses and a straw hat with a black band and went to her Japanese garden and enjoyed the outdoors while she could. Her anger had subsided, and she felt bad about taking that woman's life last night. Claudia took in a breath and contemplated, *I have a new lease on life. Maybe I'll turn Marta. We could have fun together. Two young pretty girls living the exclusive night life. Maybe, maybe.*

*　　*　　*

Roberto didn't go to the studios today. He felt that there was a reserved threat in the air. *Yes, Claudia said she would not harm me as long as I kept her secret. Her secret, how could I not reveal that there was a real existing vampire in our midst? She claims she does not kill. Ha! There had been dead depleted bodies found. My God! If she continues to exist, can there be others? Throughout time, there has always been people disappearing and never to be found. Is this their work? Will she come for me?* These thoughts ricochet through his brain all night. Roberto called a security contractor to have metal screens put on his windows and a wrought-iron door in the front and in the back of his home. Roberto also rented the old movie *Dracula* and watched it several times. He read up on vampires. Roberto now hung garlic cloves throughout his house and put crucifixes in all the rooms and wore one. He wondered, *Do they actually turn into bats and wolves? Are they super strong? Ah, Claudia does have strength. I felt it in our lovemaking. Wait, she can see her reflection in a mirror, so that point is false. Oh my God, what is true and what is bullshit? I know she doesn't come out during the day. Okay, the sun can be my weapon, hmm.*

Roberto went to his garage and with the scattered pieces of wood he had gathered, he made wooden stakes and placed them throughout his dwelling and put two in his vehicle.

Roberto then smirked and said out loud, "Baby, if you come after me, we are going to have a battle. Yes, if I go down, I'm going down swinging."

Roberto breathe hard and looked through his dating book and looked up his last girlfriend, Jennifer O'Malley. He called her at her place of employment and asked if she can meet him for dinner.

He said, "I missed you, and I know it was a mistake to break up with you. Can we at least have a bite to eat and catch up and see how things are?"

Jennifer remarked, "Robert, I'm at work right now and can't discuss anything right now. I'm seeing someone anyway." She thought a second and then said, "All right, yes, I'll meet you at the Bonaventure at seven. Remember, this is strictly a friendly dinner." Jennifer looked around at the two other girls working in the office and smiled. They turned back to what they were doing.

"Oh, okay. The Bonaventure, seven, friendly. I'll be there." Roberto hung up and rubbed his hands together and smiled.

CHAPTER 14

ELIZABETH

IT WAS TEN O'CLOCK IN the morning and Sally, Michael, and Carolynn were in the police station's artist room. Officer Benson had his easel rigged so the light from the window show directly on it. The trio had gone through the officer's illustration pages and had picked out all the various face components. There were dozens of eyes, eyebrows, noses, mouths, chins, foreheads, ears, and hairstyles that could be formulated together to give you a hard portrait. Benson would then draw the finished product, utilizing pointers from the trio, sometimes disagreeing on a feature. The finished product almost resembled Claudia.

But then the manager of the motel came in and disagreed all together. He claimed what he saw from his office that the female was taller, lean, and had blonde hair. He claimed that she had a boyfriend. He was over six feet tall, dark hair, and well-built. He had seen them when they got out of their vehicle. The license plate number he had was reported stolen. This caused a commotion until Sergeant Oberron put them all in separate rooms to wait for Lieutenant Morris. Morris had gone to speak with the Arcadia theater manager to see if he had seen anything. Morris called in and told Oberron to release everyone. He would contact them later if needed.

*　　*　　*

Michael and Olivia decided to live a better life even though they were vampires and needed blood to exist. They decided to fix up their home and not to kill their victims. It was ten o'clock when the need for replenishment overwhelmed them, so they stopped cleaning up their residence and drove around searching for food. They finally spotted a couple coming out of a Denny's Restaurant on Atlantic Boulevard. The vehicle went east on Whittier Boulevard a couple miles and the turned north on Gerhart Street. They followed the black SUV until it pulled into the driveway of a yellow stucco home. Michael passed the house and then pulled over and parked. The couple in the vehicle were unloading suitcases from the vehicle as Michael and Olivia sneaked up to them. As the female in the vehicle walked into her home carrying a small bag, Olivia jumped her from behind. She struck the woman with a vicious blow to the back of her neck. The woman fell to the floor unconscious. Olivia dragged her into the living room and began sucking on the woman's neck.

The man hassled, carrying two suitcases and two small boxes. As he reached the small porch and tried to push the door open, he yelled out, "Hey, Ruth, can you give me—" Michael attacked him from behind and then struck the man behind his head. The man went to the floor like a sack of potatoes. Michael dragged the man into the living room, lifted him, and began sucking his blood. Olivia watched her man indulge himself as she wiped her mouth.

She whispered loudly, "Remember, babe, just enough. Don't kill him."

As Michael sucked, his eyes opened and looked at Olivia and he nodded his head. Michael's victim woke startled and tried to disengage himself to no avail, and then he stopped struggling and now embraced his abductor. Olivia then went out to the car and closed it up and went back inside the house. Michael was done and had picked up the fallen suitcases and boxes and cleared the area. Michael then looked at Olivia as she began to disrobe. Michael smiled and took off his clothes. Standing there naked, they went into each other's arms and embraced and fell onto a large sofa. There, they made outrageous love. After they finished the lovemaking, they went through the house and suitcases and took anything that was valuable. At three in the morning, they checked the bodies, they both still had a pulse. The vampire couple smiled at each other and went back to their home.

*　　*　　*

Marta had a hard time in class that day. All morning, her thoughts would drift to those moments with Claudia as they slept together and made love together. Claudia expertly pressed all her erotic and emotional buttons, causing extreme pleasures beyond her belief. The multiple orgasms she went through had to be a world record. Marta giggled to herself. She may have heard just two words from the professor all day. Now, she had to catch up on her reading. Damn.

A thought brought her back to reality. *What if Claudia was the killer of the bodies they had been finding?* This thought woke her up as the class ended and the other students rose to leave. Marta got up and was about to leave when the professor halted her.

"Marta, please step to the desk, please."

Holding her books against her chest, she stepped over to the desk, "Yes, Mr. Rossi."

He cleared his throat and remarked, "Marta, it seems that you were in a daze this morning. Are you all right?"

Marta was surprised some but manage to say, "Oh, Mr. Rossi, I'm fine. It's just that for some reason, I couldn't sleep last night. I was very tired today."

He nodded and said, "I see. Okay go home and get a good night's sleep."

Marta nodded and replied, "Yes, Mr. Rossi. Yes, I will." She walked out of the building and down to her car. While sitting in her car, that thought entered her mind again. *If she is a killer, oh my, I will just leave her employment and say nothing but*— Marta took in a breath and thought—*I need to be with her one more time. Oh, she is wonderful.*

*   *   *

Morris sat at the table, nursing a scotch on the rocks waiting for Elizabeth to appear. For a moment, Morris was glued to his chair, and then, his mouth parted and his eyes broadened. He managed to stand up and view the medical doctor stepping his way. She had transformed from a lovely dove to a magnificent peacock. As she approached, Morris took in her long wavy auburn hair as it cascaded and bounced along her oblong face. Her eyebrows guarded her long dark eyelashes as they shielded her light-green devilish eyes. At closer range, he would notice the tiny gold specks glittering in the greenish irises. That straight Indian princess nose kept vigilance of her perfectly shaped lips that were hued in red. All this kept in balance by a slim long classy neck. Her white blouse with frill down the center was covered by a light vest that was sheltered by a matching jacket. Her matching skirt stopped at the knees where shapely tan limbs slipped into dark-brown high heels.

"I hope I'm not late," she exclaimed as she came up in front of Morris. He leaned in and they embraced briefly.

"You're right on the money, Elizabeth." Morris gave a big tight-lip smile and stated, "You clean up well, Dr. Morales."

Elizabeth stepped away and holding on to one another's hands, she viewed him and claimed, "You don't do so bad yourself, Lt. Morris."

Morris had changed into a dark suit with a bright yellow tie. Morris smiled and pulled a chair for her. She sat.

"You want a martini or something?" Morris asked.

She looked at him with a smirk and said, "Shaken, not stirred, and a lemon twist."

Morris nodded and chuckled and said, "Oh, a female double-oh-seven, huh?" He signaled the waitress and ordered her drink.

Elizabeth lightly chuckled and said, "Hey, I'm in company of a big-time copper. That could be intimidating. I'm leveling out the elements here." She looked at him and surrendered a sweet smile and stated, "We're being discreet, aren't we?" She kind of hunched over and looked around the room to see if anyone was listening and then whispered, "I'm also a Black Belt in karate."

"Really? Okay now. You are not only attractive, self-protecting, and intelligent, but you also have a sense of humor."

Elizabeth tilted her head and said, "Thanks for the compliment."

Morris leaned back and stated, "Yeah, I'm just wondering if I'm out of my league here?"

Elizabeth tilted her head and with a small smile, she said, "That depends on the agenda, don't you think?"

Morris took in a breath and then sipped his drink and said, "The agenda tonight is complex. Officially, it was occupational assistance, but"—Morris took another sip of his drink—"I'm open to other categories." He smiled.

Elizabeth now seemed more confident and said, "Well, in answer to your question about the league nonsense, let's see. So, in the medical agenda, I get the notch. In hand-to-hand combat"—she looked at him with a twinkle in her eyes—"that's yet to be determined. Then there's criminal science. I'd say we're even there." Morris's eyebrows rose and she continued, "Ah, criminal investigation. Yes, you're up on me there."

Morris's left eyebrow arched as he asked, "What about the itinerary of amorous development?"

Elizabeth's demeanor changed, the blood in her face seemed to drain and she looked a little pale, she then held up her hand, insinuating to wait. She tilted her head again, the blood returned to her face. As she was about to speak, the atmosphere was broken as the waitress placed her martini in front of her and asked, "You lovely folks ready to order yet?"

Morris waved his hand and commented, "Please, give us a few minutes."

The waitress nodded and walked away.

Elizabeth then picked up her menu and began reading it.

Morris brought down her menu and asked her, "Do you mind if I order for both of us?"

Elizabeth lips pursed a moment and she responded, "Ah, no, but how do you know I am not a vegetarian?"

Morris clenched his mouth and the asked, "Are you?"

She smiled and shook her head no.

Morris signaled the waitress over and he ordered for both. As he ordered, Elizabeth began sipping her drink, and over her glass, she viewed the detective. He had a hard face, but he was attractive. She thought something like Sean Connery. His thick black hair was a little wavy and he parted it on the right side. Every so often, a comma of hair would fall on his forehead. His dark eyes would shift from callous to tenderness. The slightly crooked nose must have come from some battle with someone. His lips were thin and had a maroonish hue to them. He shaved close to the skin, but you could tell he had a heavy beard. He had a slightly prominent jaw that seemed to be able to take a punch. He was tall, maybe six feet two, and at least two hundred pounds. She wondered why he wasn't married and had children.

He looked over to her and asked, "Would you take a chance and allow me to order everything, okay?"

Elizabeth nodded her head and stated, "I'll take a chance."

Morris signaled the waitress to come over and Morris cupped her ears and ordered dinner.

Morris reached over and patted her hand and asked, "You know, I'm hungry, are you? I haven't eaten all day, just coffee and a donut this morning."

Elizabeth nodded and responded, "Oh, I'm rather hungry myself."

Just then Morris noticed a good-looking man being escorted to his seat. He had an attractive woman by his side.

Elizabeth then asked, "How long have you been a police officer, Jason?"

Morris breathed heavily and answered, "Twelve years. I came in when I was twenty-two. I had just been discharged from the Marines. Signed up when I was eighteen." He smiled and sipped his drink.

Elizabeth nodded slowly and asked, "I assume you were in those desert wars?"

Morris's eyebrows rose, his eyes widened, and he took in a big breath, and answered, "Afghanistan, two years." He squinted his eyes and his complexion hardened as he said, "Please, don't ask me about it tonight." He produced a weak smile.

Elizabeth's expression showed a frightfulness and nodded, and then she stated, "Okay, uh, do you mind if I ask a personal question?"

Morris's eyes narrowed for a moment and then he smiled and said, "Shoot."

"Are you married and if not, why not?"

Morris took in a breath again and replied, "I was married once. Uh, six years ago. She was also a police officer. She was killed during a high-speed chase."

Elizabeth's mouth gaped open, her eyes reflected astonishment. She shook her head slowly.

"Oh, Jason, I'm sorry I asked. I—"

Morris interrupted her and said, "Don't fret, Liz. I'm pretty much over it now. Yeah, while she was chasing a robbery suspect, some drunk idiot ran through an intersection and slammed right into her. Doctors say she died immediately. She didn't suffer, thank God."

The waitress bought their salads and rolls in a basket and walked away.

They both watched the waitress walk away.

Then Elizabeth remarked, "Oh, so she was a police officer."

Morris's eyebrows lifted, and he just nodded his head.

"Anyway, I am sorry, and I won't ask about her."

Morris just nodded and they both started eating their salads.

After a few moments, Elizabeth looked up and said, "Hmm, this is really good. It's only slices of a delicious tomato and white onions, but the dressing is spectacular."

Morris smiled and said, "Glad you like it. I love it. First time I had it was in a restaurant in New York. It's the dressing that makes it. I told the chef here about it and it took him months to finally get the dressing right."

"I'm impressed. You went all out for something that you wanted." She looked at Morris with her left eyebrow arched and remarked, "Do you go after everything you want with that kind of gusto?"

Morris stopped his hand in midair, the fork had a piece of tomato and a slice of onion hanging on for dear life, as he commented, "When it's worthwhile and special." Morris looked into Elizabeth's inquisitive eyes and said, "I'll go all the way." He put the morsels in his mouth and chewed.

Elizabeth's eyes widened briefly. She cleared her throat and said, "I see."

They continued eating in silence, and then the waitress appeared with their dinner plates. Elizabeth looked down and there was a half-inch New York steak smothered in sautéed mushrooms and grilled onions and a baked potato. The aroma was exquisite.

The waitress then asked Elizabeth, "Sour cream, butter, and chives?"

Elizabeth just nodded, and the waitress laid down three containers with the above-mentioned condiments.

Morris then spoke, "I ordered it medium well, mine is rare. You want to switch?"

With her mouth slightly open, Elizabeth shook her head no.

"All right, let's dig in."

Elizabeth cut her steak and as she chewed her eyes opened wider and she commented, "Hmm, again. This steak just melts in your mouth. It's delicious, Morris. Thank you."

Morris smiled and, while chewing, he couldn't help but to look over at that couple he noticed earlier. There was something about the man that caught Morris's eye. As he sipped some wine, it donned on him. The picture in Claudia Brocolac's living room. *Hmm*, he thought, *he's not with Miss Brocolac.*

"Are you okay? You seem to have drifted off."

"Huh? No, I'm good. I just recognized someone in the restaurant. Can we talk while we eat?"

With a piece of meat on her fork, she pointed it at him and said, "Sure."

Elizabeth looked around the restaurant and stated, "By the way, this is a fancy place to interrogate me." She smiled, revealing straight white teeth.

Morris wiped his mouth with the napkin and stated, "Elizabeth..."

She stopped chewing and looked at him, eyes wide and head tilted some. She had an inquisitive expression on her face.

Morris took in a breath and said, "I wish you wouldn't do that. My head wanders off."

Elizabeth now had a confused look and asked. "Do what, Jason?"

Morris drew in a big breath and remarked, "Uh, never mind." She furrowed her brow and Morris then asked, "The other day, you made a comment about"—Morris looked around and then leaned in closer—"vampires."

Elizabeth's left eyebrow rose up. She put down her fork. sipped some wine, and said, "What I meant is, ah, someone is acting like one. You see, vampires cannot exist. How can a dead person come back to life? It's scientifically impossible." She picked up her fork and knife and began cutting the steak and said, "You think I can take part of this steak home? It's delicious."

Morris nodded and said, "I do it all the time." She smiled. "Why did you tell me vampires if you don't believe they exist?"

Elizabeth then took in a breath and said, "Well, Mr. Lieutenant"—she looked around really quick—"I thought you were handsome, and I wanted to continue talking with you. You abruptly wanted to leave and—"

Morris cut in, "You mislead me on purpose?"

She nodded, her eyes closed, and her mouth made straight line.

Morris shook his head slowly and remarked, "Bad girl." She continued nodding and Morris stated, "You should be spanked."

Elizabeth eyes opened wide. She leaned back and asked, "Are you the one who'll discipline me?"

Morris leaned in a little and said, "Darn tootin', I am."

They both started laughing.

Elizabeth then said, "Somebody has a tormented mind, Jason. It's really scary to know someone is out there doing these atrocities."

Morris pushed back his chair a little and asked, "Did you know there had been other bodies in LA County with similar style of killing?" Elizabeth's brows furrowed and her eyes narrowed as Morris continued, "And there have been muggings where the victims have been depleted of their blood, just enough so they won't die."

Elizabeth's eyes widened. She leaned back and shook her head slowly and remarked, "Jason, I was unaware of this."

Morris leaned in and continued, "These crimes only happen when the sun is down. Witnesses state a beautiful woman was involved and other witnesses say it was a couple." Morris leaned back as he went on, "As your report states, two different bite marks, possibly a man and a woman."

Elizabeth nodded and said, "What I am going to do is examine the bite marks more closely and take a DNA sample from them. The head medical examiner needs to give permission. A nudge from you would help." She smiled at him and batted her eyes.

The detective nodded and asked, "Do you always get your way when you bat your eyes?"

Elizabeth looked startled and said, "Moi? Never tried it before." She gave a straight smile.

Morris responded with a grunt and said, "I must look like easy pickings."

Again, Elizabeth took on an astonished look, and then she looked at Morris with an arched eyebrow and remarked, "On the contrary, you seemed to be a very hard nut to crack."

Morris cleared his throat and then said, "You know, Elizabeth, you're beginning to get under my skin," Elizabeth kind of frowned but Morris continued, "but in a good way."

Her frown changed to a happy expression.

Again, the waitress broke the atmosphere, "Is there anything else? Would you care for coffee?"

Morris looked at Elizabeth. She shook her head and Morris stated, "No, thanks. We're done, but, please, we'd like a take-home box. Thank you."

The waitress nodded. Morris handed her a credit card and she walked away.

Elizabeth drank some wine and said, "What kind of people do those kind of murders, Jason? I know you must deal with senseless killings a lot. These recent ones, they seem to be, uh, insane."

Morris nodded and said, "Insane, yes, but more. They seem to be diabolical."

Elizabeth squinted and then nodded and commented, "Yes, that's the perfect word for those killers."

Morris signed the draft the waitress brought him and said, "That word—vampires—keeps ringing in my head."

Elizabeth's eyebrows rose. She clenched her lips and said, "Hey, you wanna watch that old movie, *Dracula*? We can rent it."

Morris's eyes narrowed as he nodded slowly and remarked, "Your place or mine?"

"Oh, my place is a mess right now, but okay. Here's my address." She wrote on a napkin. "You can try to follow me, but I drive erratically," she smiled sheepishly.

As they rose to leave, Morris's attention went over to the man he had recognized from the photo at Claudia's. A woman came storming to the man's table. It was her, Claudia, and then she stood in front of Roberto's table, her legs apart, hands on hips, and exclaimed, "You rotten bastard. You break up with me and within an hour, you're out with some little hussy?"

Jennifer blinked her eyes and began to get up as she stated, "Excuse me, I'm—"

Claudia put her hand on Jennifer's shoulder and pushed her back down. Jennifer squealed oh. Claudia turned to her and gave her the evil eye. Jennifer leaned back some, and then Claudia looked at Roberto and said, "You best be silent you son-of-a-bitch, if you know what's good for you."

Roberto began to say something, but Claudia dumped a drink in his face and walked off. Everyone watched in silence. Morris took Elizabeth's hand and led her out to valet parking. There, they watched as Claudia had just got in her vehicle and sped off.

On the way to Elizabeth's, Morris went over in his thoughts the interview he had had with Claudia Brocolac. She was a confident woman and pretty sure of herself. He realized that there were two individuals taking part in these gruesome murders. As he followed Elizabeth, he found out how true her statement was about being an erratic driver. She just went from lane to lane, trying to get ahead of traffic. Nothing illegal, just erratic.

Elizabeth lived in a newer huge building complex in Montebello. She went into the underground parking, while Morris parked in a no-parking zone and placed his credentials inside the windshield so he wouldn't get ticketed or towed away. She buzzed him into the building, and he took the elevator to the sixth floor. He knocked t her door and waited.

Click-cluck went the locks. She opened the door and said, "I just needed a minute to straighten up in here. I was in a hurry this evening, I—"

Morris pulled her to him and kissed her. She didn't resist. They embraced, and then Morris pinned her against the wall. They broke for air.

Elizabeth fanned herself and said, "Man, I haven't been kissed like that since high school."

Morris wiped his forehead and stated, "I'm not apologizing for that. I wanted to do that since the first time I saw you, Liz."

She put him at arm's length and said, "I think this is the beginning of a beautiful friendship."

Morris nodded and smiled and commented, "Casablanca!"

Her eyebrows arched as she exclaimed, "You are an old movie buff."

Morris nodded. "Love 'em, the ol' black-and-whites. Bogart, Gable, Lemar, Tracy, Davis, Grant—"

"Okay, I believe you. I love them too. Anyway, don't kiss me like that again tonight. You invaded my defense system. I felt defenseless."

Morris nodded and said, "Right, may I use your restroom?"

"Yes, you may. Through the archway and turn left. While you're there, I'm gonna order the Dracula movie on Netflix."

As he walked to the restroom, he stated, "I've seen it, Lugosi is so creepy."

They watched the movie and toward the end, Morris fell asleep. At two in the morning, he awoke with a blanket on him and his shoes were off. He got up, wrote a note, and went home.

CHAPTER 15

COP KILLER

AFTER SHE LEFT THE RESTAURANT, Claudia was driving home at a speed that was ticket worthy. She was on the 110 going north toward Pasadena. It was now nine in the evening and she hadn't had her lifeblood yet. As she neared Avenue 64, those blaring red flashing lights came on behind her.

"What the fuck!" She hissed. She was on the fast lane, so she had to move over and take an exit ramp off the freeway. The 110 Freeway is the oldest freeway in Los Angeles. The lanes were made for vehicle of the 1950s. On-ramps and off-ramps, you had to be quick because the ramp lane lengths were short.

Claudia got off and pulled over and waited. The off-ramp was dark and secluded.

The motorcycle officer walked over to the passenger side window and stooped down. He poked in and said, "Good evening, ma'am, you headed to a fire tonight?"

Claudia looked up at the officer and her mascara had run some and her eyes were filled with tears. She then exclaimed, "I'm so sorry, Officer, my boyfriend just broke up with me and for no apparent good reason."

The officer has heard many stories before, some were authentic but most were lies to get out of a ticket. This one seemed real. "I'm sorry to hear that, ma'am. Guy must be an idiot. Can I see your license and registration?"

"Why sure, Officer. The registration is in the glove box. Can you help me find it?" She opened the glove box and said, "Can you flash your light inside? It's there somewhere."

The officer took off his helmet and stuffed it under one arm and spread his legs and put his head through the open window along with his arm holding the flashlight.

Claudia grabbed his arm and pulled him in further and grasped him around his neck and bit into his artery. One of his arms was trapped under him, while his other arm was held against his body by the window frame. His legs kicked for a while. As his blood seeped into Claudia, the erotic emotions heightened for both. As his legs stopped flailing, his helmet bounced along the street and rolled to a stop by the curb as his heart stopped beating. Claudia got out and turned off the motorcycle's lights and pushed the cycle into the bushes. She did the same to the officer. There, she knocked over the motorcycle and opened the gas cap. Gas filtered out around the bike and the body. She found a Bic lighter in one of his pockets and lit a rolled paper at one end, the other end was lying on the small river of gasoline leading to the fallen officer's motorbike.

As Claudia drove away, she looked in her rear-view mirror. After a couple of seconds, there was an explosion as the lit gasoline stream reached the bike. The night lit up behind her for a brief moment. The dark night flared like sunshine briefly. All went dark except for a small fire of what was left of the machine. Now, she looked at herself in the mirror and seen her blood-smudged mouth and chin. She wiped herself clean and drove home, thinking that Roberto and his girlfriend will have to be eliminated.

* * *

Roberto was taking Jennifer home going through the streets, prolonging the ride. The streetlights giving temporary lighting in the vehicle. He would glance at her and saw her sullen manner and wet cheeks.

As he drove, he looked at her again and tried to drive and look at her without crashing. "Jenny, that woman is off her rocker. She just came from Spain and—"

"Stop it, Robert. Tonight was the most embarrassing moment of my life."

"Honey, I—"

"Don't *honey* me. I can never, ever go back to the Bonaventure again."

"Ah, babe, I—"

"I knew I shouldn't have agreed to go out with you. I've known you were a player. Just take me home. Don't say another word, just take me home."

Roberto shook his head and took in a breath and just drove in silence. Jennifer turned on the radio and silently sobbed."

*   *   *

As Claudia drove into her driveway, she saw Marta's Camry. Claudia's black heart leaped as she thought, *That little bitch wants it. She did respond sensually high. We made beautiful music together. It may be time to have a vampire partner.* She parked her car, hurried into her home, and ran up the stairs with ease. She entered her bedroom and scented candles lit up the room. Marta was lying on the bed, wearing Claudia's red negligee and reading the *Twilight* series novel.

Marta immediately closed the book and stated, "Whatever you are, I want to be your lover and your friend. Since you cannot function by day, I will handle what needs to be done. Come here, Claudia, come here and devour me. Make love to me completely. I am your slave."

Claudia's face lit up and as she disrobed, she said, "Yes, my fallen angel. We will conquer the world. I will tell you my secrets and you can decide if you want to join me in an eternal life."

Marta's hand went to her mouth as she nodded. Claudia went to her completely nude and through the flickering light, Claudia took in this woman with a great body and face.

They embraced and kissed each other passionately as their hands searched and fondled their sensitive and erotic areas. No words were exchanged, just moans and groans of pleasure. They fell asleep in each other's arms.

In the morning, Marta got out of bed and went into the bathroom. There, she checked her body for bites, marks, or bruises. There wasn't anything she could find. She hugged her body and took a shower. While bathing, she recalled last night and how this woman could ignite her eroticism so feverously. She needed to speak with Claudia about the future. She decided she would stay at Claudia's today, and after Claudia got up, she would question her on what it was like to be a vampire. She wondered if it was true about them having extra strength and powers and if their senses were heightened as most myths described them to have. Marta wanted the truth. Were they immortal? Did they turn into bats and wolves? Can they drink someone's blood and not kill their prey? Yes, that was the most vital question. Marta did not want to take human lives. She also wondered why couldn't they just get blood from hospitals, the Red Cross. Would the public condemn her? Marta's curiosity was eating at her. She went downstairs and through the Netflix system, she ordered the *Twilight* series, and when it arrived, she lay on the couch and watched the love story of a human girl in love with a vampire.

The other feelings that invaded her thought process was why she couldn't wait to make love to this spectacular woman again. She knew she was not that experienced in the acts of love, but nothing has been close to what Claudia made her feel and the contentment she bathed in afterwards. So now, she contemplated on maybe being a super-being vampire and smiled unconsciously.

*   *   *

The news stations were broadcasting about the slain police officer found by a Pasadena Freeway exit ramp. Authorities and the mayor announced that there was a $50,000 reward for information that would assist in the arrest and conviction of the culprit or culprits who were responsible for this tragic killing. The reporter went on to describe the fatal style in which the officer was killed and found.

Morris was at his desk watching the news reel on the slain policeman and he became extremely interested when he heard the body was found off the Pasadena Freeway. He now envisioned that woman he had seen, Claudia, her jumping into her vehicle and hurrying away. He shook his head and thought more about it. He decided he needed to pay this woman a visit again.

*   *   *

Olivia and Victor had found that by using heavy curtains and drapes, they could function somewhat reasonably in the daylight hours. Olivia even experimented on going outside in the daytime if she was fully covered—wore a hat and sunglasses and a high-numbered suntan lotion on her face and hands. What helped also was to go outside on overcast days. On rainy days, it was nice to be outside and feel the weather. She loved walking around her neighborhood.

Victor was watching the news and Olivia took the remote and put it on mute. He looked up at her puzzled, and she sat down beside him and said, "Honey, can we suffice normally on animal blood?"

Victor looked at her his face in a frown and stated, "I don't know, babe. That's a good question. You want to try?"

Olivia clenched her hands and took on an earnest expression. She nodded and replied, "I think we should try it. If it works, we can sell this house and move to Big Bear or Yosemite. We'll get a cabin and live off the wildlife." She turned fully toward him and took on a pleading composure.

Victor stood up and paced a little. He went to a window and pulled back the curtain and peeked out, and turned to face Olivia. He scratched his head and said, "Gee, I don't know, honey. That's a big move." He sat down and put his hands on his knees.

Olivia looked at him and said, "Yeah, and?"

"Okay, first, let's try to see what happens from living on animal blood."

Olivia jumped up and clapped her hands and exclaimed, "Oh, that's fantastic! Come on, it's dark now. Let's go find a big dog."

Victor's face crunched up and an "ew" sound came from his lips. He hunched his shoulders and followed Olivia out.

They cruised the neighborhoods of East LA, and they viewed only a couple of scroungy dogs pawing through turned-over trashcans. After a while, Victor turned to Olivia and told her, "Hey, babe, it's getting late. Everyone will be in bed, and we'll have to crawl in through someone's window."

Olivia banged the dashboard and stated, "Oh, Vic, I know you're right. We need to live in the country or farm area where there's plenty of sheep and cows. We should have gone to the LA Zoo, hon."

Victor eyebrows rose and said, "Hey, maybe tomorrow we'll sneak in, okay? But tonight, we need to get fed." He looked over at her with an imploring expression.

Olivia clenched her lips and then nodded and said, "Okay."

Victor drove to a Denny's Restaurant and parked in the last row of the parking lot. They searched the lot where several autos were parked. They chose a new Camry, and Victor used his flat metal band to unlock the door. He and Olivia situated themselves in the back seat and Victor disabled the interior lights. There, they waited for their prey to return from eating.

Fifteen minutes went by, two young men came toward the Toyota. They were laughing and walking unsteadily. Victor nudged Olivia and whispered, "They're drunk."

Olivia smiled.

The taller of the two went to the driver's side and unlocked the door and the passenger door unlocked also. As they got in, the taller one claimed, "Hey what's wrong with these lights?" He tapped the overhead light cover a couple times.

His friend said, "Aw, fix it tomorrow, Ted. I'm sleepy, get me home."

Ted then said, "Aw. shoot. Okay." He turned to start the car up but at that moment, both Victor and Olivia sprang up and grabbed their prey by their chins and pulled their head back as they bit down into each of their victim's neck. Trying to scream as they waved their arms and kicked their legs. The helpless preys fought the hopeless battle for their life.

Olivia's prey began slowly to cease fighting, and then he seemed to be enjoying the depletion of his blood and life. Olivia felt the eroticism and had difficulty stopping herself, but she finally let up. She sat back on the seat, eyes closed, as she experienced the orgasmic emotion that was the height of a vampire's existence.

After some moments, she shook her head and opened her eyes and viewed Victor as he viciously continued sucking on Ted.

She panicked, and at first nudged Victor to no avail, and then she started hitting him on his back, trying to make him stop before his victim perishes.

He finally pulled off and sat back. His victim, Ted, just leaned to his right and rested on his friend's torso. The friend's head stayed leaning forward but a light pulsing vein lazily pumped on his neck.

Olivia hit Victor on the chest and screamed, "You killed him, you idiot! You killed him!"

Victor wiped his mouth, breathed in, and stated, "Aw, shit. I'm sorry, I couldn't stop, honey. I fucked up."

Olivia clenched her mouth, took a deep breath, and said, "Aw, let's get the fuck out of here. We really need to move now."

Victor squinted and frowned and just nodded. They got out of the Camry and went home and made make-up love.

CHAPTER 16

DECISIONS

THE NEXT DAY, LT. MORRIS was busy all day long. He had two morgues needed to visit and two crime scenes needed his attention. The third thing was to interview the survivor from the Denny's incident. Number four, he wanted to visit that Claudia woman again. He had a funny feeling about that female. He decided to visit the Denny's parking lot. At Denny's, he questioned the staff, but no one saw anything. Morris paced the lot and viewed where the victim's auto was. He believed the culprits were probably in the car, waiting for their prey to arrive. Next, he went to the hospital to see the survivor, a Ronald Chacon. He was a thirty-five-year-old construction worker.

At the hospital, the doctor took Morris to the side and said, "Mr. Chacon is in a bad shape and probably would not be able to speak. I'm allowing you to see him because I feel there's something awful out there and maybe Mr. Chacon can shed some light on the matter."

"Thank you, Dr. McBain, thank you very much." Morris shook his hand and then went into the room. Ronald Chacon was laying on the bed awake. He had a drink in his hand with a straw. The right side of his neck was bandaged up and he seemed pale and weak. Mr. Chacon looked up at Morris as he entered and squinted, trying to recognize who it was.

"Mr. Chacon, I am Lt. Morris, Homicide, LAPD."

Mr. Chacon lifted his head some and pointed to his throat and shook his head.

Morris nodded and said, "I'm going to ask you some questions and you can blink once for no and blink twice for yes. Can you do that?"

Mr. Chacon blinked twice.

"I know you are not feeling well and weak, but right now, it's very important to see if there are any clues we can come up with to catch these assholes who did this to you, understand?"

Mr. Chacon smiled at the word assholes and blinked twice.

Morris grinned and then asked, "You and Anthony Martin were coworkers?"

Two blinks.

"You had a late dinner at Denny's?"

Two blinks.

"Where you two drinking some place prior to your dinner? If you were could you write down the name of the establishment?" Morris handed him a notepad and pen.

Chacon blinked twice and began writing. Morris took the pad and read, "Pancho's pool hall. That's over on Whittier Boulevard near Ditman Avenue, correct?"

Two blinks.

Morris thought a minute. He knew the place. Usually, a bunch of homeboys hung out there.

"Did you notice anyone new, different, or unusual there while you were playing pool?"

One blink.

Morris nodded and then asked, "How 'bout at Denny's while you and Anthony were eating dinner?"

Again, one blink. Chacon took a sip and winced as he swallowed.

"Okay, think hard. Is they anyone you can think of that would want to do you or Anthony harm? Think about it a minute."

Chacon's eyes looked up to the ceiling as he thought. After a minute he shook his head no.

Morris clenched his lips and then said, "Well, maybe Anthony had an enemy. After all, they spared you."

Chacon hunched his shoulders and winced in pain.

Morris took out an envelope and took out a sheet of paper. He looked at it and stated, "It states here on the initial report that when you woke up here in the hospital, you wrote as best you could at the time what remembered."

Chacon's eyes opened wide and he thrust out his chin some.

Morris read, "Tony and I ate dinner and we walked to his car. As we got in, he mentioned something about the interior light not working, and then suddenly, something grabbed my chin and pulled my head back. They were very strong. I tried swinging my arms, but I was in a helpless position. After a moment I felt warm all over and then my world went blank."

Chacon nodded as he blinked twice.

"Okay, you never saw anyone and you don't know if it was a man or a woman, right?"

Chacon looked sullen as he blinked twice.

Morris put his card on the nightstand and said, "That's all I have for now, but if you recall anything, and that's anything, call me, okay?"

Chacon smiled weakly and blinked twice.

Morris then drove to the Lincoln Heights Morgue. That was where the slain police officer's remains were.

While he was speaking with the Mortician, he found out that the body was badly burned and had amputated parts from the explosion and burned as well. The head and neck were intact.

"Doctor, can you examine the neck for me and see if there's any unusual marks there."

The doctor grinned and exclaimed, "Hey, we LAPD morticians are police officers, too, you know?"

Morris frowned but nodded.

"Our disclosures and evidence had enabled you guys to catch a lot of culprits, right?"

Morris continued to frown and nodded yes again.

"So, we stay alert, we contact one another, and when there's a fallen officer, we put extra effort in our duties."

Morris chuckled, nodded, and asked, "Okay, what do you have?"

The mortician continued, "I know about the bite marks and, yes, Motorcycle Davis had two bite marks on the side of his neck right where that main vein is at. From what we can tell, his body was lacking plasma or blood."

Morris shook his hand and said, "Thanks, Doc. That helps."

Morris turned to walk away when the doctor said to him, "There's someone acting like a vampire out there. Catch 'em, will ya?"

Morris hurried down the hall and responded, "I fucken sure will, Doc."

Morris drove to the Montebello morgue. There, he would see Yolanda.

*   *   *

Marta finished class and drove to Claudia's. There, she peeked in on Claudia who was lying still on her bed. She had on a night-gown but was lying perfectly still. Marta tiptoed up to the bed and stared at this sleeping beauty. Marta decided to go downstairs and see if the maid had cleaned and straightened out the house. Then, she would go speak with the gardener and make sure they were properly doing their job. After writing out checks for bills, she would go lay down beside Claudia until she awakened. Maybe they can have a quickie before Claudia goes out and gets her medicine. *Maybe I'll go with her and see how it's done.*

*   *   *

Morris went into the morgue searching for Elizabeth. He walked down the hallway and tapped on a door, opened it, and looked inside. The first door he peeked into looked like a lab room. Counters with lab equipment, vials, and bottles lined the countertops. Nobody was in there. The next room he peeked in had two men in white frocks, one was looking into a microscope while the other stood by. They turned to look who was there.

Morris smiled and said "Oops, wrong door."

As he closed the door and turned, he nearly bumped into Elizabeth as she smiled and stated, "Looking for me, Officer Morris?"

Morris smiled and said, "You're under arrest, ma'am."

Elizabeth squinted and responded, "On what charge, may I ask?"

As Morris reached for his handcuffs and dangled them. He said, "Burglary."

Elizabeth's eyes widened and her eyebrows arched. "What did I steal?" she asked.

Morris answered, "My heart."

Elizabeth put both of her arms straight out and said, "Take me in. You can't have it back."

They both laughed.

"Are you here to see me or about the latest vampire killing?" Elizabeth asked.

Morris grinned and pinned her against the wall and stated, "Both."

"Just like most men, you need an excuse to visit a lonely-heart girl."

"I'm here because I want to catch that vampire before he bites you on the neck." He looked around and then said, "Nobody does that but me." He leaned on her and went for her neck. Just then, a door opened, and she pushed him away. They both put on their business face and Morris exclaimed, "Have you done the autopsy on the latest victim yet?"

The two scientists came out of the room deeply involved in a conversation. They looked over at Morris and Elizabeth, nodded, and went down the hall.

Elizabeth cleared her throat and said, "Right this way, Lt. Morris." She grinned.

Morris followed her down the hall. The white couldn't disguise the shape of her torso. His eyes followed her walk.

In the large morgue enclosure, all three tables had bodies on them. The first body was covered by a sheet, the second table had a woman's corpse, the upside-down Y incision from her chest to her pelvic had been done and the flesh pulled away. A technician was standing by the body and writing on a notepad. Morris gave the body a quick glance and followed Elizabeth to the third table. The dead male's nude torso was intact and the whole body appeared to have a pale complexion to it.

Elizabeth told him, "I was just gonna get started on Anthony. You wanna watch?" She looked at him and grinned.

Morris's eyes widened, and he shook his head quickly and stated, "Uh, no thanks. Maybe some other time." He looked at Elizabeth nervously and continued, "Uh, what have you discovered so far, uh, Doctor?"

Elizabeth reached over out of view from the other technician and grabbed Morris's butt playfully and said, Oh, a few things, and then she whispered, "I want to see you tonight."

Morris gently swatted her hand away and responded, "Really? Hopefully it may help with the investigation." He whispered, "Stop it. I get excited easily."

Elizabeth then responded, "Step over here." She got closer to the body and with one hand pointed to the corpse's neck and her other hand patted Morris's groin. Her eyes widened. She smiled and said, "It's hard"—she paused a moment and looked into Morris's face— "to see with the naked"—she paused again as Morris leaned down to view the dead man's neck— "eye, but here, use the magnifying glass."

Shaking his head, Morris took the magnifier and said, "I know it's hard"—he turned his head to view Elizabeth—"to see without the magnifying glass." He grabbed the handle from her and said, "The hard part"—he turned again—"is making sure you feel it"—he turned and looked through the magnifying glass—"without disturbing any evidence."

"Well," Elizabeth said as she leaned on the counter with one hand, "I guess I shouldn't touch it again." She looked at Morris with a stern look and one eyebrow arched.

Morris nodded as he saw the tiny bite marks and remarked, "Only touch it without disturbing anything else, but, it's begging for the human touch, touching verifies its existence."

At this time, the technician looked up at them and remarked, "Don't worry, Detective, Dr. Morales knows how to feel around without messing anything up." He then slipped off his protective gloves and said, "Good luck with that. I'm going to a late lunch, Dr. Morales."

Elizabeth just shooed the technician away, and he went out the door. As soon as the door closed, both started laughing.

Elizabeth leaned back on the counter with her arms crossed around her chest, but Morris pulled her to him and they embraced and kissed.

Elizabeth pulled away a little, took a breath, and asked him, "Am I going to see you tonight?"

Morris nodded and answered, "I want to see you too, Liz." He then shook his head slowly and said, "I am so busy." Elizabeth turned away and again folded her arms in front of her chest and stared forward. Morris continued, "But I will go to your place as soon as I can. If it's not too late."

Elizabeth smiled and said, "Look, why don't I just go to your apartment and wait for you? I have the day off tomorrow, so if you're late, I'll be there waiting for you." She gave him a pleading look and added, "How can I get inside?"

Morris smiled and said, "I like your thinking. I may have to arrest you for exceeding the wonderful speed limit of amore. I have an extra key."

Elizabeth faced him, and tapping his chest, she stated, "Does that include handcuffs?" She batted her eyes.

Morris shook his head at first and then nodded and said, "Yes, with a full body search."

She leaned into his arms and they kissed until they heard the door handle rattle, they pulled apart, and as Dr. Bradley entered,

Elizabeth told Morris, "And these are the same bite marks that we found on Yolanda, remember?"

Morris nodded and uttered, "Uh-huh."

Dr. Bradley walked toward them and stated, "Oh, you're here, Lieutenant. Yes, it appears there is another one of those killings." He shook his head slowly and said, "Dr. Morales was scheduled to perform the autopsy this afternoon. I know you want any information on these killings, Lieutenant."

"Yes, Dr. Morales was just answering my questions."

"Good, good." He looked at Elizabeth and stated, "Now, Doctor, you do what the Lieutenant says and help him in any way necessary. You hear me, Morales? That maniac needs to be apprehended."

Elizabeth turned away from Bradley to face Morris and said, "I'll do whatever is necessary to please the lieutenant, Dr. Bradley." She reached out, patted his groin and smiled.

Morris flinched and looked at Elizabeth with a serious look. She covered her mouth and giggled.

"Fine, fine. You let us know when you find that culprit, won't you, Lieutenant?"

Nodding, he answered, "I certainly will, Dr. Bradley." He forced himself not to laugh.

Dr. Bradley turned, walked toward the door, and said over his shoulder, "Sorry we can't chat, Lieutenant. I've a very busy schedule. I'll leave you in the hands of Dr. Morales."

Morris smiled and said, "Oh, too bad. I guess Dr. Morales will have to do." Elizabeth hit Morris on the shoulder. Morris said, "Bye, Doctor."

"Yes, yes, goodnight." He went out the door.

"I'll have to do, huh?"

"I've no time right now, hon. I want to get done so I can enjoy your company." He smiled.

"Well, then, get on with your bad self, but first, give me the key to your apartment."

"Oh." Morris pulled her to him and kissed her hard, slipped the key, walked away, and said, "You, you tonight."

Elizabeth wiped her mouth, smiled, and said, "Don't forget the handcuffs."

With his back toward her as he walked away, he lifted the back of his jacket, wiggled his handcuffs, and went out the door.

CHAPTER 17

BETRAYED

ROBERTO WAS DRIVING BACK FROM Bakersfield. He was returning from seeking a site for another movie about a 1950s kidnapping. Bakersfield "Old Town" resembled a 1950 setting. Now he was worried that Claudia was not going to keep her promise about leaving him alone. He also wanted to call Jennifer to see if she was okay. His good sense told him to report Claudia to the authorities. What would he say? "My girlfriend is a vampire?" That sounded ridiculous to him. He then recalled that one of the dead bodies found was in a different part of town where he knew Claudia was at the time of the killing. He shook his head and wondered what the hell was going on. He figured he would drive home, shower, and then go to Jennifer's and try to make-up with her.

*   *   *

Claudia woke up, cleaned herself up, and went downstairs. In the hallway, she heard voices. She peeked around the entranceway to the study and saw Marta sitting on the love seat, facing someone sitting directly across from her. It was a man and then she recognized the voice. It was that snoopy detective.

"And you say when Claudia drove home and came inside and that everything seemed to be okay with Mrs. Brocolac? She wasn't distraught or anxious?"

Marta nodded her head quickly and responded, "Uh-huh. She seemed fine to me."

"What did you two do that evening?"

"We—"

Claudia cut in as she stepped into the room, "We made love, Officer Morris. We are lovers."

Morris looked at Claudia as she strolled into the room wearing faded mustard-colored slacks and a white flimsy blouse. Her hair was piled high in a beehive and her face was scrubbed clean. For a moment, she had the appearance of a seventeen-year-old.

She squinted and peered at the lieutenant and asked, "Why are you here this evening, Lieutenant?" Her demeanor transformed quickly to someone defending themselves.

Morris had his foot over his knee, and now he set his foot on the floor and stated, "Ah, you're awake. Now I can ask you directly, Mrs. Brocolac."

Claudia lifted her chin at Morris and asked, "What do you need to ask me, Lt. Morris?"

Morris stood up and spoke, "Last night, you were at the Bonaventure Restaurant." He looked at her and then at Marta.

Claudia said, "Briefly."

Morris gasped. "Very briefly."

Claudia looked at him and tilted her head, puzzled on how he knew about that. Marta looked at him and tilted her head also.

Morris continued, "You had a dispute with a, I'd say ex-boy-friend, and you left in a hurry."

Claudia sat down next to Marta and with her chin up, she asked, "You're very informed. Is that a crime to argue in a restaurant?"

"Uh-uh, but then you raced home. I assume you took the Pasadena Freeway."

"I did."

"Well, it was the exact time that a motorcycle officer was killed by the freeway."

"I'm sorry to hear that."

Marta had been sitting there looking at them back and forth like it was a tennis match.

"So, I was wondering if you saw anything out of the ordinary as you drove home."

Claudia shook her head and said, "Sorry, Lieutenant, I didn't see anything unusual. I came straight home and Marta was here waiting for me." Marta nodded big time.

Morris nodded slowly. He thought he'd take a shot to see her reaction. "There was a witness on the other side of the freeway and recalls seeing the motorcycle's red lights flashing behind a four-door black sedan. They were too far to identify the make. Don't you have a black Kia Optima?" He waited for her reaction.

"Yes, I do. And"—she hunched her shoulders a little and shook her head—"what are you insinuating, Lt. Morris?"

Marta looked from Claudia to Morris.

Morris put on an innocent expression and stated, "It's just such a coincidence?" Morris stepped over to the fireplace mantel, leaned on it, and said, "You were extremely angry that evening, you were on the 110 Freeway, a similar vehicle as yours was spotted at the crime scene, and your only witness who states everything was normal when you arrived home is your lover." He let that sink in.

Claudia made no reaction, she kept looking at the lieutenant with steely green eyes. Marta's eyes had widened and her eyes shifted from Morris to Claudia several times.

Morris then took a breath and said, "I wonder what that fellow at the restaurant has to say about his relationship with you." Morris looked at the portrait of Demetrius for a moment. Out of the corner of his eye, he noticed a slight frightened look flashed over her Claudia's face briefly. He made a mental note to find out who that character was. The restaurant will know.

"Well, I'll leave you two lovebirds alone and get on with my investigation. Good night, ladies."

Claudia and Marta eyed him as he left the room.

Marta hugged Claudia and then grabbed her hand and asked, "That was Roberto at the restaurant, huh?"

Claudia nodded.

"Does he know about you?"

Claudia nodded.

"Do you think he'll reveal what you are?"

Claudia squinted and thought a moment. She shook her head and then she nodded.

The plans of being Claudia's lover and partner and maybe becoming an immortal super being would be all ruined if they went after Claudia. She exclaimed, "Oh no, we have to do something about him."

Claudia emitted an eerie smile and nodded.

*   *   *

Roberto had just finished showering and was standing naked while combing his hair in the large mirror in his bathroom when he heard the doorbell ring. He put on a terrycloth white robe and went to the door.

He opened the door and to his surprise, Jennifer was standing there. She seemed to have been crying.

Their eyes met, and she broke down and ran into his arms. "Oh, Robert, these past months, I really have missed you. Oh, you brute, you have women fighting for you," she blurted.

He pushed her to arm's length and told her, "I see you received my message. I was getting ready to look for you. I—"

Jennifer pulled him to her and kissed him, they embraced and as one, and they twirled into the living room. Roberto managed to kick the door shut and they continued to cling to one another, their four feet shuffling toward the sofa. Roberto's robe flung open and Jennifer at once took hold of him, moaning. He picked her up and laid her down on the couch and then laid on top of her.

Jennifer groaned as she pulled him to her, and through gritted teeth she whispered, "Oh, just make love to me, you lovely animal."

Roberto was now naked, his robe on the floor. Jennifer's skirt was up to her thighs and her blouse half open, one breast stared at him. They made passionate sensual hot love.

Half an hour later, Morris was knocking at Roberto's door.

Sharing a cigarette and a bottle of a Chateau red wine, they both turned quickly to the door and then at each other. Roberto hunched his shoulders while his eyes widened and eyebrows lifted. He then jerked his head toward his bedroom and as she scrambled to get her things, Roberto put on his robe and smoothed his hair down and went to the door. "Just a moment, getting dressed." He looked to see Jennifer's naked body and arms full of clothing dashed into his bedroom.

He pulled down the sides of the robe and tied the belt and then he opened the door. Roberto squinted as he looked at this strange man at his door, holding up a leather case with a police badge on it.

"Good evening, Mr. Clemoso, I'm Lt. Morris from LAPD, Homicide Division."

Roberto's squinted deepened and his head went back in puzzlement. He managed to express, "Homicide."

Morris grinned and spoke, "I'd like to ask you some questions regarding your ex-girlfriend, a Miss Brocolac."

Roberto's face displayed some panic, and he slowly nodded.

Morris looked around and asked, "Mr. Clemoso, may I come in? We can be more candid inside."

Roberto broke a weak smile and said, "Oh, of course, Officer, ah, er."

"Morris."

Roberto smiled and repeated, "Yes, Officer Morris."

Roberto opened the door wider and stepped aside. Morris stepped in and gave the room a quick scan. He noted couch pillows on the floor and one white high heel shoe under the coffee table. On the table were two wine glasses nearly empty. A faint hint of perfume was in the air. He smiled at Roberto and said, "Shall we sit there at the dining room table?"

Roberto nodded slowly.

They sat facing one another, and then Morris reached into his breast pocket and produced a leather notepad and pen. He looked at Roberto and told him, "I guess you are wondering what this is about, eh, amigo?"

Roberto gasped, smiled, and his hands, which were flat on the table, now clutched each other as he stated, "Why, yes. A homicide detective at my door in the evening." He shook his head. "I'm somewhat stunned. Homicide? Is this about those weird murders happening in LA?"

Morris leaned in a little and asked, "You know something about them killings, Mr. Clemoso?" Morris's detective instincts watched and tried to find any signs showing knowledge of the murders.

Roberto shook his head slowly, but his lower lip protruded and gave a quiver before he spoke. "No, I know nothing about those slayings." He shook his head, frowned, and asked, "Why do you come here to ask me about those illicit crimes?"

Morris swayed his pen between his fingers and stated, "I didn't come here to ask you about those killings." Morris's forehead creased up, "You brought it up."

Roberto's expression displayed a little fear now. His complexion paled some more. His left eyebrow arched and he asked, "Then, why are you here, Detective?"

Morris clenched his lips, breathed in, and asked, "How long have you known Claudia Brocolac?" Morris studied Roberto's response.

Roberto's eyes quickly glanced past Morris. Jennifer had opened the bedroom door slightly. Morris glanced at the large black-and-white portrait of Marilyn Monroe on the wall. it reflected the door being ajar, Roberto then looked up and said, "Oh, I met her in Spain three months ago." Roberto nervously glanced again at the opened door. "I was there conducting business for a studio. She owned a horse ranch that had the horses for a movie." Roberto then smiled and said, "We hung out, and then I didn't see her until a few weeks ago, so not really long."

Morris jotted into his notes. "I assume you two were intimately involved?"

Roberto squinted and again looked past Morris and answered, "Why yes, we had a fling." He smiled. "You know, nothing serious. I was away and single, you know." He smiled and tilted his head side to side quickly.

Morris grinned and asked, "It must have been a pretty heavy affair for her to follow you here?"

Roberto then took in a breath. His brows furrowed and he claimed, "More so on her part."

Morris nodded and then asked, "What happened at the restaurant, Roberto?

Roberto again glanced past Morris, leaned in a little, and softly said, "I had called it off with her that day. I assumed she called my work number. I let them know where I will be for emergencies when they're shooting in the evenings." He took in a breath again and continued, "I guess she wasn't used to being the one who gets dumped."

Morris nodded and said, "Hell has no wrath as a women's scorn, amigo."

Roberto emitted a weak smile as he nodded and asked, "How do you know about that incident at the restaurant, Detective?

Morris then said, "Oh, I was there. Why don't you have your friend come out here? I can be discreet."

Roberto stared at Morris a second, and then he lifted his head and yelled out, "Jenny, it's all right. Come out here."

After a few seconds, the bedroom door opened and Jennifer walked over to the dining room table barefoot and holding her shoe. She sat next to Roberto.

Roberto then said, "Honey, this is Lt. Morris. He's curious about Miss Brocolac. Lieutenant, this is Jennifer."

"Please to meet you, Jennifer."

"Hi." Jennifer's eyes widened and her expression hardened as she said, "Are you gonna arrest that horrid woman?"

Morris slightly smiled as he stated, "No, not yet. Do you know anything about her?"

Jennifer's face creased up, her body leaned back as her head shook side to side. "Why, no. That was the first time I ever laid eyes on that callous woman. Oh, she has no class, no class at all. Oh, that scene, how embarrassing!" she exclaimed.

Morris then turned to Roberto and said, "Listen, Miss Brocolac appears to me to be able to administer extreme revenge. Are you aware of that?"

Roberto thought a moment, Jennifer looked at him with brows creased. Roberto nodded a little and said, "I believe you're right, Lieutenant."

Morris took in a breath, leaned closer to Roberto, and sternly asked, "What do you know about Claudia that you're not telling?"

Jennifer touched his arm and tilted her head some.

Roberto closed his eyes as he breathed in and then let out his breath slowly and said, "She's a vampire."

Jennifer leaned back and her hand went to her mouth.

Morris squinted, he leaned back in his chair. "What? A vampire?"

Roberto nodded.

"Do you mean she thinks she's a vampire?" Morris asked.

Roberto shook his head quickly and stated, "She is the undead. She drinks blood. She is a vampire."

Morris shook his head slowly and asked, "Have you ever saw her drinking blood or bite anyone?"

Roberto shook his head no and said, "You know she lives by night." Morris nodded. "She can't be in the sun and she uses the excuse that she has some sun allergy." Again, Morris nodded. "She told me one night and swore me to silence. She believed I was going to be her next"—Roberto stopped and thought—"Demetrius."

Morris's brows furrowed and stated, "Is the portrait in the library him?"

Roberto nodded and said, "She has several portraits. She had copies made."

Morris nodded and stated, "That's why she was so angry with you."

Roberto nodded.

Jennifer shook her head and put both of her hands on Roberto's arm and asked, "Will she come after you?"

Roberto hunched his shoulders and then looked at Jennifer and then at the lieutenant and stated, "Now, she will. Lieutenant, you need to arrest her. I fear for Jennifer."

Jennifer jerked back, her hand went to cover her mouth as she said, "Me? She doesn't even know me. Why me?"

Morris cut in, "Roberto may be right. If she believes she is a vampire, she will think Roberto will eventually tell you. She dislikes you anyway for taking her man away."

Jennifer became defensive. "I didn't." She looked at Roberto. "He came after me. We had broken up months ago. I—"

Morris interjected, "She believes you took her man. She may seek revenge. Whatever she is, she may be this diabolical serial killer who's been on the rampage here in Los Angeles."

Roberto blurted out, "Lieutenant, she's a vampire, believe me."

Morris grinned and stated, "Roberto, I'm a twentieth-century detective and I believe in hard facts. I don't believe in ghost, were-wolves, and vampires. There may be people who believe they are some legendary creature, but they don't really exist. There have been serial killers who've eaten people and there's been the ones who have skinned their victims and made lampshades with their skin. These insane killers say the voice of God instructs them to do these atrocities. There is a whole lot of maniacs out there, Roberto, Jennifer. We'll try to get them, but only after they have acted on their insanity."

Roberto took Jennifer's hands and patted them. "I hope you're right, Lieutenant. I hope you're right," He said.

Morris got up and said, "You know, Roberto, it would be wise to stay somewhere else for a while." Morris tilted his head toward Jennifer.

Jennifer looked at Roberto with pleading eyes as Roberto nodded and said, "Yeah, sure. Good idea."

Morris shook hands with both of them, gave them his card, and said goodnight.

After the door shut, Jennifer went into Roberto's arms and said, "You must come and stay with me." She placed her head on his chest and said, "I'll feel safer with you there."

Roberto squeezed her and nodded yes. "Let me pack up a few things. I'll follow you, Jenny. We'll be safe. She doesn't know who you are really, and she don't know where you live," he said.

Jennifer looked up at him with a weak smile and nodded.

Half-hour later, Jennifer drove away with Roberto following her.

A little behind them, Marta followed in her Camry, trying not to be too conspicuous.

CHAPTER 18

CLAUDIA WENT OUT THAT EVENING after sending Marta to go spy on Roberto. She told her to find out where he goes. When they met later that night, she would turn Marta. But only if she really wanted to. Claudia told her that the lovemaking as a vampire is extremely more erotic and sensual than regular humans experienced. This excited Marta, and as she sat in her car checking out Roberto's apartment, she became aroused just thinking of Claudia and her beautiful body all over her. Marta closed her eyes and fantasized. Now her fantasy was interrupted when Jennifer's auto pulled to the curb and got out and went in the building. She noticed Roberto's living room light go on. Marta sat there and waited. Sometime later, she saw Lieutenant Morris pulled up and went in.

"What the fuck is happening?" She cursed to herself.

After some time, the lieutenant left, and thirty-minutes later, Jennifer came out and got in her car and waited there. Marta frowned, wondering what the hell was going on. Then Roberto pulled out from the underground parking, Jennifer pulled away and Roberto followed Jennifer. Marta followed Roberto.

*　　*　　*

While driving down Foothill Boulevard, Claudia scanned the streets, seeking someone walking alone. She realized that she needed to have some extra plasma in her tonight if she was going to let Marta feed on her.

As she passed Sierra Madre Avenue heading east on Foothill, she spotted a woman standing outside a motel, smoking. The woman was a Black female, a little heavy, and wearing a tight skirt that was a little too tight and a white sleeveless blouse. The woman had large breasts, wore heavy makeup, and had a large Afro hairdo.

Claudia pulled over. The woman came to the car, and Claudia said, "Hello there. Are you busy?"

The woman swayed over to the car, flipped the cigarette into the street, and put her arms on the window sill. She smiled and said, "Hey, baby. You's a hot looking little momma. Your husband out of town and you want some good hot pussy?" She smiled and revealed a gold-lined front tooth.

Claudia smiled and said, "You must be psychic. You read my mind."

The streetwalker looked at the automobile, the way Claudia was dressed, the sophisticated way she talked and held herself and said, "Well momma, I'm gonna make you feel so good, you is going to wanna kill your lover and move in with me, he-he."

Claudia nodded and said, "Hmm, sounds good. Listen, I'd like to take you to my home so you can take a shower and get everything squeaky clean for me. I have liquor there and we can play all night."

"Woo me! Did I hit a jackpot tonight? Hey, lady, this is going to cost you, you know?"

Claudia smiled and said, "Get in. If you are as good as you say you are, I'll give you five hundred dollars. My husband is much older than me and can't get it on anymore. Being with a woman doesn't count as cheating, yes, I'm not being fucked by a man. I'm not cheating on him."

The hooker stated, "Call me Roxanne. Always loved that name."

Claudia smiled and said, "I'm Samantha, call me Sam."

Roxanne got in and they drove away, the FM blasting rock-n-roll music. They have arrived and Claudia parked the vehicle in the garage.

Walking through the house and up the stairs, Roxanne was impressed with the home. Walking into the bedroom, Roxanne asked, "That your husband in that army uniform?"

Claudia nodded and answered, "Yes, he was an officer in the French Army. Look, there's the bathroom. Clean up and I'll be waiting for you."

"Yes, ma'am, you da boss. I'll be quick, honey. I'm all hot already. You a fine-looking lady." Roxanne began disrobing as she walked into the bathroom.

Claudia then lit candles and turned off the lights. She put the CD player on shuffle and lowered the music and then got undressed and laid on top of the bed. Claudia wanted to have fun with this woman before she fed on her. She heard the shower turn off and then the bathroom door opened. The bathroom light was on and cascaded around her. Roxanne was slightly heavy but well proportioned. Water droplets covered her light chocolate torso. Without the makeup, Roxanne had a pretty face. Her full heavy breast bore large dark nipples.

These two ladies' physical bodies were completely opposite of one another.

Roxanne stated as she walked toward the bed, "Um, um, we both gonna be in heaven in just a minute, honey. Just stay there and let big momma find your sweet spot. Here I come, baby."

Roxanne crawled on the bed. Claudia opened her legs and Roxanne crawled between them until their lips met. They embraced and rolled on the huge bed touching, fondling, and kissing one another in all exotic places.

After forty minutes of exotic lesbian lovemaking, Claudia took charge. She lay on top of Roxanne and tied her hands and feet to the bed post. Stationed there, Roxanne wiggled and twisted as Claudia kissed, licked, and massaged her. Finally, while Claudia grinded on Roxanne and Roxanne moaned with pleasure, Claudia bit into her neck and began syphoning her blood. At first, Roxanne bucked and yelled, but Claudia hung on like a rodeo cowboy on a wild bull. Soon, the resisting subsided, and Roxanne started moaning with pleasure as Claudia also groaned from the sensations emitted by the blood filling her needing body. As they both reached an orgasmic point, Roxanne quietly took her last breath as Claudia's body shivered and trembled as her orgasm reached its height, and then she collapsed atop Roxanne.

Perspiring and out of breath, Claudia rolled over and whispered, "You did it Roxanne. You made me feel so good, and now I want to kill Roberto"—she thought a second—"and that slut he was with."

Claudia then carried Roxanne's dead body and put her in the trunk of her car and drove off to dump her somewhere. She drove back to the Foothill area and up the streets, looking for an alley. It was late and hardly any traffic in the area. She found a dark alley and drove in, and to her luck, there was a large trash bin behind an apartment building. She turned off her lights, parked, and quickly dumped the body in the bin. She quickly left, turning on her lights after she cleared the alley. She drove home and smiled as she saw Marta's Camry parked in the cul-de-sac.

Claudia entered her home, and it was all was quiet except for music coming from upstairs. She went up the stairs and into the bedroom. The setting was set as earlier. Lights out, candles burning, but Marta was on the bed naked. She had a wine glass in her hand and smiling.

Marta then said, "Are you sure we can't drink wine as vampires?"

Claudia walked to the bed, tossing her clothes. She got on the bed and kissed Marta and then pushed her away and said, "It gets you sick. But drink blood from someone who is drunk and you get high. What did you find out?"

Marta reached over to Claudia's breast.

"Stop it. Later. We have forever for that. Tell me what you saw," Claudia told her.

Marta made a face and clenched her mouth and then said, "Oh, all right. I got there and parked. It was boring for a while and then this car pulled up and this gorgeous woman got out. I noticed Roberto's living room light went on, so I figured that woman went to see Roberto."

"That must be the woman from the restaurant!" exclaimed Claudia.

"Yeah, well, a little while later, Lt. Morris showed up and went into the building."

"Lieutenant Morris. Damn. He went there to question Roberto about me."

Marta continued, "Yeah, he said he would, remember? Well then, some time passed by, and then Morris came out and left. Then, thirty minutes later, that girl came out and waited in her car. Then, Roberto drove out of the building and she drove off, too, and Roberto followed her."

Claudia frowned and said, "Damn! They're trying to escape."

Marta grabbed Claudia's chin and turned her head to face her and said, "I followed them. I know where the bitch lives."

Claudia's face brightened. She leaned over, and they embraced and kissed, but then Claudia pushed Marta away and said, "Have you thought about it thoroughly?"

Marta nodded slowly but then asked, "What about Lt. Morris?"

"He can't prove anything. He'd be here already if he thought he could arrest me legally. Anyway, after I—" she looked at Marta and touched her thigh. Marta shivered. "After we take care of that imbecilic couple, we'll fly to Mexico or anywhere you want, Marta. You are my partner, and we'll take care of each other until the moon falls from the sky."

Marta nodded and took in a breath.

Claudia then asked, "Shall I give you eternity, my dear?"

Marta took in a breath, swallowed. She looked into Claudia's eyes and nodded yes and said, "Take me to your world, my lover."

Claudia rolled atop of Marta's warm body. Marta moaned as their arms encircled each other. They kissed passionately and touched one another all over. Both women were excited, and Claudia's kisses were hot, wet, and vibrating. Marta moaned and pushed her body against Claudia's. Claudia then kissed Marta's cheeks, her eyes and then she put her wet tongue in Marta's ear. Marta was writhing with excitement as Claudia's hands fondled and penetrated Marta's body parts. She shuddered with pleasure. Claudia's mouth now went to Marta's neck where she licked and kissed it until she found the pulse. The she quickly bit into her vein. Marta winced and an ow emitted from clenched teeth. Claudia began sucking and drinking Marta's blood. Marta allowed the flow to go uninterrupted. Suddenly, Marta felt an orgasm coming. She moaned and bucked with pleasure and then Claudia stopped.

Marta's eyes opened widely, and she asked, "What? Hey—"

Claudia put her finger to her mouth and said, "Shh." Claudia opened a drawer and took out a knife and made an incision on her wrist. She put her bleeding wound to Marta's mouth.

Marta's eyes opened wider and the she began sucking on the wound and the blood flowed into her. Soon, Marta had both hands on Claudia's wrist and she sucked on it like it was a baby sucking on a bottle.

Claudia felt the draining of her spirit but she was okay. She had taken all of Roxanne's blood and would not be too weak after the transition. When Claudia felt Marta had enough, she pulled her arm away and licked her arm clean. Marta sat there, licking her mouth and hands clean of any blood.

Marta then looked at Claudia and whispered, "What happens now?"

Claudia smiled and said "We rest, we sleep, and when you wake up, you'll be a new woman. Turn on your side my dear."

Marta was a little frightened but turned over and then Claudia got behind her, and they spooned and snuggled. With her arms wrapped around Marta to ensure her of warmth and companionship, they fell asleep. Marta was never to have human dreams again.

CHAPTER 19

T HE PARKING LOT WAS NEARLY filled with autos on this breezy night and the wind blew in wild dusty spurts. Small whirlwinds danced around the lot, causing debris and dirt to swirl rapidly in small circles and then die out. The dark sky was clear, leaving the stars and the half-moon to boast their existence. They seem to be battling for authority of the night heavens.

Outside of the Beverly Bowl in East LA, Victor and Olivia were having a serious discussion on obtaining their feed tonight.

"Victor, we can't go on like this." Olivia turned from facing him, she folded her arms in front of her chest and closed her eyes as she shook her head.

Victor just stared ahead and tried to keep from getting angry.

After a moment, she then turned her head and exclaimed, "You are going to get us killed, Victor. When they catch us, they'll probably hogtie us and then throw us into the sun and watch us burn. You have to stop killing everyone you bite."

He clenched his lips together and nodded.

Olivia leaned on the door and closed her eyes thinking but opened them when Victor threw up his hands and shook his head and stated, "Babe, I can't help it. Once their blood gets into my system,"—Victor shook his head again and then ran his hand through his hair—"it ignites something in me that I can't turn off." He stepped over to face Olivia and stated, "I can't turn it off. Believe me, honey, it's not my fault."

Olivia heaved in and let out her breath wearily. She then put both her hands on Victor's shoulders and shook him a little and said,

"Oh, Victor, you're such a baby. I don't know what to do." She looked down, shook her head and said, "Come on, let's see what's good inside." She pulled open the door and Victor, with a weak smile, followed her in.

The bowling alley was crowded. It was a tournament night. Teams of four in matching bowling shirts were everywhere, male and female. All the lanes were being used and there were patrons sitting anxiously in the booths on the wide aisles above the lanes, waiting. Victor went over to a large video game where a teen was excitedly pressing buttons and yelling profanities. Lights were blinking and chimes were ringing on the machine. Olivia took a walk and peeked into the café. It was nearly full but there were stools at the counter open and an unattended booth at the end. She then walked on and went into the bar. A few couples sat in red leather booths, and a few customers were on bar stools at the bar. The bar stool sitters seem to be interested on a basketball game on the TV monitors above the elongated mirror. She walked over to an empty stool and sat.

An attractive female bartender stepped in front of her and stated, "Hey, sugar, place is happy tonight. Dodgers won and the Lakers are winning. What'll you have?"

Olivia smiled and said, "I'll have a whiskey, sour, extra cherries." She smiled at the bartender.

The bartender gave Olivia a once over and stipulated, "Sure thing, sugar," she then pointed to a name tag on her chest and said, "The name's Shirley, if you want *anything* else." She had emphasized *anything*, as her eyebrows raised high.

Shirley walked away real cool and mixed the drink. After she was done, she walked back with a swagger, she threw a napkin. It floated and landed right in front of Olivia. Shirley then placed the drink on the napkin and said, "First one is on me, sugar."

Olivia's smile revealed white perfect teeth, her eyes sparkled, and she stated, "The name's, Olivia. I think this is going to be an interesting night, Shirley."

As Shirley stood there chewing her gum, a man's voice from a booth rang out, "Shirley, set us up, the same, honey."

Shirley clenched her mouth, smiled, and said, "I'll be back." She turned and began pouring and mixing drinks. She walked with a tray with two mixed drinks and two beers with upside-down glasses over them to a booth where two men were seated. She stood there talking with the gents. Olivia noticed that Shirley had a well-proportioned body. Olivia got up, took the drink, went into the bathroom, and dumped it in the sink.

She came back to the bar, and Shirley got in front of her and said, "Glad you're back. Want the same?"

Olivia placed her hand over the glass and said, "Tonight, I want to be in full senses. I want to feel everything."

Shirley's eyes widened, and her face brightened, and she asked, "Where'd you go, Olivia?"

Olivia leaned a little closer and Shirley leaned closer as Olivia told her, "I had to check on my boyfriend," Shirley's face frowned. Olivia smiled and continued, "It's okay, he'll just watch or join us if you want."

Shirley brightened up again, chuckled, and then said, "Mm, mm, tonight is a very happy night. Go, Lakers."

Olivia nodded to her and asked, "What time you get off?"

Shirley looked at her watch and said, "In half an hour, if that bozo shows up in time. But the boss can't see me walk away with you. You know, business."

"Yeah, okay. Look, Vic and I will be waiting in the car and when you come out, we'll follow you to your place. What kind of car you in?"

"Uh, I don't have a ride tonight."

"Okay, okay, that's fine. That's really fine. We'll ride together. See you outside."

Shirley walked away, and Olivia went to look for Victor. He was at the video game, pressing buttons and screaming. Olivia tapped him on the shoulder and nodded her head to follow her. Victor reluctantly left the game and went with Olivia to their car where she explained the situation.

*　　*　　*

An hour later, the three lovers were naked, wrestling, rolling, and kissing in a big round waterbed. The swishing and moving of the water and the bodies made stimulation higher for all three. Olivia knew that they were going to leave another dead body, but she thought they would not find the cadaver for days and she and Victor would soon be out of LA. After Olivia and Victor had their way and their fill with Shirley, they sucked her dry, then made love with each other again, next to the corpse.

* * *

Michael, Carolyn, Marta, Freddie, Dave, and Sally were all called in to meet with Lt. Morris in the early afternoon. They all showed up except for Marta. The group were ushered into a waiting room where they gradually broke the ice with one another as they waited for the lieutenant to arrive. Morris wanted to get testimonies from these witnesses in order to see if he could get a court order or warrant to enter Claudia's residence.

Lieutenant Morris had gotten a call from Elizabeth informing him of another body being found.

Earlier that morning, Shirley's ex-husband, Richard, came by her house to have her sign the final documents to their divorce. After knocking several times and calling her, Richard went around back and entered the house and discovered Shirley's nude sprawled body on her bed.

On his way to the morgue where Elizabeth waited, Morris received a call from Dr. Williams that a blood-depleted body was found in a dumpster in the Arcadia area.

As he drove, he exclaimed, "God damn it!" and hit the console with his hand.

Morris entered the morgue chamber where Elizabeth was examining Shirley's corpse.

"Hi, honey, thanks for calling."

Elizabeth lifted her plastic shield from her face and pulled down her mask and went over to Morris and kissed him and said, "Looks like the only way I get to see you is for dead bodies to show up."

They both grinned, and then Morris asked her, "What's up with this one?"

Elizabeth adjusted her protective gear and went to the body and then said as she pointed to various parts of the body, "The victim has several bites and puncture bites and marks. Here, here, here, and there. This body had sexual intercourse before death and after death. There is no plasmatic substance in her heart, her veins, liver, or other organs either. She was sucked dry," She looked at Morris for effect, he had winced and his brows were furrowed.

Elizabeth continued, "The bite punctures are of two different sets of teeth. The individuals were probably a male and a female. Her left arm is broken due to forcing her into an unnatural position. The bruises are of two colors and two types." Morris's brows creased tighter as she continued, "Some developed before death and some after."

Elizabeth then walked over to a counter where a microscope stood and stated, "I scraped her fingernails where I found bits of skin and after examining it I discovered the skin is from a deceased being."

Morris nodded and then asked, "Can you tell if it is male or female?"

Elizabeth's face showed triumph as she partially grinned and told Morris, "Yes, both. She was involved, I guess, in a *ménage a trois*, a male and a female partner, both partners were dead beings."

Morris shook his head and then rubbed the back of his head and stated, "Damn, I have a female suspect but this male thing throws a wrench into the mechanism here." He shook his head some more and said, "It's not her ex, Roberto. Hmm, there's someone else around, maybe he's hiding in the house." Morris rubbed his chin and then said, "Demetrius?" he shook his head quickly and said, "She claims he's dead. I'll have to check up on that with the French police or even Interpol."

Elizabeth grabbed his shoulder and said, "No one is going to believe you about vampires running around LA. Bela Lugosi has been long gone. These dead bodies convinced me that there are or something very close to the undead running around the town, killing people by sucking their blood. I want them found, baby. You and I will stake out your suspect tonight and get the proof we need." She leaned against the table and folded her arms across her chest and kept a stern expression.

Morris's face lit up as he thought a moment. Then he nodded and said, "All right, Elizabeth. You want some drama in your life and play detective? Okay, you and I will play, er, what's his name, that vampire killer?"

Elizabeth smiled and stated, "Van Helsing."

Morris smiled. He grabbed Elizabeth in his arms and they twirled once. "Yes, we'll be the Van Helsings tonight."

Elizabeth pushed him away and said, "Bring some wooden stakes and I'll bring a crucifix."

They both giggled some, and then Morris's cell phone rang. He took on a serious face and answered, "Morris here."

"Hey, you got this bunch here waiting on you. You coming in?" Oberron huffed into the phone.

Morris clenched his mouth and then spoke, "Look, Oberron, I have two more dead bodies this morning,. Have them write in detail everything that happened and what they saw and what they felt when they were in the company of Claudia Brocolac. Tell Sally to write down what happened to her in detail. No one will read it but myself and a judge."

"Okay, Morris, will do. See you when you get in."

Morris put his phone away and told Elizabeth, "Meet me at my place at six, okay?"

Elizabeth nodded and said, "I'm bringing my toothbrush."

Morris smiled and remarked, "Yes, and don't forget the crucifix," and hurried out the door.

*　*　*

At the LA morgue, Dr. Williams informed Morris of what they had discovered thus far. "The body was a rather healthy woman, at least a hundred and fifty pounds. Someone really strong put her in that trash bin. In running her ID, it reveals she had been arrested for shoplifting and prostitution. Her real name was Abigale Kingston.

She was depleted of most of her blood. Time of death, approximately seven thirty or so last night."

Morris squinted and asked, "How'd they find the body so fast?"

"It seems the dump truck was overly loaded, and the driver went on top to see if there was any obstruction and he then noticed the body."

Morris nodded and stated, "Lucky for us."

Dr. Williams stated, "The full autopsy will begin shortly, we'll have more info later today, hopefully."

Morris gave a weak smile, nodded, and said, "Thanks, Doc. Talk later."

Morris drove to the station to collect the affidavits from his witnesses.

*　　*　　*

Olivia was up, it was around five in the afternoon and still daylight outside. The blinds and curtains were drawn, and she was watching Eyewitness News. She sat up when the broadcaster stated that two similar dead bodies were found this morning and that the morticians claimed that the bodies had been depleted of their blood. One body found in a dumpster in Arcadia and the other in Montebello in a one-bedroom house.

The newscaster went on to give their names and other details, but Olivia turned it off and went to wake up Victor.

"Victor, Victor, wake up. Come on, wake up."

Victor rolled over on his back and then sat up and expressed, "Wha…what the fuck? What's going on? Is there a fire or what?" He rubbed his eyes and yawned.

Olivia stood there with her hands on her hips and said, "There's another vampire in Los Angeles, Victor."

Victor put his legs over the side of the bed, still rubbing his eyes and remarked, "What? What did you say?"

"There's another vampire here in LA."

Victor's brows furrowed. "What makes you think that?"

One hand on hip and the other waved as she talked, "I've been keeping tabs on the news on the bodies being found. And there's three that are not ours. Bodies that have been sucked dry of their blood. There's another vampire, Victor. We need to find him. He's really fucking it up for us."

Victor stretched and then said, "Hey, yeah you're right." He took a breath and then continued, "I've always known there were others in Europe. Didn't know they came to America though. Yeah, I'd like to find him."

Olivia's brows creased a little as she asked Victor, "So what happened to the one who turned you?"

Victor took on a solemn expression and stated, "I killed him. Got up early and cut off his head while he slept."

Olivia's hand went to cover her mouth and she expressed, "Why, what happened between you two?"

"My second day as an undead person, I was still so pissed he turned me, so I killed the bastard. That was in Europe, so I came here. There's an imprecation amongst the undead. We are not to slay one another. If they found out I did that, they would come after me and tie me up and let the sun do its work on me."

"Oh God, no."

"So, we need to find this vampire. Maybe he was sent to get me."

Olivia's eyes widened and a scared look covered her face.

"Where'd they find the body?"

Olivia took a breath and said, "Arcadia."

"Get dressed. We'll know as soon as one is near. We'll smell him. No cologne or perfume can hide the scent of a vampire from another vampire."

Olivia's face showed fear and excitement. Her eyes opened wide, her mouth slightly opened as her nose flared. She was ready for the hunt, they would find a friend or a foe.

*　*　*

Claudia was up and sitting on a chair staring at Marta as she slept. Claudia was content because now, she had a partner and a lover. Together they will excel in this modern world. There was so much to teach her new protégée. Marta resembled a sweet angel as she lay there sprawled above the blankets. Her long black hair cascaded across her face. She had a well-proportioned body, slim but with nice curves, tall for an Asian, and large almond-shaped green eyes. Marta had never mentioned it, but her mother must be Caucasian. Claudia recalled the day she woke up to the new world of vampirism…

*   *   *

The large canopied bed had silk sheets and Egyptian cotton blankets and were entangled around Claudia's legs. She suddenly woke up and sat up in bed. All the windows had heavy drapes blocking the outside sun. She looked around the bed chamber and candelabras emitted a pale-yellow glow in the room. Demetrius was sitting in a large stuffed chair staring at her. His nearly blindness made it hard to see her. She was now a vampire and the emptiness in her stomach bothered her. Her hands massaged her stomach.

Demetrius spoke from the chair, "That urgent hollowness will soon be remedied, my dear."

"What is this fogginess I feel Demetrius and why do I not hate you?"

"The fogginess will now be part of your existence, Claudia. Your emotions toward me is due to your emancipation from your old dull life to being baptized into the ecstasies of a new existence and the ecstasy of lovemaking. What you experienced last night was only scratching the surface of ecstasy, my love. Together, we will master this obnoxious world. Now, you will quench the elixir that gets you well, so you can let yourself go free and wild on my body. My darling Claudia, welcome to the dark world of darkness, blood, and pleasure."

*   *   *

Marta's voice brought her back, "What is this uneasiness inside me, Claudia?" Marta was sitting up, hair in disarray. her breasts jiggled and she slapped the bed.

Claudia smiled and stated, "You are a vampire, my dear. Get used to that feeling. It gets fulfilled when you drink blood."

Marta's forehead furrowed, and she asked, "And then what happens?"

Claudia smiled and said, "And then you will find that there is new heights of pleasure and desire when our bodies enfold themselves as one."

Marta nodded and clapped her hands and said, "Yes, yes, let's do it."

Nodding, Claudia held up her hand and said, "Patience, my love, patience. There is much I need to tell you, much you have to learn."

Marta frowned and then stated, "Okay, all right. I'm ready."

The first thing my dear is patience," Marta nodded. "I bet you always thought intercourse or lovemaking was when a man enters a woman." Marta nodded slowly., "Well, you have experienced that lovemaking can be accomplished without a man." Marta nodded quickly. "You see, it's the meeting of the bodies that ignite the hormones in us. The groping, the massaging, the kissing, and sucking that makes a woman excited."

Marta stated, "Yes, lots of kissing. You do it so well, Claudia. Your tongue explores my insides, once your tongue is in my mouth and then you know where else," Marta grinned and Claudia smiled.

"You will learn, and we will be each other's sounding board, and there is no limit. We are vampires, my dear. Our only pleasure is lovemaking, our only goal is orgasm. Get dressed. You'll learn every time we go out." Claudia got up and then turned and said, "Oh, there is another thing you must know." Marta stopped in the middle of putting on her panties and looked at Claudia, "There are other vampires in this city. We must find them and teach them how to hunt the right way. If they do not want to abide with us, well, we'll have to"—she took a breath—"get rid of them."

Marta's eyes bulged and then she blurted out, "How will we know who a vampire is?"

Claudia took in a big breath and let it out. She nodded as she answered, "I'll know, my dear, I'll know." She pointed to her nose.

CHAPTER 20

ELIZABETH WAS SITTING IN MORRIS'S office waiting for him to return from the carpool department. She scanned the walls and was impressed by the billboards and various reports pinned to the corkboards. As she was reading a magazine exclusively on weapons, the door opened and Morris came in.

"Hi, babe, been waiting long?" He held a cloth handbag in one hand. Elizabeth stood up and they kissed, and she said, "Hello there. big boy. What's in the bag?"

Morris stuck out his hand, and when he pulled it out, he said, "Ta-ta-ta-tan!" He held large wooden stakes sharpened to a point.

Elizabeth then pulled from her purse as she stated, "Ta-ta-ta-tan!" She showed two crucifixes.

Morris smiled and said, "I like your hunting outfit."

Elizabeth put up her arms and turned around. The ponytail gave her a young girl's appearance while her tight=fitting Levi's snugly hugged her body, her white V-neck T-shirt was a snug fit also. Her jeans met her ankles and had a nice cuff to them while her white Nike tennis finished her tomboy look.

Morris shook his head and then smacked her on the butt. She jumped and he said, "Let's go slay some vampires."

Elizabeth grinned and rubbed her butt and followed Morris out the door.

*   *   *

Victor and Olivia were in San Gabriel Valley, cruising Colorado Boulevard from the small city of Duarte into Pasadena, trying to see if they would run into the vampire who was killing in that area.

Victor looked over at Olivia and told her, "This vamp probably goes to some place that people gather and drink." He looked forward and then back at Olivia and continued, "Like we do."

Olivia nodded and added, "Yeah, a place that has a parking lot and dark spots." She glanced at Victor for approval.

Victor grinned and said, "You're learning, girl."

Olivia then looked on her side of the street and stated, "A bar, a nightclub, a bowling alley. What about a supermarket?"

Victor frowned, and Olivia went on, "You know, they have big parking lots that extend around the sides. He could have a van and just abduct them." Her eyes were wide and she nodded quickly.

Victor tilted his head side to side, contemplating. He nodded and said, "Hmm, maybe. But that's a good idea, maybe we should get a van."

Olivia sat back kind of smug and said, "I can think, Victor. You need me."

Victor grinned and just kept driving west and then turned up Fair Oaks Avenue to Walnut and went east, Walnut eventually turned into Foothill Boulevard.

*   *   *

Claudia and Marta were in Marta's Camry driving east on Foothill. As Marta drove, Claudia schooled Marta on vampire procedure.

Marta listened very intently but was very inquisitive. Claudia was patient and answered the how-comes, the whys, and ifs questions as truthfully as she could.

Marta looked over and said, "What if I drink blood that has some type of disease, Claudia?"

Claudia shook her head slowly and told her, "As soon as you taste someone's blood, you'll know by the taste and odor that it's tainted."

"What do I tell that person for biting his neck?"

"Just knock that person unconscious and get on your way."

Marta smiled and said, "So, you said if someone is intoxicated or on drugs, that I will feel the effects of that high."

"Nodding Claudia said, "Yes, my dear."

Marta then happily stated, "Oh good. I'd like to bite into a heroin user. Just to see what's it like." She glanced over at Claudia to see her reaction.

"I've done it. It just feels warm and slows you down. It's okay, I guess." She then turned to view the passing scenery of store fronts and people walking the streets and said, "There's nothing like the sensation of pure clean blood. I'm starving, my dear."

Nodding, Marta stated, "I think I am too. My stomach is churning and that fogginess is with me."

Claudia pointed and said, "Pull into that parking lot where that bowling alley is and go around to the back."

Marta's eyes widened and her anxiety heightened. She went in the driveway and followed the paved tar path to the rear on the bowling alley. There was a smaller lot and SUVs, small and large trucks were parked next to each other, and there was a couple of vans. Marta read the marquee, "Bowlmor."

Claudia blurted out, "We need to get a van."

Marta nodded and parked between two large four-door Ford trucks, she switched off the engine and they talked about specific kinds of people to feed on.

Claudia put down her window and told Marta, "Always select someone who seems alone. Try not to pick policemen unless you're forced to."

Marta was feeling her new extended eye teeth and then looked at Claudia and asked, "How do I know when to stop?" Her eyes widened and her expression showed concern. "I really don't want to be killing people."

Claudia breathed in and shook her head and then stated, "There's a thin line there between life and death. That point is right about the point of your victim and yourself start to experience an orgasm. You must pull away and usually, your victim will pass out.

If they do not go unconscious, well then, you must physically knock them out. This way, you can straighten yourself up and get rid of any evidence you have been there."

Marta's mouth was slightly open as she stared out the front window. Claudia patted her arm and said, "Don't be alarmed, my dear. I will be with you, guiding you. I may have to yank you away the first few times. You'll learn," They both smiled.

And then Victor and Olivia's vehicle passed in front of them and slowed down as they spotted the Camry. It was hiding between trucks. Claudia and Marta watched the vehicle crawl by. Victor noticed that there were two women in the parked vehicle.

Olivia asked, "What do you think?"

Victor heaved and remarked, "Looks like a couple of lesbians wanting privacy."

Olivia nodded and then said, "Park it, Vic. I'm hungry, I'll go in and lure someone out here."

Victor breathed in and told her, "Try and bring out two people so we don't have to do this again tonight." He looked at her and said, "If we drink just enough not to kill them, we'll both need a body."

Olivia gave a sideward smile and then nodded and asked, "How do I look tonight? Would you like to jump my bones if you didn't know me?"

"You're hot. I picked you to be my mate because you turn me on, baby."

Olivia smiled and said, "I'm gonna do you extra special tonight, you big hunk of sex."

They leaned into one another and kissed, but Olivia pulled away and said, "Hey, you're gonna mess up my makeup, sugar. Wait for later. She looked in the sun visor mirror really quick and adjusted her hair and checked her buttoned blouse. She unbuttoned the top button, showing more cleavage of her nice breasts."

Victor then exclaimed, "Okay, hurry it then."

Olivia got out of the car and she smoothed down her short skirt and fluffed her hair. Victor watched her walk toward the rear entrance as she exaggerated her sway. He smiled.

Claudia and Marta watched Olivia walk into the bowling alley. Marta commented, "Mm, she's hot." Claudia gave her a sideward glance and Marta stated, "You know, I was never attracted to women until you made love to me. Man, women have it all."

Claudia opened her door and then turned and looked at Marta and said, "A good hard man can thrill you too, my dear. Have you forgotten what it's like to have that manhood inside you? Come on, let's get dinner."

Marta thought a moment and responded, "Yeah, you're right, but there's nothing more beautiful than a woman's body."

Claudia smiled and just jerked her head to say let's go. Marta got out and they walked to the entrance of the Bowlmor. Once inside, they noticed that there was a party going on for teenagers at one end of the alleys. A gang of teenagers were talking, laughing, and making fun of one another as they took up four lanes.

Claudia nudged Marta and told her, "Okay, let's see how you do. Go into the bar and see what's going on. See if you can tempt someone. I think because this is your first time, we'll have to share one person."

"Marta nodded and remarked, "If it's a man, I'll hit we're two lesbians wanting to share a man"—she breathed—"if it's a female, uh, same thing."

She took a step and Claudia told her, "Marta, you look beautiful."

Marta grinned and responded, "So do you, momma."

Marta wore tight black Levi's accenting her long legs and bubble butt. Her bright yellow t-shirt was also snug, allowing her small pointed breast to stand out. Printed in front of the t-shirt were the words, "Women Power." She wore red high heels. Her long black hair was parted on one side and a large strand curled down nearly covering her left eye in a Veronica Lake fashion.

Claudia went to a video game and began playing. Marta walked into the bar. It had a plush setting. Red leather booths lined one wall and the long bar was also lined with red leather. The long gold-designed antique mirror had gold leaf borders while hundreds of liquor bottles of every shape, size, and color stood in front of the mirror.

There were couples in the booths involved with themselves. One corner booth had three men drinking and talking. Two were facing Marta. They noticed her, and one man nudged his friend and the other man turned and leaned out to get a view. At the bar, a few solo men nursed their drinks, they, too, either turned to see her or viewed her through the mirror. At the end of the bar, she saw that woman they had seen walking into the building. She sat with her back to Marta, legs crossed and revealing her flawless limbs. She was talking to an older gent who was waving his hands as he spoke.

Marta sat a seat away from the couple as the man sitting next to Olivia left his seat and went around the bar. He was the bartender.

Walking toward her, he threw a napkin that twirled in its flight and landed right in front of Marta and then he asked, "What'll it be, beautiful?"

Marta tilted her head and responded, "Vodka martini, handsome."

The bartender nodded and reacted, "I think we're going to get along fine."

Olivia was close enough overhear the conversation and slipped off her stool, and carrying her drink, she moved over and sat next to Marta. Leaning a little forward and turning her head, she addressed Marta, "Do you mind if I keep you company?"

Marta swiveled in her stool and faced the woman and then she looked Olivia up and down and said, "I don't mind at all." Marta's right eyebrow arched.

They both twitched their nose.

Olivia twisted in her stool and asked, "What's a pretty thing like you doing in a bowling alley, huh?"

Marta grinned and stated, "I was wondering the same about you. You're hot."

Olivia nodded and said, "The name's Olivia." She put out her hand."

Marta took it and said, "They call me Marty."

"Oh, cool." Olivia looked around the room as the bartender put Marta's drink on her napkin. Marta went to her purse, but the bartender put his hand over the purse. Marta looked at him and he shook his head and walked away.

Olivia touched Marta's hand and said, "See, my boyfriend and I kind of like to experiment," Olivia held back to see Marta's reaction.

Marta nodded a few times and said, "Cool. Where is he now?"

Just then, they both kind of squinted and sniffed the air some. Their perfumes could not completely cover their vampire smell.

Marta then asked, "What's that odd odor?"

Olivia hunched her shoulders and said, "Don't know. Kind of smells like wet rags and garlic."

Marta then asked, "Where's your boyfriend now?"

Olivia jerked her head and said, "He's out back. He likes to smoke pot."

Marta nodded and said, "You were saying you guys like to experiment."

Olivia smiled and explained, "Uh, yeah. Sometimes, we have a guy join us and you know, *ménage a trois*." Olivia looked at Marta to see her reaction.

Marta rubbed her groin and said, "Mm, nice. You ever invited a woman to join you?"

"Why, you interested?"

Marta tilted her head some and gave a weak smile and said, "Well, you see, me and my ol' lady, we like to mix it up ourselves."

Olivia's face lit up and her head told her perfect and she responded, "Hey, my ol' man would be in heaven to have three women in bed. Your woman around here?"

Marta's face brightened as she jerked her head toward the door. Claudia was standing there, legs apart, and her hands on her hips. Her faded blue jeans appeared to be painted on her petite curvy body. The pure white t-shirt had "I Like Me" printed across the front. Her red locks flowed around her face like burning water.

Olivia nodded and said, "Hubba hubba. We're all going to be in heaven tonight."

Marta laid her hand on Olivia's shoulder and said, "Hold on, let me go speak to her."

Olivia nodded and said, "By all means."

Marta walked over to Claudia and Claudia immediately pulled Marta to the side, out of Olivia's view, and asked her, "Who's that? What's going on?" Do you know her?"

"Whoa, whoa. Hey, she's dinner." Claudia's brows furrowed. "She and her boyfriend like to have multiple sex partners."

At first Claudia squinted and then she smiled and asked, "Where's her boyfriend?"

"He's still in their car. He's smoking pot."

"Oh, nice. I haven't been high in a while." She grinned and then continued, "I'll do the man, he may be a little stronger to handle."

Marta then said, "Yeah, sure. We'll make love after, right?"

Claudia's forehead creased as she remarked, "Of course, dear, of course."

Just then, Olivia appeared at the bar entrance. She turned when she saw Marta and walked over to them and then she stated, "Oh, you're here. I was thinking you left."

Marta then said, "Olivia, this is Claudia. Honey, this is Olivia," they shook hands and Claudia smelled the vampire in Olivia. she didn't respond and waited for a better moment.

Marta looked at Olivia and then said, "I was telling my woman here about your proposal"—Olivia looked from Marta to Claudia—"and she likes the scenario." Olivia smiled and clasped her hands together as Marta went on, "We were just wondering where you wanna meet. Your place or our place?"

Olivia tilted her head back and forth contemplating and then spoke, "Well, we have a small pad in East LA or we can rent a room."

Claudia spoke up, "No, no, no. Our place is closer, and I have a large bed." Marta grinned and nodded her head.

Olivia then said, "Groovy. Let's go out and meet Victor."

Claudia took Marta's hand and followed Olivia out the door.

Once outside, Claudia grabbed Olivia by the shoulder, turned her around, and pushed her against the wall of the building. Olivia banged against the wall, she then she sneered, showing her teeth and her hands went up as her claws are ready to attack.

Claudia took a defensive stance and shouted, "I know you're a vampire. Where's your man? We need to talk."

Olivia put her hand through her hair. She squinted and asked, "Are you both bloodsuckers?"

They both nodded.

"Oh, that was that smell," Olivia said.

"Yeah, that was that smell," came from Marta as she placed her hands on her hips.

They all turned as they heard footsteps running toward them.

"Hey, keep the fuck away from my girl," shouted Victor as he ran toward them.

Olivia stepped forward and said, "It's all right, honey. I found the other bloodsuckers we were looking for." She jerked her head toward Claudia and said, "They wanna talk."

Victor then stopped and stated, "What? What? You're kidding? Wow. Well then, howdy, my name is Victor."

Claudia folded her arms across her chest and said, "I'm Claudia." She tilted her head toward Marta and said, "This is Marta."

At first, Victor's brows furrowed and then he scratched his head. He was about to speak, but Victor's jaw dropped and his eyes bulged. "You're not the Claudia Brocolac, widow of Demetrius, king of the vampires?" he asked.

Claudia held her head up and put her hands on her hips and responded, "I am she."

Victor, at first grinned and then he smiled. "We are honored to meet you, Mademoiselle Brocolac." He slightly bowed.

Olivia stepped forward and looked at Victor and loudly whispered, "Who's she?"

Victor pushed her back and said, "Keep quiet."

Just then, four men in bowling shirts came out of the building carrying bowling bags all involved in their game they had just played. They became quiet and all looked at the four vampires, and then just kept talking and walking to their vehicles.

Claudia then nodded her head and asked, "How long have you been one of us?"

Victor's eyes squinted as he thought and then said, "Coming up on three years." He jerked his head toward Olivia and said, "She's a rookie, six months."

Claudia took on a stern look and expressed, "You are both rookies." she looked at Marta and said, "This is her first night as a"—she jerked her head at —"as your friend here states, bloodsucker."

Both Victor and Olivia's mouth opened. Marta grinned.

"Wow, she handled herself pretty well tonight," Olivia said.

Victor then stepped forward and looked at Claudia and said, "Olly here says you wanted to talk."

A car door opened, and a young couple got out and headed their way and into the bowling alley.

Claudia nodded and said, "Let's find a spot to chat."

Marta interjected, "There's a Coco's coffee shop down the ways. They have a backroom and an outside setting."

They all nodded yes and headed toward their cars.

Once inside their car, Olivia tugged Victor's sleeve and asked, "Who's this Claudia girl, Vic?"

Victor shook his head as he spoke, "Her husband, Demetrius, was a master vampire in Europe. Both of them have been around for over two hundred years. We need to learn from them."

Olivia's eyes widened, and she exclaimed, "Wow, two hundred years. I can see she has money. Yes, we need to learn from them."

"Yes, babe, so don't say anything stupid. In fact, don't say anything at all."

Olivia looked at him with annoyance on her face.

Victor noticed the expression and said, "What? Why that look?"

"I don't know how you've survived this long. You're a buffoon. I've kept things together."

"Hey, hold on a minute. I've let you hold the reins because you were new, and I didn't want you to get bored."

Olivia pulled on his shirt sleeve and asked, "And what else? Come on, what else?"

Victor swayed his head some, not wanting to admit anything, so Olivia hit him in the upper arm and said, "Admit it, damn it. Admit it or I'll be joining up with Thelma and Louise there."

Victor rubbed his arm and giggled and then said "Okay, okay. I love you, babe."

"And, and…"

"I love the way you make love."

Olivia sat back in the seat and remarked, "Don't you fuckin' forget it."

Victor nodded and followed Claudia's car.

Marta looked over at Claudia as she drove and said, "What do you think of those bozos?"

Claudia clenched her mouth and then said, "Just that, they're bozos. They will bring the authorities down on us as quick as a sneeze disappears."

Marta's eyes bulged and a sheet of fear crossed her face. "What? What can we do? What can you do?"

Claudia glanced over at Marta and responded, "First, there are too many of us." She snickered. "Bloodsuckers so close to one another. We, at times, will have to eliminate someone for various reasons, but as we deplete people of their blood, no matter how careful we are. Some will perish."

Marta's brows frowned as she asked, "How's that?"

"Some humans will have weak hearts, some will die due to shock. Demetrius and I had been careful all the years we took people's blood, but some perished anyway. We taught numerous vampires our lifestyle technique. This practice kept authorities in Spain, France, Yugoslavia, Russia, oh, all over Europe searching for us at a minimum. Yes, the witch hunts were kept to a minimum, my dear."

Marta nodded and softly remarked, "We'll teach others here how to exist with minimum risk."

Claudia took a quick glance at her protégée and smiled.

Both automobiles pulled into the parking lot of Coco's and parked next to each other.

CHAPTER 21

UNITED

AT THE TABLE OUTSIDE THE restaurant, they sat facing one another. No other patrons sat outside; it was a cool night. They ordered coffee. Traffic went by and an occasional couple would walk by. There was a half-moon, light grey sinewy clouds floated high in the dark sky, and the tiny stars fought the clouds to looked down on earth.

Claudia began, "As you know, I've existed for over two centuries now. Most of those years were in France and Spain at one dwelling in each country."

Her three counterparts took on solemn expressions. "This life was coordinated by my late husband, Demetrius." Three heads nodded. "He conditioned me to be satisfied by only drinking enough blood to hold me over. The sexual sensations were immense, but with practice, they can be overcome, knowing that later, I will get my fulfillment with my husband." She looked at Victor and continued, "It's good you have a mate."

Victor took Olivia's hand. they smiled.

Marta interjected as she looked at Claudia, "And you have me."

Claudia smiled and nodded, "One of the things you must learn is how to invest and save money. Money buys silence. Money keeps you existing. Try and subdue wealthy-looking preys. Take their belongings, get to know the underground individuals who purchase stolen items." She looked at her three students.

They were transfixed on her knowledge.

A waitress came by and asked," Would you care to order anything or need more coffee?"

The bloodsuckers had dumped their coffee into the plant pots and shook their heads as Claudia explained, "No, thank you, dear. It's getting late. This is my sales team and we're having a late-day pep talk."

The waitress smiled and left.

Claudia continued, "Find a location that you want to call home. Find a housekeeper who needs the job and make up a reason why you stay indoors during the day. Keep your home in good shape, not to cause neighbors to get nosy or complain. If possible, get into a small business that does not need too much of your attention. Stocks are fine as long as they do not drop too much. Maybe you can find a stockbroker who can handle finances for you. I hear that marijuana is a thing these days and gold is always good to invest in."

Victor nodded and stated, "Yeah, marijuana is legal now and dispensaries are popping up all over."

They all smiled.

Claudia put down her hands on the table, her expression turned serious and stated, "If you two want to keep depleting people's blood until they die"—she looked at Victor and Olivia with a lethal stare—"you must move from Los Angeles. This will be home for Marta and myself. We don't want to be dodging the law. We will travel but always come home. Victor,"—she looked at him with malice in her eyes—"you do not realize how powerful I have become. Do not challenge me."

Victor sat back, swallowed, and his brows furrowed. "Don't worry about us, Claudia. We want what you have. If I can't discipline myself, we will move on," he managed to express.

Claudia looked at him and nodded.

Marta sat there proud of her woman.

Olivia thought, *The hell with Vic. Will this woman take me in?*

Marta broke the mood and said, "I'm hungry."

The other three smiled and nodded.

Marta then said, "Hey, there's this wild nightclub down the ways in Eagle Rock called Kabuki's. Mostly everyone is young and rowdy there. They like to get high on weed, and everyone is drinking and dancing. We all can pick someone up. Easy pickings and then we can celebrate tonight."

Claudia debated this scenario. Deep down, she didn't like the idea of four vampires out hunting together. She reluctantly agreed.

They all gave big nods. Their chairs scraped as they rose to leave.

*　　*　　*

Earlier that evening when Morris and Elizabeth were about to leave, they were confronted in the lobby of the police station.

A handsome older Caucasian woman was sitting on the bench, waiting anxiously as the sergeant behind the desk called Morris as he and Elizabeth came into the lobby.

"Hey, Lieutenant, this woman has filed a missing person's report on her daughter and—"

Morris put up his hand, smiled, and stated, "That's Missing Persons, Miller."

"I'm aware, Jason, but I overheard you talking with Oberron, and the name Marta came up."

At the sound of her daughter's name, the woman stood up, her hand went to her mouth.

Miller went on, "This woman here, Mrs. Yamamoto, is looking for her daughter named Marta. That's not a common name." His eyebrow lifted as he spoke.

Morris went over to the lady and guided her to the bench where they sat down. "Is your daughter a very pretty tall girl that has Asian-looking eyes?" Morris asked.

Mrs. Yamamoto gasped and said, "Why, yes. That's her. What…where, uh…has something happened to her? Oh my God." Her hand went to her mouth, her eyes watered.

Morris nodded and said, "No, no, no. I saw her yesterday."

"At Miss Brocolac's residence?"

Morris nodded and said, "Yes, she's probably out having a fling. She's a young vibrant college girl."

"I know she's only been gone one day, but that's not like her. Since my husband died, we've been in touch every day."

Morris didn't want to alarm her so he said, "I'm on my way to check on some things in that area. I'll drop by Brocolac's home and see what's going on. Give your address and phone number to Miller there, and I or she will contact you later."

"Oh, thank you, Lieutenant. Thank you very much."

"You go home now. I'm sure she's all right."

Elizabeth looked at Morris with a leery glance. Mrs. Yamamoto looked from one to the other and nodded. She gathered her purse and sweater on the bench and went out the door. Morris looked at Elizabeth and hunched his shoulders and gave her a weak smile. Elizabeth slightly shook her head and followed Morris out the door.

In his car, Elizabeth turned down the radio and asked, "What does this Marta girl do at this vampire's home? You seem to know her."

Morris glanced at her, his face had a puzzled flare to it. "I don't really know." He grinned and went on, "I think she kind of takes care of the household duties."

Elizabeth nodded and remarked, "Yes, since"—she glanced at Morris's notepad—"uh, Claudia doesn't go out in the daylight."

Morris smiled and nodded.

Elizabeth kept reading and stated, "It says here that Marta is an Asian girl, tall, and good-looking."

Morris squinted.

Elizabeth asked, "Did you flirt with her?"

Morris gave her another glance. His face creased in annoyance and answered, "No, what I note are details. A good detective describes important details, so another detective can be aware of what to look for. I might get assigned to another case, hon, and someone else would take over."

Elizabeth smiled and said, "You're being defensive, Jason."

Morris's eyes squinted but he kept quiet.

"By the way, where are we headed?" She looked around at the streets.

Morris looked at his watch and checked the skies. The sun was setting into the Santa Monica mountains. "Claudia will be up by the time we get there." He looked at Elizabeth. "You'll meet both of them."

"What about those deaths that may not be hers? You think there are other undead beings in LA?"

Morris quenched his mouth. He nodded slowly and answered, "Looks like it. First, we take care of what we believe. I'll deal with that matter after."

Elizabeth just drew in a breath and let it out.

Morris drove into Claudia's driveway where Marta's Camry was parked.

"That's Marta's car," Morris said.

Elizabeth just nodded.

Getting out of his vehicle, Morris went to his trunk and slid two wooden stakes under his coat, Elizabeth took out her crucifix and slipped it into her jacket pocket. He knocked on the door and they waited. He did this several times to no avail. Elizabeth stood on the porch as Morris went around the house looking through the windows. The double garage doors had small windows. Morris jumped up to peek inside.

He then went to where Elizbeth stood waiting and shook his head and said, "Her car is gone."

They both got in his car and sank into their seats.

Elizabeth looked over and asked, "What now, Sherlock?"

Morris grinned and said, "It's elementary, my dear Watson, we search the streets for them."

Elizabeth nodded and said, "While we goose-chase, do you think we could get a burger somewhere? I skipped lunch so I could meet with you."

Morris grinned and said, "A good detective always comes prepared. Look in the back there. There's a lunch bag waiting for you."

Elizabeth frowned some, she turned but was restricted by the seatbelt. She heaved, unbuckled the belt, and twisted so she was on her knees and reached over and grabbed the paper sack. She pulled out a thick sandwich in a sealed baggie.

Morris told her, "Ham and cheese, lettuce, tomato, mayo, and mustard. There's a pickle too."

Elizabeth bit into the sandwich. Her face lit up and she said, "Mm, honey baked." She then reached into the sack and pulled out a Twinkie and a pickle in a baggie. "Gee, you really know how to treat a lady."

Morris smiled.

"What do you do for an encore. Can you sing a little tune or soft-shoe?"

Morris looked over and stated, "I'll be your after dessert, dessert."

Elizabeth's eyebrows arched. She nodded and said, "Is that with a cherry on top?"

Morris nodded

Elizabeth smiled and said, "Can't wait."

They drove around Pasadena, Arcadia, and Duarte and then returned west and went through Alhambra and Glendale. They went through so many parking lots searching for Claudia's automobile. It was almost ten o'clock.

Finally, Elizabeth said, "Why don't we try Eagle Rock and then we can retire for the night? Then I can have my dessert after dessert." She looked over at Morris, her expression showing a pleasant demeanor.

Morris took in a breath and nodded and responded, "I knew there was an ulterior motive for you to tag along."

Elizabeth grinned and stated, "A good detective always has an ulterior motive." She slapped him on his leg.

Morris flinched and said, "There will be payback for that."

"Mm, can't wait."

*　*　*

Kabuki's was really jumping this night. The darkened night-club had Christmas lights along the long bar and on the ceiling as well as strobe lights that would flicker every so often, making all movement seemed jerky. There were two male bartenders and four waitresses. The bartenders wore black T-shirts that had a tuxedo silk-screened on the front. The waitresses were very attractive and wore short black pleated skirts that swished while their walk, revealing nice thighs and red panties. Their white T-shirts had the sleeves removed, the front was cut short showing flat stomachs, and the collars were also removed and sliced down the middle a few inches so their breast could breath.

Claudia, Marta, Victor, and Olivia sat at the back in a booth, watching the wildness of the crowd as the youthful patrons danced while some walked through the crowded aisles with drinks in their hands. The bloodsuckers were eyeballing everyone, trying to locate prey. The tables in the middle of the club were mostly filled with females, while the male studs sat at the bar or stood around the dance floor watching couples dance. Some couples were hot females. Everyone seemed to be having fun. The DJ was witty and entertaining, and he played a variety of rock-n-roll music, old and new.

The vampire seekers were in Eagle Rock, driving down Glendale Boulevard headed for the 134 Freeway. They were exhausted from their searching most of the San Gabriel Valley. As the headed north, Elizabeth spotted the Kabuki nightclub and nudged Morris and said, "Hey, let's try this place before you serve me my dessert after dessert."

Morris faced creased. He tilted his head side to side and then agreed, "Oh, all right. I was called here a couple years ago. There was a big fight and someone got stabbed."

"Oh, wow. Look, the parking lot is full. Drive slow. What kind of vehicle does Claudia drive?"

"A new black Kia Optima."

They entered the driveway and saw a small crowd of youths smoking. Clouds of smoke drifted into the air and then dissipated into the cool night air. The new vaper fad had smokers addicted to them. The blast of huge dark smoke almost became a competition for the smokers of who can make a bigger haze of smoke. The crowd watched the seekers drive by as they were being assessed.

They scanned all the vehicles in the lot and did not see Claudia's car.

Morris hit the steering wheel with his palm and said, "Ah well, let's go home.

Elizabeth sat up in her seat and said, "Hold on. The parking lot is full. People had to park on the street Jason. Go up a couple of these side streets."

Morris nodded as his mouth clenched down. "My oh my, honey. Here, take my badge."

"Shut up and drive, Lieutenant Morris."

They both kept quiet and had clenched smiles as Morris drove out the driveway and went up the dark narrow street. Morris drove up two blocks and turned around. They didn't see Claudia's Black Kia.

Morris looked at Elizabeth and said, "I may as well try the other street too."

Elizabeth smiled and in voice said, "May as well."

Morris squinted and held his tight lips together.

Halfway up the block, Morris spotted the Kia. There was a parking spot two houses up. After parking his car and again arming themselves, they sneaked their way to the Kia's front door. No one was in the vehicle.

They walked over to the doorway of the nightclub, Elizabeth's arm through Morris's. At the doorway, Elizabeth pulled Morris to the side as the door opened. Two Asian males and one Asian female busted out the door laughing and almost stumbling. They immediately lit cigarettes and the girl took a flask from her purse and took a swallow.

The taller male asked, "Who's driving?"

The female stated, "Not me. Jimmy is." and started laughing.

The taller one then asked, "Jimmy, you know where that party is in Alhambra?"

Jimmy blew out a cloud of smoke and said, "Yeah, it's down the street from Trader Joe's."

They walked to the parking lot mumbling to one another.

Elizabeth had Morris pinned against the wall, when the trio was out of range she backed up and asked, "What's the plan, Detective Jason Orville Morris?"

Morris frowned and then grabbed Elizabeth by her upper arms and pulled her to him and shook her a little and said, "You looked through my desk."

"Hey, big boy, watch it. You want to be arrested for abuse? Gee, I was looking for a nail clipper. I have this hangnail, see." She put her finger in his face. "It's bothering me. Ever have one?"

Morris nodded and said, "I just bite it off."

"Here then, do it," she put her finger to his mouth.

Morris just kissed it and then pushed it away as he said, "Later." He looked around and said, "If she's in there, well, I can't do anything yet, but I want her to know I am on her. We'll follow her and mess up her trying to feed on someone."

"You going to keep tabs on her all night?"

"Till the sun comes up."

Elizabeth then said squinted at him and asked, "What if she isn't a vampire, just a serial killer?"

He took a breath and responded, "Either way, she needs to be stopped."

Elizabeth displayed a sad face and stated, "There goes my dessert after dessert." She pouted.

Morris took her hand and said, "Business before pleasure. I'll make it up to you."

Elizabeth smiled.

*　　*　　*

All the while, the four undead made their plan to abduct four young women who were sitting two tables away from them. They had been drinking and men sent drinks to their table.

The vampires' keen hearing had overheard the gossip about a big party in Alhambra. Marta had suggested that she and Olivia should mosey on over to their table and let them know about the party. When they got up and went to their car, the Vamps would grab them. They all nodded even though Claudia's forehead creased. Deep inside, she knew this foursome wasn't a good idea—too much commotion, too many things could go wrong, too many bodies. She would tag along tonight but this would be it. If Victor and Olivia could not comply with not killing their prey, she would eliminate them.

Morris and Elizabeth entered the club to be confronted with loud music, darkness, strobing lights, and patrons of all shapes and sizes dancing, walking around, and standing.

The badged couple squeezed through to the bar. There was one seat and Morris offered it to Elizabeth. She hopped on and Morris stood beside her with his back to the bar.

Morris yelled above the music, "Order me a scotch and water." He then started scanning the bobbing heads on the dance floor. The strobing flickering light show made it difficult to ID anyone. Now he and Elizabeth both were trying to scrutinize their surroundings. The back tables were in dim lights and only silhouettes could be made out.

Elizabeth leaned up to his ear and loudly stated, "We should get on the dance floor. We'll get to move around the floor and check everyone out." She laid her jacket on the stool.

Morris's face creased but he nodded. They got pushed and shoved but made their way onto the dance floor. Now Elizabeth got into the swing of the music, while Morris kept his head high and bobbed a little. He was out of rhythm with the beat. As they moved around the floor, couples moved all around him and Elizabeth, some more wildly than others. After dancing through the middle of the crowd and near the edge of the dance floor, Morris felt a hot stare on him. it was as if he were under a magnifying glass.

Claudia was staring at him from a booth where she sat with another couple. Marta was not there. Elizabeth caught him gazing and looked in the same direction and viewed the vampire for the first time.

This straining moment was broken when a dancer purposely bumped into Morris and Elizabeth. He turned to see who it was.

Marta was grinning at him. Her partner, a female Asian was all involved into the music and was unaware of the collision.

Marta yelled up at him, "You here on business or pleasure?" She glanced at Elizabeth and wet her lips.

Morris moved Elizabeth away from Marta's perilous stare and shouted back, "Both." he grinned. He sensed that something was different about Marta. Something evil.

Morris then took Elizabeth's hand and pulled her through the crowded dance floor to their spot at the bar. He leaned down and told her, "Let's get your things and wait outside."

Elizabeth nodded and retrieved her jacket.

Morris put his mouth to her ear and said, "Let's swing around the crowd and go by her table. I want to get a better look at her company." He took her hand and maneuvered through the crowd and when they got to the table, it was empty. Morris looked around and then he noticed a back door with a green neon exit sign above it.

"Shit!" he exclaimed. He then hurried to the door and they went outside. The night had gotten windy and debris swept at their feet.

Morris stood there looking around when Elizabeth pulled his sleeve and said, "Hey, let's go see about that party. They booked out of here. They need to get fed." She took in a breath and rubbed her stomach and said, "Just like me."

Morris took her hand and pulled her toward his vehicle and said, "What do you mean? You scarfed up my lunch."

"I only ate half. I want warm food in my tummy before I try that dessert after dessert you're boasting about." She looked at him with an innocent face.

Morris looked at her, he half smiled and then just pulled her along to the car. He opened her door but before she got in, he turned her toward him and kissed her hard and deep.

Her eyes widened. She grinned and stated, "That's what I'm talking about."

She sat smiling and Morris quickly went around and got in and took off. *"Jew taste ma-vo-lust,"* he said.

Elizabeth nodded her head as she continued smiling.

Driving Morris stated, "Here's my phone. Look up Trader Joe's in Alhambra, honey."

Elizabeth like it when he called her honey. She responded, "Yes, dear."

He side glanced her and grinned.

"Here it is. On Huntington Drive and Rosemead."

"Hmm, I know where that is." He stepped on the gas pedal and the car lifted. He dashed through the streets with just his red light flashing he had placed on the roof of the vehicle.

The detective and his mortician partner arrived at the Trader Joe's Mart fifteen minutes later. He turned off his red light. He drove down Rosemead a few blocks and then down Huntington Drive. Traffic was scarce and there were no signs of a party. Morris then scanned the side streets, and to their luck, one street had many cars parked bumper to bumper. At one residence, three cars were parked in the driveway and one on the front lawn. A small crowd of youths stood around the vehicles on the driveway, cigarette and marijuana smoke filtered into the air. The vampire seekers searched the streets for Claudia's Kia Optima. Down at the end of the street Morris noticed a parked SUV but the brake lights were flashing off and on and nobody was around, and no heads could be seen through the tinted windows.

Morris parked and went over to the big SUV. The passenger was locked and so were all the doors. Elizabeth tried the back hatch and it clicked open. Morris hurried to the back and opened the door. A female body lay sprawled in the trunk. Morris felt her pulse and she was still alive.

He reached over and unlocked a side door and crawled out and gave his phone to Elizabeth. "Call 911," he said and went around to the side door.

When he opened the door, another female body upper body slumped out and he had to catch her. He dragged her outside and laid her down and checked her vitals. There was no pulse, she was dead. Morris shook his head as he looked at Elizabeth on the phone. She squinted and shook her head.

In the front seat, there were two more female bodies. One girl had her hand on the brake pedal, her hand was shaking. Both girls were alive. All four women had the puncture wounds on the neck.

Elizabeth shrieked into the phone, "There's more bodies, yes, three, no four. Hurry, they're still breathing."

Morris had lain the girls on a lawn and they waited for the ambulances to arrive.

"Those fuckin' monsters," Morris stated. "Shit, I fucked up. I should have…" He got lost in thought. "I should have…" He shook his head.

Elizabeth cut in, "There was nothing you could have done, Jason." She shook her head and said, "There's still nothing you can do. There's no proof."

One of the attacked girls stirred and moaned and tried to touch her head, Elizabeth took her hand in hers and soothed her cheek.

Morris grinned and said, "These girls know who attacked them. They will be our witnesses."

Elizabeth then whispered to the wounded girl, "You're safe now. You're going to be okay."

The three survivors all had nasty bumps on their heads and blood on their faces.

Morris looked down the street waiting for the ambulance and ran his hand through his hair and said, "I'm getting the forensic team out here to go over this car. Every inch." He breathed in and out. "There has to be a fingerprint here."

Just then, four ambulances came rolling down the street, sirens blaring and red lights twirling. This excitement brought many of the partygoers out front to see what was going on.

Down the street in Victor's car, the four vampires watched with disdain at the detective as he helped the fallen women.

Victor then said, "That fucker needs to go, man. From what you told us, he knows, Claudia, he knows."

As Marta and Olivia looked at Claudia, she nodded and stated, "He thinks he's pretty cocky. I will set a trap for him."

Marta frowned, she had liked Morris and did not like the idea of murder. Ah, but she now is a vampire, and she had to follow what the cult demands to be able to continue to exist. She then just nodded slowly.

CHAPTER 22

SURVIVORS

MORRIS NOW DROVE TO THE hospital. He wanted to be there when the girls woke up. He wanted to at least get a description from them. He and Elizabeth sat in the emergency waiting room going over the victims' purses for IDs for the record and for the hospital. The deceased girl's name was Katherine Woo. She was twenty and a student at Cal State in the San Fernando Valley. One of the Asian girl's name was Tanya Maeda, another twenty-year-old and also a student at Cal State. The other two were Emily Cota, twenty-one, a Hispanic attending UCLA and Veronica Simms, twenty-three, Caucasian, her ID stated she worked at NASA in Pasadena.

After forty-five minutes, a doctor came into the emergency waiting room and confronted Morris. He pulled down his mask and there was gloom on his face. He stated, "Sorry to inform you, Lieutenant, but we lost Veronica. Too much blood was depleted from her." He took in a breath and continued, "We were able to save Emily and Tanya. They are stable but cannot be disturbed until morning." The doctor looked at the two disheveled officers and told them, "You two should go home and get some sleep. You'll be able to question them in the morning. They need continued transfusions and rest right now."

Morris looked at Elizabeth and nodded, "Thanks, Doc, we'll be back." Morris helped Elizabeth up, and she held on to his arm as they walked out of the hospital. At the car, he turned Elizabeth to face him and told her, "Hey, you were a real trooper tonight. I want to get to know you and…" His brow creased as he searched for the words. "I want…"

Elizabeth just pulled him close and said, "Shut up," and she kissed him.

*　　*　　*

The four bloodsuckers were sitting in Claudia's library. Olivia was impressed with how Claudia has managed to sustain her existence all these years. As they sat facing one another, she gazed around the room and nodded her head. She liked the surroundings.

Victor looked at the portrait of Demetrius and asked Claudia, "So that was the king of vampires, huh?" He nodded, "He was a handsome brute, wasn't he?"

Claudia didn't respond and was thinking that it indeed was a mistake to hook up with these two low-life Americans. But they were of her brethren now and she needed to respect that.

While Victor and Olivia got up and examined the artifacts in the large library, Marta clicked on the large flat screen wall TV.

It was eleven o'clock and Eyewitness News was on.

"And we are receiving an update on that mass attack on four young women in Alhambra while they attended a birthday party. We have Dale McCormick at the Huntington Memorial hospital where the girls were taken. Dale?"

"This is Dale McCormick broadcasting from the ICU room at Huntington Memorial hospital. Yes, four young girls were attacked in their vehicle they were driving in. Yes, you heard right. In their vehicle. Their names are being held back until next of kin can be notified. There is disturbing news on the girls' conditions I'm afraid. In speaking with the doctors, I was informed that one of the young women was pronounced dead at the scene and now a second victim passed on the operating table due to loss of blood and a drastic blow to her head. At this time, it is undetermined what caused the death, her loss of blood or the head wound."

The four vampires looked at one another with concern.

"The doctors stated that the two surviving victims have excellent chances of being okay. Three of the victims were college students, the fourth a NASA employee. We will keep you informed. Back to you at the studios."

"Thank you, Dale, for that disturbing report. It's so—"

Claudia clicked the TV off and looked at Victor and Olivia, "You two are complete idiots. The deaths of those two girls will alarm the public and the authorities will have no choice but to put together a task force to capture us."

Victor slammed the arm of the lounge chair and exclaimed, "Wait a fuckin' minute. How do you know who was the culprit here? I—"Hold your tongue. I monitored Marta and pulled her off when I knew she had enough. I, myself know when to stop."

"Uh, well, maybe. What about those two who are alive?" He looked at Claudia and Marta and continued, "What did they see? I know we crept up to the vehicle and as soon as the driver turned off the ignition and placed it in park, the doors unlock automatically. We each took a door handle and immediately opened the door and I bashed them. They had a second to view us. Was it enough?" Again he looked at his accomplices and stated, "I say it was good to kill them. You fucked up," he pointed at Claudia.

Her eyes widened, and her jaw dropped a little.

Victor went on, "Now, we'll have to go to the hospital and eliminate them before they can talk, that fuckin' copper already suspects you. He found the girls. He's a smart cookie. We'll have to get rid of him too."

Everyone kept quiet for a moment and then Marta spoke, "Victor is right about putting those girls to sleep, but I don't know about offing the lieutenant. Cops get angry when one of their own gets murdered."

Claudia then got up, she squinted her eyes and looked at her fellow fiends and said, "Best we disappear from Los Angeles. I agree we need to keep the girls quiet. I will come up with a way to get rid of the lieutenant and make it look like an accident."

Her brethren nodded.

Victor sat in his chair and said, "All right, that sounds pretty convenient for you. You have what it takes to vamoose out of here at a moment's notice." He jerked his head toward Olivia and continued, "It's not so easy for Olly and me." He grinned and said, "You're going to have to help us make that getaway."

Claudia paced the room and went to the portrait of Demetrius which was behind where Victor was seated. Leaning on the wall was Demetrius's sword, as she spoke she touched it. "I agree, I will do what's best to see that we get away safe." She silently pulled the sword from its sheaf, Marta was facing her and her eyes widened some. Olivia leaned over and picked up a small statue of Napoleon seated on a horse that was on the coffee table. It was solid silver. As she examined it, Claudia stepped behind Victor's chair and then she stabbed into the back of the chair with a mighty thrust. The blade went through the chair and into Victor's back.

His face showed surprise and fear as his mouth screeched out, "Claudia." He leaned forward and stood up and turned to face Claudia, anger blanketed his face. In that moment, Claudia swung the sword and the blade met Victor's neck. In a flash his head wobbled and then fell to the floor. Blood gushed out five feet high. His body froze, his arms stuck straight down, and then his body wiggled and slumped to the floor.

Olivia's and Marta's hands went to their face and mouth. They looked at the shaking body on the floor. The head had rolled to Olivia's feet, and she kicked it away.

Claudia faced Olivia and then said, "Don't worry, my dear, I am sparing you. You can leave and fend for yourself."

Olivia's face displayed puzzlement, fear, and query. Her head shook involuntarily.

Claudia went on, "Or you are welcome to join Marta and myself in our existence. You will be our lover and companion. But you must obey me. What do you choose, my dear?"

Olivia's face brightened some. She tried to speak but she had lost her voice. She cleared her throat and squeaked out, "I want to stay with you and Marta."

Marta smiled and clapped her hands quick.

Claudia then said, "Fine. You both will learn how to live dignified and with sophistication."

They both nodded their heads quickly.

"Now, I will get this body ready to be disposed of." She looked at her girls. "You two clean up the blood. After, we will pack what is valuable, put Victor's remains in his car, and we will drive it somewhere secluded. We will go to Mexico. We will have to stay in a hotel or motel before daylight. There, we shall make love, sleep, and we'll think about what to do and then continue our journey to Mexico."

The girls stood there, their arms straight down, their jaws somewhat open. Then slowly nodded and then Olivia said, "Claudia…"

Claudia turned quickly and looked at her.

"Uh, Victor has a house in East LA. We can stash his body there."

Claudia thought a moment and then said, "All right, good. Let's get to work. Right now, time is our enemy." She clapped her hands and exclaimed, "Get with it."

The girls broke out of their trance and ran to the kitchen to get cleaning equipment.

* * *

Elizabeth stayed overnight at Morris's apartment, but they were too tired to get involved and just fell asleep in each other's arms. Morris woke up all tangled up in the blankets. He felt around, and Elizabeth was not next to him. He sat up and smelled coffee. He hopped out of bed and went straight to the restroom. Fifteen minutes later, he walked into the kitchen in jeans and T-shirt, barefoot, and his hair still wet from showering. He caught Elizabeth standing over the sink rinsing a frying pan. Her hair was pinned up, exposing her slender long neck. Her scrubbed face without makeup resembled a young pretty country maiden. Morris's dress shirt hung loosely on her body. The sleeves were rolled up, collar was up, and the shirt covered her top, thus the bottom of the shirt revealed bare tan limbs and nicely formed thighs and calves which led to feet swimming in the lieutenant's slippers.

He stood at the doorway. He nodded at her and looked at her feet and stated, "I was looking for those."

She turned grinning. "Well, good morning to you, too."

He smiled and walked over to her and put his arms around her and said, "Good morning, honey. Gee, this is kind of nice."

Elizabeth twisted and faced him. She placed her arms around his neck and said, "Can you get used to this?"

Morris's face showed panic briefly, and then a brightness flowed as he smiled and stated, "I think so."

They kissed.

The kiss continued until Elizabeth pulled away and said, "Breakfast is getting cold."

Morris's eyebrows went high on his forehead as he said, "Breakfast. You're spoiling me."

Elizabeth kind of frowned and told him, "Your fridge was kind of bare, but I managed to make you a cheese omelet."

"Well, let's test the waters then."

As Morris fed himself, Elizabeth poured him a cup of coffee and then sat down and looked at his face to see his reaction to her cooking.

"Ah, just the way I like it. The egg cooked thoroughly and the cheese melted on top as well as gooey in the center."

She smiled and said, "Mom said that a way to a man's heart is through his stomach."

As he buttered his toast, Morris claimed, "A way to a woman's heart is to never criticize her cooking."

Elizabeth smacked him on his arm and sipped her coffee.

Morris looked at her and asked, "What are you doing today, hon?"

Elizabeth's expression displayed some stress as she explained, "Well, Jason—"

Morris interjected, "I love it when you say my name. Everyone calls me lieutenant or Morris."

"Well, Jason, the two bodies from last night will be in my jurisdiction. I'll need to go in and at least give a fundamental examination and summary prior to a full autopsy."

Morris clenched his mouth, nodded, and then said, "I'll be at the hospital, baby, but first I need to talk with my superior about raiding Claudia's residence."

Elizabeth nodded and told him, "Eat your breakfast. You're going to need your strength later." She wiggled her eyebrows up and down.

"I'll be ready, darling, I'll be ready." He stuffed two forkfuls of eggs in his mouth and wiggled his eyebrows at her.

Elizabeth smiled, picked up her coffee cup, and went into the bedroom.

*　*　*

Morris came out of Commander O'Reilly's office with a smile.

Sergeant Oberron nodded to him and asked, "What's up?"

Morris grinned at Oberron and told him, "There's going to be a raid at the Brocolac residence and you're leading it."

Oberron frowned and asked, "What about you? This is your case."

Morris nodded and took in a breath and responded, "Yeah, I'll be at the hospital interviewing the survivors. As soon as I get confirmation, I'll call you. You get the squad ready to leave at a moment's notice. I'll meet you there. The warrant is being processed as we speak."

Nodding, Oberron stated, "Yeah, downtown is really upset. Too many bodies, Morris. The mayor is on the commissioner's ass. He's on the chief's ass and he's on the commander's ass. He's on our ass. You haven't been here when he gave us the riot act."

Morris smirked and said, "Well, we're close now." Morris shook his head and said, "That prick still don't believe there's actual vampires here in LA."

Oberron sank in his seat as he stated, "Well, it's kinda hard to believe, Morris. Vampires?"

"You too, huh? You'll see. That's why you're leading the raid, ha-ha-ha."

Oberron just stared at Morris and then said, "The forensic crew picked up a print on the outside door of them victim's vehicle."

Morris's jaw dropped. He nodded and said, "Yeah, yeah."

"It belongs s to a Victor Eriksen. Last known address was in Seattle, Washington, before he flew to Europe. He was a movie extra. Got you some pics and blew 'em up for you along with pictures of Claudia Brocolac and the college girl Marta Yamamoto." His eyes shifted to a briefcase on the desk.

Morris picked up the case and said, "Hey, Sarge, you're a buddy, man. A real buddy."

He saluted Morris and said, "We'll get those fuckers."

Morris grabbed his jacket and said, "See ya at the Brocolac's," and scooted out the door.

CHAPTER 23

GETTING CLOSE

MORRIS CHECKED AT THE REGISTRATION desk to find out what room the girls were in., he was carrying a small leather briefcase. Walking down the hall, he stopped a doctor to inquire how the girls were doing.

"Emily is awake and is pissed this morning. She has an attitude, but it helped her recover more quickly." Doctor shook his head and then said, "This Tanya girl, well, she's still in shock. They're both gonna need counseling, yes, the Asian girl is a wreck. Take it easy on her if you need to speak with her."

Morris nodded and asked, "Are they in the same room?"

"Uh-huh, we thought it might help Tanya to be with her friend."

"Thanks, Doc," Morris then went to the room. It was slightly open, and he tapped on it and went in. Tanya was under the covers, she seemed to be asleep, bandages on her scalp. Emily was sitting up in pajamas. She had gauze around her head and a large bandage on her neck. She was talking on her cell phone.

She gazed at the detective as she nodded into the phone and said, "Yeah, we just got to Richie's, uh, hold on." She covered the phone and gave a nod to Morris and asked, "Who are you? What do you want?"

205

Morris grinned and pulled out his wallet with his badge and said, "I'm Lieutenant Morris. I'm here to ask you some questions."

Emily spoke into the phone, "Nancy, I'll get back to you. The cop who found us is here." She smiled and said, "He's good-looking too." She hung up and placed the phone on the nightstand. "Did you catch those suckers yet?"

Morris tilted his head. He gave her a straight smile and said, "Almost. Maybe you can help us nab these culprits."

"You want me to go with you to ID them? Come on, let's go."

Before Morris could react, Emily hopped off the bed and took a step and then collapsed into Morris's arms.

"Whoa, there. Doctor says you need rest and nourishment." He laid her back on the bed.

She shook her head slowly and stated, "Oh, gee. Wow, my head is spinning."

"Yeah, it should be, Emily. You almost died last night."

Emily closed her eyes and rubbed her forehead and said, "Yeah, I know."

Morris shook his head and asked, "Maybe you need something. Let me get the nurse."

Emily then said, "No, no, no. I'm okay, really. How can I help you? it's Lieutenant Morris, right?"

Morris nodded.

"You're on the news, you know. They say you were on these killers' trail that night. You're really a Sherlock Holmes."

Morris shook his head and responded, "Emily, the media builds things up. I'm just doing my job. Anyway, I brought along some photographs."

Emily sat up and put a pillow behind her for support and said, "*Pasa, calabasa.*"

Morris frowned quick but smiled and brought up the briefcase. He unstrapped it and took out the black-and-white eight-by-twelve photos. He first showed her the photo of Marta. "Best you can, tell me what you remember."

Emily grabbed the photo and held it with two hands and scrutinized the photo a moment and then shook her head and said, "Uh-

uh. The girl I saw wasn't Asian. A pretty blonde chick. It was only for a second though. I heard the door open, and suddenly, a face was in front of me and then something conked me. Next thing I knew, I was in the hospital. But I did see this chick at Kabuki's. She invited us to a house party. She was sitting with two or three others. It was too dark to make them out.

Morris squinted and said, "A blonde Caucasian, huh? Take a look at this one and imagine her with blond hair." He handed her the photo of Claudia.

Again, Emily examined the photo closely and shook her head and said, "She's not the one who attacked me." She clenched her lips together and then said, "I did see the guy who jumped Katherine. He came through the back door just before my door was opened."

Morris quickly gave her the photo of Victor.

She immediately nodded her head and exclaimed, "That's the fucker. That's the guy, detective."

Morris took out his cell phone, and when Oberron answered, Morris just said, "Go."

Morris looked at Emily and said, "I'm off to get the fucker."

Emily laughed as she yelled yay and clapped her hands. As Morris was leaving, she yelled after him, "Let me know what happens."

In the hall, he yelled, "Will do."

*　*　*

Morris arrived at the same time the task force did. Oberron instructed two men to go round back, while he placed one man on each side of the garage. Oberron had two officers with him at the front door, one with a hand-held battering ram, plus Morris tagged along at the rear. At a designated time, they would burst into the front and back doors and place anyone in the house under arrest.

Oberron looked at his watch as the men looked at him, he silently raised his arm and hand signaling five, and then four, three, two, and then he yelled, "Now!"

The officer with the ram charged the door. The door splintered and flung open. The men rushed in, weapons held at the ready and they searched each room. The officers in the rear did the same. Each officer yelled clear as they cleared each room. A rear and front officer met in the hallway and motioned each other to go up the stairs. Morris followed them up. The upstairs rooms were also empty. Morris then noticed some of the antiques were not there as well as the portraits of Demetrius. The picture of Roberto was torn to bits and the pieces lay on the floor. The garage was empty also.

Morris and Oberron met in the kitchen and sat facing one another at the dining room table.

"Shit. We missed them. They must have left early this morning," Morris said.

One of the officers came in and told them, "You guys need to see this."

Both men rose quickly and followed the officer to the neighbor's trash barrels. He picked up the lid and inside were towels and rags stained with blood.

Grinning, the officer said, "I was throwing this empty cartridge box away and went to the neighbor's bin, bingo."

Morris told him, "Bag it."

Oberron told him, "Good work, Smith."

Morris looked at Oberron and said, "Get that crap to forensics and tell them it's a 711, top priority."

Oberron nodded and said, "Will do. Where are you going now?"

"Morgue."

"Uh-huh."

Morris looked at him and said, "Come on, business."

Oberron grinned and wave his hand and said, "Go on."

*   *   *

Earlier that day, a moving van was at the Brocolac residence with instructions to remove certain items and store them in a self-storage located in Seal Beach.

*   *   *

When Morris entered the morgue, Elizabeth was standing over Katherine Woo's corpse, sewing up the surgical wounds made for autopsy purposes. Veronica Simms's body lay on the next table.

She glanced up as Morris came in as he held a surgical mask to his nose. She put up her hand, indicating that Morris should stop, he did. Elizabeth finished the patch up and covered the body with a sheet and then walked toward Morris. She jerked her head for him to follow and he did.

In the hallway, she leaned close to Morris and told him, "Cause of both deaths are loss of blood. The blunt to the head didn't help, but they would have died anyway. They both have the puncture wounds on the neck. Katherine's were a wider berth and more violent."

Morris kept looking down and shaking his head, and then he banged the wall and told Elizabeth, "Liz, we raided that bitch's house and she's wasn't there. All her valuables were gone too. What the fu—"

Elizabeth put two fingers across his lips and said, "Hey, they're running. They're scared. You're gonna get them. Think. You're a class-A detective. What is she thinking? What can she do right now? Where can she go?"

Morris squinted as he thought. He pounded the wall as he think. Then he looked like he found gold. "Yes, she had somebody store her valuables. The neighbors might have seen something. She knows we know what she is. She probably wants to leave the country. Mexico is her best shot right now. From there, she can go anywhere. She can't use her name or Marta's name to get tickets. There's someone else with them. A young pretty blonde and that Victor character. Thank you, babe. I'll contact you later." He kissed her quickly and ran down the hall.

CHAPTER 24

DRIVING, MORRIS WAS ON HIS phone talking to Oberron, "Check the moving van companies and see who went to this address and where did they take her stuff to. I'm checking hotels and motels. They're here somewhere. Send out the regular red-light notice to the airports and train and bus depots and to report if either one of them buys tickets. They'll probably use cash. Get the fraudulent squad to help you infiltrate her accounts. They have experience with this shit. They can illegally barge into her accounts and sniff around. Find out what bank she uses, block her accounts along with her credit cards."

Oberron kept nodding and nodding.

"Okay, get back to me with anything you get."

"Will do. Later."

"Later."

*   *   *

The sun was hanging low as it said goodnight to Los Angeles. A hazy reddish sunset smeared the western skies. It would be dark soon. Suddenly, Morris felt a flood of fear penetrate his body. The fear was not for him but for Elizabeth. How much did Claudia know about his personal life?

Morris was on his way to the Double-Tree Hotel on Huntington Drive in Monrovia when the thought of calling Elizabeth hit him, that's when he received a call from Sergeant Oberron.

"We have an address on that Victor fellow."

Morris said, "Good, what is it?"

"234 North Ditman, Boyle Heights in East LA."

"I'm on my way."

"I discharged a unit to check it out."

Morris shook his head and told Oberron, "Have them wait for me. We don't know what these demons are capable of."

Oberron's brows furrowed and he asked, "You think he's one of these vampire people?"

"I'm pretty sure of it."

"Okay, they'll be waiting."

*   *   *

234 North Ditman was a rear dwelling. A black-and-white police cruiser was parked three houses down, two officers sat there waiting. Morris pulled up next to them and then nodded for them to follow him.

Morris parked and got out of his vehicle and went to his trunk. The two uniformed policemen stood there waiting for directions. Morris pulled out three wooden stakes and handed one to each officer. They looked at it with puzzled expressions.

Morris told them, "If you are attacked, bullets may not have any effect on the culprit. Try and stick these in its heart." The officers grinned a little and the older of the two said, "Sir, are you serious?"

Morris responded, "Serious as a heart attack. Please, no questions."

They nodded. At the front door, Morris indicated that both go to the rear door. they had a surprise look but nodded. Morris gave them enough time to get situated.

Morris held his weapon in front of his face and the stake stuck in his waist as he kicked in the door. He needed to kick it again and it flung open. He stepped in cland announced, "Police officers, put your hands up and on your knees." He heard the back door bust open. The living room was empty, he yelled clear and went into the bedroom on the left. He heard an officer scream clear from the kitchen. One officer went into the other bedroom, Morris yelled clear and the officer yelled clear and they met in the small hallway. the second offi-cer went into the bathroom and came out almost vomiting. Morris and the other officer frowned and went into the restroom. There in the tub was Victor's lifeless body and his hands were holding his head on his stomach.

Morris told them, "Call it in and wait for homicide to arrive. Check around outside and see if there is any weapon that could have done this. I'll contact headquarters later."

The officers looked at one another and nodded. Morris went out the door.

In his car, he called Elizabeth.

She answered after four long rings, "Hello, Detective, you com-ing to give me the dessert after dessert?" She was wrapped in a towel in the locker room of the morgue.

"Baby, I wish. What took you so long to answer?"

"Just got out of the shower, getting squeaky clean for my dessert after dessert." She grinned into the phone.

"Look, honey, I'm kind of worried. Those killers know where I live, and I don't think they know where you reside at. Just stay at home tonight, lock the windows, and bolt the doors. Wait there until you hear from me, okay?"

Elizabeth frowned but she nodded and stated, "You think they'll come after me? Why?"

"I've got this feeling she feels that she can get to me through you so I will stop chasing her. Even if that's not true, I'd feel better knowing you're safe."

Elizabeth thought a moment and then said, "Safest place is with you."

Morris took in a breath and then said, "You may be right." He then shook his head and told her, "Wait a minute, I may be in the eye of the storm."

"They say that's the calmest place. Come on, big strong detec-tive, I'll feel safer with you. You have me scared now."

"Okay, look, I'm just hitting hotels and motels trying to find her. I believe Marta is somehow involved in this caper and there may be others."

"Really? Oh no. You think that Claudia made her into a vampire?"

Morris was near his destination and stated, "This is the craziest case I've ever been on. Anything is possible. We, uh, I don't really know if there are really vampires. She may become deranged psychopath and somehow got others to follow her. In either scenario, she's dangerous."

Elizabeth nodded and replied, "What do you want me to do, Jason?"

"Is there someplace you can stay until I can pick you up?"

"Why don't I just stay here? There will be a night watchman coming in soon. There's a lounge here that's comfortable."

"Okay, okay, yeah. I'll be there in about two hours." He looked around and said, "Shit, it's already getting dark."

Elizabeth looked out the window, the twilight tonight looked scary. It was windy and the moon had a mustard haze to it. she bit her lower lip and said, "Forget about them tonight, Jason. Just meet me here."

"All right, I'll just check this one place and drive over to the morgue. It's not far from where you're at. See you in a while."

Elizabeth smiled and stated, "Okay, I'll just finish up here and wait for you here. I feel better now."

Morris put the phone in his jacket and headed for the Double-Tree.

*   *   *

That day, Claudia was first to rise, she stepped out of bed nude and walked over to the sky-rise window. She peeked out and dusk was beginning to flood the streets below. The street lights had not been turned on yet. She turned and looked at the bed and Marta and Olivia were still sleeping, sprawled naked and entwined in the sheets and pillows. They had gotten in just before daybreak that day, all three engorged themselves in Victor's remaining blood. Arriving at the hotel, they hurried to their room and jumped in bed. There, they excitedly disrobed each other and together, Olivia and Marta sexually engaged themselves on Claudia for two hours.

"Get up, you two muffins. We can't stay. That detective will not give up so easily."

Marta stretched and pushed Olivia over with her foot.

Olivia yawned and placed her head on Marta's stomach and said, "You were insatiable this morning, Marta."

"Me? You couldn't stop touching on me."

Smiling, Olivia remarked, "You can't blame me. It was my first time with a woman." She rolled her eyes and continued, "And there were two gorgeous ones at that."

Marta smiled and smoothed Olivia's hair and said, "It gets better, wait for—"

"Girls, girls. You both were wonderful. Let's get cleaned up and make ourselves presentable." Claudia, clapped her hands and said, "I want to get that lieutenant's girlfriend's work place before she leaves."

Marta and Olivia looked at her with a puzzled expression.

"She will be our ticket to safety. We will kidnap her, and then I'll threaten Morris with turning her. He will stop chasing us, believe me."

Marta and Olivia looked at one another. They nodded and smiled and then they gave each other a high five.

"Hurry now, get moving."

The girls jumped out of bed and rushed to the restroom.

*　　*　　*

As Morris and an attendant went up one elevator, Claudia, Marta, and Olivia were descending in another. At their door, the attendant slid in the pass card in the slot and backed away. Morris pushed the door open with gun in hand. He scanned the room. The quarters were empty. Blankets were in bundles and pillows on the floor. He checked the bathroom and it was in disarray and no one was in there either.

Morris stepped out of the restroom, and the attendant was standing there, wondering what was going on.

"You said there were three women checking in to this room?" Morris asked him.

He nodded and said, "Yes, I brought them up, there were only two suitcases. I didn't know if they were tourist or college girls on a binge. They were all attractive though."

Morris looked at him and asked him, "What time do you get off?"

He kind of frowned and said, "In an hour. I had a twelve-hour shift today. Why?"

"I'm going to send over a departmental artist. I'd like a drawing of the women."

The attendant smiled and said, "Hey, we have a video of everyone checking in. Check with the supervisor."

Morris smiled and said, "Great, somebody will be over to get it. Let them know downstairs that this is a police matter." Morris looked at his watch and said, "I've got to run. pal. Later!" He quickly ran down the hall to the elevator.

*　*　*

Elizabeth was finishing up closing up a cadaver when her supervisor came into the medical room.

"What's up, Dr. Bradley?"

"I'm glad you are still here, but I'm sorry to inform you that I need that report on Rosily Romero finished tonight. The court proceedings were moved ahead, and the prosecutor needs it in his hands in the morning."

Elizabeth frowned but nodded and responded, "I'll get on it now."

Dr. Bradley smiled and said, "Thank you, Doctor. You've done all the examining and documentation already, just type it up. Shouldn't take you more than fifteen minutes. I'm leaving. you'll be here alone so lock up when you leave."

Elizabeth nodded and said, "Will do. Dr. Bradley, will do."

The door closed, and Elizabeth put a sheet on the corpse and then went to the wall where the refrigeration section stood and

215

opened the door and rolled the body into a slot. She then went to her office and began typing the report.

Outside in the morgue's parking lot. Claudia parked her car in the shadow of the building. The girls got out and inspected their surroundings. They kept out of view of the surveillance cameras and Olivia went to the front door and rang the doorbell. Claudia and Marta stayed on either side of the large front door.

There was a speaker system there and Olivia pressed the intercom button and spoke, "Federal Express."

Elizabeth heard the doorbell and the message. She stopped typing as she squinted at the clock and took in a breath. She turned in her chair and said out loud, "Federal Express, really?"

She walked to the front door and viewed the monitor and saw a young pretty girl standing there with a small box in her arms. She didn't recognize her.

Elizabeth took in a breath and spoke through the phone system, "Hey, you can leave the package on the floor. I'll get it when I leave."

The girl smiled, nodded, and replied, "Look, it's late and you're my last stop. I wanna go home too. You have to sign for this. It must be something expensive or important."

Elizabeth closed her eyes and then shook her head. "Okay, hold on."

As she unlocked the door, out of habit, she glanced at the monitor again and she saw another person's arm, trying to stay out of view. As the door began to open, she pushed it back but before she could lock it, the force from the other side began to push the door open. Elizabeth managed to push it closed again but then more pressure was pushed against her. She looked at the monitor and she recognized Claudia and Marta, all three were now pushing the door as Olivia held the door handle so Elizabeth couldn't lock it.

The door was moving inward slowly and now, Elizabeth looked around, nothing was available. She took off her watch and braced it under the door. She knew she only had a few moments, so she ran to her office. There, she locked her door and looked for something to defend herself. She saw her large letter opener with the small skull handle. As she picked it up and braced herself against the door, she felt the pounding on her door. She managed to grab her cell phone from her desk and called Morris.

As the door got banged and began to splinter, Morris answered, "Hey, I'm almost there."

She screeched into the phone, "Jason, they're here! They're gonna kill me—"

The door busted open, knocking Elizabeth to the floor. The three demons burst into the room with havoc on their faces.

Elizabeth rolled into a corner, her knees up and her arms hugged her body and she cried out, "What do you want from me? Why do you want to kill me?" She shook her head in distress.

The three vampires encircled her and looking down, Claudia stated, "Don't worry, my dear. We're not here to kill you. You'll be our hostage. We want your boyfriend to stop chasing us."

Olivia reached down and pulled Elizabeth to her feet. They faced each other, and Olivia said, "You are a pretty thing, girl. I wouldn't mind doing you."

"Stop the nonsense. Bind her," Claudia said as she grabbed the duct tape from the desk and gave it to Marta. Olivia twisted Elizabeth's arm and made her turn around. Marta grabbed her other hand and put it behind Elizabeth's back, and they taped her wrists together. Elizabeth displayed scorn on her face as her captives grinned at one another.

Claudia led the way down the hall. Olivia followed, pulling Elizabeth by a small chain around her neck and Marta was in the rear.

CHAPTER 25

DEATH OF A VAMPIRE

MORRIS SCREECHED INTO THE PARKING lot as he saw the single line of women heading to a vehicle. They momentarily stopped and looked at the crazy driver skid to a stop as the car hit a planted tree in the middle of the lot. The driver's door flung open and Morris rolled out of the vehicle his forty-five caliber at the ready.

"Freeze right there! Freeze or I'll shoot!"

Claudia yelled out, "Eat shit, Lieutenant," as she ran to her car.

Olivia was behind her, pulling Elizabeth. Marta ran at the lieutenant. Morris fired three quick bursts. First bullet hit Marta in the right shoulder, and she stopped running. The second and third bullets hit her in the stomach. The force of the hits knocked her back and she fell backward, but she immediately sprang back on her feet and jumped for the detective. He was quick enough to avoid contact with her as she bumped into his open door.

Marta gave a high pitch snarl and said, "You're going down, motherfucking pretty detective!" Then she pounced at him and swung at him hitting him on the shoulder. The quick blow took Morris by surprise. He flung back and bumped into his front fender, his forty-five flew out of his hand. Then Marta grabbed him, and they rolled on the parking lot pavement.

Claudia stopped for moment and then grinned and kept going to her car while Olivia was close at hand, tugging Elizabeth. Elizabeth's expression of fear changed itself to shock when she saw her hero on the ground, struggling with that vampire woman.

Marta wrapped her legs around Morris's thighs, locking him in position for her to take full control. Her right arm held his body to hers. Morris swung his one free arm pounding on Marta's upper shoulder. She laughed at his feeble attempt to escape. With her other hand she grabbed Morris's hair and yanked his head back, exposing his vulnerable pulsing neck. Marta then reared her head back, she opened her mouth fully, her ferocious white pointed teeth seem to gleam in the early evening moonlight. As she came down onto the detective's neck, Morris had managed to pull out the stake he had stuffed in his beltline. As her teeth penetrated his vein, with all his might, he stabbed Marta in the heart.

With a screeching yell, Marta pushed Morris away and with both hands she yanked at the stake from her heart.

The stake was embedded and blood spurted out in streams. Marta rolled on the ground and yelled, "Claudia!"

Claudia and Olivia pushed Elizabeth into the back seat and Olivia got in with her. Claudia screamed, "Oh, Marta, no!" She looked at Morris who crawled and retreated his pistol. Claudia's eyes closed and she stated, "You will pay for this, Detective! You will pay for this!" With that, she sped away as Morris emptied his weapon at the getaway vehicle.

Morris ran to his vehicle, and quickly as possible, he got into the chase. He saw Claudia's vehicle a block away. It turned west on Beverly Boulevard. Morris placed his portable light on the top of his car and the red light flashed. There was light traffic on the Boulevard tonight, and both cars weaved in and out of traffic. Morris called in and within minutes, there were two blac- and-white vehicles behind Morris with flashing red lights and blaring sirens.

Claudia turned left on Garfield, another wide boulevard, she was still a block ahead of Morris. He drove with one hand, stopping the blood seeping from the teeth wound on his neck.

Olivia grabbed Claudia's shoulder and said, "I'm gonna get rid of this bitch. He'll stop for her."

Claudia gritted her teeth and nodded and exclaimed, "Yes, go ahead, at the next turn. I'll come back for her and him some other night."

At Whittier Boulevard she slowed enough to make the turn and Olivia opened the door and kicked Elizabeth out the car. Elizabeth landed on her butt, her white medical coat bundled up to her face and she rolled on the street several times and lay in the middle of the street.

Morris made the turn and saw Elizabeth on the street. He swerved his vehicle which almost flipped over and he T-boned a parked car. The police officers made the turn, and avoiding Elizabeth, the police car turned and hit Morris's car, the other police vehicle made the turned but to avoid any collision, the driver turned hard and his vehicle flipped over and rolled on its top.

The smell of burnt rubber and gasoline filled the air. As the smoke and dust dissipated and the looky-loos gathered around. They viewed wrecked cars. Doors squeaked and clanked open and police-men squeezed out of their smashed vehicles. Morris had to wedge himself out of his window.

On the ground, he ran over to Elizabeth and unraveled the white coat and chain around her neck and body and held her to him and said, "Elizabeth, Elizabeth, are you all right?"

She blinked her eyes and she shook her head and stated, "I feel like somebody threw me in a dryer. I hurt all over, honey," She then smiled and said, "But, thank you, you bad-ass detective. You saved my life. Get this tape off my hands so I can hug you."

An ambulance siren blared down the street and then stopped. Two attendants came over, one with his first-aid kit.

Morris kissed her quickly and said to the attendant, "Patch her up for me, will ya?"

The attendant nodded and got down on one knee and started wiping at the scrape marks on Elizabeth's legs and arms. Blood seeped from Elizabeth's forehead and forearm. The medic began cleaning her wounds. The other attendant took Morris's hand from his neck and said, "Come to the cab with me. I should patch that up for you."

Morris looked around and asked, "How are the officers?"

A big black officer replied, "We're all good. Nothing serious but the vehicles are totaled. What's going on here? Stolen car? robbery?"

Morris ran his hand through his hair and told them, "The blood depleters and killers just got away."

The officer remarked, "Damn, really? Shit."

A young crew-cut Latino officer stated, "Yeah, but it looks like you saved someone."

They all nodded.

*　　*　　*

Claudia turned right on Naomi Street and parked the vehicle. They both got out and took what suitcases they could carry and went to the bus stop on the corner and called for a taxi.

Sitting there waiting, they saw the red lights flashing and the sirens of police vehicles drive by and then a police helicopter flew by. A few minutes went by and a yellow cab came for them. They got in and asked to be dropped off in downtown LA. They got off the cab and walked two blocks to the Bonaventure Hotel. There, they got a room in Olivia's name and then rented a car. In the room, they cleaned up and Claudia finally sat on the bed. With her head in her hands, she sobbed. "Oh, Marta. My lovely, lovely Marta. That horrible detective. Oh, that horrible detective."

Olivia sat next to her. She placed her arm around her and said, "Claudia, you are my queen. I am yours. I will be your new Marta."

Claudia peeked through her hands and viewed this pretty country girl. Her straight blonde hair was full and thick. She had piercing deep blue eyes, a small perfect nose, and two full lips. Yes, she was actually beautiful, and she had a teenager's body.

Claudia pulled her to her, and she hugged her. "Yes, my darling, we will thrive together. For now, we must eat. The night is young."

Olivia nodded. Then she switched the TV on. She got up and started brushing her hair as Claudia pulled off her dress boots.

A newscaster was at the crash site announcing information regarding the incident.

"A task force is being assembled to locate two renegade women, one has been identified as Claudia Brocolac, a French resident who was living in Spain and owns a high-breed horse ranch in Spain. Her accomplish has not been identified yet. Authorities claim she is a young female, maybe twenty, blonde, and approximately five feet five—"

Claudia turned it off and Olivia said, "I'm five seven."

Claudia's face took on an enraged look. She stood there with her arms straight down and her hands clenched. "That son of a bitch! I will make him suffer just as Demetrius made my fiancé suffer. Yes, Demetrius did not kill Beaudin. He made him watch me sucking blood and killing someone. After that, Beaudin could not be a policeman no more. He took to drink and disappeared. I will take his love, and she will be one of us." she uttered.

Olivia looked at Claudia and asked, "Why did your Demetrius do that to him, honey?"

Claudia sat on the bed and grinned as she told Olivia, "Beaudin killed his love, Liberte, and blinded Demetrius."

Olivia nodded and softly said, "Revenge is best served cold." She smiled and said, "That's from the movie *Kill Bill.*

Claudia stood up, and looking at Olivia, stated, "And cold it will be." She turned and paced the room, and then she turned and told Olivia, "We will find someone close to him, and when we find that person, they will be the one his girlfriend will be sucking on when he sees her as a vampire."

Olivia's eyes brightened as she responded, "Wow, there's no fury as a woman's scorn."

Claudia smiled and asked, "Another movie?"

"Uh-uh. Something that's just a popular saying."

"Oh, well then, someone was hurt badly I see."

"Yeah, you're going to put a dagger in this cop and twist it as you put salt on the wound."

Claudia just smiled and went to Olivia and took her in her arms and kissed her.

Olivia then said, "You're my queen. I'll follow you anywhere."

"My love, we will have to take care of certain things first. First, I will dye my hair brunette and so will you. We will find the crud of this city and get new IDs, and I will contact my associates in Spain to transfer my wealth in these new names. We will lay low for a while. When we feed dear, no more deaths. I will teach you when to stop. We will reside out of Los Angeles so our trail will become cold. We will outfox this detective. Revenge will be, as they say in French, déjà vu." Claudia then petted Olivia's head and again said, "Déjà vu, my love!"

*　　*　　*

Morris and Elizabeth were at her home because Morris felt they would be safer there. They just watched Eyewitness News and Morris switched it off. Elizabeth lay propped up on some pillows on her overstuffed sofa. Her legs and arms had bandages on them from her fall from the car. The wounds were just scratching cuts from rolling on the ground. She also had a bandage on her forehead.

"Honey."

Morris looked at her. He was sitting across from her on a La-Z-Boy chair. He had a bandage on his neck and his fists were scraped from the fight with Marta.

"Yeah, babe," he responded.

"You think that news broadcast will help get them any faster, so we can go on to a normal life?" Her expression showed pain.

Morris grimaced a little and he answered, "Maybe, but not really."

Elizabeth pouted.

"Claudia is probably a smart woman. Both girls will dye their hair and try to get different IDs." He reached over and rubbed her shoulder and said, "If they are real smart, they'll just leave the country." He shook his head and continued, "Or at least get out of LA. She has money to do just about anything."

Elizabeth nodded and said, "Well then, we should be safe, huh?"

Morris shook his head and responded, "I don't know, hon. I'm not taking chances. If you don't mind, I'm staying with you for a while. I'll drive you to work and pick you up. If no bodies show up, then we might be safe. I'll tell you, when I was struggling with Marta. She was exceptionally strong. It was just by luck I got a hand free. She had me, babe. I thought if she bit me, I was a goner."

"Oh, Jason, it wasn't your time. I was freaked out the whole time. That bitch, Olivia, held that chain on me tight. I was so powerless."

Morris nodded and said, "I took out one of her girls, hon. She might want revenge."

They looked at one another and weakly smiled.

CHAPTER 26

SERENITY

THREE MONTHS HAD GONE BY, and it seemed that the vampires had disappeared from the planet, Los Angeles, anyway. The task force had ceased making rounds to the hotels and motels in the county of Los Angeles. The news media had died down and concentrated on the president's policies, police chases, and the weather.

Time had healed the scrapes and bruises, and Morris and Elizabeth became more involved. They decided to live together and found a new place and moved in together. Their quaint two-bedroom home in Sierra Madre was in a quiet neighborhood, and it seemed that life was getting to feel safer, securer, and content for them. Occasionally, Elizabeth would wake up in the middle of the night with a scream, and Morris would console her back to sleep. Morris had a new vehicle and was back to investigating homicide cases. Elizabeth was back at work and was promoted to senior staff member. No dead bodies were reported with depleted blood as the cause of death. Los Angeles continued to have its cool mornings, hot afternoons, and colder nights. Summer was around the corner, and dress codes would become skimpier. Authorities found the abandoned rented vehicle in Riverside, but the trail ended there. Prints were wiped clean. Authorities still did not know the true identity of Olivia.

*　　*　　*

On that horrid night of Elizabeth's abduction, Claudia and Olivia had driven to Riverside. There, they took in with two homeless men, fed on them, and then left them in their tent alive. They covered the windows with foil and slept in a stolen car. Later, they ditched the auto and had taken a bus to Lake Elsinore where Olivia had a cousin. The vampires made up the story that their vehicle had blown its engine and they had walked and were tired. That evening, they left and had taken a bus to San Diego. There, they rented a motel room and bought a used car from a man needing money.

The weather was now getting warmer and people were taking more walks, either in pairs or walking their dogs, and more individuals were jogging and strolling on the beaches. This made the pickings easier for the vampires. They had developed a teamwork style of feeding themselves. They would find a solo individual, Claudia would abduct the prey from behind, cover their mouth with one hand and give the individual a vicious judo chop on the back of the neck. Olivia would the grab the feet and secure them. They would drag the person out of view and then bite into a vein in different areas. They would drink enough to quench their thirst and then drive to a different location and repeat their actions.

This seem to be working for them. An occasional newscast would announce the assault and robbery, but San Diego had many suburbs, they worked them all. After two weeks at the motel, they rented a two-bedroom condo on the Mission Beach. Claudia had Alphonse convert her savings into an alias and he sent her new IDs and passports for her and Olivia. The horse farm was still bringing in money from sales and rentals. European and American movie companies used her horses many times.

In their bedroom, Claudia had Demetrius's portrait on a wall and Marta's eight by ten photo on the dresser to remind her that revenge was still due.

It was eight in the evening now, and the tip of the sun peeked over the horizon of the Pacific Ocean and left a trail of an orange blaze reflecting on the waters. The night air was warm, and the night and sky were clear and inviting. Claudia and Olivia walked the sands near the shore. The small waves lapped on the wet sand and formed foamy suds and then disappear as the waters ebbed back out to sea. The girls were in their bikinis, Claudia in black and Olivia in white. Thin sheer see-through coats hung on them and covered their shoulders and down their bodies. They held their sandals in one hand and a towel in the other as they strolled along, jumping out of the way of dying waves. They appeared to be like a natural loving lesbian couple.

Down the ways, a beach party was going on. It appeared to be of rowdy college students. A large bonfire was fuming high. Sparks and smoke grabbed for the sky and dwindled away quickly. A group of eight or nine young people sat around, mostly drinking beer. A five-gallon keg stood on wooden legs inviting anyone to indulge themselves.

One long-haired boy strummed a guitar and was singing, "Don't know the reason, been here all season. Nothing to show but this brand-new tattoo. But it's a real beauty. A Mexican cutie. How it got here, I haven't a clue." Then most of the crowd sang the chorus, "Wasting away again in Margaritaville, looking for my lost shaker of salt. Some people claim that there's a woman to blame, but I know it's my own damn fault."

One tall thin male got up and yelled, "Hold it, hold it. There's a group of dolphins out there."

Voices roared, "Where?" "Can't see 'em," "How many?" "Too dark."

He pointed and stated, "Look, about a hundred yards to the right of the setting sun."

"Oh yeah," came a voice.

"I see the fins," said others.

Wows and neato were heard.

A tall muscular guy yelled out, "I'm going in, who's coming with me?" no one answered. He removed his T-shirt and ran into the water. The crowd looked and then went back to the bonfire as a woman's voice stated, "That Rick, always the daring stunts."

Olivia and Claudia were about fifty yards away and their keen sense of hearing caught the commotion and all the dialogue. They looked at one another and took off their wraps and ran into the water. They headed toward the disappearing sun which now took its last breath and hid behind the horizon. As they swam, they listened for another swimmer. Soon, they heard him and then then saw the white water as he paddled in the water. He was now swimming toward them.

Olivia spoke out, "Over here, Rick."

He stopped and was treading water and asked, "Who's that? Victoria, is that you?"

Olivia then told him, "Yeah, baby, come here. I'm naked."

"Oh, man, just wait there." He swam quickly toward Olivia and then reached her. She was facing away from him and he said, "I'm here, mama, come here."

Olivia turned around and his face twisted. "You aren't—"

Just then, Claudia attacked him from the rear, one hand on his mouth the other around his chest, pinning one arm to his body. Olivia attacked him from the front and pinned his other arm. Together, Claudia and Olivia kicked their feet to keep them afloat and simultaneously bit into his neck. After two minutes, his struggling ceased, and they drank until they had their fill. Done, they took the body out where the ebb was flowing out, and then they swam back to shore. They gathered their belongings and immediately went to bed and made love.

After twenty minutes, the partiers started wondering what happened to Rick. He was an excellent swimmer. After another half hour, they called for him. They searched the shores and finally called authorities. A coast guard boat and two police boats scoured the sea for Rick to no avail. They combed the waters for three hours and told the college kids that the search would resume in the morning.

The party ended, and they all went home bummed out. The morning news had a brief report on the missing boy, and then the weather and traffic reports were aired.

*   *   *

The body had drifted, and many small fish had nibbled on the corpse as it sank. It then floated north, the remains drifted and tumbled with the tide. The ocean current took the body northward and finally came to shore just south of Seal Beach which was in the county of Los Angeles. The city of Long Beach had jurisdiction and their morgue recovered the body.

Jacob Johnson, they called him J.J. at the morgue, was the examiner and inspected the body when he became aware of an oddity. The body had been in the water for ten to twelve hours. It was tattooed with hundreds of bites and chewed marks, but the texture of the flesh was very limp and rubbery. He cut into the organs and there was no blood in the body. He was puzzled for a moment, and then a light went on in his head. He went to the wall where bulletins were pinned. He grabbed a clipboard and started flipping through them. He pulled out the one he had been looking for. All depleted corpses must be reported to the LAPD Homicide Division immediately. He called the number on the sheet.

"Lieutenant Morris here."

"Uh, Lieutenant Morris, I am Jacob Johnson, a medical examiner here in the Long Beach area."

"Go on."

"Well, you see, this body washed up to shore this morning, and upon examining it, I discovered that there was no blood anywhere in the body. Organs and all were sucked dry."

"Have you determined the cause of death yet?"

"No, sir, that's my next step. You see, the bulletin says to call you immediately."

"Yes, yes. Jacob, go ahead and do what you need to do. I'll be there in half an hour."

"All right, detective. See you then."

Morris scuffled through his desk and then the drawers and found the wooden stakes. He shoved them in a briefcase, put on his jacket, and was gonna leave when Sergeant Oberron stopped him, nodded to him, and asked, "What's going on?"

Morris grimaced and said, "They found a bloodless body in Long beach. It washed up on the shore. Gonna check it out."

Oberron nodded and asked, "You want me to tag along?"

Morris thought a second and said, "Sure, come on."

Oberron got his jacket, and together, they went to the police garage.

While driving on the Long Beach Freeway, Oberron asked Morris, "You still believe they were vampires?"

Morris looked over at Oberron and said, "Did you read the autopsy report on that kid Victor?"

Oberron shook his head no and said, "Not yet."

"That corps had been dead for over three years. What was he doing that night at that party? Emily Cota identified him. You tell me he wasn't one of the undead. That Marta Yamamoto. I emptied my gun in her. She just brushed it off and pounced on me. I stabbed her with a stake. Just like the fuckin' movies, Obie, she died after I used the stake on her."

Oberron grinned and asked, "That's why you brought them sticks, huh?"

"You're damn tootin, man. Them girls are vicious."

"Okay, I'm with you all the way."

Morris put out his hand and Oberron gave him a high five.

Next, Morris pulled out his cell and called Elizabeth.

"Hi, handsome, whadup?"

"They found a body in Long Beach."

Elizabeth's eyes opened wide and she asked, "You on your way there now?"

"Uh-huh."

"You have those things?"

"Uh-huh."

"You be careful, you hear?"

"Uh-huh. Look, if you have to work late and it gets dark, don't leave the building until I get there. You got that?"

"You got that right, handsome."

"Okay, it's not lunch yet so there's plenty of time. I'll see you later."

"Uh-huh."

"Stop saying uh-huh. Love you, bye."

"It really worked out with that mortician doctor, huh?" Oberron asked.

Morris nodded and uttered, "So far." He grinned.

They arrived at the morgue and had to go down the elevator to the morgue.

In the morgue, Morris put on the protective gloves and turned parts of the body this way and that way looking for bite marks. There were plenty of fish bites all over the torso, legs, arms, and face. The neck had human teeth marks on each side of the neck. He found that out after he asked Jacob to do DNA on those wounds.

Morris looked at Oberron and said, "She's back." Then he asked Jacob, "How long do you figure the body was in the water?"

Jacob rubbed his arm and said, "Oh, about ten, twelve hours."

Morris and Oberron simply nodded their heads.

Morris asked Jacob, "Can you or someone take me to the spot the body was found?"

Jacob nodded and got on the phone. After a minute, he told Morris, "Just drive down to Seal Beach. It's about four miles down the coast and look for life guard tower number five. Ruben will be waiting for you."

"Thank you, Jacob. See ya." They all shook hands.

At tower five, Ruben came down from the tower after seeing the detectives in their street clothes. "Hi there, officers. I'm Ruben Ornelas. I'm the guy who found the body."

Nodding, Morris asked, "Where exactly did the body wash up at?"

Ruben pointed straight ahead and said, "Right there. That's where all the driftwood and floating trash washes up, Officer."

Morris squinted in the direction and asked Ruben, "Since that's the gathering spot, where do you believe that debris come from?"

Ruben smiled and said, "That's simple. The flow of the tide comes up from the south, uh, er like San Clemente, Oceanside, you know, like the San Diego area or even Mexico."

Oberron then asked, "If the body was in the water say ten or twelve hours, where do you figure it began its trip up here?"

Ruben closed his eyes a sec and then said, "I'd say the San Diego beaches."

Morris looked at Oberron and they connected. He then looked at Ruben and told him, "Okay, thank you, Ruben. I'll get in touch if I have any more questions. Here's my card. If you can think of anything, call me."

Ruben's eyes widened. "That guy was pretty messed up. Was he murdered or something?" he inquired.

Oberron butted in and told the boy, "We're waiting for the coroner's report."

He nodded, and the detectives left the beach.

Driving home, Oberron mentioned, "Looks like she's out of our jurisdiction, Jason."

Morris gave him an adverse quick look and said, "I don't care, I'm gonna find her."

"Unless she finds you first," Oberron stated, staring straight ahead.

*   *   *

There was no further news about the missing college student that evening, and the vampires were feeling content. Claudia and Olivia were sitting in their patio, reading and viewing the ocean and the walkway that paralleled with the shoreline. Couples would walk by, skate boarders would zoom by, and bicyclist would ride by. Some would wave, some nodded, and a few would say good evening. Local papers informed readers of a gang of muggers in the South Bay area and warned the neighborhood inhabitants to refrain from being outdoors alone at night.

Olivia crumbled up the paper and tossed it aside.

Claudia looked at her and asked, "What is wrong, my love?"

Olivia grimaced and then banged the chair with her hands and said, "I've really allowed myself to get settled here. I feel like I have a home. And because we have to do what we have to do to exist, we may have to move again. The locals are getting leery of us, and they will put pressure on the authorities to stop us." She grabbed onto the chair, straining. "Oh, I'm so mad."

Claudia reached over and soothed her head. "Look, honey, I want to stay here too. We will just go farther out to eat, up to, uh, where is that big Indian casino?"

"Pechanga? In Temecula."

"Yes, Temecula. That's only an hour's drive, babe. After that, there's Lake Elsinore and Corona." Claudia stood up and stamped a foot and continued, "No one is making us move. We will move when we want to."

Olivia got up and they embraced.

Olivia whispered in her ear, "Let's go to that casino, sugar, and get fed. I'm going to fuck your eyeballs out tonight."

Claudia broke a big smile and said, "Hell, I can't wait. I will get us a room there." Olivia hugged her and lifted Claudia's chin, kissed her, and said, "I fuckin' love you."

CHAPTER 27

PECHANGA

T HE LOS ANGELES POLICE ACADEMY was celebrating a huge graduation this evening with awards and medals. Before the announcement of the outstanding rookie, there will be a speaker. The speaker was last year's rookie winner. During the day, there will be workshops from the different fields in police work, homicide, robbery, fraud, vice, juvenile, and forensics. Morris and Oberron will be the speakers at the homicide workshop. It will be an all-day affair followed by a banquet dinner and then the award ceremony. Morris was not aware yet of his assignment.

The celebration site for this gala event was the Pechanga Casino in Temecula. Pechanga was chosen due to their contributions for their sponsorship for the Fallen Officers Family Fund.

Two days before the event, Morris entered his office. Oberron tossed an envelope on his desk. Morris looked up at him as he sat and picked up the envelope.

Oberron stated, "I have one too."

One eyebrow high and a twisted grin, Morris opened the envelope, took out the document, read it, and then dropped it on the desk. "What the fuck?" he exclaimed.

"That's exactly what I said."

"Don't they realize I'm in the middle of a murder investigation?"

Oberron tilted his head side to side and responded, "Yeah, Jason, but the trail has been cold. Sanders was supposed to be the instructor. He's laid up, got into a wreck chasing high school kids racing."

Morris glanced at him, and then he balled up the invite and tossed it in the waste paper basket. "Shit, I heard. Hell, I better call Elizabeth, so she can do what women do when they go to big functions."

*   *   *

It was seven in the evening, and Claudia and Olivia stopped in front of the Pechanga Hotel and allowed the valet to take their car and the porter to carry their luggage. They decided to stay for at least two days. They used false IDs and were now situated in their room.

Sitting out on the patio, Olivia told Claudia, "What a view, honey. There's a whole lot of cars coming in, most of them toward the casino."

Claudia smiled and said, "People like to gamble, sweetheart. Most people want something for nothing. One spin of the wheel and win a small fortune." Claudia stepped behind Olivia. "Gambling, it could be a sickness, like alcoholism and drug addiction."

Olivia turned and took Claudia's hand and told her, "You're my addiction."

Claudia smiled and pulled Olivia up and they embraced and kissed.

*   *   *

Down in the casino were Michael, Carolynn, and Sally. Since meeting up at the LA police station for questioning, the witnesses had kept in contact, mainly it was Sally contacting them occasionally due to her fixation on Carolynn. Earlier today, Sally called Carolynn and asked if they would meet at Pechanga for dinner, since it the site was between their two residences and the fact that Sally likes to play the slot machines and Michael likes to play poker.

As they were finishing up their cheeseburgers and fries facing each other in one of the eateries in the casino, Sally asked them, "Hey, have you guys heard any more about that fiend, Claudia?"

Michael shook his head no, but Carolynn answered, "Well, I've kept in touch with that Sergeant Oberron. He was more polite then the lieutenant, uh—"

"Morris," Michael added.

Sally reached over and patted Carolynn's hand and then walked her finger up her arm and lightly rubbed it. She looked at her and nodded and said, "And…"

Carolynn felt the smooth warmness of Sally's touch and didn't mind the connection. She gave a small smile and told her, "Well, the sergeant told me that there were four of these horrid killers and they found one of them dead."

Sally's eyes widened and her mouth opened. "Dead? What do you mean they found him dead?" she exclaimed.

Michael gritted his teeth as he responded, "Yeah, found him depleted of his blood and his head was cut from his body."

"Ew, no, really?" Sally frowned and asked, "Do they know how many there are?"

Michael nodded and stated, "There were three females. Morris killed one, so now there's two female vampires."

A glow spread through Sally's body. She then rubbed her hands on her thighs. Being across from Carolynn and remembering what it felt like when she was in Samantha's or Claudia's arm, she closed her eyes quickly and then opened them and looked at the couple and said, "If that Claudia Babe is a vampire, I just wonder what it's really all about to be one. I mean, what I've heard is that vampires have all these super powers." She looked at the couple and continued, "Like super strong and the only way you can kill them is with a wooden stake."

Carolynn drearily uttered, "Or slice off their head."

The three innocent souls sat there in silence a moment and then Sally said, "Well, I'm finished."

Both Michael and Carolynn patted their stomachs and said, "Me too."

Sally smiled and said, "Well, I promised Carolynn I'd show her how to play the slots on the penny machines. What do you like to play, Michael?"

Michael shook his head. He then looked up and said, "Well, before I met Carolynn, I used to play poker almost every Friday with the homeboys."

Anxious to get some time alone with Carolynn, Sally stated, "Hey, you're in the right place. They have one-to-two and three-to-five dollar no-limit Texas two-card hold'em poker here."

Michael's face lit up and said, "Hey, hold'em! I could sit in on that. I won't lose more than a hundred dollars though, okay, Hon?"

Carolynn nodded.

Sally told him, "Think positive, dude. You might win tonight."

Both he and Carolynn nodded and smiled.

They decided to meet in three hours at the bar.

Michael went off to the poker room which was in an enclosed area at the back of the casino. Sally and Carolynn searched for two open penny machines that were next to one another. After they found a secluded area at a wall near the rear of the casino, they settled in.

Carolynn sat in front of her machine and Sally instructed her from behind her, leaning her body on Carolynn's back.

Sally told her, "Okay, put in a twenty-dollar bill." Carolynn did so, and the machine made some twirling noises. The monitor turned colors and at the bottom of the screen numbers displayed what she had banked, what she would bet, and what she would win with each turn.

"Okay, see all these buttons with numbers on them?"

"Uh-huh."

"So, one unit is one cent, these buttons allow you to bet all the way to a dollar and twenty-five. Right now, you have four hundred units of twenty-five cents. To start, I would bet a quarter. The more you bet, the more you lose or win."

Carolynn smiled and said, "Twenty-five cents will do right now." She leaned back a little and snugged against Sally's warm body.

Sally then put her hands on Carolynn's shoulders and kneaded them softly and said, "Okay, sugar, I'll be right next door."

Carolynn twisted, rubbed her head on Sally's hands, and said, "That feels nice. Are you a masseuse by any chance?"

Sally grinned and said, "Not professionally, sugar. I do have the touch though. I can give you a *full* body massage. It'll get you all relaxed and warm inside."

"Mm, I'd like that. Just stop before I get excited."

"That's when I apply the finishing touch."

"Oh, that's something to look forward to."

"Yes, it's vital to finish what is started." Sally reached down and squeezed Carolynn's upper arms.

Carolynn turned her head and asked, "Um, you do have that touch. You think you can make money doing it?"

Now Sally reached down and gently rubbed the Carolynn's shoulders and move down and rubbed her chest and the tops of Carolynn's breast and then quickly went up and rubbed her neck and said, "My lovers have never complained. Maybe I could do it for a living."

Carolynn swallowed and stated, "Gee, don't know about love-making with a girl, but a massage sounds wonderful and your touch is a turn on."

Sally kept massaging Carolynn's neck and put her mouth close to Carolynn's ear and she whispered in her ear, "I'll make your body feel things you never imagined."

Carolynn hunched up her shoulders and giggled and then she said, "Okay, here it goes." She pressed a button and pulled the slot machine's arm.

The screen's three roles of symbols rolled up displaying small faces of cartoonish people, assorted colored sevens, a wild card, and jackpot signs. When they stopped rolling, two sevens and a wild card symbol displayed.

"Oh, what does that mean?" she exclaimed.

Sally looked at the screen and said, "You just won one five hundred units, that's five dollars."

"Oh, really." Carolynn jumped out of her seat, turned, said really, and then pecked Sally on the lips. She sat down again, pressing the buttons and pulling the slot machine's arm.

Sally touched her lips with her fingertips and stated, "Hmm, hope you win a million dollars."

Carolynn's expression showed embarrassment, but then she smiled and said, "Me too."

Sally sat down in the adjacent seat and started playing her machine.

*   *   *

Morris had conducted a workshop on investigating procedure in the afternoon and was now waiting in his room for Elizabeth to show up. The awards ceremony and banquet would commence in forty-five minutes. His room was two rooms to the left from the vampire's room. Every two rooms had one extended wall on the balcony, allowing you to only view your neighbor's patio on the right. You had to lean way over to see the other balconies. Morris was sitting out on his balcony, enjoying a scotch on the rocks and a cigar. He looked out at the new assembled golf course and the dark blue sky. The heavens were clear tonight, which allowed the millions of stars in God's universe to give their salutations to the inhabitants of earth. The moon was full and glared down at the green planet as if it waited for the cow to jump over it. Morris laughed to himself as he thought of that old nursery rhyme.

His room door opened. Elizabeth stood there with an overnight bag in one hand and a dress in a plastic in her other hand. "Hey, handsome, nice to see you."

"Hey, gorgeous. You have forty minutes to shower and get ready. That's if there's no interruptions." He smiled devilishly.

She stepped in and laid her things down, took Morris's chin in her hand, and told him, "No dessert after dessert before dinner, honey. I need all those minutes to make a suitable transformation from working girl to prom princess. Get out of my way."

Morris hopped out of her way and went back to the patio.

*   *   *

At that moment, as Morris was leaning over the railing looking out at the world and the people below, Claudia was on her balcony leaning over her railing looking at her world, she could only indulge life in the night so she breathed in the air and let the night surround her. They both turned and looked in the direction of each other's room. At that angle, you really couldn't make out who was on the next two balconies. You had to lean and focus. Just as each of them were going to focus on each other, a couple in the middle room backed into the railing. A man was kissing a woman, she leaned back, so this couple, at the last moment, blocked the view of Morris and Claudia seeing each other.

*   *   *

Claudia felt some disturbing vibrations and sensed danger vibes. She wrapped her arms around herself and snarled and went back inside.

*   *   *

Morris sensed something but wasn't sure. A coldness went through him. With his hands on the rail, he shuddered and shook his head and entered the room and put on the TV.

*   *   *

Claudia went in the room and Olivia was waiting for her. She had on a tight white slacks that caught her delightful curves and a red T-shirt cut above her abs that exposed her flat, hard stomach. Claudia smiled and told her, "Darling, you look scrumptious."

Olivia grinned and stated, "You don't look too bad either, momma." Claudia put up one hand and twirled. Her full-length tight black dress hugged her body. She would surely turn heads.

"Let's go gamble and find dinner, my dear." Claudia said as she nodded for Olivia to follow her.

*   *   *

Morris turned and stopped at the entranceway into the room. Elizabeth was standing there for Morris to say something. The red high heels made her look taller and her hair was teased around her face and cascaded around her shoulders. Her makeup was perfect but the snug, sequin red dress was on her body like a glove. It stopped just below her knees revealing smooth, flawless calves and ankles. With a hand on her hip and a tilted head, she stated, "Well?"

Morris shook his head and took in a breath and finally said, "I will be the envy of every man and every lesbian in the room. Don't get too far from me. Don't want to lose you."

Elizabeth shook her head and said, "You had me at I."

They both simultaneously said, "Jerry Maguire," and laughed.

CHAPTER 28

SALLY

THE AWARDS CEREMONY WAS OVER, and everyone went to their seats in the banquet room. The tables had pitchers of water and coffee with glasses and coffee cups. Baskets of warm rolls and butter were waiting to be eaten. As the guest sat, the waiters and waitresses began to deliver their dinners. The guest had a choice of chicken or beef, a couple ordered a vegetarian plate. As some buttered their rolls, others prepared and ate the small salads. There was a small buzz in the room and plates could be heard being move along with the sounds of knives and forks. The hustle of the workers walking between the tables was the only movement throughout the room.

After dinner, cheesecake for dessert, and coffee, the Los Angeles mayor went to the podium and gave a speech commemorating the police department and praised the training academy that was set next to Dodger Stadium. Now a band went to their instruments sitting behind a curtain on the podium which overlooked the banquet hall. The front of the stage had a squared off wooden tiled area so those wishing to could dance.

The lead singer stepped forward with a mic, he tapped it, and then spoke, "Hello there, officers and detectives. It wasn't me, it was the butler." There was scattered laughs. "I want to congratulate all you young men and women who graduated tonight and who will be arresting me for a DUI later tonight." Again, more laughs. "But really, you guys have a tough job. Risking your lives and making less than them LA senior trash collectors." More laughs. "But anyway, let's have a good time tonight." He turned to the band and stamped his feet and created a tempo. The music blasted the room and a chorus sang, *I shot the sheriff, but I did not shoot the deputy.*

Morris leaned over and told Elizabeth, "Hey, honey."

She turned to face him smiling.

"Cap gave me this nice Cuban cigar. I need to go outside to take a couple puffs. You wanna come with me or listen to the band?"

"Oh, I'll step out with you. I need to walk, I'm a little stuffed. Need some air, baby."

They got up and made their way to the front of the casino.

*   *   *

Claudia and Olivia were sitting at a minimum twenty-five-dollar blackjack table near the roulette table. The seats on each side of them sat a young guy and an older gentleman. The younger guy, Bobby, wore holey jeans and a black T-shirt which had a statement across the chest, "don't worry, everything will be all right." The older man, Henry, wore slacks, and loafers with no socks. His solid black T-shirt was mostly covered by a neat gray blazer.

Bobby placed his four twenty-five-dollar chip on the bet circle and looked at Claudia and asked, "So how long have you two known each other?"

Claudia placed her bet, the same as Bobby's, and answered, "Oh, the last four years. We were in college together, USC."

Henry slightly grinned and cut in and stated, "Oh, my granddaughter is attending there currently. Maybe you have run into her." He placed his hundred-dollar bet.

Olivia had already bet her four chips and cut in, "Hey, you guys. We're here to have some fun. We really don't want to talk about school right now." Claudia nodded.

The pretty dealer dealt the cards, Bobby received a ten, Claudia a seven, Olivia a nine, and Henry a five, and the dealer dealt herself a queen. The next cards were an eight, a three, an ace and a six, and the dealers card went face down.

The dealer looked at Bobby. He had eighteen and he said, "I stay."

She looked at Claudia and she said, "Hit me." The dealer dealt her a ten, that made her twenty. "I stay."

Next, Olivia had twenty and said, "I stay."

Lastly, Henry looked at his cards and said, "I double down, hit me." He received a king, that made it twenty-one. He said, "Nice."

The dealer looked at everyone and flipped over her card. It was a seven that made her seventeen, a mandatory stay amount for dealers. She smiled and said, "Looks like it's a community win here. Good for you, guys."

Picking up her winning, Claudia asked the group, "Anyone want to join me for a breather outside?"

Bobby stated, "I could use a smoke."

Olivia uttered, "Hmm, good idea, Claudia."

Henry slipped off his chair and said, "I don't smoke but some fresh air and your company would be a winning hand."

They all got up and Bobby turned to the dealer and said, "Hope you're still here when we return."

The dealer smiled.

The two naïve men followed the vampires as the demons found their way through the tables and wondering patrons milling here and there in the casino.

*　　*　　*

Sally and Carolynn were at the bar now which was situated in the center of the casino. Sipping on their drinks, Carolynn sat on a stool and Sally stood at her side, rubbing Carolynn's back. Having two drinks, Carolynn was beginning to feel a buzz and enjoyed the fondling of Sally.

Sally was such a manipulator. She massaged Carolynn's neck and asked her, "Hey, let's go do a dobie."

Carolynn turned in her stool, patted Sally's behind, and said, "I'm feeling good right now. Will you take care of me if I get too high?"

Sally grinned and pulled Carolynn off the stool and said, "You're in safe hands with me." She led the way, pulling Carolynn by the hand.

Carolynn uttered, "Those hands are soothing."

Sally remarked, "Hope someday I can give you a full massage."

Carolynn smiled and responded, "Does that include a happy ending?"

Sally turned to face Carolynn and just nodded her head slowly.

*　　*　　*

Morris and Elizabeth were sitting side by side at twenty-five cent slot machines located at the entrance of the casino. Oberron was two seats away.

Morris was interrupted by a waitress, "Sir, would you and your lady friend care for a drink?"

Morris looked at Elizabeth and nodded to her. She shook her head no but said, "Water."

Morris looked at the waitress and said, "Two water."

At that moment, he saw Sally and Carolynn walking toward the exit.

He frowned and nudged Elizabeth. She looked at him and he bobbed his head toward the exit doors. She frowned and then shook her head. Morris realized Elizabeth didn't know the witnesses.

He weakly smiled and told her, "I just saw two of the witness women of the killers walk by."

Elizabeth shook her head and said, "So they might be gamblers." She grinned.

Morris grinned and said, "Yeah but one of them has a boyfriend and he wasn't with them."

Elizabeth stuck out her tongue and wiggled it.

Morris nodded yes and went back to playing.

Outside, the vampires and their escorts sat on the concrete benches and breathed in the cool night air. The two men were on each side of the women.

Finally, Olivia broke the ice and said, "Hey you guys, my room-mate and I are pretty much adventurists." The men looked at her their eyebrows rising. "So we kind of like you, guys. We'd like to have some undisturbed company with you two. Either one of you have a room here?"

Henry stood up and responded, "What a coincidence. The casino has comped me a suite here. My company awards our employ-ees with rooms here."

Now Bobby stood up and said, "Hey, that's so cool. Let's head up there and party."

The girls smiled, nodded, and clapped their hands.

Henry took a breath and said, "The night is young, let's make it a memorial one."

As the vampires stood up and began to follow Henry, Sally and Carolynn were behind a pillar, embracing and kissing. Claudia had put her arm through Henry's arm as Olivia did the same with Bobby.

Sally broke away from Carolynn to get a breath and to sug-gest they go to the vehicle when she noticed the couple walking by and the female was that woman, Claudia, the suspected killer and assumed vampire. She looked at Carolynn and said, "Look, it's the vampire."

Carolynn's hand went to her mouth as she exclaimed, "Oh my God."

Sally then told her, "Go inside and call Lieutenant Morris. Here's his card. I follow them and find out where they are going. They're headed to the hotel right now."

Carolynn nodded and said, "Okay. You be careful."

Sally crept behind them and pretended she was a detective. Carolynn hurried into the casino looking for a phone. As she past Morris's slot machine he called to her.

"Carolynn, what the hell is going on? Where's Michael?"

Carolynn froze, turned, ran over to the detective, and excitedly exclaimed, "Oh, Detective, you need to hurry." Elizabeth leaned over listening. "We've just seen Samantha the vampire, her friend, and some men walking toward the hotel. Michael is playing cards."

Morris grabbed her by the shoulders and exclaimed, "What? Where? Are you sure? Where's Sally?"

Carolynn was nodding her head, trying to follow Morris's questions and then she said, "Sally is following them into the hotel to see where they are headed."

"What? Oh, shit. Okay, look, go find Michael. I'll handle this. Go." Carolynn nodded and then Morris said, "No, here's my phone. Call Oberron and tell him to get some men and meet me at the hotel lobby."

Carolynn's face showed fear, but she nodded and walked away.

Elizabeth was now standing next to Morris. He looked at her and then said, "Babe, come with me. As soon as I find out what room they're in. I'll send you to get Oberron and some men. They'll be in the lobby. We have to stop them before there's more casualties." Elizabeth nodded. "Come on." They walked out and headed toward the hotel.

In the lobby, Morris didn't know where to go. He went to the registration desk and showed his credentials and asked to view the hotel's list of residents on the computer monitor. He was looking at the names, trying to see if there was any clue for him to see where they could be. Elizabeth was looking at the elevator doors hoping Sally would appear as Morris's frustrated expression hardened his face. The lines of names scrolled down the computer screen to no avail.

Elevator doors number two opened and Sally jumped out and ran toward the exit. Elizabeth yelled at her, "Hey, Sally."

Sally halted and turned to see who called her. Morris got up and looked at Sally.

"Sally, what do you have, honey?"

Sally's face broke into a huge smile and she stated, "Detective, what are you, uh, hey, they're in room 9007. Better get up there and save them dudes who are with them."

"Liz, you and Sally, stay here. Oberron will be here shortly. I'll do what I can." Morris told the registry attendant, "Hurry, I need a pass key."

The young and pretty short-haired brunette nodded and went to a drawer and pulled out a card and ran it through some slot and handed it to Morris. The girls went to the doorway as Morris ran to the elevators. While there, he pressed and pounded the up buttons. It felt like forever, but the door finally opened, and Morris jumped in, the doors closed, and up he went.

Elizabeth and Sally talked with one another as they waited for Oberron. He was not in sight yet. Elizabeth panicked, she looked around frantically and then saw Oberron trotting their way. He was slightly puffing as he and two other officers reached the entranceway.

They entered, and Elizabeth shouted to them, "She's in room 9007."

He nodded and waved to the officers to follow him to the elevators. He pressed all the buttons and they waited.

Morris was at the room 9007. he was breathing hard and took out his revolver and tried to listen at the door. He knew every minute counted, he wouldn't wait any longer. He slipped the card into the slot and a small green light came on.

He braced himself and then, as quickly as he could, he turned the door latch and pushed in the door and rushed in, pistol at the ready and yelled, "This is the police! Everyone freeze!"

The view of what he saw stunned Morris. At one side, a tall naked man was standing. He was in the clutches of a nude Claudia. They had been embracing and the interruption had them stop kissing and turned their heads at Morris. Puzzlement covered their faces. To their right stood another younger man all entwined in the clutches of a lovely woman, both were nude. They also turned to view the intruder. They were confused and had perplexment on their faces.

Claudia's expression quickly turned to anger, and she scowled at the detective, revealing her deadly teeth and her hands went up in a clawlike maneuver. Olivia mimicked Claudia and hissed at Morris.

The men overcame the initial shock of the intruder and roughly stated, "What the fuck?"

Bobby screamed out, "He has a gun."

Claudia pushed Henry away and he fell on the bed, still in shock. He had two bite marks on his neck, he sat there, and placed a hand on the wound. He frowned and was still confused.

Claudia the said, "I'll take care of Lieutenant Morris."

Bobby expressed, "He's a cop?" And then felt his neck and saw blood on his hand and said, "What the hell is going on?" Olivia punched him and he collapsed to the floor.

At that moment, Claudia lunged at Morris. He fired once, twice, and a third time. The first bullet hit Claudia on her right shoulder, the force stopped her in her tracks. She uttered, "Oaf." The second round struck her in her stomach, her hand went to the wound, blood seeped through her fingers as she screamed, "Shit!" She took a step toward Morris. The third shot hit her in the middle of her chest. The impact knocked her back and she fell back on her butt, a spray of blood shot out, but then all the wounds stopped bleeding.

Henry came to his senses and said, "Are you a madman?"

"I'm here to save your fuckin' lives! Get out of here, you two!"

Henry was confused and slipped off the bed and was trying to stand when Olivia quickly went to him and slugged him on the jaw. He fell eagle spread on the bed.

Claudia turned and smiled. "Your measly attempt will not kill me, you imbecile. I won't kill you Lieutenant. I'm going to turn your lover into one of us. Live with that. Get him, Olly."

Olivia pounced toward the detective and he fired four, five, six rounds at the on-coming demon. The bullets hit her all over her torso, each round knocked her back a step. Claudia's eyes bulged, and she lunged at him. At that moment, Oberron and three officers burst into the room. They all started firing their weapons at both fiends. The vampires were hit several times and the force knocked them back. They screamed at the assault, the shots continued, and the vampires were knocked backward toward the balcony. Claudia took Olivia's hand and took her to the rail of the balcony, and then holding Olivia's hand, they jumped over the side.

Morris and Oberron ran to the railing and looked down. They didn't see any sign of the vampires.

Morris exclaimed, "They may be headed to the casino, we need to go after them."

With that, the detectives ran out of the room.

Oberron yelled to the officers, "One of you stay here, call an ambulance. You two, come with us."

One officer stated, "Jesus, the bullets didn't stop them."

Waiting for the elevator, Morris exclaimed, "They're not humans."

Going down in the elevator, an officer scratched his head and asked, "Not humans. What are they, aliens?"

Oberron turned his head sideways and uttered, "They're vampires."

Morris slightly grinned.

The other officer asked, "Jesus, like in the movies?"

The elevator stopped, the doors opened, and as Morris stepped, out he said, "Exactly. Come on, let's find them."

The four policemen trotted over to the casino.

*   *   *

As the vampires landed on the grass, they hit hard, their legs broke, and they rolled away into the flower garden. Their legs were all twisted, and bone perturbed through the flesh. They didn't feel pain, but they couldn't stand or walk. They lay there hidden in the brush. Claudia grabbed Olivia and pulled her over and they embraced on the ground. As they hugged their legs began to heal. In minutes, they stretched their legs. Olivia was about to stand when Claudia pulled her down and pointed to the hotel entrance. The four officers came running out.

Claudia then got up and said, "Come, let's get some clothes and feed ourselves." They sneaked around the hotel and looked up at the second story. They saw a room that had the lights on and silhouettes on the sheer drapes. They climbed up and went over the railing and peeked in.

A male was sitting on the bed watching TV. He had a drink in his hand and then the bathroom door opened, and a woman stepped out in a bathrobe and they heard her say, "I'll be ready in a jiffy, honey." She playfully opened her robe and closed it and said, "You win tonight, baby. This is all yours." She smiled and went back int the bathroom.

Claudia tried the sliding door but it wasn't locked. She slowly pulled it open enough to squeeze through. She got down on all fours and crept into the room and then she pounced on the unsuspecting gentleman. The force knocked him back, knocking the drink from his hand, it hit the wall and splattered. Claudia immediately covered his mouth and embraced him and bit into his neck. His arms were waving, and he tried to kick his feet to no avail.

As Olivia opened the bathroom door, she viewed a naked woman examining herself in the mirror and she exclaimed, "What's all the racket, hon?" and then she screamed, "Oh God!" as Olivia jumped on her. They fell to the floor, and the woman tried to fight this maniac off, Olivia was just too much for her. As the fight subsided, the only sound in the room was the slurping of vampires feeding themselves.

The vampires placed the corpses under the bed and went through the woman's clothes and the man's belongings. His hotel valet ticket was on the dresser. They decided to spend the day there and leave the next evening. They placed a "do not disturb" sign on the door and waited. Sirens could be heard and flashing red lights reflected everywhere. Any odd noise made them leery. For a while, they sat on the bed hugging each other.

*　　*　　*

Outside, the grounds were being searched, and all departing vehicles were stopped and inspected, even the delivery trunks were being inspected. The casino had uniformed policemen walking through the aisles with snapshots of Claudia. The drawing of Olivia was not a good portrait of her except for her flowing blonde hair.

CHAPTER 29

THE LA AND SAN DIEGO police joined in the manhunt for the vampires at the Pechanga grounds. With dogs, they searched the parking lots and then went over to the golf course. Night-lights were turned on and the roads in and out of the casino had roadblocks. They began knocking on the room doors and searched the room if no one was there. When someone answered the door, a policeman would see if the individuals were appropriate and okay and then they'd go to the next room. When they arrived at the room where the vampires were, Olivia answered the door wearing a platinum blonde wig she found in the dead woman's belongings.

Olivia opened the door, smiled, and asked, "What's all the commotion about, officers?"

Her low-cut blouse revealed smooth mounds and the cleavage gave an attempting invitation.

First officer, "Sorry to disturb you, ma'am, we're looking for a couple of renegades. Have you seen or heard anything unusual tonight?"

Olivia smiled and said, "Except for you guys flashing your lights and stuff, why no, officer. We're just here entertaining one another, if you know what I mean." She opened the door wider and they saw a man standing in the balcony smoking a long cigar.

Olivia told them, "It's against the law to smoke in the rooms, you know."

The second officer tapped his buddy's shoulder and said," Come on, Rick, there's a thousand rooms in this hotel."

First officer tipped his hat and said, "Sorry for disturbing you, ma'am. Have a nice night." They walked away, and Olivia closed the door.

Claudia came in and disrobed the man's suit and the hat she had stuffed her hair into. She stubbed the cigar and said, "Ew, I don't see how they enjoy these nasty things."

Olivia pulled her close and said, "Come here and make love to me, you beautiful monster."

Claudia smiled, and they embraced and fell on the bed.

*   *   *

Morris and Oberron were seated in the huge command post van. The van was littered with computers, monitors, and communication systems covering the walls. Elizabeth, Sally, Carolynn, and Michael were waiting in the hotel manager's office with two uniformed policemen.

The manhunt went on until three in the morning. There was no news about the two renegade vampires. Henry and Bobby were examined at the nearby hospital and released. They would never forget that night's experience. The dogs had lost the scent of Olivia and Claudia in the grounds by the hotel dwelling.

Oberron looked at Morris and said, "What the fuck? did they turn into bats and fly away?"

Morris chuckled, nodded, and responded, "Shit, maybe. We don't know what they can do. I put numerous slugs into those bitches, and they kept coming, and then you guys filled them with lead that would bring down an elephant."

Oberron nodded and told him, "That stake you shoved into Marta seems like the only way."

Morris glanced at his partner and mumbled, "Yeah."

By four in the morning, everything went back to normal at the Pechanga hotel and casino. The police department gathered all their equipment and the freeways were cluttered with police vehicles, some headed towards LA and the rest going to San Diego. Morris was driving home as Elizabeth napped in her seat, her head on Morris's shoulder.

* * *

Morris didn't get to his office until three in the afternoon the following day. Oberron was at his desk. They looked at one another and nodded hello.

Morris went to the coffee counter and was about to pour himself some coffee when Oberron told him, "I wouldn't do that if I were you. It's been there all day. It's mud by now."

Morris lips clenched and he went to his desk when Oberron told him, "Captain wants to see you."

Morris frowned and nodded and went to the captain's office.

Captain Jeffreys nodded at a chair and told him, "Sit down, Lieutenant."

Morris sat and crossed his legs and waited.

The captain was looking at a commentary lying on his desk and stated, "I got a flimsy report you faxed from home, I guess, regarding the proceedings you and about two hundred officers last night."

Morris gave a weak grin and answered, "Yeah, yeah it was late, and I thought you should see something about the force's undertakings in trying to capture the blood-depleted killer, he-he. I'll make an official report today."

Captain Jeffreys shook his head and said, "Wait on that. I got a lot of details from Oberron."

Morris gave a half grin and nodded.

The captain pointed at the report and stated, "It states here, you and three other officers practically unloaded your weapons on two women, and they just jumped off the ninth story balcony and just disappeared."

Morris's face grimaced and he uncrossed his legs. He leaned forward and said, "These women are not human."

The captain nodded and said, "Not human?" He shook his head and asked, "Well, what are they?"

Morris took in a breath, he straightened up, and responded, "Sir. Did you read my report on the Marta Yamamoto killing and the young man's decapitated body that we found? His named was Victor something."

"Yes, I just returned from vacation and Captain Lewis briefed me on all the turmoil that's been going on. Fantastic stories. But, putting all that flair aside, with the Yamamoto girl, I gathered you were out of ammunition and used what was available to defend yourself. And that beheading, wasn't that incident just the result from some cult or devil worship group?" The captain sipped his coffee.

Morris shook his head and explained, "Sir, what we are dealing with"—he took in a breath and straightened his tie—"is something out of the supernatural." The Captain frowned as he listened. "These women are vampires."

Captain Jeffreys shuddered and asked, "Vampires? You expect me to go to the commissioner and tell him that Bela Lugosi is out there, sucking blood from the public?"

Morris nodded and answered, "You tell the commissioner anything you want. I'm just telling you what we are combating against."

"Lieutenant, this is outrageous. I need something concrete."

"Yeah, okay. Ask the men who were with Oberron and ask Oberron. You'll get the same story. They weren't two individuals high on PCP and immune to bullets. Them old stories don't hold water anymore."

"Lieutenant, go and get these killers. Do what you have to do. Don't panic the public whatever you do. Keep me informed, I cannot disclose a story about vampires. Take Oberron with you. Bring me some results."

Morris got up and left the office frustrated. Before going back to his office, he went to the armory and spoke with Trinidad Heinz, the police weapons expert and maker of hand-held weapons.

As they spoke Trini told him, "Yeah, those would be easy. I have these six-foot wooden dowels and can cut down and sharpen them on the leigh. What are these for? A new competition game?"

Morris nodded and said, "Something like that. Can I get them I a couple of hours?"

"Sure, no problem."

Morris shook his hand and walked out. Trini stood there scratching his head.

* * *

Sally, Carolynn, and Michael were comped a room at Pechanga and slept in a two-bedroom suite. They were pretty exhausted, and they slept most of the following day. It was now five in the afternoon and the trio were eating in one of the smaller restaurants; the hotel has twelve restaurants. Sally and Carolynn kept their attraction with one another private. Sally was waiting for an opportunity to jump on Carolynn's bones.

Michael was too naïve to notice anything going on between the girls. The early evening was warm, and Sally suggested they use up the free time left by hanging out by the pool.

At six, they were lying lazily on lounge chairs, watching youngsters playing around in the pool, they were drinking mai tais, Sally had them laughing. Michael was getting buzzed and the girls milked their drink, hoping they'd get a chance to get it on.

* * *

Claudia and Olivia were all rested up and ready to go home. They used their female prey's belongings to dress themselves. They thought they'd leave Pechanga right after the night sky shed its stars. Olivia looked down the hallway and saw one of the maids pushing a cart down the hall. She appeared to be Hispanic and was a little overweight. Olivia nodded her head for she knew that this woman would be enough for her and Claudia to fed on and be well for another day.

Olivia waved to her and called out, *"Señora, Señora, viene aqui."*

The maid weakly smiled and left her cart and walked over to the vampire's doorway.

Olivia smiled and told her, *"Como se abre el seguro?"*

The mad smiled and responded, *"Oh, es muy sencillo, mira,"* and she walked in and Claudia and Olivia attacked her. When they were done with her, they left the body on the floor and called valet to have the dead man's vehicle put out front. They left and placed with the "do not disturb" sign on the outside door handle. The two demons left the room, and as they walked to the awaiting auto, Sally and Carolynn were headed to their room. Michael had fallen asleep in the lounge chair. The two couples passed each other, and then Sally's mouth opened and she tried to speak.

Carolynn looked at her and hunched her shoulders. Sally's eyes bulged and she pointed. Carolynn followed Sally's finger, and when she saw the vampires getting into the car, she ran to the registration desk and hollered, "Give me a phone, give me a phone. The vampires!" she pointed out to the exit.

The vampires didn't notice the commotion and drove away.

*   *   *

Morris was about to leave the office when his cell phone rang. "Morris here."

"Lieutenant, the bitches are leaving the hotel."

Morris frowned, he looked at his phone and said, "Who's this?"

"It's Carolynn, I'm still at Pechanga, and I just saw them vampires leave the hotel."

"Damn, they were there the whole time, Shit. What kind of vehicle were they in?"

"Look, the hotel has that info. I'll let them give it to you."

"Fine, put them on."

Five minutes later, Morris was at the police switchboard, giving the make and model of the vampires car.

"They should be on the Fifteen going south but have some choppers search the north-bound lane as well. I'll be with you guys shortly."

Morris and Oberron were now on the roof, waiting for a helicopter to pick them up in order to pursue the demons.

Ten minutes later, they were flying over Los Angeles in a southeast direction, catching up to Air-Mobile One. Air-Mobile One had identified the late model BMW heading south on the 15 Freeway which led to San Diego.

Morris informed Oberron, "Them beaches drift everything to LA beaches, you know."

Oberron nodded and said, "That puts another piece into the puzzle."

The pilot handed over a pair of earphones to Morris and said, "There's a call for you from the dispatcher."

Morris took the phones and put them on, "Yo, this is Lieutenant Morris."

"Lieutenant Morris, we got a call from security from the Pechanga resort." Morris frowned and said, "Yeah, go ahead."

"There's been three more bodies found in one of the rooms."

Morris grimaced and said, "Hell, three? get them bodies to an LA examiner before the San Diego people get wind of it. Any IDs yet?"

"Two visitors and a maid. The maid was a fresh body. She was still warm when her floormate found her. We'll get the bodies to LA, that's a roger, Lieutenant. Good hunting tonight."

Morris removed the headphones and Oberron nodded to him.

Morris shook his head slowly and told Oberron, "We gotta get them this time, Sarge, they just found three more bodies at the hotel."

Oberron took on a repulsed look and commented, "The bitches were hiding in a room, huh?"

Morris nodded, "Yeah, and we were combing the entire countryside. Damn."

"Them vampires are either smart or lucky."

Morris displayed a weak smile as he said, "A little of both, man. A little of both."

*   *   *

After Carolynn informed the hotel management of Claudia and Olivia's departure, Sally went to her car and was gonna try to catch up to them. She wanted to see what happened to the vampires. Carolynn refused to accompany her and went to go find Michael.

Sally took a chance and flipped a coin. Heads, north and tails, south. The coin landed on tails.

*   *   *

Olivia kept looking behind to see if any police were following them. she advised Olivia, "Just drive the speed limit. We don't want to be pulled over for anything."

Olivia grinned and responded, "You gonna be a, mother hen, baby?"

"You are in the big game now, Olivia. We have to anticipate their moves and be ready to countermove."

Olivia frowned, she looked over at Claudia, and said, "We are going to make it, baby, we are going to make it. Once we get over into Mexico, we'll be home free."

Claudia nodded and responded, "Yes, I've heard that Mexico is pretty open. Money will knock down walls for you."

"You know what? I knew there was a reason for me to take Spanish in high school. I speak it pretty good."

Claudia smiled and said, "So do I, my pet, and French, German, and some Russian. We can go anywhere we want."

Olivia said, "I love your pretty ass, Claudia."

Claudia smiled and said, "It's yours, my pet, anytime."

*   *   *

The helicopter above kept behind the vampire vehicle, avoiding suspicion.

"Air-Mobile Seven, this is Air-Mobile One. Your package has exited the 15 south on California 117, Oceanview Avenue and has headed west, over."

"Air-Mobile One, this is Air-Mobile Seven. Received coordinates, keep informed, over."

Ten minutes later, "Air-Mobile Seven, this is Air-Mobile One. Package has reached destination, confirm address, 1219 Alta Vista Road, Mission Beach."

Morris's pilot confirmed the address and handed the note to Morris who looked at it and put it in his pocket. He then opened the overnight bag and took out four neatly detailed wooden stakes. Each one had moisture resistant tape at the handle while a plastic cap covered the honed tip.

Air-Mobile One returned to base to refuel.

Morris looked at Oberron intently and handed some stakes to him and told him, "Your forty-five will stun them for a moment. You need to shove one of these into their hearts."

Oberron swallowed and stated, "It's going to be a hand-to-hand combat, huh?"

Morris squinted his eyes and advised Oberon, "This is the plan. When we find them, fill them with lead and then in that moment of nil, plunge one of these babies into them." He looked at Oberron and smiled.

Oberron nodded and responded, "Do we get overtime for this shitty detail?"

"Not even a medal," Morris uttered.

The helicopter began its decent and landed atop a San Diego Police substation. A black SUV vehicle was waiting for them. They put their gear in the vehicle, and Oberron drove to the culprits' dwelling.

*   *   *

The wind from the shore were not as gentle as the previous nights. Stars glittered, and the half-moon shed its faded yellow gleam on the waters below. The vampires arrived at their picture-perfect bungalow set on the sandy shore, fifty yards from where moderate waves lapped onto the shoreline. As the waters ebbed back to the mother lode, small sand crabs scuttered to find shelter. Olivia parked their stolen BMW on the side of the dwelling and covered it with a heavy tarp.

Inside their home, Claudia told Olivia, "We are fed, we have the night to do as we please. What do you wish to do, my love?"

Olivia took a breath and clapped her hands together and said, "Oh Claudia, I would love to go someplace that has music and be in your arms and dance the night away."

Claudia's head went up and down as she agreed and smiled. "Oh, Ollie, you are going to be the love of my life. Come, let's change and make the men and the women want us."

*　　*　　*

Sally was driving down the coast and was ready to turn around and go back home when a brisk wind came through the area. The wind blew the tarp off the stolen vehicle just as Sally was driving by. She saw the car and she parked down the road and sneaked toward the quaint bungalow. As she got to the house, she crept to a window and peeked in. Olivia was in the middle of the living room dancing to the music from a radio. She was clad only in skimpy panties and bra. She had that blooming teenage body, firm pointed breast, a solid round butt and flawless limbs. She was singing alone with the tune of "You're More Than a Woman to Me" by the BeeGees.

This scenario aroused Sally. Then Claudia entered from the bathroom. Her hair all teased up and she was totally nude. She accompanied Olivia in the disco steps.

Sally became really turned on. She kept staring at the disco couple, and she started to rub herself. At this point in time, she thought, *God, there are having fun. Being like them may be exciting, they can have anyone they want.* She turned and sat on the floor and recalled her episode with Claudia and how sensual and sexual the ordeal was. She remembered that she was at the edge of an atomic orgasm when she blanked out.

She whispered to herself, "I want that."

The music ended, and the DJ blabbed about some contest. One of them turned it off and Sally got up and peeked in again. The women had gone into the bedroom and began dressing. Sally sat again and thought on how to approach the vampires.

Finally, after fifteen minutes, the female demons walked into the living room and admired one another. Olivia had on a short black shirt and black sleeveless blouse with a low neckline and black patent leather high heels. Claudia wore ad all-red short skirt tonight that revealed smooth knees and her loose-fitting blouse allowed her firm breast to jiggle.

They faced each other and held their outstretched hands. They looked at each other with admiration.

The door suddenly slung open and Sally stood there, legs apart and hands on her hips.

Olivia gave a short scream and Claudia took a defense stance and moved her head side to side waiting for enemies to attack.

Sally exclaimed, "It's only me, girls. Don't fret."

Both vampires had puzzled expressions as Claudia asked, "My pretty little Sally, what is the reason for this unexpected intrusion? Perhaps you miss me?"

Sally took a step inside and said, "Perhaps."

Claudia smiled.

"Don't try anything funny." Sally held out her hand with her cell phone and claimed, "I've been in touch with Lieutenant Morris and once I press send, your address will be sent to him. He's driving somewhere nearby now, waiting."

Olivia's face exhibited fear and she looked at Claudia. Claudia squinted her eyes staring at Sally and then she asked, "What is it you really want?"

Sally took in a breath and told them, "I want to be your day keeper."

Both Claudia and Olivia frowned. "Hmm, and what does that consist of, my dear?"

Sally relaxed some. She stepped in some more and shut the door and explained to them, "I will take care of all the daytime stuff. Travel arrangements, hotels, motels, and inns reservations. I'll make sure you are not bothered in the daylight hours."

Claudia's left eyebrow rose. She took on a serious face and probed her, "And what do you get?"

Sally smiled widely and expressed, "I want to join you in your orgies. I will be your third leg that handles all that you cannot, and I will learn how to pleasure both of you."

Claudia straightened her posture and stretched her neck. She then stepped back and turned to Olivia to face her and softly spoke, "What do you think, my pet? You will be part of the decision making?"

Olivia turned her head to view Sally, and then turned around and told Sally, "Take off your clothes."

Sally frowned. She hesitated and then she took off her clothes and stood there in her white Vans. Sally was petite but firm and very cute in all areas.

Olivia then said, "I like the idea."

Claudia then said, "It's settled then. We will be the Three Musketeers. Come here, my dear."

Sally ran to them and they embraced her.

"We are going out to celebrate! We must find something for you to change into. Come with me, dear, to the bedroom," Claudia said.

CHAPTER 30

MORRIS AND OBERRON WERE CLOSE to the address of the vampires. They had stopped for a Starbucks coffee to keep them alert. A task force team was prepared to advance on the dwelling immediately when summoned. They were stationed one block from the address.

Morris saw a different vehicle parked in front of the address and nudged Oberron. Oberron nodded and they passed the home and pulled over and parked. Morris now remembered that the car parked there was Sally's.

"That's Sally's car. What the fuck is she doing here?" \

Oberron hunched his shoulders.

With a frown, Morris said, "Aw, come on."

The officers then went to the trunk and prepared themselves. They removed their jackets and slipped on these sweaters that had turtle necks that contained meshed material like the ones used by English knights. They also put on belts that had loops for the wooden stakes. They put on their jackets, checked their weapons, and Morris picked up the automatic shotgun. They sneaked down to the dwelling and braced themselves against a wall.

Morris took out the walkie-talkie and whispered, "Widow-Maker One, you ready to advance?"

There was a quick squelch noise and then, "This is Widow-Make One, all set. Give us the word."

"Widow-Maker One, hold on." Morris signaled to Oberron.

Oberron crept up to the window and peeked in. Oberron shook his head and said, "Looks like nobody is home."

Morris grimaced and stood up and looked in. He signaled Oberron to go to the rear of the bungalow, Oberron nodded.

Morris went to the front door, braced himself and kicked the door open and yelled, "This is the police, everyone lay on the floor!"

There was complete silence. Oberron came in from the kitchen shaking his head. They searched the small bungalow and found no trace of the vampires.

"Fuck, where'd there go, partner?" Morris asked.

Oberron hunched his shoulders as he picked up a small pair of jeans and kicked away a pair of white vans, "Maybe Mexico. There's a bunch of scattered clothes in the bedroom."

Morris nodded and then he called the task force team, "Widow-Maker, this is papa. False alarm. No bandits. Go home."

"This is Widow-Maker. That's roger, papa. Over and out."

Morris slammed the device on the coffee table and let it go.

Oberron put his hand on Morris's shoulder and said, "Hey, man, they'll show up again. We'll get 'em."

Morris shook his head and said, "Aw, hell, let's go home." Oberron nodded and Morris looked down to pick up the walkie-talkie and saw a local phone directory book on the table. It was open and something was underlined.

He picked it up and read it, "Captain Smith's Dine and Dance." He looked at Oberron and said, "Feel like dancing?"

Oberron took the book, saw the underlined script, and said, "Let's boogie."

They hurried out the door and were driving down the coast.

*　　*　　*

Claudia was sitting at a table watching Olivia and Sally dance. The DJ was playing Under the Moonlight and Olivia and Sally were dancing the swing. There were about six or seven couples on the dance floor and it looked like a scene from Dick Clark's *American Bandstand.* The bar and grill had a large picture window at the rear of the nightclub which viewed the dark sandy beach and the ocean. Small waves rolled over on the shoreline making the wave ends form foam that turned a fluorescent orange hue caused by the ginger moonlight. A big mirrored ball twirled from the ceiling, producing tiny silver spots throughout the room. The bar was upholstered in an aqua-blue front and the long wall mirror had Christmas lights all around it. The DJ was a hi-looking Black man who, between tunes, had commentary full of one-liners and witticisms. Captain Smith's Dine and Dance was a fun place to be in. The dining section on the other side was half-full of couples and small groups celebrating a birthday, a farewell, or a promotion. The dance section was almost at its limit. Tonight, the vibes in the club were from cheerful to ecstatic.

The detectives rolled in and parked in a handicap slot. Oberron placed the official LA City plaque on the windshield, Morris looked at him with a "really" look. Oberon just hunched his shoulders. There were two swinging front doors also upholstered in aqua, and there were diamond-shaped windows on each door. As they got to the front, the club the doors swung open and the detectives jumped back, reaching inside their jackets, as two young men exited the bar and grill. They went to the sidewalk and lit up cigarettes.

The detectives looked at one another and smiled. Then Morris looked through a window, the lighting was vague except for the bar section, all the tables had a small blue glass bowl with a lit candle flickering its radiance, causing shadows on faces.

Morris looked at Oberron and told him, "Can't make out shit from here. Maybe you should go around back. I'll give you a minute. You're packing right and have the stakes?"

Oberron produced a thin smile and pulled away the sides of his jacket, revealing the stakes and his forty-five in its shoulder holster.

Morris nodded and then jerked his head and Oberron walked around back. Morris pushed the door open into a small hallway. The walls had blinking colored lights around several posters on the walls. He waited for his eyes to get accustomed to the dark setting and walked to the bar and stood at one end with a view of the whole room. Through the dimness of the flickering candles, he could only make out the chest portion of individuals sitting there. He waited and then he saw Oberron at the other end of the nightclub. He was also scanning the room. He seemed to have a better view. Oberron signaled Morris.

He held both hands up with two fingers pointing down and moving his fingers back and forth, thus indicating two people dancing.

Morris nodded and put his palm up, signaling Oberron to wait and then a woman stood next to him and said, "Jason, what in the world are you doing here?"

At first, Morris was caught by surprised and uttered, "Uh, wha, oh, gee, Susanna. My God. Hi there." He looked around and saw Oberron nodded to him. Susanna was a girl he dated in high school.

Susanna looked at him up and down and remarked, "Well, you're looking as good as ever. You seemed to have put on a few extra pounds though." The stakes made him look bulky.

"Uh, yeah, listen, I'm kind of working right now and—"

"Oh, that's right. I heard you're a big-time detective in the city of LA."

Morris took on a serious face and explained to her, "Susan, there are a couple of murderers in here. My partner and I are gonna apprehend them. There may be some trouble. I advise you to step outside for now."

Susanna's eyes widened, and her eyebrows arched, and she shook her head, and said, "Murders, here? I can't leave. I own the place. I...I—"

Morris cut her off by putting her hand on her mouth and said, "Hey, maybe you can help me."

She stared at him, her face white with anticipation and fear, but she nodded quickly.

Morris calmly explained to her, "Look, so none of your patrons gets hurts and sues no one," Susanna nodded some more, "in about five minutes, turn on all the lights, turn off the music, and announce that there has been a fire threat drill ordered by the fire department and that everyone should calmly leave. Can you do that?"

"Yeah, yeah, uh-huh. Oh my God. Murderers here, my mother was right, I should have gone into real estate." She grinned and said, "And made a killing."

"Jesus, Susanna, still a court jester."

"What are you doing after the arrest, Jason? I'm divorced you know."

Morris quickly looked her over and she still had a great shape. He shook his head quickly and said, "Sorry, it's inviting, but I'm engaged. Look, five minutes, okay?" He put up his hand with five fingers extended.

Susanna gave a grim smile and nodded. Morris went over to Oberron and told him the plan. Then they both went out front and waited.

Morris spoke to Oberron, "When they come out, there's two we have to worry about. I'm gonna tackle Claudia and you cuff her and then we'll both jump the other one. Sally is not a vampire threat, yet. What she's doing here, only heavens knows.

*   *   *

Claudia, Olivia, and Sally were now seated and were talking among themselves.

Sally then questioned Claudia, "Who in here would you like to do?"

Claudia smiled and said, "That big redhead with the white shorts. She looks healthy enough to feed Olivia and me."

Olivia nodded and said, "I like that tall handsome blond guy sitting two tables over. He has big arms."

Sally then said, "Claudia, you owe me a dance. I hope they play a slow one."

Then the DJ put on a tune, it was a slow love number. "*Kiss me each morning, for a million years, hold me each evening by your side.*"

Sally grabbed Claudia's hand and said, "Come on, they're playing our song."

Claudia smiled and took Sally's extended hand. They got to the dance floor and Sally placed her arms around Claudia's neck and laid her body on Claudia's chest. Claudia had her arms around Sally's waist, and they swayed to the tempo of the tune, "*Sweeten my coffee with a morning kiss. Soften my dreams, with your sigh…*" Then Olivia got behind Sally and put her arms around both of them, they swayed, "*Tell me you love me for a million years. If it doesn't work out, if it doesn't work out, then you can tell me goodbye.*"

Then, suddenly, all the lights went on and the music stopped. There was a loud static sound from a microphone. From the bar, holding a microphone, Susanna announced, "Please, everyone, do not panic. I say again, do not panic. Walk out slowly through the front door. This is a fire drill ordered by the fire department." Ahs and ohs rang out from the crowd. "Just comply, exit, and then we can get back to dancing."

A few screams were heard and oh-nos sprang up along with oh-shits as chairs scraped the floor and drinks were knocked over. Susanna went on, "Again, do not panic. Everything is under control. Use the front door, please."

The patrons were headed toward the front door. It bottlenecked at the entrance and got crowded. There was grumbling and words flaring.

Claudia grabbed Olivia's and Sally's hands and said, "The hell with this, come on." She led them to the back door. When they got there, it was chained up and locked.

"All right, Olivia, just be ready to fight. Sally, you run and get the car if this is a trap. We may have to go to Mexico tonight." The girls nodded.

Morris, Oberron, and the security guard were out front. Oberron and Morris on either side of the door, the security guard stood in the middle, shining his flashlight in the people's eyes and then telling them to move to the side.

Finally, the trio emerged, Claudia was ahead of the group and the light blinded her for a second. Morris jumped at her legs. She somehow sensed the danger and jumped up high, Morris went under her but grabbed on to Olivia's ankle. She fell over and Morris scrambled on top of her. Oberron managed to get her handcuffed.

The crowd of patrons began screaming and scattering.

Sally ran to their vehicle.

Claudia then picked up Oberron and tossed him against the club's doors. They gave, and he rolled back into the club. Morris rolled on the ground and pulled out his revolver and emptied the gun on Claudia. She stumbled back and fell to the ground. Morris flipped out the cartridge and put in another one. Olivia had gotten up and stretched her hands apart, the chain stretched and then broke. She then lunged at Morris and had him by the neck and was choking him. He managed to slip out a stake and he shoved it into her stomach. She screamed and let go of Morris. She stepped back, trying to pull the stake out. Morris shook his head and lunged at Olivia with another stake, this time he went straight to her heart.

Her mouth opened wide, her eyes bulged, she fell back, and landed on her butt and then closed her eyes and fell backward, dead.

Claudia yelled, "No! No!" She looked at Morris and with rage and fury. She pointed and said, "You! You!" and sprang at him.

Morris took out a stake, but Claudia knocked it away from him. She grabbed him and shook him like a rag doll.

"You'll be sorry, you'll be sorry!" She held him helpless. Then, she opened her mouth wide, showing her glowering fangs. As she came down to his neck, Oberron came out the doors and threw a stake at the demon. It hit her on her upper arm and stuck there, blood spurted out.

She screamed and released Morris. he slumped to the ground and she pulled the stake out and turned to face Oberron. He had his forty-five in one hand and a stake in his other hand.

Just then, Sally stopped in front of the club, honked the horn and yelled "Claudia, come on, let's go."

Claudia looked at Oberron then looked at Morris, and then threw the stake at Oberron. He ducked, the stake stuck in the door. Claudia ran to the vehicle. Morris got to his feet and ran after her. As she got to the door, Sally kicked it open and moved to the passenger side. Claudia jumped in and sped away. Morris emptied his revolver at the speeding vehicle.

Oberron joined him and they ran to their car. When they got there, the two left sides of the vehicle's tires were slashed.

Oberron went to the police radio and called in an all-points bulletin on the getaway vehicle. They looked at each other and Oberron said, "We got one."

* * *

Driving up the highway and then going in and out of neighborhood streets, Claudia finally slowed down and she glanced over to Sally and smiled. "You did well, my pet. You did really well." She then the hit the steering wheel and began to sob. "They took my Olly from me. They took Olly, Sally."

Sally was silent. She was just sitting there. Her head resting on Claudia's shoulder.

"Sally, did you hear me? They took Olly, our third musketeer. Sally! Sally!" she yelled. Claudia pulled over and shook Sally. Sally just fell over, and Claudia saw the blood on the back of her head.

"Oh no! Not you too!" She sobbed. "Not you too! not you too!"

One of Morris's bullets had hit Sally.

Claudia grasped the steering wheel. Squeezing, she broke a piece off.

"You will pay, you bastard. You will pay." Claudia took in a breath and said out loud, "It is déjà vu time, you swine, it's déjà vu time."

CHAPTER 31

DEJA VU

TWO WEEKS WENT BY WITH no further incidents involving Claudia and dead bodies being found. Dispatches were sent to the Orange County, Riverside County, Bakersfield, San Bernardino County, and as far as San Francisco, describing Claudia Brocolac as the blood depleter and murderer and was also branded as a serial murderer. The warrant stated she was wanted dead or alive. Precautions were indicated to take heed and not to apprehend suspect alone and to use zappers to hinder and to use heavy-duty shackles to detain the suspect. The California police force united in the apprehension of this wanted criminal.

Morris and Elizabeth continued their relationship and announced their engagement. An engagement party was scheduled for the upcoming event at the new home they were residing in.

Morris and Elizabeth had resumed to their regular schedule and the eeriness of the threat of revenge aimed at him had dwindled down some. The adorable three-bedroom home they were renting with an option to purchase was quaint and charming and located in the San Fernando Valley in the area of Sylmar. The garage was attached to the home that had access to the laundry room. The home had a large indoor patio which was converted into an extra living quarters with large picture windows that viewed the pool and backyard barbeque grounds. A sundeck sat left of the pool.

The stolen vehicle that the vampires had used during their getaway from the Pechanga Resort was found in Mission Viejo with the body of Sally Jennings. The report indicated a bullet wound to the left side of the brain, damaging the parietal lobe, causing immediate trauma and death. Status of the body specified the victim was of human stature until time of death. Body was not depleted of blood. *Vampires cannot drink blood of a deceased human being, it would be fatal to them.*

*   *   *

Claudia had worked her way to the San Fernando Valley by drinking animal blood—cats, dogs, pet pigs. She had dyed her hair blonde. She now wears brown contact lenses and was has holed up in a large house in the Agua Dulce area of the Santa Clarita Valley. The home belonged to a Mr. and Mrs. Cantrell and their seventeen-year-old son. The three family members are now bound with duct tape, feet, hands, and across the mouth. Each evening, she would feed a little on each family member. The homes in this area belong to horse owners, thus they were secluded, and the properties were huge. All this was to Claudia's advantage. She used this time to spy and observe the going-ons of Lieutenant Morris, his girlfriend Elizabeth, and her ex-boyfriend, that rascal Roberto.

Each evening, she would spy on one of these people she hated. Her plan was to kill Roberto and then kidnap Elizabeth, and then turn her, and then let her feed on the Cantrell family and then turn her back over to Morris.

Claudia looked in the mirror and told herself, "He has taken my loves from me. I shall take his love from him. Déjà vu, motherfucker. A fate worse than death! Ha-ha-ha!"

*   *   *

This day, Roberto had played a round of golf at the Van Nuys golf course with studio friends then went home to do home chores—laundry, cleaners, grocery shopping, and home cleaning. It was now four-thirty, so he lay down to take a nap before he cleaned up and got ready to meet Jennifer. They had tickets for a Justin Timberlake concert at the Forum. Because of Jennifer's weekend schedule, they were to meet at the concert.

It was now six in the evening and Roberto stirred on his couch. Something was wrong though. He felt paralyzed, he tried to move and tried to turn over but he fell to the floor.

A voice stated, "Well, my love, was that a good nap?"

He tried to move and speak, he had tape across his mouth, and now he realized his hands and feet were taped up tightly. He couldn't move.

"Your next nap will be eternal."

Oh God, he thought. *It's Claudia, the vampire.*

"Yes, it's me, my love. I think in time I may miss you. You were so good in bed."

Roberto wiggled and rolled back and forth. He mumbled and pleaded through the tape, but nothing was audible.

"For you, my love, it will be slow and intent. In the end, you will become aroused, maybe you will feel an orgasm before all your senses cease to function and you go to that darkness that never lightens. Goodbye, my love."

Claudia straddled Roberto. He tried to move his head back and forth. Claudia put a hand on his cheek and forced him to look one way. She leaned down and slowly allowed her fangs to touch the pulsing vein on his neck. She held there for a moment. He yelled a muffled scream into the tape. Then, Claudia's teeth went into his vein. Blood squirted, but Claudia's expert lips clenched in and captured the small geyser of blood. She sucked slowly and savored in the salty warm taste of his blood. As she kept feeding herself, Roberto's struggles began to diminish. Soon he was in euphoria and Claudia's moaning with pleasure excited him. Claudia now groaned with desire, they both were sexually excited. Roberto now completely stopped resisting and jerked his body when Claudia's hand rubbed his groin. He was stiff for a moment, but as Claudia sucked his blood, he orgasmed. He then went soft and then his eyes closed forever. Claudia sucked his last ounce of blood and she wiggled on his body as she also orgasmed.

Claudia got off Roberto and straightened herself up and went to the Cantrell's vehicle and drove to the home of Jason and Elizabeth.

*　　*　　*

The house in Sylmar was full of warmth and intimate friendship tonight. In the kitchen were Elizabeth, her mother, and Elizabeth's best friend from college, Betty. Betty was preparing a huge salad, cutting tomatoes, red onions, avocados, celery, Fiji apples, mushrooms, and walnuts, tossing it all into a bowl with spinach and Romaine lettuce leaves. The assorted dressings stood close by. Elizabeth's mom was slicing up the honey-baked-ham, the aroma filled the kitchen. Elizabeth was washing some glasses and looking at the friends in the living room. The kitchen counter displayed a potato salad, a bowl of macaroni and cheese, and baked beans. Girls were standing and talking with one another while others sat across from each other, all chatting. A couple of men hung out, eating the chips and dip and dipping into the veggie tray that had roasted onion and salsa dip. The avocado slices disappeared early. They were mostly women because a lot of the men were out back smoking cigars and telling dirty jokes. A make-shift bar was set up with milk cartons and a wooden board on top. Oberron was the bartender tonight. The only bottles of booze sitting on the bar top were vodka, scotch, Seagram Seven, and Jamaican rum. There were assorted mixers and a large bowl of ice. Olives and cherries had their small containers to sit in. It was a family-and-friends gathering, simple and innocent.

There were people there that Morris did not know and there were people there that Elizabeth did not know. That was Claudia's ace up her sleeve.

A DJ was at one end of the pool. He was an apprentice rapper, trying to break into the big times. His library of assorted tunes was phenomenal and his chatter between numbers was witty and funny.

The front door continued to open and close and friends came in and out. Soon the door was just left opened.

Because it was early summer, the men were in dress shorts and Hawaiian shirts and tennis shoes or sandals. The women also wore stylish shorts and dressing tank tops or sleeveless blouses. There were married couples and singles all interacting and getting to know one another.

An attractive blonde with baby-pink lipstick, wearing a black sexy-mesh-sheer-see-through blouse with long sleeves and white dress slacks was mingling among the guest. She held a small tablet and pen in her hand and was asking people if they had a request for the DJ.

Betty looked up and viewed the pretty blonde and asked Elizabeth, "Who's that seductive blonde over there?"

Elizabeth looked up and squinted and answered, "I don't know. It must be one of Jason's friends at the force or she may be with the DJ."

Betty half-smiled and stated, "Whoever. Keep her away from my man."

Elizabeth grinned.

The gathering went on and the ladies put out the spread on a long table that was set up outside. There were rented chairs all around the pool, and Betty then yelled, "Come and get it before we serve it to the inmates." There was laughter and remarks hailed the air. Individuals got in line and served themselves what they wanted.

Morris and Elizabeth stood on an elevated sundeck and viewed their companions as they frolicked and stood in line, chatting and sitting and eating.

Elizabeth asked Morris, "Who's the blonde chic there, serving herself a plate of food?"

Morris looked and saw the blonde who now walked over to the DJ and handed him the plate of food. The DJ smiled and they conversed. Morris then said, "I don't know her. I thought she was one of you friends."

"No, must be with Rudy-the-Rapper."

Morris nodded.

The party continued for another hour, and then Oberron announced the engagement of Morris and Elizabeth. A toast was made, and everyone gathered to hear commentary from the engaged couple.

Morris went first, "I met this doe-eyed beauty while on the bloodsucker case." There were ohs and ahs. "She as wearing that stylish doctor's frock covered in blood." Ews rang out. "To get my attention, she quickly removed the frock and pushed out her chest." The men whistled. "And I was mesmerized. Someone must have told her I was a bust-man." More whistles and a couple of halleluiahs sprang out.

With a big elbow into his side, Elizabeth responded, "Ladies, always wear a cup two sizes bigger and stuff with a sock, just like the men do to their groin."

The women yelled, "We know that, Liz" and "Man's pride and joy is a sport sock." There was much laughter and another statement, "Tell us something, we don't know." More laughter.

Elizabeth then grabbed Morris's arm and said, "And then this man held out handcuffs and said he'd arrest me if I didn't marry him."

"Oh yeah," "That's right," "Only way to go," and other remarks filled the air.

Morris then turned Elizabeth and looked her in the eyes and said, "She said yes." He kissed her and the crowd clapped and hoorayed the couple.

The party went on for another three hours with dancing and drinking. The party ended, designated drivers and Uber cars took everyone home, and the blonde had disappeared sometime during the night.

The house emptied. Betty was the last to leave, except for the DJ who was packing all his gear.

Elizabeth went over and asked him, "Where's your assistant?"

Rudy frowned and asked, "Who? What assistant?"

That blonde beauty who brought you a plate of food."

Rudy made a dumb face and said, "I thought she was one of your friends."

Elizabeth shook her head and then said, "She must have come with someone we invited."

"She was pretty though and very nice."

"Hmm, all right. Thanks for your service, and did Jason pay you?"

Rudy nodded and patted his breast pocket, "Got the check right here."

"You are a very good entertainer. There were lots of people here tonight. I'm sure you'll be getting calls."

Rudy smiled and said, "Well, I gave out a lot of business cards."

"Good for you. So long and good luck in your career."

"Well, thank you guys for having me.

Rudy was the last to leave. The house was kind of messy, and there were things that needed to be washed, so they straightened out some, and then they decided to do the rest in the morning. Morris and Elizabeth were beat and went to bed. It was twelve-thirty in the morning.

*　　*　　*

At two in the morning, there was a slight creaking sound at the side of the house. The old wooden gate was pushed opened slowly. Elizabeth stirred in her sleep. Morris was dead tired and did not move. Morris had most of the sheet, so Elizabeth pulled on her end and covered herself, leaving Morris half-covered. Light footsteps padded the concrete pathway. Again, Elizabeth rolled over, pulling the sheet off Morris. The intruder was now at the glass sliding door that led into the indoor patio that was converted into a game room. There were sofas and lounge chairs that surrounded a large coffee table/poker table and had shag carpet. Many board games were on the shelves attached to the wall. The intruder took slow exaggerated steps through the darkened house. The living room and hallway that led to the bedrooms was linoleum. The creeper made it to the hall-way without a sound. The stalker was clothed all in black including a hoodie, blonde hair protruded out the sides resembling golden wings. Claudia went to the first door on the right, she peeked in and through the moonlight from the window, she saw that it was set up as an office. There was a bookcase on one wall and a desk adjacent to it. She backed out. The door on her left was a bathroom. Claudia cursed herself for not checking the rooms when she was at the party. There were two more doors, one straight ahead and one more on the left. She went to the end of the hall to the end doorway. She turned the knob and it made a metal click. She froze.

Elizabeth sat up, the room had one large candle burning on the dresser, so if someone needed to use the restroom in the middle of the night there would be light, so they didn't stumble around. Elizabeth sleepily looked around, the room flickered, shadows mostly on the ceiling. She slumped back down on the bed and curled up next to Morris. He stretched his legs and put an arm over his face. Elizabeth wrapped an arm around Morris's torso and fell asleep quickly.

The demon vampire pushed the door open and tried to adjust her eyes to the dark. A helicopter passed above, and its search light fanned the homes in this area. The brief light brightened the room for a brief second, Claudia saw that the room was empty. Claudia clenched her teeth and went to the last bedroom door. It was ajar, and the slayer pushed it slowly, a slight breeze rushed in from the hallway. Morris's nude chest received the blunt of the cool air. He stirred and rolled on his back, his legs stretched wide apart. The move pushed Elizabeth off him and with her, all the sheet. Except for his shorts, Morris's muscular body lay exposed. Elizabeth rolled up in the sheet.

Claudia stepped over to Morris's side of the bed and stared down at her prey. The candlelight shimmered shadows on his body. Claudia licked her teeth. She scanned the room looking for something to hit Morris with. The only thing available was the lamp on the end table. She nodded to herself and picked it up, and with both hands she swung down.

The cord caught on the end table drawer knob and stopped the blow's full force. The lamp hit Morris on the top of his head. He jerked and rolled over Elizabeth who was now screaming and kicking her legs and swinging her arms wildly.

Claudia made a desperate leap at Morris who continued his roll off the bed and landed on one foot and one knee. He reached between the mattress and withdrew his revolver. Claudia was now standing on the bed one foot on Elizabeth's chest, holding her in place. Elizabeth squirmed under the powerful force.

Morris fired three shots, hitting Claudia in the chest and stomach, the blow knocked her off Elizabeth and she banged into the wall. As Morris grabbed his love and pulled her off the bed, her hysteria and wild arm swing knocked the weapon from Morris's hand. Claudia was now hysterically angry, and she stood there screeching a horrible noise, her hands out in front like bear claws and her mouth wide open, fangs dripping with saliva.

The demon vampire jumped over the bed. Morris pushed Elizabeth aside and Claudia landed on Morris. They fell to the floor and rolled to the wall, Claudia wrapped her arms and legs around Morris. She wanted to bite down on his neck. Morris's two hands were free, and he pushed at her head. Claudia was now bringing her head down. She had remarkable strength and her mouth was getting closer to Morris's neck. He strained, and as he pushed up, she forced her head downward. Morris's muscles were straining, and he was losing strength. The veins in Claudia's neck were bulging as she forced her head toward Morris's neck. She was closer. Three inches, two inches, one inch. She now had her fangs on Morris's neck. One tooth penetrated his skin, a thin squirt of blood shot out. It hit Claudia's cheek, her wicked tongue swiped her face. She screamed again with delight. The second eye-tooth now penetrated the skin. Claudia smiled.

Just as she was about to make a final push, she suddenly let go of Morris and screamed bloody pain. Her hands went behind her and felt the wooden stake that Elizabeth had plunged into her spine.

Claudia stood standing and turned in a circle trying to get a hold of the stake.

"You swines! Both of you! I shall destroy you both!" she screeched.

Elizabeth backed to the wall. Claudia got hold of the stake and yanked it out. She held it high as she looked at Elizabeth and told her, "You want this in your eye, or do you want my teeth in your neck, my pet?"

Elizabeth squirmed and fell to the floor and rolled into a ball.

"Then it's the stake in your eye! Ha- ha-ha!"

Morris had composed himself and grabbed the other stake that was between the mattresses and yelled at Claudia, "She'll take neither!"

Claudia turned toward Morris and he lunged at her heart with all his strength.

The stake made a slurp sound as it embedded itself between ribs and into the black heart of Claudia. All the heart chambers burst, and blood gushed out through the wound.

Claudia grabbed the stake and tried to pull it out. She fell and sat on the floor, her back against the wall. Once more, she tried to yank out the stake, but then Elizabeth hit the end of the stake with the heel of Morris's shoe.

In a dying voice and in French, Claudia uttered, "*Demetrius, je veins a toi, animal de compagnie.*"

Morris climbed on the bed and pulled Elizabeth up. They hugged each other, and he asked, "What did she mumble Hon?"

Elizabeth pushed away a little and looked at her man and stated, "Demetrius, I come to you, my pet."

Morris pushed back a large strand of hair from Elizabeth's brow and told her, "We're a hell of a team."

Elizabeth grinned and said, "This looks like the beginning of a beautiful friendship."

Morris shook his head and whispered, "Casablanca."

End

www.ingramcontent.com/pod-product-compliance
Lightning Source LLC
Chambersburg PA
CBHW021305190726
48288CB00003B/700